A SCANDALOUS MATCH

JANE DUNN

Boldwood

First published in Great Britain in 2024 by Boldwood Books Ltd.

Copyright © Jane Dunn, 2024

Cover Design by Alice Moore Design

Cover Photography: Lisa Webb / Arcangel / Shutterstock

The moral right of Jane Dunn to be identified as the author of this work has been asserted in accordance with the Copyright, Designs and Patents Act 1988.

This book is a work of fiction and, except in the case of historical fact, any resemblance to actual persons, living or dead, is purely coincidental.

Every effort has been made to obtain the necessary permissions with reference to copyright material, both illustrative and quoted. We apologise for any omissions in this respect and will be pleased to make the appropriate acknowledgements in any future edition.

A CIP catalogue record for this book is available from the British Library.

Paperback ISBN 978-1-80483-545-6

Large Print ISBN 978-1-80483-546-3

Hardback ISBN 978-1-80483-547-0

Ebook ISBN 978-1-80483-543-2

Kindle ISBN 978-1-80483-544-9

Audio CD ISBN 978-1-80483-552-4

MP3 CD ISBN 978-1-80483-551-7

Digital audio download ISBN 978-1-80483-548-7

Boldwood Books Ltd
23 Bowerdean Street
London SW6 3TN
www.boldwoodbooks.com

To My Friends

* * *

'Kindred spirits are not so scarce as I used to think.
    It's splendid to find out there are so many
    In the world.'

— *ANNE OF GREEN GABLES*: L.M. MONTGOMERY

'All I know
    Is that "thank you" should appear
    Somewhere.
    So, just in case
    I can't find the perfect place –
    "Thank you, thank you."'

— *I HAVE JUST SAID:* MARY OLIVER

1

MAY A CAT LOOK AT A QUEEN?

The Member of Parliament for Abingdon strolled home from the Palace of Westminster where he had been chairing a committee on the controversial move to protect children under the age of nine from working in the cotton mills. They had started business much earlier than usual and had now adjourned for the day. As it was a beautiful spring afternoon, he thought he would take the rural route home through St James's Park. Ivor Asprey was a tall man with striking looks, austere and distinguished rather than conventionally handsome. He had fine cheekbones, a prominent, aristocratic nose and straight black eyebrows, below which deep blue eyes gazed coolly on the world. As a highly respected and wealthy lawmaker, he was perfectly content with his life and the elevated position in the society he bestrode with grace. This current parliamentary work, however, threatened his habitual *sang-froid*. He did not like to consider the life of poor children working more than twelve hours a day in such harsh and dangerous conditions. It disturbed his natural respect for the status quo.

So it was, that as March 1814 drew to its bright spring-like close, Ivor Asprey could be seen making his elegant way through the Park with an easy athletic gait, a commanding figure immaculately if soberly dressed, swinging his cane as he walked. In a mood of abstraction he watched the coots and moorhens gliding over the water in the Canal, chattering to each other, busy foraging amongst the reeds: his mood was lifted by the happy thought of his own extensive lake at home, so much grander, with interlocking cascades and sinuous vistas contrived to embellish his acres of fertile land, just upriver from London. Such comfortable ruminations of ancestral good fortune restored his mood.

This peaceful contemplation was interrupted by a cry. 'Asprey!' He turned to see a spirited bay cantering towards him, Lord Rackham in the saddle. His lordship reined in his horse and dismounted to offer a hand in greeting. Ivor Asprey's feelings were ambivalent towards this libertine colleague who rarely attended Parliament and was contemptuously unconcerned with his constituents' interests.

Asprey met the glittering eyes in a handsome but ruined face and wondered if he was already half-foxed, despite the early hour. His voice in response was cool. 'Good afternoon, Rackham. On your way to Westminster?'

'Devil take me, no! It's torture. Closest thing to being buried alive. Don't you feel in that chamber we're just waiting to die?' With a discontented expression he continued, 'Luckily, I'm not burdened with your conscience. The thought of benighted brats in Manchester's satanic mills so lowers the spirits, don't you find?'

The two men walked on a hundred yards or so together, drawing interested glances from the fashionables promenading in the Park. Their demeanours were arresting in different ways and they were both well-known. Although still youthful at thirty-four, Ivor Asprey was an ascendant star in the Whig party and a rich and eligible man on the social scene, who scheming mamas wished to snare for their cleverer daughters. It was obvious to them that he needed a wife to play the political hostess and assist his rise on the national stage. The fact he was so elusive, some said arrogant, merely spurred them on, as did the added piquancy of his past with a dead young wife, a motherless daughter, gossiped about when his name was mentioned.

His companion's repute had quite a different source. A few years older, Cato Rackham's dissolute life had made him cynical in his search for increasingly extreme experiences to revive his jaded palate. That and his name, as well as his habit of always dressing in black, had also earned him the soubriquet amongst his peers of 'Black Cat', with all the ill omen that implied. Having inherited his father's seat, he was a Member of Parliament for the Tories, but thought of Westminster as just another of his many convenient clubs for meeting, drinking and pleasurable diversion. His appearance at assemblies and routs during the Season caused mothers to shield their daughters from his calculating gaze. Some of the more perverse-minded and spirited young women, however, found his reputation and raddled good looks rather thrilling.

The two men talked in a desultory way about the progress of the Prussian coalition's approach on Paris in their grinding war against Bonaparte, the coming owners' race at Newmarket and a water spectacular at Sadler's Wells Theatre that Lord Rackham had reluctantly attended. With a sneer on his face, he said, 'Half the sottish audience ended up cavorting in the vast tank on stage filled with filthy water.' He emitted a mirthless laugh. 'One of the riff-raff youths nearly drowned. Ape-drunk he looked to me. I should have left him there, gasping like a gudgeon. But of course they had to fish him out.'

Ivor Asprey was used to his lordship's predictable disdain and responded drily. 'The theatre's but our great city in miniature. Everyone from the royal princes to the scape-gallows are there to be seen. I'm surprised you went.'

'There was a certain young vestal playing the part of a mermaid, very affectingly I thought.' Lord Rackham's predatory smile made Mr Asprey recoil but he strove to maintain his civility, whatever his lordship's transgressions in the past. He saluted and turned away. His lordship bowed and swung himself into the saddle to trot in the direction of Birdcage Walk.

Quickening his stride, Ivor Asprey walked north towards Pall Mall which was filled with carriages and promenaders out to enjoy the late afternoon sunshine. The handsome buildings, the bookshops, clockmakers and gentlemen's clubs confirmed his belief in the established order of things. He glanced up, as he always did, towards the monumental frontage of what used to be the Shakespeare Gallery when he was a boy. He particularly liked the carving in relief of the apotheosis of England's greatest playwright. He stood for a moment, reassured by its intimations of national supremacy and the historic thread of certainty in his settled world.

As he walked on, greeting a few acquaintances on the way, Mr Asprey began to look forward to getting back to his mansion in St James's Square for a restorative whisky before setting out for Brooks's. At his club, he could count on being able to find convivial company where it was relaxing and unchallenging to be amongst men as secure and fortunate as himself. He turned into the handsome Square. The peace and quiet after the bustle of Pall Mall was always a balm.

Walking up through St James's Square he noticed a grand town coach-and-four pulled up in front of his house. A familiar gloom settled over him. The great gilded crest of the Duke of Arlington glinted on the carriage door; this meant his sister awaited him within. Ivor Asprey mounted the steps and his front door swung open to reveal the smiling face of Goodall, his butler. 'Good afternoon, sir,' he said, taking his master's coat, cane and hat. 'Your sister is in the library.' His cheery face almost twinkled into a wink until quelled by his master's forbidding frown.

Ivor Asprey strode through the wide hallway with its elegant stone staircase curving up to the drawing room floor. He opened the mahogany door to his favourite room in the house. The carved Jacobean bookcases that lined the walls had come from an earlier mansion, now demolished, and added the gravitas of dark oak and age. They were filled with his books whose gleaming leather backs he recognised like old friends. But the peaceful atmosphere that usually greeted him was disturbed.

Edwina, Duchess of Arlington, was sitting in his favourite chair by the fire, an imposing figure in aquamarine silk, wearing a turquoise turban and one of the many magnificent Arlington necklaces she inherited on her marriage. This one was of foiled garnets which drew the eye to her generous bosom and emphasised the deep brown lustre of her hair. She was tapping her foot with impatience and looked up as she heard the door.

Her bright blue eyes met his deeper colder blue. 'Ivor! You've arrived at last. Goodall couldn't say when you'd be back and I thought I'd wait half an hour before leaving you a billet.' Her voice was emphatic and her opinions were rarely gainsaid.

He walked over to kiss her lightly on the cheek. 'Edwina. To what do I owe this unexpected pleasure? May I request some tea for you, or ratafia?' His impassive gaze rested on her face.

'Goodness no! But a whisky would do.'

He noticed she was unusually agitated and his heart sank further; Lord Charles Latimer, her cossetted son and heir, was probably involved in some scrape from which he would be required to extricate him. He poured out two glasses and sat down in the chair across from hers.

'How is the Duke?' he enquired. He was sympathetic to the tragedy that had befallen the family when his brother-in-law was struck from his horse at the Battle of Alexandria, some thirteen years prior; bleeding from the ear and badly trampled, his fellow dragoons had dragged him from the mêlée of horses' hooves and fallen men, but he had never been the same again.

'Oh, little changed,' the Duchess said brusquely. 'He keeps to his chambers. Still obsessed with snuff boxes.'

'What is his tally?'

'Oh, he's not challenging Petersham yet, only about two hundred and fifty, but I didn't come to talk to you about poor old George.' Her bright bird-like eyes missed nothing and were usually focussed on his face demanding answers, but now evaded his gaze.

'What's troubling you, sister?' He looked at her more closely, noting her pillowy cheeks and disappearing jawline, but was taken aback to see she was close to tears, a weakness she did not readily allow herself, or others.

'Charles intends to offer marriage to a young trollop!' Her voice trembled with outrage. Ivor Asprey knew she was a stickler for propriety and had very pronounced ideas about who would be worthy to become the next Duchess of Arlington, a noble line of which she was possessive and proud. He watched his sister take a gulp of whisky and the fiery liquor seemed to give her the strength to meet his eyes.

'And pray who is this lucky young woman?' He had to suppress a curl of amusement at his nephew's unexpected rebelliousness. Fundamentally, he agreed with his sister; it was essential for social stability and the conservation of wealth that the status quo be maintained. Marrying out of your class weakened the very structure of society.

The Duchess could barely contain her feelings. 'There's a young minx, an actress at Covent Garden Theatre, cavorting about as Ophelia. Charles is there nearly every night casting lovelorn eyes her way.'

Her brother smiled, then checked his amusement when he saw her face. His languid words were meant to be consoling. 'Oh, Edwina, you have nothing to worry about. All young red-blooded youths fall in love with an actress at some point. It's a trifling matter. Mere animal spirits. At that age, Maria Campion was the focus of my calf-love. I would've given up my life for her.'

'Don't ridicule my concerns, Ivor!' she said sharply. 'The capricious boy is serious. He's taken the Latimer jewels out of the bank! His inheritance from his grandmother, you know; she'd be turning in her grave.' She wrung her hands. Her brother had never seen her in such distress, not even when the Duke was brought back from the battlefield insensible and close to death.

'I presume you're here because you want me to interfere, Edwina? But the young greenhead is almost come of age; I can hardly justify throwing a rub in his way.' He crossed his legs and smiled at his sister. 'At least he's not rolled up in debt.'

Her Grace had got to her feet and to relieve her feelings paced to the window and back. 'I'd rather it was debt. That at least has a solution, even though it's costly.' She paused and stood in front of him, a challenging light in her eyes. 'I want you to offer the young woman money to return any family jewels and rebuff my son's pretensions. To tell him she will never marry him.'

'You know I can't do that.' His relaxed way of speaking of such matters of moment irritated her greatly. He continued, his voice still calm, 'If you feel so strongly, why not get a contract made out and signed by the Duke?'

His sister could have stamped her foot with frustration, as she used to when a girl faced by her younger brother's obstinacy. She restrained herself, instead hissing through clenched teeth, 'George may not be able to look after himself or the estate but he still has opinions, unfortunately. He's all in favour of his son and heir marrying a beauty as he calls her! He's lost all sense of proportion and propriety.'

Ivor Asprey was surprised. 'You mean he's seen her?'

'Yes! My perfidious son took the young hussy to meet his father. George, of course, was completely bowled over. The designing harlot brought him a present of a Scottish mull, made from a ram's horn, filled with his favourite snuff. She said it had been given to her by an admirer and she'd prefer him to have it. The poor gull was beside himself with delight.'

'Tell me, what's this young woman's name?'

'I thought you already knew. She's quite the thing. Her Ophelia titillates men's fancies and touches women's foolish hearts.'

'I don't have the time for such entertainments, Edwina.'

'Well, the title-hunting Mistress Minx is called Angelica Leigh. She's nightly at the Garden Theatre.'

Ivor Asprey rose to his feet, hoping to usher his sister to her carriage, when the door opened and a bright-faced girl, no more than eleven years old, peeped into the room. Her eyes alighted on him and she dashed forward with delight. 'Oh, Papa! You're home already.'

She was stilled by his frown as he indicated the presence of the Duchess. 'Elinor, where are your manners? Aunt Edwina has come to call.'

The young girl skidded to a halt and the delight on her face faded as she went across to take her aunt's hand and offer the appropriate curtsey. 'How do you do, Ma'am?' she said in her most demure manner.

'Very well, my dear. And where have you been this afternoon?'

The girl's blue eyes looked from her father to her aunt, aware that conversations with the Duchess were fraught with unforeseen peril, and answered with care, 'It was such a nice afternoon, Miss Stafford thought we could practise my Latin declensions while walking round the Canal in the Park.' Elinor Asprey was slight and pretty, a fairy wisp of a girl, with fine light brown hair and an expressive pale face, alive with imagination.

The Duchess huffed, 'Sounds very lax and negligent to me. Where is your governess?'

'She's gone to see Mr Digby, I think,' the young girl said quietly, casting a despairing glance at her father.

'Edwina, I have absolute confidence in Miss Stafford's teaching methods,' he said then turned to his daughter with a smile of encouragement. 'Elinor, can you ask my secretary to come through to me in five minutes. I have some letters to sign after I've seen your aunt to her carriage.'

As the door closed behind his daughter, his sister put up a hand. 'Not so fast, Ivor. We haven't finished our business.'

He cocked an eyebrow and murmured, a hint of fatigue in his voice, 'Have we not, dear sister? What more can I do for you?'

'You haven't agreed to do anything for me!' she responded in an exasperated voice. 'I would be grateful if you'd at least meet Miss Leigh and see if you can ascertain her purpose in this pursuit of my son.'

Ivor Asprey inclined his head in reluctant acceptance of his mission and was about to open the door when the Duchess put a hand on his arm and added, 'I think for Elinor's sake you should marry again. For your political future too.' Her brother's face turned dark but she was undeterred and continued, 'What's become of your courtship of Lady Linus? I thought Portia Linus a good serious young woman. And an heiress too. Property and good family never go amiss in a marriage, you know.'

Ivor Asprey's equanimity was beginning to fray. It was hard not to show his irritation as he ushered his sister towards the door. 'Edwina, you have the most managing disposition. It's a national tragedy that you were not born a man. You could have taken command of one of Lord Wellington's armies and no doubt the war against Boney would have been shortened by years.'

She took this in good heart, in fact, chose to see it as a compliment and gave her brother a friendly thump on the arm as he bade her goodbye. Elinor joined him on the doorstep to watch her stately figure being helped into her carriage by the Arlington coachman, in full gold-braided livery. Father and daughter waved her off, and turning back to the house, both sighed.

'Oh, Papa,' was all the young girl said, and her shoulders drooped.

'I know. Your aunt can be a bit of a trial.'

Her face lit up as she clutched his arm and said, 'I'm so glad you agree with me.' Ivor Asprey had found it difficult to know how best to bring up his daughter, motherless these last six years and himself immured in grief. He strove to combine discipline with affection, as befitted a young woman's education, to ready her for adulthood and marriage, but feared he sometimes erred on the side of discipline and perhaps was too repressive. Certainly his secretary, Nicholas Digby, implied he thought so. But his sister, who had iron opinions on everything, including bringing up daughters despite not having any herself, considered the household far too lenient and lacking in a firm woman's touch.

Elinor tiptoed to brush a kiss on her father's cheek before running up the stairs to her room. Mr Asprey returned to the library, his spirits worn thin. There, a sweet-faced young man was waiting for him with a sheaf of papers in his hand. Nicholas Digby had been one of the best scholars at Westminster School when his father died and he was forced to seek a living rather than proceed to university. He was recommended to the Member of Parliament for Abingdon who had been gratified by his intelligence and how hard and cheerfully he worked. He found, however, some of his secretary's Godwinian ideas on social reform rather jarring to his own overriding desire for peace and prosperity and the comfort of the status quo.

Beside Mr Digby stood a tall young woman dressed simply in a grey cambric dress, its plainness relieved by a ruffle of cream lace round the neck and wrists. She turned at her employer's entry, a faint blush colouring her cheeks. Her face was symmetrical and serene; her intelligent brown eyes and chestnut hair twisted into a low bun added distinction to her agreeable looks. She inclined her head. 'Good afternoon, Mr Asprey. May I borrow your edition of Mr Goldsmith's *The Vicar of Wakefield*?' She held out a red leather volume in her hands.

'Certainly, Miss Stafford. But tell me, do you intend to read it with Elinor?'

The young woman looked at him, hesitated and then replied, 'I thought it might amuse and instruct her.'

'Oh, I'm sure it will. She'll start her plaints again about wanting a sister.' His voice was amused. 'Just don't read her *The Deserted Village* else I'll have to sacrifice my Capability Brown vistas to rebuild the village and small-holdings that once inhabited my parkland.'

Nicholas Digby smiled. 'Ah, but that desecration of rural cots and productive land happened in your grandfather's day.'

'You know, Nicholas, that to you radical social reformers it don't much matter when it happened. It must be redressed.'

The young man laughed in acknowledgement. He then noticed his employer's usually unruffled manner was a trifle discomposed. 'Are you heading for Brooks's later, sir?' he enquired in a mild voice.

Ivor Asprey had taken the letters from his secretary's hand and was reading and signing them with an abstracted air. Eventually he answered, his usual languor returned. 'I will tonight. But, Nicholas, could you get me a ticket for the theatre at Covent Garden tomorrow. There's a performance of *Hamlet* that's proving very popular.'

'Just one ticket, sir? You may have to share a box.'

'Yes, just one. This is family business, not entertainment.' His voice was grim.

Both Nicholas Digby and Miss Stafford exchanged a fleeting glance before the young governess bade her farewell and left the room, the volume of Goldsmith's novel in her hand.

* * *

'I'm late! I'm late!' Two young women ran across the Piazza towards the artists' entrance to Covent Garden Theatre. The building with its grand colonnaded façade had been rebuilt after a devastating fire six years before and the stone was still gleaming, the pillars rising nobly above the busy street where grubby urchins played, hawked cheap goods and begged.

Laughing, the girls dashed into a small dressing room in the ill-lit warren of spaces backstage. One was Mary Summer, dark-haired with a whimsical cast to her features, always in motion and full of humour. The other, her mistress, Angelica Leigh, was so astonishingly beautiful that strangers paused in conversation at the sight of her. This was as much to do with a sparkling sweetness and humour in her expression as her remarkable colouring. She was blessed with clouds of fine wavy hair of a brilliant red-gold which owed nothing to the cosmetical administrations of beet juice or saffron and carbonate paste.

Angelica threw herself into the chair by the glass, undid her loose bun and began to drag a comb through her long curling hair. She turned to her maid, who was happy to act as her theatrical dresser, and said in a low musical voice, 'Mary, can you make sure that diadem of myrtle and honeysuckle is not wilting or dead? And that the rosemary, pansies and daisies will last another day before we get more from the market tomorrow?' She turned back to the looking-glass. 'Oh, how I wish I could cut this hair!' she muttered almost to herself, disentangling the comb.

'Your contract demands your hair remains long, Miss Angelica.'

'Fiddlesticks!' Her face was fine-boned with translucent skin, enlivened by her large, heavy-lidded eyes of a striking hazel-green. She was small and slightly built but emanated an energy and sensibility that made her such an affecting tragic presence on stage.

The white muslin dress for the 'mad scene' hung on the wall behind her, ready for the evening's performance. Mary had stitched silk forget-me-nots onto the bodice and skirt in a delicate tracery of green and pale blue. This was the second identical costume that had been made for her as the first was still drying after the previous evening's performance. Beside it, Mary hung the evening dress they had brought with them, a gauzy green affair in tulle and silk ribbon with a low tucked bodice and a ruffled hem.

Angelica had slipped out of her day dress and was instead attired in a dressing gown of pink satin that she tied round her narrow waist. 'Miss Angelica, shall I assist with your *cosmétique*?' Mary was beginning to prepare the pearl powder to dust over her skin to make it paler and more translucent in the soft stage lights. She then reached for the Indian cochineal pigment and corn starch stored in a small glass-stoppered pot to add a flush to the cheeks and lips.

At this point there was a rap at the door and without permission, Mr Dunbar, the theatre manager, entered the room. He was middle-aged and had been an actor himself but now was balding and corseted, with a harassed, irascible air. 'Miss Angelica, the tank for the stream was leaking. We've put mastic in it now. But when it's refilled the water will be colder than usual.'

Angelica turned her large eyes towards him and shivered. 'It's frigid enough as it is. You don't want your Ophelia getting pleurisy and really dying, do you, Mr Dunbar?' Her voice was light but the death scene was an ordeal she had to go through every night. The management had been envious of the success of the theatre at Sadler's Wells with its water extravaganzas and mock sea battles on stage and Mr Dunbar had decided that Ophelia should not drown off-stage, as Shakespeare had intended, but stumble beneath the 'willow grown aslant' and slip into a real stream in full sight of the audience. This affecting death scene had been a triumph. Those of a more sensitive disposition almost fainted with sympathy and grief while the rowdier elements, carousing in the pit, savoured the sight of Ophelia being retrieved from the water, her flimsy chemise so sodden it clung to her lovely, lifeless form. Even the most drunken and prurient were silenced by the pathetic sight.

Mr Dunbar congratulated himself on this innovation, together with his foresight in engaging Edmund Kean to play Hamlet for a season. This young actor had taken the theatrical world by storm with his portrayal of Shylock earlier in the year and was newly hailed as a great tragedian. Both attractions ensured a full house every night, but Dunbar was insensible to the demands it made on his young actress.

He was about to leave as abruptly as he had arrived, but at the door turned with another thought. 'Miss Angelica, this play and your performance seems to have attracted more disreputables than usual.' He looked uncomfortable. It was not in his character to reassure, but the audiences had been particularly rowdy and he thought it necessary to show some sympathy for his troupe. 'It is hard for you actors to endure the bawdy catcalls when the Prince speaks unchastely to Ophelia. Silence them with the power of your acting.' He nodded and left.

Angelica looked at Mary with her eyebrow raised. 'I don't think I've ever heard Mr Dunbar show any concern for us before. Perhaps he's afraid my delicate spirits won't survive the rudeness from the floor and I'll cry off and leave him in the lurch?' She was tucking her luxuriant hair into a net, ready for the wig. 'What do you think, Mary?'

'He's a prosy fool and knows nothing other than how to turn a penny. Pay him no heed, Miss Angelica,' Mary said over her shoulder as she pulled an orange and purple brocade dress from the closet and retrieved the long corset from behind the door. Mary had grown up on the streets of Covent Garden, picking up discarded fruit and vegetables for a living, until Angelica's mother had stumbled over her one night after the theatre. The scruffy, half-starved child had been trying to sleep in a doorway and Mrs Leigh, knowing too well the dangers of the street for young girls, took her home to train as a maid. She was not much older than her own daughter and so Mary and Angelica grew almost as close as sisters, despite the disparity in their positions in the household. They were each protective of the other.

Angelica slipped out of the dressing gown and stood before Mary in the flimsiest of chemises over which the corset was fitted and tightly laced. 'I don't know if I'll ever get used to the discomfort. To think our grandmamas had to wear these every day!'

'Your grandmama might but mine would 'ave bin toiling in the fields with everything hangin' out, no doubt.'

'Oh, Mary!'

'Just tellin' as I know it, Miss Angelica.'

The production had been updated to a Georgian tragedy, with costumes from the end of the last century, and Angelica stepped into the richly embellished dress with a triangular bodice that emphasised her tiny waist. This too was laced up the back. She then lifted a white powdered wig from the wig-block on her dressing table and placed it over her netted hair. Both women inspected her reflection in the speckled looking-glass. Angelica appeared grand but impersonal in the armour of boned corsets, brocade and elaborate wig. The contrast with this and her later dishabille in her last scene added drama and pathos to her performance. The 'mad scene' became all the more shocking for the audience when for the first time they saw her natural hair undressed and flaming in colour, her garments reduced to a simple lawn chemise.

Angelica was in full costume and seated, leaning towards the glass, outlining her eyes with a sooty waxy paste when there was a soft tap on the door. They turned to see the handsome face of a young man with wavy brown hair and amused eyes peering into the room. 'Miss Leigh, are you accepting visitors?' he asked with a flirtatious smile.

Angelica jumped up and put out her hands, a laugh in her voice. 'Lord Latimer, of course! But just for a moment. You can help me with my final preparations.'

The young man was followed into the room by another and Charles Latimer, still holding Angelica's hand, turned to introduce him. 'Miss Leigh, may I introduce my friend, Dante Locke. He's a poet y'know.' This young romantic bowed very low over Angelica's proffered hand. He was dark with soulful black eyes and unruly locks that curled to his shoulders. His full mouth looked as if it rarely smiled but instead had been formed specifically to effect a soulful pout.

'A poet?' Angelica asked, marvelling at just how influential Lord Byron was on the pretensions of the susceptible young.

'Yes, Miss Leigh. My mother is a Venetian and from my birth had determined I would be a poet.'

'Hence your name?'

'Indeed. I'm working on an epic poem inspired by the tragedy of Ophelia. She will become my Beatrice.' The young gallant tossed his head and smouldered into the middle distance then roused himself to utter in dramatic tones, 'If I didn't write, I think I would end up mad.'

Angelica was taken aback by the vehemence of his last words but Lord Latimer ignored his friend's outburst, saying equably, 'He's been inspired by your performance, Miss Leigh. He was overcome with your interpretation of tormented delusion.' Lord Latimer was in some awe of his friend's romantic temperament.

Angelica bowed her head, a smile on her lips. 'I am gratified that I may have helped you in your poetic vision. But, gentlemen, I have to prepare myself for tonight's performance. Will you excuse me?'

'Not before you allow me to place a patch on your lovely cheek,' Lord Latimer said with unexpected boldness.

'Ah, my lord, I may be in a costume that befits our grandmothers, but I do not wear the patches they wore. Ophelia is but a young girl and unsophisticated.' Seeing his face fall, she added, 'But of course, you may apply some of this pearl powder to my cheek before you go.' She sat down in front of the looking-glass again and he bent across to pick up the pot, meeting her eyes in the reflection. He paused, mesmerised for a moment.

Angelica broke the spell by glancing away from the glass and up into the flushed face leaning over her. She murmured, 'Have a care, Lord Latimer, this powder will spoil your coat.'

He dabbed the swansdown puff into the powder then delicately pressed it onto the curve of her cheek. Without permission, he moved the swansdown slowly down her slender neck and then across her collarbone. His face was very close, as if he longed to trace the same trajectory with his lips. His breathing was fast as his eyes glittered in the candlelight. She felt a disconcerting quiver of excitement pass between them as his dark gaze held hers for a moment.

'Thank you, my lord, for your help.' Her voice was matter of fact as she extracted the powder puff from his hand. 'Now, I must prepare.'

'Don't forget, Miss Leigh, you promised to come with us afterwards to Lady Marwood's rout. The whole town is full of rumour about the war. It'll be quite a summer of parties and balls if we're victorious.' He gazed at her with the look of a man who could not believe his good fortune in having such beauty within his grasp.

'Of course.' She indicated the green dress hanging on the wall. 'I've come prepared. But I will only be able to stay for a few dances. I have to get some sleep. Unlike you, my lord, I have work to do.' She wrinkled her nose with a teasing smile.

Both men bowed. Dante Locke took Angelica's hand. 'Your craft is as mine, Miss Leigh. We are the rainbow in the storms of life.' The young men then kissed their own finger tips in a theatrical farewell.

As Lord Latimer was pulling the door to behind them, he said, 'We'll be in the first box on the left. Good luck, Miss Leigh. Look after her, Mary.' With this they were gone.

Mary tutted disapprovingly. 'You shouldn't lead the young lord on so, Miss Angelica.'

'Oh, Mary! I don't. It means nothing. He's in love in the way young men fall in love, so easily, without meaning. It's courtly, like the poet, Dante's love for his Beatrice. It's no more than that. It will pass.'

'I don't think you're right. He looks at you in a hungry way.'

'You fanciful goose. If I was a gambling woman I'd bet you ten guineas we would not see him again after the Season's over. Thus it goes.' Her voice was subdued. She gazed back at her reflection, her artificially pale face making her eyes seem all the larger and more striking. 'We have fifteen minutes. Can you hear my lines in that difficult Scene V? And where is my lyre?'

* * *

Angelica was relieved to be back in the dressing room once more. The crowd had been as boisterous as usual but were mostly on Ophelia's side. Knowing the play well, they shouted advice and encouragement, and abused Hamlet in a good-natured way for his crueller jibes. Her death scene never failed to quell their noise and the drowning scene on stage always shocked, as it did Angelica, sinking into the chill water.

With Mary's help she was quick to clamber out of her cold wet clothes and into a dressing gown, shivering while her maid dried her hair with a towel. Mary had already timed her dash across the Piazza to Mistress Pastow's tavern to collect the nightly cup of hot chocolate to restore and warm her mistress. She put the bowl into her cold hands.

'Oh Mary, thank you. This is the thing.'

'How was the audience tonight, Miss Angelica?'

'Not so bad. And very affected by my last scenes. I'm tired and yet we have this party to attend.' She stifled a yawn. 'Can we be ready to leave as soon as Lord Latimer arrives?'

Mary had already hung up the dripping chemise to dry and returned the heavy gown, corset and wig to their frames for tomorrow's dressing. She handed her mistress her under-chemise, stockings, stays and then helped lace them up. Angelica slipped quickly into her evening dress and pulled on her long satin gloves as Mary piled her still-damp hair into an unconventional but fetching style of burnished gold curls. Both women put on their pelisses and Mary picked up a small portmanteau.

By the external door they found a large, belligerent-looking man with a broken nose and a jaw like a gammon. 'Oh, Mr Brunner, I'm so pleased you're early. I've promised a friend I would go with him for a short while to a party in Lady Marwood's house in Leicester Square.' Angelica tucked her hand into the pugilist's meaty arm and his other hand took the portmanteau from Mary. Usually it was he who escorted them on fine nights for the twenty minutes' walk to her mother's house in Berkeley Square, but tonight their destination was just a few minutes' stroll away. They heard a shout and turned to see Lord Latimer and Dante Locke dashing up the road behind them. 'Miss Leigh, another performance to touch the heart.' The young lord grasped her free hand and brought it to his lips.

Angelica felt Brunner stiffen beside her, his protective hackles up. She disentangled her arm and turned to greet the young men. 'Lord Latimer, this is Mr Brunner, my walking companion. Mr Brunner, Lord Latimer and his friend, Mr Locke.' All three men bowed. Angelica continued, 'I've told Mr Brunner I'm accompanying you to a party. Just for a short while. It's on our way home anyway.' The men bowed again and all five of them set off into the noisy night, pressing through the evening crowds that milled around the alehouses, brothels and gambling hells of Covent Garden.

In this area round the theatre, Angelica was always recognised, despite her distinctive hair being twisted up into a loose chignon and covered by the hood on her cloak. She was addressed in a familiar manner by people who considered her one of their own, even though her talent and beauty had elevated her to fame and a little fortune.

'Angelly, give us a kiss, wee lass,' was a common cry from men and women alike. 'Oh, chick-a-biddy, ye make us proud, our angel.' She nodded and smiled and let them grasp her hand in passing. Lord Latimer looked startled at just how lacking in deference they were in their address, but Angelica seemed completely at ease, welcoming their good wishes. How shocked his mother would be to see this scene. He looked at the young actress with new interest and some concern.

She felt she should explain. 'I've grown up amongst these people. I have known what it's like to live precariously.' This information, so casually imparted, would only have increased the Duchess's disdain.

They entered the wide spaces of Leicester Square with its shops and mansions and were soon mounting the steps of a grand house, its windows ablaze with light. The sound of an orchestra drifted out onto the street. Carriages were still arriving, disgorging brightly plumed guests. Lord Latimer had leaned in to murmur in Angelica's ear, 'At the height of the Season, fashionables are like migrating birds, fluttering in one evening from soirée, to grand dinner, to a ball, as the whim takes them.'

They were met by a very smart butler, fully braided, bowing low in greeting before taking the men's top coats and Angelica's pelisse. Mary and Mr Brunner had already descended the basement steps at the front leading to the kitchens to join the other servants with their own drinks and merriment below stairs.

Divested of her outer garment, Lord Latimer saw Angelica for the first time in evening dress and his eyes widened in amazement. 'Oh!' It was more an intake of breath. 'Miss Leigh, that dress so becomes you.' At last he had managed to persuade her to accompany him to a party and could hardly believe this prize would be his for an hour.

'I thank you, my lord. I hope it not improper that you appear so publicly in my company. Or improper that I'm here without my mama as chaperone.'

'Never fear. My mama and her friends do not move in Lady Marwood's circles. She's not quite of the beau monde, you see. She welcomes a more raffish and amusing crowd.' They were walking up the thronged stairs, Angelica between the two handsome young men, and many eyes were drawn their way. The young actress was known across all social strata from the costermonger in the market to the Prince Regent and his cronies. Wherever she went, she cut a striking figure and seeing her in the company of someone of such noble family as Lord Latimer fuelled speculation and gossip about the exact nature of her relationship with one of the most eligible young men about Town.

When they reached the ballroom, the throng parted to let them pass into a great gold-ceilinged room with four full-length windows giving views of the shadowy garden of Leicester Square. The light from thousands of candles in the chandeliers was reflected many times in the tall rococo look-ing-glasses filling the spaces between the windows and lining the opposite wall. The faces and dresses of the guests were reflected in brilliant frag-ments, gleaming in the soft light. Angelica gasped with the ever-shifting beauty of the scene as dancers swirled around the room and people preened, catching sight of their gorgeous reflections in the glass.

It was a more colourful and exuberant throng than was usually the case at society balls, for Lady Marwood's liberal social policy allowed men to bring their mistresses and more informal paramours to the party and everything was made merrier with a great deal of alcohol and laughter. The orchestra was playing a lively reel and Angelica forgot her tiredness and longed to dance. A small middle-aged woman dressed in gold and wearing a plumed turban, its feather almost as tall as herself, dashed to Lord Latimer's side. 'My lord, what an honour.' She took his hand.

'Lady Marwood, the honour is mine.' He bowed. 'May I introduce to you Miss Leigh and Mr Locke?' Angelica found herself being scrutinised by the wisest pair of dark eyes, sparkling with intelligence.

Their hostess took her hand. 'Miss Leigh, I am honoured too to welcome the finest Ophelia I have seen.'

Angelica looked into the still charming face, so lively with sympathy and experience and recognised a fellow outsider making her way in the world. 'I am delighted to be able to dance in your beautiful ballroom, surely one of the loveliest in London?'

Dante Locke seemed to be as struck as Angelica by this bird-like woman who had alighted in their midst and grasped his hand to pass it to Angelica. 'Young man, I am loath to feed the gossips further about this young beauty. Would you partner her for her first dance?' Dante Locke had long professed not to dance. What poetic young man who wished to be taken seriously in his melancholic reveries could ever be seen to caper and laugh like jokers and fools? But now in thrall to their hostess's energetic force, who could demur? With grace he accepted defeat, bowed and held out his hand to lead Angelica onto the floor.

She was naturally light and graceful on her feet and had been well taught and he accomplished in all the social graces. They managed to join a set seamlessly, slipping into the figures of eight, weaving out and together and then looping round, with a clap and a skip, to repeat the geometry again. It was great fun and Angelica's face was shining with delight. She was aware of Lord Latimer lounging against a sofa watching them, a peculiar expression in his eyes.

'I thought poets don't dance? Yet you dance so well, Mr Locke.' Angelica could manage only a few words as they came together before parting again.

'I don't usually.' His dark moodiness lightened with the ghost of a smile. 'But it takes a more determined man than myself to resist your charms and Lady Marwood's force of will.'

She laughed as the reel separated them again. When their hands met he continued, 'I learnt in Venice where my mamma has a palazzo. We go in the winter.'

'Where is your family in the summer?'

'For the Season, we come to Town. To Duke Street.' So their conversation continued in fragments. When he wasn't smouldering in poetic distraction, Dante Locke had an attractive, mobile face with a mouth that curled with humour on the occasions he forgot to look disconsolate.

'And you've known Lord Latimer since schooldays?' she asked him as they came together again.

'Yes. He was one of the popular boys who protected me from the bullies. Our friendship was forged in blood.' He tossed this last sentence over his shoulder with dramatic emphasis, as the dance parted them again. Too soon for Angelica, the music stopped and the dancing couples drifted off to the refreshments on offer in the adjoining room.

Before Angelica could join the crowd, Charles Latimer grasped her hand and said with urgent fervour, 'Miss Leigh, I insist on the next dance.'

She bowed her head in acceptance. 'Of course. I shall look forward to it.' Having been so quick to dismiss his romantic interest in her she was beginning to wonder if he was unlike all the other young men who fancied themselves in love after the barest acquaintance. His animal spirits aroused in her an occasional and disconcerting thrill.

In the corner of her eye she saw the dark figure of Cato Rackham approaching and held her breath. He was a habitué of the theatre and had a carnivorous look about him; her instinct in his presence was to become as still as a vole in the gaze of a hawk.

'My dear, what a pleasant surprise.' He bowed over her hand. 'And Lord Latimer, too. Doubly delightful,' he drawled, showing his teeth more in a grimace than a smile.

The young lord looked coldly at this interloper and gave him a brusque nod in greeting. 'Lord Rackham, sir,' he said as he turned to take Angelica's arm.

'Not too fast, my dear. May I request you as my partner for a dance?'

Angelica squeezed Charles Latimer's arm in a mild panic. The previous week, Lord Rackham had arrived uninvited in her dressing room and she sensed he was a man who liked to hunt. She knew, however, she could not publicly refuse him. 'I am promised for the next two dances, my lord. I fear I will have to leave soon after that.' Her words drifted off lamely.

'I'm sure you could manage one dance before fleeing like Cinderella at midnight.' He gave her a mirthless smile. A few years ago, *Cinderella* had been a sensation at her theatre and his allusion to the gulf of social difference between the servant girl and the prince was not lost on her. Colour rose in her cheeks and she was grateful when the orchestra struck up again and Lord Latimer swept her off to the dance floor.

With some trepidation, Angelica recognised the strains of a waltz. This was a new continental dance that shocked the old but was embraced with delight by exuberant youth. Without saying a word, Lord Latimer encircled her waist and pulled her close. Taken by surprise, she gasped. She had only danced the waltz with her dancing master and her mother who had learned it from a Viennese gold trader. With them as partners it had been a practical enterprise without any sensual awareness of her own body and that of the person with whom she danced. She looked up into Lord Latimer's eyes and realised how close their faces were, aware of his breath on her cheek, and her heart missed a beat.

'My lord, I haven't danced so in public before. I hope I don't disgrace you.'

'You could never do that, Miss Leigh.' He seemed to be inhaling her scent, and continued with eyes half-closed, 'I'm afraid this is the only way I can take you in my arms without creating a scandal. I've wanted to hold you from the moment I first saw you on stage as Ophelia.'

Angelica shivered. The excitement was unexpected and made all the more heady by being in the arms of a young man who could dance. So different from the distance and formality of the country dances and reels, this required a physical closeness that was thrilling. They were meant to dance with air between them, except for any fast turn, but she felt his hand insistent on her back, his free hand entwined with hers. He held her close, hip to hip, with enough contact for her to be acutely aware of the movement of his muscle and the hard contours of his body. So intimate was the embrace, Angelica felt quite breathless, amazed that such liberty was permitted in public.

Lord Latimer smiled down at her, a dreamy expression in his eyes. 'I feel I was only half awake in the years before I met you. Now everything is sensation and possibility. I don't think I can properly exist without you, Miss Leigh.' The last words were said in a rush that seemed to surprise him as much as they did her. The music had come to an end but he did not release her; he stood at the edge of the ballroom floor with Angelica still in his arms.

'My lord, take care to allay the worst of tittle-tattle.'

Lord Latimer released his hold on her and whispered fiercely, 'The devil take 'em! I don't give a tinker's curse what anyone thinks. What my virago-mother thinks.'

Dante Locke had joined them and heard the last of the conversation. 'Oh Charlie, you're such a contrary son, you know. The Duchess ain't so bad. You should meet my mother. Venetian mammas are proud and fierce as panthers. There's no way she'd approve marriage for me to any woman less immaculate than the Virgin Mary.'

Angelica had forgotten her tiredness in the excitement of the dance but now a wave of fatigue overcame her. 'Gentlemen, I fear I must take my leave. I'm suddenly in need of sleep. But I don't want to spoil your night.'

The young men both decided to leave with her. 'Without you, there's no reason to stay. We'll accompany you home and then go on to our club at St James's.'

There were so many guests in constant flux, leaving and new ones arriving, that Angelica and the young men thought they could slip away unnoticed but Lady Marwood, her eyes bright as a robin's, was suddenly at their elbow. 'My dears, are you leaving so soon?'

Lord Latimer took her hand. 'The orchestra is wonderful, but Miss Leigh is fatigued after this evening's performance. She needs to rest and we will escort her home.'

Angelica took her other hand. 'Lady Marwood, thank you for your hospitality.'

Their hostess smiled. 'It's always a treat to welcome youth and beauty to the rout. Join us next time. I try to have a monthly ball during the Season.' Then she was gone, called away by two young beauties who had arrived on the arm of a disreputable-looking man who appeared to know her.

Angelica saw the sleek head of Lord Rackham bent over another young woman's hand and was relieved to evade his attentions. They went to ask the butler to call Brunner and Mary from the servants' party and were soon out in the cold air. Mr Brunner gazed up to the dark sky and said, 'It's a fine night and we're only about fifteen minutes from Berkeley Square, it's probably quicker to walk than wait to hail a Hackney.' Everyone agreed and they set off west towards Piccadilly.

They walked in silence. Then in Prince's Street their passage was blocked where a roof had collapsed into the road and Brunner led them on a detour into Rupert Street. They walked past the shuttered milliners and drapers' shops and the small enclave of French goldsmiths. Angelica felt her pulse quicken. 'My mother used to work for a gold trader here.' She did not expect to be so immediately transported back to her earliest memories when she was six years old and the street was her playground.

She pointed to a ramshackle building and said in a small voice, 'Mama and I used to live here.'

'Well, ye be in a better place now, thank the Lord.' Brunner hooked her arm tighter into his.

Dante Locke paused, seemingly rapt in thought. 'A shining flame arose from these ashes.'

For Angelica, the neighbourhood aroused such powerful memories, long suppressed, and in a moment of insight she realised her mother's harshness with her had come from a determination to ensure a better life for her daughter. Almost to herself she said, 'How I longed for a father to whisk me away to some warm house with a bubbling pot on the range.'

Lord Latimer heard her words and took her other arm in sympathy. 'You have that now?' he asked, peering at her face in the gloomy light.

Angelica nodded. 'And I even have father figures, in Mr Brunner and his employer, Mr Breville.'

As they walked down the street, she gazed with sadness at the shuttered shop fronts and the accumulated rubbish through which they picked their way. The jeweller and most of the goldsmiths had left, the milliners were now purveyors of cheap bonnets and the draper's shop had become a drinking den and worse. Outside the Blue Posts tavern there was a hubbub and knots of pleasure-seekers and sots had spilled into the street, arguing loudly and flashing their fists. When Mr Brunner passed, the ex-pugilist warned fiercely, 'Step aside, gentlemen!' Even through the haze of alcohol he was recognised by his distinctive bulk and menacing expression as an ex-boxer, and most fell back in respect.

Lord Latimer took her arm. 'You should not be exposed to such dangers, Miss Leigh.' They all walked briskly towards the greater safety of Piccadilly with its flow of carriages, the pavements full of people on their way to or from their evening's entertainment.

Brunner agreed. 'I'll tell Mrs Leigh we'll use the carriage from now on.'

'But on a fine night I enjoy the walk. It helps me leave Ophelia at the theatre, and I'm never afraid when I'm escorted by you, Mr Brunner.' Angelica gazed up into his large, pugnacious face. 'And you too, Lord Latimer,' she added with a cheeky tilt of her head. 'I like London at night. I've known it all my life.'

'But there are hell-hatched things no young lady should see or hear.' Mr Brunner's face was grim and Angelica knew his abject childhood in the cotton mills of Manchester had left him with nightmare images of poverty and degradation. She squeezed his arm in recognition of his care.

'I warrant you're a handy practitioner of the art, Mr Brunner.' Lord Latimer cocked his head.

'Came to London as a boy; brawn and dancin' feet helped in the ring.'

'Then you met Mr Breville in the Daffy Club and we all were lucky that day.' Angelica's voice was warm with the memory.

'Yes, Miss Angelica. Ye were just a sprite when yer Mama moved into Berkeley Square. We helped each other out.'

Dante Locke had been quiet and pensive and when he spoke everyone turned to listen.

> 'The exulting sense – the pulse's maddening play
> That thrills the wanderer of the trackless way?
> That for itself can woo the approaching fight
> And turn what some deem danger to delight.'

Lord Latimer clapped him on the back. 'Damned good. One of yours?'

Mr Locke looked aghast. 'No, no! It's our own poetic Lord Byron, been reading *The Corsair*.'

'Well, it's as good as anything I've heard of yours, Dante,' Lord Latimer said generously. 'And truth indeed that a good fight turns danger to delight. What think you, Brunner?' He was in a fine mood and glanced across at Mr Brunner with a sense of the comradeship of the ring.

Angelica took Mr Locke's arm and he looked into her eyes with a smile. 'It's said in Persia that a beautiful face is balm for wounded hearts and the key to locked doors.'

Angelica chuckled. 'That indeed is a nice thought, but not all doors, Mr Locke, I assure you.' In the dim light her eyes gleamed.

Lord Latimer had not forgotten Mr Brunner's words and the thought he had known Angelica as a child made him curious. 'What was Miss Leigh like when you first met her?'

'A fairy with a halo of golden hair.'

'Tush! Mr Brunner. I was tougher than I looked. I had learned young how to care for myself.'

'Miss Angelica, yer safety is my first care. Be no better than an unhanged blackguard if anything should befall ye.' He spoke these words with so much force, Angelica peered into his face with some concern.

She said reassuringly, 'I promise I'll not give you cause for anxiety, Mr Brunner. Your care is much appreciated.' They arrived at number seven, where she and her mother lived under the protection of Mr Breville, a big corner house that dominated Berkeley Square. Angelica turned to say farewell to the young friends. 'Well, thanks to you, I've had enough excitement to last me a month.' She laughed.

'Good night, Miss Leigh, Mary. And Mr Brunner too.' Lord Latimer bowed. 'For us, the night is still young.' They waved as they retraced their steps in the direction of St James's.

As Angelica entered the house she smiled at Martin, the butler who had waited up to let them in. 'Huzza! Mr Brunner, our Perseus has brought beautiful Andromeda safely home.' A retired actor, Martin had been reluctant to relinquish his sooty eye make-up and rouge and managed the household with the informal flamboyance of the theatre.

'Thank you, Martin. He is indeed a hero. Is Mama still up?'

'The beauteous lady of the house retired an hour ago.' With a dramatic flourish, he flung his arm towards the staircase. Bidding goodnight to Mary and Mr Brunner, Angelica walked up the stairs. Tiredness overcame her. The unexpected detour down the street where she and her mother once lived had stirred thoughts on which she did not care to dwell and she longed for bed. As she reached her door she heard

Amabel Leigh's lilting voice from across the landing. 'Angel dearest, come in.'

She knocked on the door and entered to find her mother resplendent in lemon satin, sitting up amongst the banked linen pillows in her great four-poster bed. Her face was still pretty, her cheeks pink and shiny, her fair hair rolled in curling papers; Angelica knew she could not be expecting a visit that night from Mr Breville. Her mother patted the bed in invitation, then noticed her daughter was wearing an evening dress. 'Angelica, where have you been? And at this hour too?' She peered at her face with suspicion.

Angelica sighed. 'Oh, Mama, there's too much to tell you. And to ask. But I'm dog-tired. I'll see you in the morning.' She leant over and kissed her mother's soft scented cheek and headed for the door before she could be recalled to explain herself.

Amabel Leigh's face fell in disappointment, but she acquiesced and waved from the bed. 'Sleep away all fatigue and sorrows, my darling.'

2

PRIDE COMES CALLING

Ivor Asprey was at breakfast, discussing the day's Parliamentary work with Nicholas Digby. The room was at the back of the house overlooking the mews and painted a sea-green, the shadows from the beech tree in the garden flickering on the wall and across the oval table laden with sweet pastries, a pot of coffee and a jug of ale. In the centre was a baked gammon and a large loaf of bread. Both men were plainly dressed in dark navy coats, but Mr Asprey's had a certain style to the immaculate cut and a lustre to the cloth that revealed its expensive provenance from one of the leading tailors of the day. Papers requiring signatures were arrayed on the table as Mr Digby poured out another cup of coffee for his employer. Just as they bent their heads, intent on business, there was a giggle at the door and Elinor skipped into the room.

'Oh, Papa! I'm so glad you're still here.' She danced up to him, ignoring his forbidding look, and kissed him on the cheek. 'Good morning, Mr Digby,' she said impishly and helped herself to a currant bun.

'Good morning, Elinor. When do your lessons start?' Her father gazed at her with a speculative expression.

'You know they don't start until nine. I still have ten minutes with you before you go.' She sat down beside him and slipped her arm through his. Nicholas Digby watched this affectionate gesture with a smile. He had been in the Asprey household for the last five years and had seen this motherless child grow up from the age of six, remarkably sunny in nature and unconcerned with her father's austere moods which could quell the spirits of grown men. He put much of the credit at the door of the girl's governess, Miss Stafford, whom he considered to have brought intellectual rigour and a maternal sensibility to her job of educating Elinor Asprey.

His employer shifted in his chair and, turning to his daughter, said in a matter-of-fact way, 'Well, Mr Digby and I have business to transact before I make my way to Westminster, you know.'

'What time are you back?' Her eyes, not as deeply blue as her father's, twinkled at him. 'I want to play you the Haydn etude I've been practising.'

Ivor Asprey's pen was poised over a letter and he responded in a distracted voice, 'I won't be home until you're in bed, I'm afraid.'

'Oh, Papa! I never see you. You've always got something more important to do!' She pulled her hand from the crook of his arm. 'Where are you going?'

He put down his pen and cast his intense gaze over her for the first time that morning. 'You look very charming, my dear,' he said with a warm smile. 'I like that dress. Is it new?'

'No, Papa! It's my old calico I wear for lessons. You know that,' she said in an exasperated voice, and he laughed.

'My sweet daughter, you can't expect me to keep up with all your costume choices.'

'Well, at least tell me where you are going tonight.'

'I'm going to see Mr Kean in *Hamlet* at the theatre.'

'Oh, I'd so like to see Mr Kean. Can I come?'

'No. I don't know that the play is suitable for a young girl of sensibility.'

'Well, I'm reading Shakespeare with Miss Stafford. She says all of life is in his works.' Elinor Asprey's face turned serious and she looked into her father's eyes. 'And life is sometimes tragic, is it not, Papa?'

These words made him glance at his daughter with apprehension. There were times when he feared she was too wise for her years. He nodded and appeared to soften his stance. 'Miss Stafford is right. I'll see what the production's like and perhaps I can take you at a later date.'

'Are you taking Lady Linus tonight?' Her teasing tone had returned.

Ivor was brusque. 'No. I'm going on my own. This is business not pleasure.'

'But Papa, that would be perfect then for Lady Linus, don't you think?' She met her father's surprised look with an innocent gaze, while Nicholas Digby suppressed a smile.

It was well-known in the household that Portia Linus considered herself the perfect wife for Ivor Asprey, taking pride in how clever and rational she was, a veritable *bas-bleu* continuing the worthy tradition of her intellectual forbears. The Duchess also approved of her as a suitable help-meet for her brother. But that brother's daughter, his secretary and governess all thought her a prosy, nosy personage with strong improving opinions on the lives and behaviour of others, that she chose *not* to keep to herself. Elinor had confided to Miss Stafford how she dreaded the thought that Lady Linus might become her stepmother.

'I hope you're not being pert, young miss!' Her father's voice was stern. When she dropped her eyes, the colour rising in her cheeks, he added more equably, 'Lady Linus is an admirable young woman and you'd do well to heed her care of you.'

'Yes, Papa,' Elinor Asprey said just as Sarah Stafford knocked and entered.

'Good morning, sir, and Mr Digby. Elinor, it's time for your French conversation. I would be pleased if you would come and join me.' An attractive young woman, the governess had a warm friendly manner that hid her quiet authority. Elinor Asprey had learned early that she could not get round Miss Stafford as she could the maids. But for six years this young woman had been the nearest she had to a mother and had embarked on not just educating her intellect but also nurturing her heart.

Elinor flung her arms round her father's neck and buried her face in his immaculate cravat. 'Oh, Papa. Take care. I don't want anything to happen to you. You're all I have.' Her words were muffled but tumbled out with such feeling that those in the room felt the poignancy of her fear of loss.

Her father put down his pen and enclosed her in a quick embrace. He held her close for a moment then recovered his poise and said with a steady voice, 'Run along now. And you be a good girl and I'll see you tomorrow.' He kissed her pale cheek.

'You promise?' Her anxious eyes searched his face.

'I promise. We'll have breakfast and I'll tell you about Mr Kean and you can read me your latest Latin prose. What are you reading?'

Her face lit up. 'Miss Stafford's book of *Aesop's Fables*. There are beautiful pictures of the animals and it's in Latin, English and French. So I can read it all.' She followed her governess from the room, turning at the door to cast her father a mischievous smile.

* * *

Ivor Asprey set out to walk across St James's Park to Westminster rather later than he had hoped. It was a fresh morning; the overnight rain had washed the air clean and the birdsong seemed even louder than usual but he was distracted by the thought of a speech he was due to give the following day on the hours and conditions of child labour in the mills. Parliament did not sit until late afternoon but he had work to do. Various men and women hailed him as he passed. He had just reached the Canal when he heard the hooves of a galloping horse. Nothing faster than a canter was allowed in the royal parks and he turned with some asperity to see his nephew astride a beautiful grey stallion, his flying white tail catching the morning light. The young man pulled his horse up and leapt to the ground.

'Uncle Ivor, sir! Forgive this rude intrusion but I wanted you to be the first to know. Boney's been forced to abdicate! The war is over!' His youthful face was flushed and laughter bubbled up with excitement and relief. Despite the usual reserve he felt with his forbidding uncle, he grabbed him in a hug.

Mr Asprey returned his embrace, then asked urgently, 'How do you know? Who told you?'

'I've just seen Castlereagh's private secretary riding in the avenue. We were at school together. He hailed me, only just conveyed the intelligence to the King. The generals insist on Napoleon's exile.' He was still breathless with the import of it all.

'It is indeed tremendous, Charles. Rumours were rife, I know. Once Paris fell it would not be long. After all these years, good news indeed.'

One of his parliamentary colleagues came up to them, having heard the report too, his genial face beaming. They shook hands and exchanged words of relief and congratulation.

Lord Latimer could not suppress his emotion, aware of the personal repercussions for everyone. 'I can barely remember when we weren't at war with that Corsican fiend! Nurse used to make me say my prayers to ask God to protect us from The Devil's Favourite, so she called him. All were affrighted, sir!' He grasped his uncle's arm with the memory.

An almost imperceptible shudder went through Ivor Asprey as he recalled his initial excitement, along with most of the young and the radical, at Napoleon's cry for freedom. The thought that a new egalitarian order was beginning gripped the imagination and Bonaparte embodied this revolution. 'You were too young to know the exhilarating dream of liberty from every ancient régime. It was your generation who lived through its terrible souring.'

'So, God be praised! My papa's sacrifices were not in vain. When he came home I thought he could not live.'

'The Duke's bravery was never in doubt.' Asprey met his nephew's sorrowful eyes. 'We were victorious in Egypt and he played his part.'

'Now Boney can never be a threat again.' Lord Latimer's voice was fervent.

'I wouldn't be so sure this is the end of his ambitions. He's still a prodigy and is a force not spent yet.'

The young man swung round and with an emotional voice cried out, 'Don't say that, Uncle! He's a fiend who's caused such destruction. He almost destroyed my father and my family, the Devil take him and fry him in Hell!'

He was met with a sympathetic smile. 'You're right young hotspur, he is a fiend, but he's a genius too. Today let's celebrate the shift in European power at last. Shall I meet you at your club tonight for champagne?'

'I'm busy until ten. What time after that, sir?'

'I'm attending Kean's *Hamlet* tonight. So I'll come to White's on my way home.'

Lord Latimer was about to remount his horse when he paused and gave his uncle a sharp look. 'What's up, Uncle? I can't recall your last visit to any playhouse. Always much more important things to do,' he said with a mocking laugh.

'Be gone, young shaver! There's much interest in the thespian Kean.'

'No doubt in his beautiful Ophelia too,' Lord Latimer grimaced as he swung into the saddle. 'I hope Mama has not asked you to intervene. I'm about to reach my majority and what I do with my affairs is entirely my own business.'

'I couldn't agree more, my dear Charles,' Ivor Asprey drawled, amusement in his eyes as he met his nephew's scowl. The young man wheeled his horse round and cantered away.

* * *

Angelica slept late. She awoke to the spring sunshine seeping through the heavy silk curtains casting a gleaming light over the room. It had been ten years since she and her mother had moved into Mr Breville's grand house but she never took for granted the pleasures of a room of her own and freedom from the corrupting grind of poverty and uncertainty. Last night she had been shocked to be reminded just how afraid, cold and hungry she had been as a child. But thanks to the heart and open purse of her mother's protector she had been educated to be a lady, even if her provenance and her profession suggested otherwise. Her mother had always had great expectations on her behalf. Angelica knew that some alchemy meant she could express emotional truth through her acting that her audiences, however crass or intoxicated, recognised and responded to with feeling. She was grateful to be able to earn a modest living this way, doing something she enjoyed, rather than having to be a lady's companion or a governess to other women's children.

The resourceful Mrs Leigh had discovered her own talent for furniture buying and interior decoration, having wheedled a generous budget of 8,000 pounds out of her indulgent benefactor. She had transformed the house into a palace of colour and oriental detail to rival the Prince Regent's Royal Pavilion at Brighton. When Angelica opened her eyes, the first sight was of small brilliant-plumed birds appearing to flit amongst twining stems of jasmine, clematis and periwinkle. She had loved this hand-painted wallpaper since she had been ten years old and her room was newly decorated; as consciousness dawned each morning she still found it hard to believe she was waking in paradise, and it was hers.

Not knowing quite why, Angelica felt a pulse of excitement ripple through her at the prospect of the life awaiting her, though still unknown. She slipped out of bed, impatient to start the day. Mary had placed in her dressing room a pitcher of hot water and a large Delft bowl ready for her morning wash, and laid out her day dress. She put on the sprigged green muslin gown, simple with its scoop neck and small puff sleeves over straight inner sleeves, and tied the sash just above the waist. Pulling a comb briefly through her mass of wavy hair, she plaited it loosely and coiled it into an informal bun at the nape of her neck. She ran down the stairs to breakfast and found her mother with a cup of coffee, poring over a book of fabric swatches.

'Good morning, Mama.' She kissed her on the cheek.

'You look very sanguine, Angelica.' Mrs Leigh lifted her shrewd gaze and with a smile inspected her only child. 'So, tell me what happened last night.'

'The performance went well enough, but Lord Latimer was keen that I accompany him and his friend to a ball at Lady Marwood's house afterwards. I agreed but just for a couple of dances.'

'This sounds very promising, my dear.' Mrs Leigh purred with pleasure at the thought that matters might be gathering to a head between her precious daughter and this most eligible of young men.

Angelica ignored her mother's aperçu to continue with her tale. 'Then Mr Brunner brought me and Mary home, and Lord Latimer and his friend, Dante Locke, decided to accompany us before going on to their club.'

'So I should hope.' Mrs Leigh nodded in a satisfied way.

'Oh Mama, I wish you could think of things other than my capturing a duke's son!' Angelica said in an exasperated voice. She had been so dismissive of Lord Latimer's interest in her, aware of how unlikely it was that anything could ever come of it, but her own feelings had surprised her and made her vulnerable. It was exciting to elicit such desire in a handsome young man and impossible not to recognise that pulse of her own animal spirits in response. This realisation unsettled her and her mother's blatant matchmaking made her recoil.

She changed the subject to another which exercised her more. 'We had to take a detour home down the street where we used to live. Seeing it so derelict and dangerous made me think of our life there.'

Amabel Leigh's face was stricken as she spoke, 'I am reluctant to remember, Angelica, such desperate times. I wish things had been other-wise. The neighbourhood mothers and I had to scrabble where we could just to feed our children. It was hard for you and for everyone. Don't judge me.'

Angelica leaned forward earnestly, tears springing to her eyes. 'Mama, I'd never judge you. I am more grateful than I can say that you kept me, that I didn't go to the Foundling Hospital. Now I understand why you intro-duced me to Mr Dunbar at Covent Garden Theatre.'

'I wanted you to have a chance of a better life. You see, I knew your wit and beauty needed a bigger stage.'

'But now you have Mr Breville to care for you, we have a better life.'

''Tis true, but you would have an even better life as a duchess if you marry that young Lord Latimer.' She smiled at her daughter.

'Oh, Mama! He's just a young man who thinks he's in love. It means very little.'

'That may well be, but if you're a clever woman you can *make* it mean more.' Amabel Leigh's voice had grown brusque. She had little time for the niceties of sensibility; the young of today were self-indulgent in their senti-mental expectations of life. 'You may have been born in penury, but you've been schooled to be the wife of a nobleman. You have great beauty and feminine accomplishments; you would make a fine duchess.'

'Mama, you don't realise just how much his family would resist a lowly actress being so elevated amongst their ranks.'

'They should consider themselves fortunate to have your beauty and grand disposition added to their ancestral line. From what I hear the Arlington family tree is so enervated it's barely upright.' Mrs Leigh's maternal ferocity was roused.

Angelica explained as if to a child, 'You know as well as I that a noble family as elevated as the Arlingtons do not consider marriage as a matter of predilection. It's a contract between two equal nobilities where the woman brings as much property and status to the match as the man. I have nothing to offer but myself.'

Her mother remained irrepressible and said in a triumphant voice, 'But the Duke approved of you, my darling.'

'He did. But he was so damaged in Alexandria he no longer has any power in the matter. The Duchess is the force in the family, and according to Lord Latimer, so is his uncle. And he's a stiff-rumped martinet.'

'Is that the Mr Asprey who's a Member of Parliament? Don't see how that gives him any authority over his nephew's marriage.' Her mother's mouth turned sulky.

'He's clever and ambitious and Lord Latimer says he'll be the next Prime Minister when the Whigs come to power.'

'May Jove help us!' Amabel Leigh threw up her hands in disgust. 'Politicians! All concerned with their own ends.'

It was Angelica's turn to be sly. 'He's been involved in the Catholic Emancipation Act,' she said quietly and watched her mother's expression change from disgust to a dawning appreciation. Amabel Leigh had long been bitter that her younger brother had been unable to take up a minor post in the Civil Service because of his religion.

'So, in favour of emancipation? Well, that would be a thing,' she said thoughtfully. 'This brother of the hoity-toity Duchess may be more than a well-breeched swell after all.'

'Now Mama, I have to get on with reading this script for my new play.' Angelica picked up the play she had to learn.

'What's it called?'

'*The Child of Nature*, translated from the French by Mrs Inchbald.'

'I'm glad you'll be offered a new contract, my dear.' Mrs Leigh poured out another cup of coffee for them both. They sat in easy silence, Angelica reading her play and her mother poring over her swatches, planning her next decorating scheme. After some minutes Angelica looked up, an expression of impatience on her face. 'Mama, Mrs Inchbald is meant to be a radical, a friend of Mr Godwin's. Yet she's made my character, Amanthis, prepared to give up happiness with the marquis she loves in order to demonstrate filial piety to a *disgraced* father whom she was told was dead.

She's about to follow him into penury and exile!' She was surprised to see her mother's expression lose its equanimity as she quickly returned her gaze to her sample book.

An uneasy thought clutched at Angelica's heart and her voice was insistent as she asked, 'Mama? When did my father die?'

Amabel Leigh composed her features and responded lightly, 'My dear, you know he was a petty officer in the British Navy under the command of Rear Admiral Nelson. He died during the Battle of Aboukir Bay, when you were five.'

'Did they bring his body home?'

'No, all sailors lost in action were buried at sea.' Her pretty face appeared downcast.

'Mama, what was he like? You've never told me anything other than he was handsome and Irish and a very good singer and dancer. You thought I got my talents from him.'

'Did I?' She looked startled. 'I think your beauty and facility for music and theatrics come from me.' She seemed disinclined to talk any further on the subject and this fuelled Angelica's uneasiness. Her mother deflected the conversation back to the play. 'I hope you'd show more sense than that heroine and grasp the chance of happiness with a nobleman!'

'Oh, Mama! You are incorrigible.'

Mrs Leigh jumped up in irritation. 'Don't be so jingle-brained, Angelica! You have no idea of the realities of the world. You say Lord Latimer is not serious, well, you have enough wit and beauty to ensure he becomes so!'

There was a knock at the door and Martin entered carrying a silver salver with an envelope, embellished with a self-important crest, at its centre. With a bow he presented it to Angelica. 'A liveried groom delivered this for you, Miss Angelica. He did not wait for a reply.' Mrs Leigh was immediately alert to the possibilities in another noble admirer for her daughter.

Angelica did not recognise the crest or the black spidery handwriting and opened it, curious herself. She read aloud to her mother, '*My dear Miss Leigh, I will call on you after your performance tonight, to commend you on your art. As it will be well before midnight I hope you will not be impelled to flee. Rackham.'*

She looked up and met her mother's bright eyes. 'Don't raise your hopes, Mama, I assure you Lord Rackham has no intention of making me Lady Rackham in the near future,' she laughed. 'He's notorious among the theatre girls and is not to be trusted.'

'My dear, I hope you won't live to regret such high-mindedness. Without money or breeding we women take what opportunities we can.'

'Mama!' The argument Angelica was about to enter was cut short as the door opened and a tall, large-chested man entered the room in a rush.

'Bella! The news of Bonaparte's abdication is now official. No more false hopes, the long war is truly over!' He flung out his arms and Mrs Leigh flew into his capacious embrace.

Pressed against his chest, she became soft and kittenish and with a winsome twinkle, gazed into his face. Adept at flirting, she purred, 'So Neddy, can we go to Paris soon?'

He released her with an indulgent smile and turned to acknowledge Angelica. 'Forgive me, my dear. This is indeed such welcome news. At last I can begin to rebuild my continental business.' Pulling Mrs Leigh close again, he smiled into her excited face. 'And yes, we will go to Paris in the next few weeks. I am set on importing French porcelain again; we'll visit the factories of Sèvres and Limoges, and you'll come with me.'

Edward Breville was large in body and character. His big square face belonged on a statue of a stalwart adventurer, heading into the unknown. Fortitude set his jaw and his dark shrewd eyes were intent and watchful but quick to find amusement in the vagaries of the world. He had escaped the poverty of his Rochdale childhood where he had withstood the gruelling conditions as a child labourer in Mr Vavasour's woollen mill. Like Amabel Leigh and Mr Brunner, he had come to London in search of his fortune. Where Mrs Leigh had used her beauty, guile and charm to advance her prospects, Brunner his strength and courage in the boxing ring, Edward Breville's more ambitious dreams had been reliant on the brilliance of his mind and a hard-schooled determination.

His memory and mathematical ability meant he could reckon the odds so fast in games of chance he made his first fortune gambling at Hazard.

Always disciplined, he did not succumb to running his luck in the gambling hells off St James's and Covent Garden. Instead, he gambled to a scheme and when he'd won a sufficient amount, he invested in his business, the import and export of fine porcelain for the increasingly prosperous and discerning middle classes.

Mr Breville had left his homely wife back in Rochdale in comfortable circumstances in the bosom of her family. When he had met the comely Mrs Leigh she persuaded him how much it would profit him to have a beautiful woman in his bed who was able to preside over the management and decoration of his grand London house, as befitted a very wealthy man indeed.

Edward Breville's forthright Yorkshire manner, bluff ways and the fact he had earned his immense wealth through his own enterprise in trade meant that the highest echelons of society were closed to him. This merely made him declare in his bull-headed way he couldn't give a curse. But in fact, just a week before he had approached White's Club for membership and this most aristocratic of gentlemen's clubs had unanimously blackballed him, intimating he was not sufficiently 'high born'.

Angelica knew that beneath his confident braggadocio, Mr Breville longed for some recognition from the ruling classes. She had put her hand on his arm and said with sympathy, 'I've never known an estimable man who is a member of White's. You're too singular for them, Mr Breville.' He'd squeezed her hand in thanks.

Her mother had said archly, 'Lord Latimer's a member is he not, Angelica?'

'I said *estimable,* Mama.' They laughed and Angelica continued, ''Tis true, Lord Latimer has many personal virtues, he is charming and has every advantage of exalted nobility and wealth but what will he do with such good fortune?' She paused for dramatic effect then turned with a smile to Edward Breville. 'No doubt he'll live an unexceptional, even useless life.'

All three of them knew they were disqualified for different reasons from being considered members of the *haut ton*. For the sticklers of social propriety, Angelica's profession as an actress placed her only one rung above a bordello dweller, subject to all kinds of unwelcome advances, from the elevated membership of the gentlemen's clubs to the soakers and card sharps scrabbling for a living on the streets. Her mother's dubious beginnings and shady amorous past meant that no amount of beauty and fine clothes would make her acceptable, unless she married into the upper classes and could gloss her social status with her husband's nobility.

However, money could buy a certain sort of celebrity and immortality and Mr Breville had paid a pot of gold sovereigns to the most famous and flattering society portraitist, Thomas Lawrence, to create a painting of the beauteous Mrs Leigh. In his delight on seeing the completed portrait he relapsed into his native accent, blurting out, 'Ee lass, it's almost as grand as the original!' He had immediately got his footman to hang the painting above the drawing room fireplace where the image of his mistress welcomed all-comers with her beauty, and the clear evidence of his wealth.

When she first saw it, Angelica had gasped, admiring the enhanced charms of her mother. The artist had shortened her nose a touch, added lustre to her glorious hair, and a suffused colour as delicate as a blushing peach to her cheek. 'Mama! You look very welcoming indeed,' she said with a naughty smile. The portrait was a glossy embodiment of seductive beauty with Amabel Leigh's creamy bosom almost bursting from the constraints of her ivory satin bodice, her eyes sparkling with promise.

Now, as Mr Breville's energetic presence filled the room, Angelica greeted his news of the end of the war with a smile. 'This is a happy day for everyone, but tonight the theatre will be even more unruly.' She thought of the usually rowdy pit and knew that during her performance more alcohol would be drunk and wild revelry ensue.

Mr Brunner insisted on taking her and Mary to the theatre in the Breville carriage. They both clambered into the chaise to make the short trip to Covent Garden Theatre through roads already filling up with celebrating Londoners. As they approached the Piazza, Angelica was increasingly recognised by the crowd. Men with red faces staggered towards the coach, their eyes bleary and smiles lopsided as they hailed her. The women on their arms cried, 'It's our angel! God love yer, dearie,' as they waved their work-worn hands and blew her kisses. Angelica waved back; she believed only luck had separated her fate from theirs.

The young women disembarked and dashed through the stage door, nodding to the keeper who guarded the entrance from unwelcome visitors.

As they were settling into the dressing room Mr Dunbar appeared round the door. 'Ah, good. I wanted to discuss our next play with you, Miss Leigh. Mary, would you be so kind as to go to Pastow's tavern for some ale?'

Mary looked doubtfully at her mistress but Angelica nodded for her to go. The manager lounged in the chair and gazed at Angelica speculatively. She noticed how pale and doughy he looked as if he never saw the sun. His hairline was receding and he had affected a tousled hairstyle in the hopes that the side curls would disguise the thinning on top. His pale eyes narrowed. 'What did you think of *The Child of Nature*?' he enquired in a mild tone.

'It's fine enough. There are some fair passages and I think the audience would find it entertaining. Why, what think you?'

'It would be a fitting play after we finish this run of *Hamlet*. As you know I'd like you to play the part of Amanthis, *"in which perfect beauty, and enchanting grace, timid innocence, with matchless sensibility, were all united."'* With his eyes half-closed he recited the description of the main character as if in a kind of trance.

More irritated than enraptured, Angelica briskly replied, 'It's her vapid innocence that galls me. But I can see it would be an affecting part to play.' She was grateful for any first-rate employment in the premier theatre in the city, although she thought the male parts had more meat on their bones.

'Well then, Miss Leigh, the part may well be yours.' His expression changed from neutral benignity to something more malign. 'Why not show your appreciation and come and sit in my lap,' he said in a wheedling voice. 'A little thank you kiss and a fondle would do no harm, surely?'

Angelica felt a shock of surprise, then her good spirits faltered. She knew her profession was held in low regard but did not expect this from the usually inoffensive Dunbar. She swung round from the dressing table and said with disdain, 'Sir, if you think me good enough for the part then I will accept with gratitude. Should you be unsure and need persuasion then I suggest you offer it to someone else.' She knew this was a risk and her future work depended on men like him, but she also knew that he considered her presence a boost to ticket sales and she hoped such mercenary thinking would prevail.

With a flash of anger he spat out the words, 'Hoity-toity! Beware you don't become a Covent Garden doxy. Your sights may be set on that notable sprig, Latimer, but believe me, madam, women like you, however beautiful and clever, do not marry into the higher reaches of our nobility.' He leapt to his feet, his pride stung.

Angelica tried to keep her voice calm and said, 'Mr Dunbar, I'm a good actress. I know I can get work at other theatres, should you wish to dismiss me.'

David Dunbar was not used to being challenged by a young woman who depended on him for her livelihood; having her disdain his power to make and break careers unsettled him. His voice rose. 'You'll come to rue the day you treated my patronage with such disrespect. You'll learn to know your place!' He grasped her arm as if to forcibly embrace her.

Just at that moment the door opened and he stepped back. Mary entered with the tankard of ale and handed it over with distinct lack of grace. She did not care to be ordered about by someone who did not employ her. By the colour in her mistress's cheek and the scowl on Mr Dunbar's face it was obvious her mistress did not care to be imposed on either. The door closed with a bang behind the manager's departing back and the women exchanged glances that spoke of their trials.

'Thought he'd be up to something.' Mary's sniff was freighted with disapproval.

'Yes, thank you for being so quick and turning up in time.'

'He's a hog-grubber. Always was, always will be. I'm not running any more errands for him so he can impose on you, Miss Angelica.'

Angelica hugged her. 'There's another man visiting tonight after the performance, hoping to importune me too. Lord Rackham.'

'Oh, 'im. He's a hog-grubber too, only a noble one, and handsome too, so he's that more dangerous!' The women managed to lift their spirits with a laugh.

'I'd better get dressed. With the news of the victory in France, it's going to be a reckless night.'

* * *

Ivor Asprey had to leave the Houses of Parliament sooner than he would have wished but in order to settle his sister's mind and gain some peace he needed to at least show willing and see the play, perhaps meet the offending actress and be able to relay some sort of consoling intelligence back. He strode into the brilliant low sun of a late spring evening and joined Parliament Street thronged with revellers, heading north towards Covent Garden. His mind was full of the speech he was due to make and he stopped occasionally to take from his breast pocket a small notebook in which he jotted down new ideas or a particularly resonant phrase that came to him as he walked.

His thoughts were soon wrenched to the present and the world of the senses. Arriving in the foyer of the theatre, he was faced by a brilliant caravanserai of people in high plumage and of every persuasion. The fashionables who had paid for the best boxes were beautifully dressed and mingled for a while with the rougher elements, more foxed than not, heading for the pit or the even more unruly upper terraces. Two strands of *beau-monde* and *demi-monde* came together at the entrance, the young dandies and older libertines jostling and soliciting the painted ladies who congregated like butterflies, fluttering and coquettish around them.

Ivor Asprey stood for a moment surveying the merry scene, half expecting to see his lovelorn nephew enlivening the view. His brow darkened, however, as he caught sight of Lord Rackham, even more vulpine than usual, weaving his way through the crowd with a very comely lady of indeterminate age and reputation on his arm. The sight of his lordship on the prowl always incensed him. He could not forgive his predatory interest falling on his own wife all those years ago. Not wanting to be drawn into conversation with his lordship and companion, Ivor Asprey turned away and found himself looking into the upturned face of a lady he knew somewhat better.

He bowed. 'What a pleasant surprise, Lady Linus.' The young woman gazing at him in an unnervingly clear-eyed way was smooth-faced and handsome, her fair hair swept off her face in a neat chignon with a modicum of tendrils softening the restrained style.

'Mr Asprey, I am surprised to see you at the theatre when you have such important work to do.' She smiled as if they shared a secret. 'I'm only here because my mother needed accompaniment.'

He was reluctant to reveal anything of his mission and so deflected with a languid comment. 'Mr Kean is causing a sensation as Hamlet, I hear.'

'I heard the sensation was more his counterpart, a young upstart girl who reveals rather too much in the dying scene.' There was a small frown between her brows as she looked across at the milling crowd of men around the birds of paradise, chattering in a flirtatious flock in the foyer.

With a serious voice she took his arm. 'You and I, Mr Asprey, are engaged on important work in this new century. The licentiousness and tumult of the previous age is now past. You, with your social reforms and I with my concerns for public morals, are at the forefront of change.' Her eyes were cool and challenging.

Ivor Asprey had been attracted to Portia Linus's intelligence and conversation when he'd first met her some months before and she had discussed her translation of Hesiod's *Works and Days* and compared it to Vergil's *Georgics,* but he had not suspected such a zealous, managing nature underneath that cool cerebral manner. As the noise from the foyer had increased he bent his head closer to hers to ask, 'How so? M'lady.'

With her eyes still on the young unaccompanied women peeling off in pairs with the young men, she said in a low confiding voice, 'I've joined Lady Dartmouth's committee seeking to rehabilitate the unfortunate young women of the streets. Make them fit for employment. Mostly as maids and kitchen assistants; no responsible employer would want them working in the nursery.'

Ivor Asprey admired her for her lack of priggish sentiment in discussing this pervasive underbelly of city life. He liked her rational, even masculine, turn of mind. Perhaps Edwina was right, she would make an admirable wife for a reforming Whig politician on the rise. Then Lady Linus's mother appeared at her elbow and claimed her daughter's attention.

Ivor Asprey saluted them as they bade farewell then turned on his heel to discover which box was his. He was no longer single-mindedly focussed on his forthcoming speech and sat down in the luxurious red plush seat feeling unsettled and pensive. He entertained the alien thought that perhaps his sister was not always wrong. He glanced across at the opposite box and glimpsed a familiar profile and an unexpected stab of longing further undermined his equanimity. Arabella, Countess of Hilperton, had just taken her seat alongside her husband and mother-in-law. He looked on her disconsolate beauty, that exquisite tip-tilted nose, the curve of her cheek, and was reminded why, against reason, he continued his unsatisfactory affair with her. She must have sensed his piercing gaze for she turned and, as the light dimmed, their eyes met, gleaming in the semi-darkness.

He sat back in his seat thoroughly discomposed. How much he disliked to be in the sway of his emotions. Since the death of his wife he had sought to minimise his emotional vulnerability by burying himself in work and choosing to express any romantic needs with the beautiful Countess, herself dissatisfied with marriage to a sporting earl who preferred his horses to her. Ivor Asprey thought it fortunate that each desired nothing much from the other beyond a pleasurable few hours in the afternoon. But his heart, so long cauterised, was stirring back to life, he knew not why, and was disturbed by these unruly feelings that surprised him at unexpected moments.

The play had started but his mind was elsewhere. In the low light he was aware of the Countess who was aware of him, stealing the occasional glance his way. And somewhere in another box, Lady Linus and her mother were sitting, perhaps as distracted as he was. Even the arrival of the ghost, clanking onstage, and the excitement of the pit did not hold his attention. A great cheer at the sight of Hamlet made Ivor look up to see Edmund Kean, already hailed as the new great tragedian of the age, dressed in his embroidered frock coat, satin breeches and a towering powdered wig. Ivor Asprey thought the production had made a mistake in choosing eighteenth-century dress but despite this sartorial disadvantage, Hamlet's presence was mesmerising. Regardless of his diminutive stature, Mr Kean compelled all eyes as he stalked about the stage, his voice thrilling with emotion.

When Angelica, as Ophelia, eventually arrived on stage with her brother, Laertes, Ivor wondered what all the fuss was about. This slip of a girl was undistinguished, overborne by her heavy costume and the white powder on her face and labouring under an elaborate wig. But when she spoke her voice was lyrical and full of feeling. He leaned forward to catch her words better. The drunken crowd had begun their bawdy catcalls from the moment she appeared and the excitement reached a crescendo when she spoke the verse:

> *'Do not, as some ungracious pastors do,*
> *Show me the steep and thorny way to heaven;*
> *Whilst like a puff'd and reckless libertine,*
> *Himself the primrose path of dalliance treads,*
> *And recks not his own rede.'*

A slew of shouts almost drowned out Laertes' farewell to his sister and father. Ivor Asprey winced in sympathy for the actress as one stentorian voice bellowed, 'Ee lass! That's telling the whore's-bird, that is.'

He heard a woman's voice cry, 'They're all scabs and varlets, miss. Keep away from 'em!' to much laughter. And then another rough voice from the opposite side of the pit shouted, 'Eh, miss! Don't believe Mister 'Amlet else it end in a bath of tears.'

Watching from the safety and privacy of his box, he admired how this young woman through force of character managed to act with such dignity and pathos that the audience grew subdued, despite reeling as they did with cheap ale.

Ivor Asprey was intrigued. Such skill and her exercise in subtle authority would be a lesson for politicians dealing with the rowdy floor of the House of Commons he thought, and wondered whether it was in technique or character that her power resided. As Ophelia left the stage his thoughts returned to his speech and the sudden realisation that it would be given extra force if he used first-hand accounts of the children in their own words, telling of their daily lives and suffering. He was busy making notes when a great roar from the pit startled him.

His pencil mark jagged across the page as he looked to the stage and beheld a vision that completely took him unawares and stopped his heart. It was as if one of Botticelli's Graces had wandered out of mythology and into their mundane lives. The crowd too fell uneasily silent, rapt in their attention on the divine figure before them.

For a moment it seemed that Ophelia had appeared entirely unclothed, so frail and vulnerable was she now in a simple white chemise having cast aside the brocaded armour of her previous costume. No longer hidden by her powdered wig, Angelica's hair was like liquid gold as it tumbled to her waist from a coronet of columbine and daisies; her face, free of white powder and paint, revealed the beauty of her translucent skin and her large, heavy-lidded eyes. Carrying her lyre and an armful of wild flowers which she strewed across the stage, she sang fragments of an unearthly song. All eyes were upon her. Her movements were a dance, her presence mesmerising; there was a sense of the audience holding its breath. With a chilling thought, Ivor Asprey realised that Ophelia was not about to die off-stage, her death to be described later by the Queen, but to drown in front of them.

He could not look away as the young woman, deceived in love, deprived of her wits, of everything, wandered distractedly and in despair to the back of the stage where the willow branch bent over a manufactured stream. Almost in a trance it seemed, she slipped into the water, still singing to herself, flowers floating around her body, her arm raised, her fingers holding the lyre until it too fell away. Then without a cry or struggle she disappeared beneath the water. A great sigh went up from the pit, a woman sobbed, 'No!' A man struggled to climb onstage to save her but was held back, and Ivor Asprey felt an unfamiliar clutch of sympathetic anguish.

The drunken element of the crowd then recovered its bawdy humour when the body of Ophelia was carefully extracted from the stream and the actress's form was unexpectedly revealed to the audience, the wet muslin clinging to her limbs, long tendrils of her hair trailing as she was carried into the wings.

Mr Asprey sat back deep into his box, unsettled, transported. Since his wife's death, a steel band had constrained his heart but he felt something shift and suddenly his emotions were at sea. He shut out the catcalls of the crowd who had turned so roundly against Prince Hamlet, and could barely follow the remainder of the play. His mind was exercised with the heart-wrenching vision of this young beauty so stripped of artifice, so undone.

He was touched to the core, yet he knew it was this very power that made Miss Leigh such an affecting tragic actress. But he had to resist her sorcerous art. Charged with his sister's mission, he now had to discourage her son's love affair with this young woman who no doubt had cast a spell over him as surely as she did the unruly audience. Mr Asprey felt lacking in the authority to intervene in his nephew's life and ill-equipped with any weapons of persuasion. It was disconcerting to recognise, in his own heart's reactions, something of Miss Leigh's emotional power. But most of all, he was startled by his own heart's susceptibility to Shakespeare's ageless tragedy and how it unlocked memories of the past. His wife, Emma, had been almost as young as Ophelia, her face as pale. It had been a long time since he had allowed himself to feel, to remember.

As the curtain fell he left his box in a hurry, not wanting to be in a queue of admirers waiting to see the actress. From his days as a young buck, courting Maria Campion, he knew well the secret passages that led directly to the lead actress's dressing room. Unnoticed by either Lady Linus or the Countess of Hilperton, he slipped into the corridor and through the hidden door that led backstage. One dark lord however saw him go, his face registering sly amusement that such an Honourable Member of Parliament was clandestinely visiting a young actress and taking such care not to be seen.

* * *

Angelica was sitting in her dressing robe, her damp hair falling in spirals round her face, sipping her hot chocolate and puzzling why she had forgotten two of her lines. 'Mary, in my response to Laertes's advice on maidenly virtue, I forgot the first couplet, "*I shall the effect of this good lesson keep, as watchman to my heart*". I had to be prompted to continue. Why, d'ye think?'

'The audience was so rumbustious, I could hear the hubbub back here. Perhaps you were disturbed?'

'Or just resistant to my brother's tedious jobation.' The young women laughed. There was a knock on the door. Angelica pulled her robe about her and tied the sash round her waist. 'Oh no, it's probably Lord Rackham. I'd hoped we might be gone before his threatened visit.'

Mary went to the door and there found a tall stranger with the bluest eyes she had ever seen. 'Sir, what can I do for you?'

'My name is Ivor Asprey. May I have a word with your mistress?' He had recovered his equanimity and his voice was businesslike.

Angelica sighed with relief. 'Let Mr Asprey come in, Mary.' She stood to greet her visitor.

'Forgive me intruding, Miss Leigh.' He bowed as she surveyed him with interest. 'My name may not be familiar to you.'

Angelica interrupted him with a delighted laugh and came forward to take both of his hands. 'I am relieved it is you and not another of your colleagues. And yes, I do know your name.'

Such a warm greeting took him aback. 'Has my nephew mentioned me?' His voice was wary.

'No, no. I know not whom your nephew may be. I have heard your name from a friend of mine, a Mr Brunner, who used to work in a woollen mill in Yorkshire when he was a boy. He very much approves of your efforts to address conditions in the mills.'

This unexpected sally put Mr Asprey on the back foot, however he determined to carry through his original plan. 'I am gratified that my work might make a difference,' he said stiffly, standing very tall in the small room. Angelica motioned him to the only chair, Mary whisking away the brocade dress that had been tossed there in the middle of their costume change.

Angelica was still smiling when she said, 'I think I do recall your nephew mentioning you. Is he, by chance, Lord Latimer?'

'He is indeed.'

'So you have been involved in trying to promote a bill on Catholic emancipation?'

Mr Asprey was surprised this young beauty was so up to snuff on his political work. It disconcerted him to be confronted by her in the flesh, so charming and welcoming, yet having to follow through with his disagreeable mission. He was further deflected by Angelica's amusement.

'Have I said anything untoward, Miss Leigh?' he asked, narrowing his blue eyes as he looked at her.

'Not at all, Mr Asprey. I'm just delighted to find you're not stiff-rumped at all.' Her words ended in a peal of laughter.

He found her laugh oddly infectious and smiled. 'That incorrigible boy! Did he really describe me thus?'

'Only with affection.'

'He is a rattle-pate, I fear.' In the expectant silence that hung between them, Ivor Asprey launched into the purpose of his visit. 'Apart from congratulating you on a most affecting performance, Miss Leigh, I have come on other business.'

Angelica sat down in front of her looking-glass. 'And what might that be, sir?' she asked, her remarkable eyes flashing with merriment.

Ivor Asprey looked disconcerted again; it embarrassed him to think he had implied ulterior motives in visiting a young actress in her dressing room. 'Oh no, no! Not on my own business, Miss Leigh. This is to do with my nephew, Charles Latimer.'

Angelica's smile faded as she turned to her maid. 'Mary, perhaps you should leave us so that Mr Asprey can talk freely.'

Seeing her in profile, he was struck once again by how beautiful she was in person. Her remarkable colouring, charm and intelligence of expression made it almost impossible not to gaze on her with a little wonder. But someone of his sophistication, experience and sense of self was not about to reveal admiration to any woman, least of all an actress, practised in the art of attraction and pretence. He hardened his recently sensitised heart. 'Miss Leigh, you cannot be unaware that Lord Latimer is heir to a great dukedom and extensive fortune?'

Angelica would have found his pompous delivery amusing if she had not sensed that something more serious was about to be presented to her. Disinclined to help him with his presumptuous mission, she responded sweetly, 'Indeed, I am not unaware.'

'His mother, the Duchess of Arlington, is concerned that his intentions may be more serious than mere flirtation.'

'I must admit, Mr Asprey, I am not privy to such intentions. Have you, or she, spoken to Lord Latimer of the matter?' Angelica still had a faint smile on her face but her blood was rising. 'Perhaps I am mistaken, but is not his lordship about to reach his majority and is therefore will be free to do as he pleases?'

Ivor Asprey's practised *sang-froid* came to his aid as his increasingly fragile moral ground crumbled beneath him. He said with unruffled hauteur, 'He will indeed. But the Duchess requested me to offer you, in good will, significant compensation if you should agree to discourage his pretensions, and also return any gifts of ancestral jewellery.'

Angelica leapt to her feet and paced towards the door. 'What Lord Latimer, and indeed I myself, choose to do with our lives is entirely our concern. And what makes you think I can be bribed? It is insolent in the extreme that you should even consider making such an offer.'

Ivor Asprey remained seated and to her exasperation appeared amused by her fiery response. 'Certainly, Miss Leigh, how you choose to live your life is entirely your own concern. However, Lord Latimer has an ancient lineage to consider. Does not Ophelia's own brother warn her of the disparity in the destinies of herself and Prince Hamlet?' and with a sardonic smile he continued, 'If I recall it right: "*his will is not his own; for he himself is subject to his birth: he may not, as unvalued persons do, carve for himself...*"'

Angelica whirled around to face him. 'What pretensions, sir! Lord Latimer is no prince and I no green girl. Mr Asprey, I would be grateful if you would leave. I need to dress.' She stood imperiously by the door, ready to open it and usher him out, unaware of the discrepancy between her manner and the dishabille of her attire.

But he did not move and instead merely crossed his legs and, ignoring her defiant eyes, murmured, 'I'll leave, Miss Leigh, when I have your answer for the Duchess.'

'I refuse to honour such insolence with a reply. Do as you please, sir, but excuse me while I change. I am becoming chilled.' Angelica walked behind his chair, slipped behind a narrow screen and began to remove her robe.

The sound of rustling silk swept the last support from Ivor Asprey's moral stand and in an instant he knew she had check-mated him; it would do his reputation no good at all to be found in the dressing room of a semi-naked young actress. He rose unhurriedly to his feet and as Angelica covered herself decorously with the protective garment he bowed. 'Thank you for your time, Miss Leigh. And once again, congratulations on your performance.' He lifted his cold blue eyes to meet hers which sparkled full of amusement and even a little triumph.

Feeling less in control of his life than he liked, Ivor Asprey stalked out of Angelica's dressing room and almost bumped into the last man he would choose to meet in such a place. 'Good evening,' he said with a curt nod to Lord Rackham.

'Asprey, I didn't think I'd see you here. Although it's entertaining enough, is it not, to contemplate the gay congregation of mistresses and divorceable wives, recognised courtesans and regular mercenaries?' His usual expression of disdain had hardened into a sneer. 'I presume you commended Miss Leigh's touching performance?' His lordship's knowing manner seemed to implicate Ivor Asprey in his own licentiousness and in swift recoil Ivor doffed his hat and turned away to stride towards the entrance and fresh air.

The audience was leaving in a largely cheerful mood, the high tragedy they had just witnessed barely deflating the alcohol-fuelled celebration of the end of Emperor Bonaparte's domination of Europe. Ivor Asprey joined the throng that spilled onto Bow Street.

His nephew, Charles Latimer, was expecting him at White's, the club just a footfall away from his own house in St James's Square, so he decided to walk the mile or so rather than hail a Hackney. He turned down Hart Street and headed for Leicester Square. It was a fine evening and the cool air helped settle his disconsolate thoughts. Tonight three women had intruded on his usually well-ordered mind: Lady Linus reminding him of his social and paternal duty, the Countess of his carnal desire and Miss Leigh, somehow conflated with Ophelia and his wife, Emma, had speared straight to his soul. These young women each represented something different, stirring his long-famished heart and the forgotten joys of youth and hope.

St James's Street was busy with gentlemen arriving at their clubs for the night's play. Drinking and comradeship were almost as important as gaming but Ivor Asprey had long abandoned the Hazard tables and card games of his wild youth. He walked past Brooks's, his own club, and crossed the road to enter the edifice of White's. The atmosphere in the overflowing clubs and on the street was exuberant.

As a prominent Whig politician, Ivor Asprey's appearances at this Tory club were always greeted with ribald good humour. The noise and bonhomie had noticeably increased; pretty much everyone was more than half-cut, a few passed out on the sofas. He ascended the grand staircase and entered the card room, greeting acquaintances as he progressed. It was slightly quieter here, until his young nephew bounded to his side. 'Uncle! Come, I've ordered a bottle of champagne.'

He followed Lord Latimer's elegant back through the boisterous crowd until they stopped by a table where a game of Hazard was drawing to a close. As the dice were scooped up and the winnings collected, Charles Latimer gripped the shoulder of his friend sitting at the table and addressed his uncle, 'Sir, you've met Dante Locke before.'

'I have indeed. How d'ye do?' Ivor Asprey looked down at the bleary-eyed young exquisite whose long dark curls were tousled decoratively around a pale finely boned face. The young man smiled uncertainly, alcohol and exhaustion taking its toll on a delicate constitution.

'He's a poet, you know,' Lord Latimer added helpfully.

'Really? You surprise me,' Ivor Asprey murmured as he joined his nephew at a quiet table by the great window overlooking the street. He poured out two flutes of champagne and said, 'To continuing peace and prosperity.'

Charles Latimer leaned in excitedly, his face shining. 'Well, what did you think of her?'

'I take it you're talking about Miss Leigh?' Ivor leant back in his chair and surveyed his young nephew. He was a fine-looking young man full of appetites and vivacity but not over-endowed with wit. Even his school, used to the unruly sons of the aristocracy, had found him hard to handle and threatened expulsion. Eton was Ivor Asprey's old school too but he had been one of its stars; inevitably his sister had called him in as a mediator.

The young reprobate, whose school career he had salvaged, took a gulp of champagne. 'Of course I mean Miss Leigh. Who else?'

'Well, it's true she's an affecting actress.'

Lord Latimer was exasperated at his uncle's deliberate obtuseness. 'She's an angel. Her name so becomes her. I love her, you know.'

'I can understand that, Charles; half of London seems to have fallen in love with her.' Ivor Asprey watched the young lord's face darken at this attempt to point out that an ecstatic response to Miss Leigh was not unique to him. He continued in a reasonable voice, 'You do understand, dear boy, that you're not entirely a free agent when it comes to managing your conjugal choices.'

'Oh, Uncle, don't be so stuffy and pompous!'

'It may seem irrelevant but I'm afraid the fact you will become the next Duke of Arlington comes with certain constraints and responsibilities.'

'You've been talking to my mother, haven't you?' The young man leapt to his feet.

'Oh, do sit down. Can I give you some fatherly advice?'

'What? You're not that much older than me.'

'I'm afraid I feel very much older.' His uncle gave a rueful smile.

'Anyway, Papa has already met Miss Leigh and approves of her.' His lordship's petulant expression transformed into a grin. 'He said he thought the genealogical tree could do with a new grafting of beauty.'

Ivor Asprey laughed, then grew serious again. 'I'm not surprised. She's a very taking young woman. But I'm afraid your dear father's opinion does not matter as much as your mama's.'

This statement chilled the atmosphere between them and the young man said with a scowl, 'I've almost reached my majority; there's nothing Mama can do to stop me.'

The men fell silent and refilled their glasses. Both were sizing each other up. Lord Latimer had always treated his uncle as a hero figure, thirteen years his senior and as fine a horseman and sportsman as anyone he knew. When he confounded his family and friends by putting aside the profligate ways of a rich young man to become instead a reforming politician concerned with the suffering of the poor, the young lord was as nonplussed as they. From that point, Lord Latimer considered his uncle had become less amusing.

Gazing at his nephew's youthful face, Ivor Asprey attempted some advice. 'I too, at your age, was in love with an actress. I could not imagine finding any other woman as worthy of my love. But you know, Charles, 'tis a stage many young men go through.'

His nephew bridled. 'Oh no, sir, don't try to persuade me this is just calf-love.'

'Well, dear boy, there is no denying that Miss Leigh is an actress and, however fine, is in no way suitable to become your duchess.'

'I never thought I'd hear you spouting such fustian cant!' Lord Latimer had sprung to his feet again, so irritated was he with his uncle's patronising tone. 'Where the New Man? Where the reforming politician? You're no better than the rest of 'em. The bang-up Corinthian become the dullest of dogs. It's a tragedy!'

'I'm sorry you're so disappointed, Charles.' His uncle's voice was dry and amused but he wondered if there was not a scintilla of truth in this; that he had indeed lost his spark. At this point, Dante Locke meandered towards them. His friend hailed him, 'Dante, come and save me from my prosy relation.' The queasy poet subsided into a chair, elegant even while drunk. He gazed up at Charles Latimer and Mr Asprey and opined, in a voice made all the more affecting by his slurring lisp, 'The best of life is intoxication, is it not?'

Lord Latimer shook him. 'No it's not, my friend. Your poetry is more important than wine.' He turned to Mr Asprey. 'Uncle, Dante's writing an epic about the tragedy of Ophelia.'

'Yes, Miss Leigh has inspired me, the fragile beauty of her pale cheek, her hair aflame.' Alcohol and fatigue made his words falter. 'I could read you some now.' He fumbled in his coat pocket.

'Some other time, Mr Locke. I still have work to do. But I must say it is rather remarkable how Miss Leigh's charms seem to affect so many.' Ivor's blue eyes looked coolly at his nephew. 'Charles, do me the honour of at least considering what I have said. Good evening, gentlemen.' He doffed his hat and headed for the door.

'The devil take him!' Lord Latimer looked sadly at his uncle's receding back. 'He used to be such a dashing buck, an out and outer, but look at him now, it's midnight and he's going back to work!'

'Well, like all self-respecting Trojans we're returning to the gaming tables. Come on, Charlie.' Dante Locke grasped his friend's arm with an uncertain hand and hauled himself to his feet. With their arms around each other's shoulders they wove their way back to the card room. The gambling dons, strict about their own drinking, greeted the two rich, befuddled young men with keen avaricious eyes.

'Don't overdo it, Dante. We're going riding tomorrow. There's always a chance we might come upon the divine Miss Leigh. She often exercises her prancer in the afternoon and we need to be at our best.' Lord Latimer's smile sparkled with the thought.

While the two young men returned to the dice, Ivor Asprey walked down Jermyn Street at a brisk pace and was soon home. As he entered, Goodall divested him of his coat and hat and then presented him with a complexly folded piece of paper. He recognised his daughter's hand and walked across the stone-flagged hall to enter the sanctuary of his library. The fire was glowing in the fireplace, the whisky was on the table and his favourite chair awaited. He sank into it as weariness engulfed him and he wished he could ignore his work and head upstairs to bed. His long fingers unfolded the paper and there, written in his daughter's best hand was a message.

My dear Papa, I hope you Enjoyed seeing Prince Hamlet. I have been Reading in Latin about the Frogs who wanted a King and the Vain Crow and the Crafty Fox. I will see You tomorrow.

With coloured inks she had illuminated the P of Papa as if it were a medieval manuscript. And she ended with an elaborate signature, *Elinor*, that owed not a little to Queen Elizabeth's famous flourish.

3

THE MASQUE OF TRAGEDY

Angelica passed her mother's rooms on her way downstairs to breakfast and noticed the door was open and clothes were strewn across the bed. She knocked and entered. 'Mama!' she called and Amabel Leigh bustled from the dressing room with an armful of shawls.

'Angelica, I can't find my best Kashmir. I am *désolée*.' She had taken to sprinkling French words into her conversation, in part because it mimicked the social mode of talk of aristocratic women but also to acquaint herself better with the language she would need on her expedition to France with Mr Breville.

Angelica kissed her mother on the cheek. 'But you have so many shawls, surely one of those would do?'

'No, no!' Mrs Leigh was agitated. 'These are passably good but my Kashmir is so striking it draws all eyes. Neddy bought it for me when he was in Amsterdam and chose the finest from one of the great trading warehouses there.'

'You're not packing for Paris already, are you?' Angelica laughed.

Her mother frowned in irritation. 'You have too much levity of spirit, young miss. Your *joie de vivre* will chase away every suitable gentleman. There are still those who consider feminine laughter to be close to ill-bred, you know.'

'Oh, Mama,' Angelica sighed.

'And you're lacking in a proper appreciation of the things that should matter to a young lady.'

'I know, an elevated place in society, preferably with a town house, an estate in the country and 50,000 pounds a year. Mama, it may sound foolish, but I'd hope that love might have a place in my life.' Angelica moved the clothes to one side and sat on the edge of the bed.

Her mother was busy admiring her new pelisse of saffron silk and, exasperated by her daughter's obstinacy, turned from the looking-glass. '*Absurdités*, my girl! For women like us, without family or fortune, it is an indulgence to talk of love. Such only belongs in novels and plays. You and I have to exhibit more sense.'

'Well, Mama, thus is the world we live in. Last night, Lord Latimer's uncle came to the theatre and offered me a substantial settlement if I would quash his nephew's designs on a shameful marriage.'

Amabel Leigh dashed to her daughter's side and took both her hands. 'What! To you?'

'Indeed, it seems marriage to a mere actress brings down on a noble family too much scandal for them to bear.'

'Angelica, *quelle insolence*! Such lofty behaviour, attempting to pay you off like a mercenary streetwalker. I am lost for words! I'm so sorry, my dear.' Her expression of outraged sympathy then turned thoughtful. 'It does give me pause, however,' she said with a sly smile. 'Lord Latimer's family are clearly exercised by the matter, perhaps a proposal may be more directly on the cards after all?'

Angelica shook her head. 'You are impossible, Mama. To be fair, his uncle, Mr Asprey himself, did not seem to think his nephew serious. I think he was a reluctant go-between. But the Duchess is the main antagonist.' Angelica draped one of the discarded shawls round her shoulders and said with a faint smile, 'Lord Latimer declares his mother is more high and haughty than our Queen and has a great opinion of her family's place in society.'

Undeterred, Mrs Leigh pressed for more information. 'It does seem peculiar that Mr Asprey should be despatched to do his sister's will. The Duke is still alive, is he not?'

Her daughter was growing restless, wishing for breakfast and fatigued at any more discussion. 'Mama, I suppose the Duchess thinks her brother has more authority than the poor injured Duke. Mr Asprey has made a name for himself attempting to reform child labour laws.'

Amabel Leigh looked up, startled. 'Really? How curious he should care. But I suppose there's no accounting for rich men's whims.'

'He's certainly not whimsical. In fact, more supercilious and cold.' Angelica felt a small shiver slide down her spine and quickly changed the subject. 'I'm going with Mary to Bond Street this morning to take my Leghorn bonnet in for re-trimming. Can I get you anything? A new romance novel, perhaps?' she teased, recalling her mother's view of where love rightfully belonged. But Mrs Leigh was already distracted by the next sartorial challenge and had headed back to her dressing room, humming to herself.

After a quick breakfast Angelica dashed up the stairs to slip on her new green silk spencer, corded and toggled in silver braid. She barely stopped to check her appearance but grabbed a bonnet trimmed with pink feathers which matched her gown then picked up the bandbox with her favourite hat for refurbishment.

Martin, the butler, was adjusting his white powdered wig in the large looking-glass in the hall. He was a small man but his exuberance and histri-onic air gave him presence. Excessive drinking had coarsened his once good looks but the twinkle that had made him a passable comic actor was undiminished. He liked the clothes and manners of the last century and even occasionally sported a patch on his cheekbone. 'Oh Miss Angelica, what a picture you are!' He turned to open the front door.

'As are you, Martin. Thank you, we won't be long.'

Mary had joined her in the hall and they tripped down the front steps into the late spring day. Berkeley Square was sparkling after a brief shower of rain. Two blackbirds were pouring out their liquid song, defending terri-tories at opposite ends of the Square. The young women walked through the gardens, noticing how the stately plane trees and topiary hedges were bright with new growth.

As they approached the east of the Square, the front door of number thirty-eight swung open and the unmistakeable figure of Lady Jersey emerged. Angelica caught Mary's arm and they paused to watch the strikingly tall society queen and patroness of Almack's sweep down the front steps, her fur-edged cloak billowing behind her like a theatrical Valkyrie's. She climbed into her waiting carriage and the coachman drove it away at speed, rattling over the cobbles.

Ever since she was old enough to understand the subtle gradations of class, Angelica had known her lack of high birth, fortune or influence debarred her from Almack's and being presented to the assembled guests and scions of the nobility as an eligible young woman worthy of marriage into the upper echelons of society. She was further disqualified by a profession that placed her truly beyond the pale of respectability. Despite these barriers to conventional advancement, Angelica felt a sense of anticipation and excitement about her life rise in her breast. Perhaps her mother was right, she had too much levity of spirit to be acceptable to the *ton*, especially if overlaid on her social disadvantages, but she could not wish to trade this lightness of being for anything.

She and Mary turned into Bruton Street where the houses were almost as grand as Mr Breville's. Soon they were in the bustle of Bond Street. The parade of smart carriages and knots of well-dressed pedestrians visiting the drapers, milliners, shoemakers and jewellers' shops, each with glittering windows filled with their wares, added to the kaleidoscope of passing faces and fashionable clothes. Angelica took a deep breath and joined the swirling throng.

'Here's Madame Vigier's.' She led the way into a pretty bow-fronted shop, its window filled with a display of elaborate bonnets, their flaring brims trimmed with silk flowers, striped satin ribbons, veils of lace and plumes of ostrich feather.

Mary was transported by the range of ribbons that were brought out for Angelica to choose. After she had requested a striking Venetian silk of grey, pink and green Angelica asked Mary which she would like for herself. She chose a maroon and navy silk to trim her own bonnet, and Angelica asked Madame Vigier to add two yards to her bill. She thanked Madame and turned for the door.

As they rejoined the pedestrians on the street, the young women had to thread their way through the sauntering crowd. The road was so dirty with mud and horse dung no one wished to have to step off the raised pavement. Without warning, a young woman bumped into them. She raised startled eyes to Angelica's face. 'I beg your pardon,' she whispered as she attempted to pass, but the press of people was suddenly too great.

Angelica had a chance to study this stranger more closely; she looked distraught, pretty but pale with glossy brown hair swept up into a fashionable topknot with carefully arranged fine ringlets framing a heart-shaped face. Her eyes would have been fine if they were not red-rimmed with crying. Angelica touched her arm and said quietly, 'What's the matter? Is there anything I can do?'

'No, no. It's very kind...' She broke off, gazing for the first time into Angelica's face. After a moment, her eyes widened with amazement. 'Are you perhaps Ophelia, I mean Miss Leigh?'

'I am.'

The young woman was overcome with embarrassment and babbled, 'Forgive me! How rude to accost you, but for a moment I thought I knew you and you might be a friend. But you are so beautiful...' Her voice died away once more.

'Don't concern yourself. People quite often think they know me. I am perfectly content with your addressing me so.'

'Oh, how fortunate.' The young stranger's face brightened. 'Miss Leigh, I am happy to make your acquaintance. I've seen you at the Theatre twice. I am Isobel Fitzjames.' She spoke as if she too expected her name to be recognised. When Angelica waited for her to elaborate, she continued, subdued again and close to tears, 'I apologise for such liberty, Miss Leigh, but I have no one to speak to. I'm so much in need of advice.' The young woman's voice was breathy and her words tumbled out, unheeded.

Angelica smiled and gave a small laugh. 'It all depends what advice you seek.' By now the two young women, their maids standing discreetly behind them, had become an obstacle on the busy pavement and pedestrians were stepping into the muddy road to pass. Some of the Bond Street dandies, who habitually strolled the area hailing their friends and ogling the women, recognised Angelica, and their address became more familiar and jocular.

A young man in yellow pantaloons and an exaggeratedly tailored coat bellowed, 'Oi! Miss Ophelia, don't mind Lord Hamlet. I'll give ye a johnnie, that'll see ye right,' to general guffawing amongst his peers. Miss Fitzjames looked shocked, but Angelica was used to the vulgar liberties taken by a few of her audience when they saw her in the street.

She took her new acquaintance's arm and said, 'We shouldn't talk here. Would you like some tea or ratafia? I live just a short walk away.'

'Mrs Fitzjames thinks I've gone to Bullock's Museum; I won't be missed for an hour.' They began walking back down Bruton Street, their maids trailing behind, gossiping.

'Is Mrs Fitzjames your mother?'

'No! Mama died when I was ten. My father married again.' The way Isobel Fitzjames wrinkled her pretty nose was so expressive of dismay and disdain that Angelica wondered if this was a fraught relationship and part of her distress. They walked on in silence and soon had crossed Berkeley Square and were mounting the steps of Mr Breville's house.

Martin opened the door and Miss Fitzjames seemed taken aback. 'Welcome home, my dears.' He bowed low with a flourish, discreetly holding on to his wig with his free hand, as the four young women entered and removed their bonnets. The maids headed for the kitchen and Angelica asked Martin if he could bring some ratafia to the library where she knew a fire would be lit.

She ushered Miss Fitzjames to the chair opposite hers. Once Martin had left and they each had a glass by their sides, Angelica leaned forward. 'Now we can talk,' she said.

Isobel Fitzjames was suddenly shy. 'I apologise again for my temerity. It's just I have no sisters and few friends since...' Her voice faded away and she looked steadfastly at her hands, tightly clasped in her lap.

'There's no need to apologise. I too am without a sister. Treat me like one, if it pleases you.'

The young woman looked up and smiled and for the first time Angelica could see what a charming face she had, if rather lacking in vitality. 'That would make me very happy.' She sipped her ratafia and then launched into a tale of woe. 'My step-mama insists that I marry a man I cannot love so that the Fitzjames fortune is restored to the family,' she said in a rush of words.

'How so?' Angelica's sympathetic expression met her guest's forlorn one.

'My father was a gamester and during a long night and a day he lost all our family's wealth to the man I now have to marry.'

Angelica's spirit recoiled. 'Is the sacrifice of you part of the deal?'

Isobel Fitzjames nodded in misery. 'It seems the only way my family's patrimony can be in part restored.'

'And what does your father say to this prospect?'

'Sadly, he is dead.' She sighed and met Angelica's eyes; the shadow of grief hung between them, then she added, 'By his own hand.' Her voice faltered as her head drooped. Angelica was shocked. Those words *by his own hand* carried so much personal suffering and the censure of society and the Church. She involuntarily reached out to touch Miss Fitzjames's arm as the young woman continued haltingly, 'He could not bear the shame. But now it's for me to try and make it right.'

Angelica's natural sisterly sympathy was replaced by a flash of anger on Isobel Fitzjames's behalf. She had been grievously let down by both men. 'Who, pray, is this reprobate who will happily deprive a man and his family of their home and means to live?'

'Oh, he's Lord Fulsham. I think he's well-known in the clubs and gambling hells. But we aren't quite destitute yet. We've relinquished our house in Grosvenor Square but have managed to rent a smaller one in Charles Street, just around the corner from here. When the marriage settlement is legalised I think we'll all move back into the Fitzjames mansion.'

'But my dear, you can't marry someone you dislike so. A man so morally corrupt.'

'I don't think he wants to marry me either. Perhaps he feels obliged after the tragedy of my father's death. My family is an old and venerable one and after my father died Lord Fulsham was blamed by some.' Colour rushed to her pale face as she recollected the reason for her bartered future. Her voice trembled with a tragic outrage. 'And Mrs Fitzjames is a termagant whose son's patrimony has been lost.'

A sudden thought occurred to Angelica. 'Perhaps something so easily gambled away can be as easily won back?'

Isobel Fitzjames looked at her aghast. 'No, there's no one who can play better than Lord Fulsham. No one with his luck.'

Unlike her young guest, Angelica was temperamentally disinclined to accept the hard hand dealt by fate. Her mind was already busy with possibilities of resolution. 'You don't think anyone has Lord Fulsham's skill. Well, I know someone who possibly does.' Angelica then felt embarrassed at having confided to a stranger such an audacious idea, an idea that was not hers to suggest. She put down her glass and got to her feet. 'Miss Fitzjames, do you ride?'

'Oh yes, and I still have my mare.'

'I'm riding with my groom in Green Park this afternoon. As you live so close, would you care to accompany me?'

'I'm still in mourning,' she said, gesturing to the dark fabric of her dress, 'but riding with a friend is not considered disrespectful by anyone other than my stepmother.' Her face looked more hopeful.

Angelica linked her arm in Isobel Fitzjames's and led her into the grand hall where Martin returned her bonnet. The young woman's spirits seemed improved. She crammed the pretty straw onto her springy brown hair and grasped Angelica's hand in farewell. 'I'm so glad to have met you. Do you think you would be happy to call me Isobel?'

'Of course.' Angelica smiled. 'And you can call me Angelica. I'll have Storm saddled for three. Shall we meet outside and ride up to the Park together?'

* * *

Elinor Asprey was waiting for her father in the breakfast room. She had taken greater care than usual in dressing in her new spotted muslin and tied a blue ribbon in her hair. Sitting quietly munching on a caraway bun, she looked up when Nicholas Digby entered the room carrying a sheaf of papers for his employer to read and sign. He smiled at the sight of the pretty child, the early sun making a halo of her light brown curls. 'Good morning, Miss Elinor,' he said, an amused warmth in his voice. 'I didn't think to find you here. Are you waiting for your papa?'

She nodded, looking up into his friendly face. She liked the way his brown eyes always seemed to be smiling. 'I want to hear about Mr Kean and Prince Hamlet. And read him my Latin text of "The Fox and the Crow".' Her eyes were striking but not as deeply blue as her father's, with none of his piercing and chilly regard.

'Aha, that's a useful fable indeed. What, Miss Elinor, do you think of the moral?' He poured himself a cup of coffee and settled down in the chair across from hers.

The girl wrinkled her brow in thought. She liked being treated as if her opinions mattered. 'Well, I think it is a warning against vanity.'

'Indeed. And the dangers of flattery. Something we could all be mindful of, perhaps?' Mr Digby cocked his head and smiled.

'Do you mean, like Papa when he's courted by people who desire his approval?'

Nicholas Digby laughed. 'Actually, your papa is probably proof against all flattery. No, the danger comes for those with less *amour propre* than Mr Asprey.'

The girl nodded her head in agreement. She was not quite sure what he meant but she appreciated that he had thought she would understand, and knew enough to suspect it was complimentary about her much-loved but elusive father.

At that moment the door opened and Ivor Asprey entered, surprisingly quiet and light on his feet for such a tall man. He looked as immaculate as usual, his dark hair slightly curling after his morning ablutions. His eyes alighted on his daughter and softened. 'Elinor, what a treat to see you. I thought you might have already gone to your lessons.'

'Papa, you promised to tell me about last night and I promised to read you my Latin translation.'

'Aha. So I did.' He quickly bent to kiss the top of her head, then took the cup of coffee proffered by his secretary and sat down beside his daughter. 'Nicholas, can you spare me a few minutes? I will attend to business afterwards.'

Elinor took his arm in hers and attempted to snuggle close. 'Papa, what did you think of the play last night?'

'It was very affecting. Mr Kean is a funny small fellow but with a rich voice that conjures the tragedy of the situation. It's no wonder he is fêted.'

'And what about Ophelia?'

'The actress is young but seems to manage the part creditably, I'd say.' His voice was cool and clipped.

'Oh, I'd so love to see it.'

'I'm still not sure it's suitable for a young lady of your sensitive nature, Elinor.' He looked at her but his mind appeared to be elsewhere.

His daughter pulled at his sleeve and said with some exasperation, 'Papa, Mr Digby treats me as if I have understanding and good sense. Why cannot you do the same?'

He gave an unexpected chuckle. 'I'm sorry you find me so wanting as a parent. Perhaps I'll ask Miss Stafford's advice on the matter. She is your governess, after all, and a good one too.'

'But Papa, it's you I want to accompany me.'

'I'm sorry you have no mama or sisters as company. I'm a poor substitute, I know.' He met her eyes with a sorrowful glance. 'Now where's this Latin translation?' He had taken out his watch and checked the time and his mind was suddenly on the work that awaited him.

His daughter shyly produced the book that had been hidden on her lap; its battered old red leather cover bore the legend in worn gold, *Aesop's Fables*. 'This is Miss Stafford's. It's very old and I love the illustrations.'

Ivor Asprey took it from her hands and opened it at random on an engraving of a magnificent shaggy lion. ''Tis a beautiful book indeed. I see the stories are in Latin, French and English; is the translation you're about to recite yours alone?' He lifted his gaze, meeting her eager face with a smile.

His daughter giggled. 'Of course, Papa. You know I wouldn't cozen you.' Turning to the page with an illustration of a fox gazing up at a crow in a tree with the fable written out in Latin, she slowly translated as she read. *'They who love to be flattered with artful praise'* – she looked up shyly – *'are for the most part shamefully punished by a late repentance.'*

Her father surprised her with a laugh. 'Is this aimed at me, pert miss?'

'Oh no! Mr Digby said you were proof against all flattery.'

'Well, I'm glad to hear it. Continue.'

When she came to the final moral of the story of how ingenuity prevails and wisdom *is always an over-match for strength*, she closed the book triumphantly, having barely hesitated over any of the meanings.

'Bravo, my dear,' her father said and kissed her hand. 'I am impressed by your facility with Latin, and I trust with French too? Now I must get on with my work. Would you ask Nicholas Digby to return and we'll start?'

'I will, Papa. Mr Aesop thinks ingenuity should prevail, so can I ask again if you will take me to see Prince Hamlet?'

He smiled. 'If I say yes it will not be your ingenuity that prevails but rather your perseverance. And my very lack of such qualities.' She crept an arm around his neck. 'Oh, I surrender, even though your aunt, Edwina, would utterly disapprove of my weakness. You can ask Mr Digby to get me another three tickets.'

'Three, Papa?'

'Yes, I think it would be polite to take Lady Linus with us, if she'd like to come. She has already been once before, with her mother.' He had turned to address the sheaf of papers left by his secretary and did not see his daughter's face fall.

* * *

Once Angelica and her mother had moved into Edward Breville's house, Mrs Leigh lost no time in persuading her generous *cavaliere servente* to spend a portion of his fortune on educating her beautiful young daughter in the ladylike arts. Angelica might be barred from entering the *beau monde* by the irregularity of her birth and her profession but Amabel Leigh was determined that should her beauty and gifts attract a noble suitor, as she deserved, her daughter would be able to acquit herself well in any company.

From their first meeting, Mr Brunner had taken the child under his bluff wing and taught her to ride. Angelica was blessed with natural balance and grace and this, allied with her devil-may-care courage, meant she was soon riding as well as anyone twice her age. Then Maestro Zampolli was engaged to teach her how to play the piano-forte with unshowy grace while singing a small repertoire of charming country songs, and an elderly dancing master, the famous Mr Cherry, taught her the steps of the minuet and the quadrille, and even the new and faintly shocking waltz, together with some country dances and Scottish reels for fun.

Edward Breville had given Angelica a special palfrey for her eighteenth birthday. As a particular treat he had arranged a private meeting with the great bloodstock trader, Richard Tattersall, for her to choose her own mount. They had gone early to the stables at Hyde Park Corner and she had been so excited to see the horses, stamping and whinnying, ready for their morning exercise, their breaths wreathing in the chill air.

Then came the moment when a grey mare was led into the courtyard and Angelica gasped at the sight of the beautiful creature. Gazing into the horse's dark eyes, she fell in love. The early sun made the mare's pale coat glisten as if frosted and as she began to trot everyone who saw her was transfixed by the elegance and refinement of her lines, the fluidity of her high-stepping movement and her beautiful mottled grey coat. Angelica immediately knew she would call her Storm; her name suggested an inclement day and her mane and tail, almost white and very long, flying behind her as attendant cirrus clouds.

The afternoon was sunny and Mr Breville's groom, Robert, brought Angelica's horse from the mews, fully saddled for her expedition to Green Park. Angelica had quickly slipped into her riding dress and asked Mary to help lace it. It was a flattering outfit with its full skirts of green batiste nipped into a small waist emphasised by a form-fitting jacket with a military air, corded and toggled with navy braiding. Mary quickly twisted her mistress's mass of gold-red hair into a low bun so Angelica could wear the stylish shako that completed the fashionable hussar look. Angelica dashed down the stairs to find Martin opening the door to a visitor.

Isobel Fitzjames stood on the threshold looking a picture of elegance. Her riding habit had all the extra distinction of the finest dark blue cloth and a perfect line that declared it to be a garment made by someone of the highest skill. Angelica had been told by her mother that before the war, Parisian women would come to London to buy their riding clothes from the best of the men's tailors in St James's, so incomparable was the fabric and fit. She wondered if this exquisite garment had been created by Mr Meyer of Conduit Street, the military tailor par excellence, famous for making Beau Brummel's uniform.

Martin had exclaimed and clapped his hands in delight at the sight of the two young women as they settled into their side-saddles with the help of their grooms, their skirts decorously arranged over their knees to show merely the barest glimpse of booted ankle. Isobel Fitzjames looked appraisingly at Angelica mounted on Storm. 'She is such a striking horse you look like you're riding Pegasus.' Her own mount, Merry, was handsome enough but not showy. There was something about the grey mare paired with her beautiful Titian-haired owner that demanded attention from everyone who saw them.

Green Park was much less extensive than Hyde Park to the north but it was pretty in its smaller scale with naturalistic copses of trees and shrubs and a few grazing sheep in an enclosure. Its grassy avenues and gravelled walks led to the reservoir for St James's Palace, a welcome expanse of water where ducks and waterfowl frolicked, much to the entertainment of dogs and children. There was still a light-hearted atmosphere of celebration and a group of young men, drunk from the night before, were playing bowls under the trees with two hussars, resplendent in their uniforms. Their shouts and laughter drifted on the breeze.

Angelica called over her shoulder, 'Shall we canter to that oak tree by the lodge?' She put a hand on Storm's neck and felt her horse tremble with anticipation. Isobel Fitzjames nodded and their grooms followed as the young women gave their mares their heads. The speed and freedom were exhilarating and too soon Angelica had to rein her mount in, laughing with sheer enjoyment. They trotted over to the shade of the oak and let their horses graze while they surveyed the groups of revellers in the distance. Two horsemen were coming towards them at speed; one raised his arm in salutation. Angelica recognised Lord Latimer and waved.

'What a pleasant discovery.' He rode up on his handsome grey and inclined his head. His friend, Dante Locke, joined him in greeting, his dark eyes registering surprise at the sight of Isobel Fitzjames.

'Good afternoon, my lord, and Mr Locke, how good to meet again.' Angelica nodded towards the young bloods on their restless, snorting stallions. 'May I introduce you to Miss Fitzjames.' She looked towards her companion who brought her horse forward to offer her hand.

'But we have met before,' Dante Locke said and bowed low over her gloved hand.

The colour rose in Isobel Fitzjames's cheek as she murmured shyly, 'I think it was at Lady Lyon's rout, was it not?'

'No, that cannot be,' Lord Latimer broke in with a mischievous gleam. 'I was there with you, Dante, and I would have remembered such a charming encounter. Could you be mistaken, Miss Fitzjames?' And he too bowed over her hand with an elaborate flourish.

She met his eyes fleetingly then turned her face away with embarrassment. 'Perhaps so, it has been some time since I have been in company.' Angelica was irritated by Lord Latimer's teasing manner. The death of Isobel Fitzjames's father would have been gossiped about in the gentlemen's clubs both these young men frequented and they would have realised she was the daughter in this tragedy. Angelica was taken aback that he seemed to show so little concern for the young woman's feelings. Luckily, his friend drew Miss Fitzjames aside and they seemed to be deep in conversation about horses.

Angelica turned to Lord Latimer. 'You surprise me, my lord.'

'Why the clouded brow, milady? It does not become you.' He was still in a jaunty mood.

'Why the unmannerly banter, Lord Latimer? It does not become the situation when a lady is in mourning for her father.'

Unused to being admonished, especially by a young woman whose beauty so disarmed him, he quickly changed the subject. 'I was on my way to apologise to you for my relation's visit to the theatre last night.'

Angelica looked at him with a question in her eyes. 'And how did you know you'd find me here?'

'I saw you crossing Piccadilly. You and your horse, Miss Leigh, are as dramatic a sight as a comet's flaming flight.'

Such hyperbole made Angelica laugh, despite her mother's entreaty to be less light-hearted. 'Well, there is no need for apologies. I know what your family think of me.'

'All but the Duke, who is very much in your favour.'

'Ah, but has he more sway than your mama and stern uncle?'

Lord Latimer did not answer but turned in the saddle to look across to where his friend was still in soulful conversation with Angelica's companion. 'I am sorry for Miss Fitzjames. 'Tis indeed a woeful business. No noble gamester would deprive a man of everything, including his honour.'

'Do you know Lord Fulsham?'

'I know him by sight; he's often in the club but I have never joined him in play. He's known for being reckless in running his luck.'

Impetuously, Angelica confided to him her nascent plan. 'I wondered if there was anyone who could win the Fitzjames patrimony back, playing him at his own game?'

Lord Latimer leaned forward in his saddle to catch Angelica's arm. 'That is a ruinous idea. How could you even consider it possible? The only person I know who's as good at computing the odds in Hazard is my uncle and he gave up gaming when he went into Parliament. Why are you so interested in Miss Fitzjames's fate?'

'Because her stepmother is insisting she marry Lord Fulsham in order to restore the family's wealth, specifically for the benefit of her son. It is shameful.' Angelica could feel her cheeks growing warm with her frustration at the unfairness of things.

Lord Latimer sat back in the saddle and whistled softly. 'Sad chit.'

Angelica looked across at Isobel Fitzjames and Dante Locke whose conversation had come to a natural halt. She nodded at Lord Latimer. 'I think we should be heading home. I have to get ready for tonight's performance.'

'If you want to avoid the self-important Uncle Asprey, don't go via Hyde Park. He said he would tool around the Serpentine with Lady Linus, before heading off to Westminster.'

Angelica was surprised by her own curiosity in the matter and blurted out, 'Pray, who is Lady Linus?'

Lord Latimer snorted with some derision. 'She's the lady my mama thinks should become the next Mrs Asprey. She frequents the public lectures at the Royal Institution, useful only for those who know little and aspire to less.'

'That's rather dismissive, my lord. Professor Davy is a great hit with his chemical and galvanic experiments. I think such interest admirable in Lady Linus.'

'Admirable indeed. She is a very superior woman, but rather encumbered by *virtue*.' He emphasised the last word with a smirk and Angelica had to stop herself joining in with his mirth. She wheeled her horse round and Isobel Fitzjames joined her. They saluted the two young blades and set off towards Piccadilly.

The women were trotting side by side, their smartly dressed grooms following, and their appearance drew many interested glances from the other horsemen and carriage drivers. Miss Fitzjames said, 'Talking to Mr Locke I realised I met him at a musical evening at Lady Sefton's.'

Angelica was interested to hear that one of the patronesses of Almack's Assembly Rooms, the gateway to all young ladies' entrance to London Society, had invited her to a private social event.

'Have you been admitted to the Assemblies?'

'Before my father died I was rather well-courted and attended a few of the evenings. But lately I have been in mourning. Also, I fear now that scandal is attached to my family name...' Isobel Fitzjames's voice was lacking in expression and tailed off, as if she saw no alternative to her fate. Glancing across at Angelica, who had eased Storm into a slower trot, she asked in a shy voice, 'Are you fortunate enough to still have your papa?'

'No. I never knew him. He was killed while under Admiral Nelson's command at the Battle of Aboukir Bay. I was about five years old at the time.'

'I am sorry. Perhaps I was favoured in having my father's protection for nineteen years of my life. It was just such an ignominious end. Unlike your father, who died a hero's death.'

'I don't know how much of a hero he was. My mother evades any talk of him, which makes me wonder.'

'Of course he was a hero. He was fighting to protect his country.' Isobel Fitzjames's face glowed with romantic fervour. 'I like your friends, Lord Latimer and Mr Locke. Mr Locke says he's writing an epic poem on an alternative fate for Ophelia. Isn't that clever?'

'It all depends.' Angelica looked across at her friend and smiled. 'I'm sorry Lord Latimer was rather tiresome when he first met you. He's young and has had every praise and opportunity placed upon his table. And is the heir to a mighty Dukedom.'

'And has a certain *tendresse* for you?'

Angelica swung around in the saddle to meet her eyes. 'Is that what Mr Locke told you? Well, his lordship may think thus about me but I recognise it merely as youthful fancy. 'Twill last a season, if that. There'll be another more suitable lady to catch his interest.'

'But how could anyone compare to you, Miss Angelica?'

Angelica put her gloved hand on her friend's. 'That's very kind of you, but you forget the small fact of my lack of fortune, not to mention my disreputable profession.' As Isobel Fitzjames demurred, Angelica continued, 'I really don't mind. I know we women are often denied the liberty of choice, but I still have an unreasonable optimism about life.'

'Oh Miss Angelica, if only I could share your hope.' They had dismounted and grasped each other's hands. 'I fear my future looks bleak indeed.'

'Come, come, my dear. Who knows what life has in store for us?' She so wished she could share some of her blithe spirit with her wilting friend. 'Just think how fortunate we both are. We have our health, some education, you have good breeding, we both are warm at night and don't go hungry.' She glanced up at the bright spring sky and thought of the unfair advantages of beauty, saying, 'Above all, we both have our good looks. Such privileges open many doors.' Angelica released her friend's hands and smiled at her. 'We have every reason to be optimistic, don't you think?'

'It's hard to be so when one's heart is heavy and one's spirit fails.'

Angelica tried another tack. 'I so enjoyed our ride. Shall we meet again in two days' time? At three?' Isobel Fitzjames smiled and Angelica quickly embraced her and ran up the steps of Mr Breville's house while Robert took Storm back to her stable in the mews. Miss Fitzjames and her groom, with the horses' reins in his hands, walked the short journey to her stepmother's house in Hill Street.

* * *

Elinor Asprey was dressed for her trip to the theatre hours before she and her father were due to depart. She was pleased with her new velvet spencer, the colour of cornflowers which matched her eyes. Pretending to read at the window seat in the morning room, she watched the road. She had infor-mally borrowed her governess's set of the *Forest of Montalbano* hoping for an exciting historical tale but found volume one heavy going and was unlikely to struggle through the next three. She put it down and with impatience gazed out on the few horses and carriages that circled St James's Square, longing to see her father's distinctive figure with his cane and curly beaver hat walking up from Pall Mall. Then he was there. She leapt up to tap on the window and wave. Ivor Asprey's expression softened as he caught sight of his daughter's eager face.

'Papa!' Elinor bounded into his arms as he came through the front door. 'I'm so glad you're home early.' Her expressive nature seldom failed to penetrate his long-practised reserve as she usually ignored his admonish-ments, her blithe spirit percolating through his *sang-froid*. He could not resist her smile.

Mr Asprey divested himself of hat and coat and followed his daughter into the library. He poured himself a whisky and sat by the fire while his daughter perched on the sofa facing him. 'Well, young lady. You look delightful. Have you and Miss Stafford discussed the play?'

'Yes, Papa. But it's so gloomy and confusing. Is the ghost real?'

'This is why I said it was not suitable for you to see yet. But you are a determined miss and I am just your weak-minded pater whose opinion you ignore.'

Elinor giggled. 'You don't mean that Papa. Nicholas says your *amour propre* is proof against all.'

Her father looked seriously into her merry eyes and murmured, 'Do you discuss my failings with all my staff? Perhaps Aunt Edwina is right, you need a new mama.'

Elinor Asprey looked horrified. 'No, no! I don't want a new mama. I have you, that is enough. And Miss Stafford is like a mother to me. I am happy as we are.'

'Well, I'm not about to offer for Miss Stafford's hand.' He chuckled.

Elinor's face grew serious. 'I wish it was just you and me, Papa, going to the theatre tonight.'

He frowned as he looked at her. 'I hope you won't forget your manners, my dear. Lady Linus is an admirable woman with your interests at heart.

Please be more welcoming to her than last time you met.' Elinor's spirits were cast down at the mention of the sorry occasion she had been over-heard telling Miss Stafford she thought Lady Linus's character was a cold collation, borrowing the description of the villain in a novel she was reading.

Looking across at his daughter's meek face, Ivor Asprey rose to his feet, took her hand in his and squeezed it gently. 'I'll go and get dressed. The chaise will be ready in three quarters of an hour.'

When the carriage eventually set out, Elinor sat beside her father, full of excited anticipation for the evening ahead. The coachman, resplendent in his distinctive Asprey livery, turned the horses' heads north-west to Bruton Street and Lady Linus's house. The streets were filling with the evening's revellers, carriages-and-four, smart curricles for two, the occasional sedan chair, its chairmen squelching through the malodorous mud, and the pavements thronged with the less genteel on their way to the taverns, cockpit, theatres and gambling hells.

Elinor slipped her arm in her father's and shivered. 'Papa, this is so diverting. To see everyone dressed up and merry.'

Ivor looked down at her and smiled. 'Everyone is relieved the war with France is over.' Their carriage clattered to a halt outside a handsome house with a portico. The coachman opened the chaise door and Ivor Asprey strolled up the front steps as the great door was opened and Lady Linus emerged, elegant in a pelisse of lilac silk with a matching toque and curling feather. Elinor Asprey watched her father offer his arm and felt a trickle of unease as he bent his face towards hers, the better to hear her words of greeting.

They entered the carriage and sat together on the seat Elinor had shared with him. She now settled herself on the opposite side with her back to the horses, watching with a polite smile on her lips.

'Good evening, Elinor.' Portia Linus's cool grey eyes settled on the young girl's face as she extended a gloved hand. 'You look very charming tonight.' She had a glacial kind of beauty that attracted admiration rather than desire.

'Good evening, Lady Linus.' Elinor took her hand and fleetingly bowed her head.

'I hope your governess has prepared you for the play tonight. When I saw it first I was shocked by some aspects. I don't approve of the production. I fear it plays to the baser instincts in man.' She had turned her gaze to Mr Asprey's face and Elinor relaxed into the seat. Her attention was caught by the excitement of the evening crowds outside, and she shared in their exuberance. She only heard occasional snatches of conversation in the carriage above the clatter of the wheels and horses' hooves.

Elinor, however, could not curb her curiosity about Lady Linus completely. Her attention was piqued by her low confiding voice saying to her father, 'Mr Asprey, have you considered a more sophisticated companion than your current governess to prepare Elinor for her entry into Society? I can help you interview suitable candidates if you so choose.' A sense of foreboding made the girl shiver. She did not wish to appear uncivil by listening in but could not quell her inquisitive nature.

Her father's voice was low but she was relieved when she heard him answer in his usual languid way, 'My dear Lady Linus, I am grateful for your concern but I think Miss Stafford will be more than adequate. There is help too from my sister – the Duchess of Arlington is an unquenchable fount of advice.' Elinor shared her father's sense of humour, and in the darkening interior of the family coach, without even catching his eye, knew in that moment that he and she had that private understanding.

When they arrived at the theatre, Ivor Asprey shepherded his daughter quickly through the pillared portico where thronged the usual egalitarian mix of persons of quality, befuddled beefy men and wanton women in full plumage, chattering like parakeets. Her eyes were wide with excitement. As they settled into their seats in their box she deftly manoeuvred herself between her father and Lady Linus and perched forward in her seat as she gazed out at the carnivalesque sight before her.

The horseshoe auditorium was ornately decorated in cream and gold, the audience's boxes set in ascending serried ranks facing the stage, on which a heavy red velvet curtain remained tantalisingly closed. Elinor Asprey peered into the pit below them, filled with a colourful roistering crowd of men and women who were standing or strolling about greeting friends, ignoring the lines of benches meant to encourage them to sit. She laughed as she watched a young man juggling with two apples and a pear, before catching one of the apples in his mouth. Food and alcohol was being consumed everywhere. The atmosphere was more festive than usual, the air febrile with excitement.

Elinor felt Lady Linus's hand on hers and she turned to see the woman's earnest face, a small frown creasing her forehead, as she quietly said, 'Elinor, my dear, don't look up into the higher boxes. I know they're called the gods but more surely they're the Infernals.' This immediately made the curious girl wish to see what could be so alarming and when Lady Linus had turned away to greet a passing acquaintance she stole a glance into the regions from where apple cores and pie crusts were lobbed into the pit, accompanied by shouts of laughter. Her eyes opened wide at the sight of an even more profligate crowd of revellers where half-dressed women could be openly seen in the arms of leering drunken men. She was reminded of an engraving of a Bacchanal in one of Miss Stafford's books, considered unsuitable for a girl her age, but she had peeked anyway.

There was a sudden stir as the stage curtain rose and although the hubbub of talk and laughter did not cease completely, people's faces turned, intent. Elinor shivered in anticipation. The lights were low and a gothic castle loomed out of the dim recesses of the stage. A soldier stood sentinel dressed in a hussar's uniform. He challenged a servant of the King. It was hard to hear their conversation above the audience's revelry, but the characters seemed to be exercised about an apparition seen on the ramparts.

Suddenly the air was rent with a great groan and the sound of clanking metal. Elinor grabbed her father's arm and for a moment hid her face. Even the rowdiest in the audience were silenced. Pale faces strained to see through the low light a ghostly figure in full armour enter slowly from the left.

'Is this the King's ghost?' Elinor whispered urgently to her father, remembering her reading with Miss Stafford.

'Yes, don't fear. It's only an actor.'

'I'm not afeared. But where's Mr Kean?'

Her father pointed as Hamlet entered in a royal group with lords and attendants. The actor dominated the stage. The crowd fell silent again to properly hear Kean's rich voice speak the words, known so well by many in the audience.

She felt herself drawn into the drama and leaned into her father, asking in an urgent whisper, 'When will we see Ophelia, Papa?'

'Don't be so impatient, child.'

Her curiosity was soon answered when Ophelia, in full eighteenth-century dress and a powdered wig, walked onto the stage arm in arm with her brother. The audience was roused again to interaction with the play as catcalls and friendly jokes were hurled at her when she spoke. The girl watched Angelica's face closely and found her large eyes mesmerising as they swept over the auditorium commanding silence with her words of despair at the change in Hamlet.

Ophelia ended with the sob, '*O woe is me, to have seen what I have seen, see what I see.*' And Elinor's heart was wrenched. 'Papa. It's so sad.' She buried her face in her hands.

'We can leave now if you'd prefer.'

'No, no! Papa. I want to see Ophelia again.'

'It ends tragically, you know.' He spoke gently, putting his hand on hers.

'I know. I read the play with Miss Stafford, but we can't leave now.' Her eyes returned to the stage. Many in the crowd knew the great soliloquies and intoned them along with Kean.

Lady Linus was obviously irritated by how much interaction the audience in the pit thought they could have with the play. She leaned across to catch Ivor Asprey's attention and said clearly in her crisply enunciated voice, 'I wish the lower orders would hold their tongues so we could enjoy Shakespeare's words, spoken by the actors alone.'

A tall man below them in a neat coat and with hair waxed into a frozen seascape glanced up with a frown and lobbed a half-eaten currant bun into their box. It landed plumb in Lady Linus's silk lap. Elinor suppressed a giggle and quickly picked it up and lobbed it back, hitting another man on the back of the head.

'Elinor! Don't encourage this unruliness,' Portia Linus said crossly, her colour rising.

Ivor looked across at his daughter's bright face with an inscrutable expression and said quellingly, 'I don't expect my daughter to start a bread-throwing war with the pit.' His tone was remonstrative but his eyes gleamed as they met hers.

The restive audience stilled. Onto the stage drifted a vision that made Elinor and half the audience gasp. Ophelia was almost unrecognisable in her floating chemise, her cascade of golden hair released from the formal powdered wig curling in fine ringlets down her back.

'Papa!' The word was more an exhalation.

'This is the scene where Ophelia has gone mad. Recall now, she's only acting.' The audience had fallen into a tense silence. Elinor's eyes were fixed on the figure as she meandered through the glade, playing her lyre and singing disjointed phrases in a distracted voice.

'She is so beautiful. Like an angel.' The young girl was mesmerised by the sight of her flitting through the shadows to the back of the stage where a stream appeared to flow under a willow tree. She knew from her reading that Ophelia drowned but was unprepared to see it happen on stage. 'No!' she cried, turning to her father. 'She can't die with us watching, doing nothing.'

Some women in the audience seemed to agree with her for there were stifled cries at the sight of Ophelia slipping into the stream. Audiences had a life of their own and each night was different. This time there was a palpable sense of the tragedy of it all as her lifeless form, dripping with water, was carefully carried away, her hair almost sweeping the ground. A mournful lament from the pit followed her tragic passage.

Elinor Asprey turned her face and buried it in her father's chest, sobbing with a heart-rending whisper, 'She can't die. She's so young. It's too sad.' Her father put his arm around her thin shoulders and patted her gently, aware of the echo of the tragedy that had befallen their own family.

Lady Linus leaned across to stroke her hand as she said consolingly, 'It's only acting, Elinor. She's not really dead.'

'She looked dead.' The girl hiccoughed.

'The actress is very good at her craft,' her father said, his expression grim.

'Will she come on at the end and show us she's alive?'

'No, I don't think she will. She will be warming up backstage.'

'Well, then can I see her? Or I'll be haunted for ever,' Elinor said with melodramatic emphasis.

'Now you're being a bit affected and missish, Elinor.' Lady Linus was disapproving of girlish histrionics.

'Well, I am just a miss, so why should I be any different?' was her tearful but defiant reply.

Her father stepped in with a soothing drawl, 'Come now, Elinor. I'll take you to see Miss Leigh after the play is over, but we can't stay long.'

'If so, I'll wait for you in the chaise,' Lady Linus said in a clipped tone of voice. 'You know I don't approve of the thespian professions.'

'Of course, my dear. I'll only take Elinor backstage after I've found my groom and can settle you comfortably.'

* * *

Angelica was particularly exhausted by the evening's performance and was feeling the cold more acutely. Her teeth were chattering as Mary put her chilled fingers around the cup of hot chocolate. Her damp hair tumbled round her face and she pulled her gown close. There was a light tap at the door and Mary opened it to the dissolute face of Lord Rackham. 'May I enter for a moment?' he purred.

Angelica's heart sank. Cato Rackham was a determined and practised seducer who enjoyed as sport the pursuit of reluctant lovers. This was his fifth visit backstage. She knew how influential he was, in Parliament and Society, and she was reluctant to cross him. He was capable of ruining her in many different ways. She rose to her feet and extended a hand.

'My dear, how chilled you are,' he protested as he brushed her fingers across his lips, prolonging the gesture for just a few seconds longer than propriety decreed.

'Lord Rackham, how kind of you to come.'

'How could I not, when you have just conjured the most affecting Ophelia in my memory.'

'Would you take a chair?' Mary once again scooped off the brocaded gown Angelica had worn during the first part of the play as Cato Rackham subsided into the seat that last supported Ivor Asprey. Angelica motioned to the table beside him and said, 'I have only some Canary sack to offer you.'

His lordship waved the offer aside and gazed speculatively at Mary, who was busy hanging up and brushing the costumes for the following evening's performance. It was obvious to Angelica that he wanted to speak to her in private but she was loath to be alone with him. 'Are you returning to your club, Lord Rackham?' she asked sweetly.

'That depends on whether a more attractive offer comes my way.' His voice was quiet and matter of fact but he glanced at her, askance through lowered lashes, and the look was full of suggestive meaning. Angelica shivered. She knew his reputation and was afraid that he might entrap her in some way.

He continued in a conversational way, 'I'm returning to my estates for the weekend. I think you might like the good riding country there.' His lordship had a way of talking in a dispassionate way but conveying his true meaning with the glitter of his eyes or the inclination of his head.

'Lord Rackham, I am grateful for your kindness but until the play's run is over I am not able to leave town.' Angelica was aware of his pale beringed hand reaching for hers.

She was greatly relieved to hear a further soft rap on the door. Mary opened it to a pretty young girl with wide eyes as blue as cornflowers. Behind her stood the tall, stern figure of Ivor Asprey. Discomforted, Lord Rackham stood up and bowed low over Angelica's hand. 'I should be going, Miss Leigh. Thank you for a consummate performance tonight.' Nodding briefly to Mr Asprey, he slipped from the room.

Angelica was surprised at how pleased she was to be rescued by a man whom she had thought insolent just a few days before. She looked from his impassive face to the girl's, as pale as his was dark, as sunny as his was obscured. The girl seemed astonished to see her and when Mr Asprey introduced her to Angelica she stammered, 'Miss Leigh, I am pleased to see you well.'

'My daughter was so convinced by your portrayal she would not believe you still lived.' Mr Asprey's expression was serious but his eyes betrayed a certain amusement.

Angelica smiled and put out her hand, which the girl grasped with both of hers. 'Come, Miss Asprey, you can see I am perfectly well, if rather cold. I am pleased to meet you.'

She answered Angelica shyly, 'I imagined you as poor Ophelia.' Then she gazed up with an ecstatic expression. 'But you're even more beautiful, Miss Leigh.'

'Well, I thank you. And you are beautiful too,' Angelica said as she smiled and brushed Elinor Asprey's cheek with a finger.

Her eyes met Mr Asprey's over his daughter's head. An unspoken recognition of imaginative sympathy for the child united them for a moment. Then he looked away. 'Elinor, we must go. We cannot make Lady Linus wait too long.'

'Oh, Papa.' His daughter wrinkled her nose and his face darkened in irritation.

Angelica laughed. 'Miss Asprey, you're lucky to have a courteous papa. I never knew mine, mannerly or not.'

Ivor Asprey indicated to his daughter to follow him, and bowed to Angelica. 'Thank you, Miss Leigh, for reassuring my daughter about your health and vitality.'

The child had skipped to Mary's side and was busy examining the costumes and appeared too engrossed to notice his command. Watching them, Angelica recalled her new friend, Isobel Fitzjames, and the tragedy that had befallen her family. She took the opportunity to take Mr Asprey aside. 'May I ask you, sir, do you play at Hazard?'

He paused and looked at her, puzzled. 'I used to.'

'Do you perhaps know Lord Fulsham?'

His face stiffened. 'He is a member of my club. I've seen him occasionally but he is part of a different crowd. May I ask why your interest?'

'He's ruined the life of a young woman I know.'

'I'm afraid he's quite practised at that.' His words were dry. 'How so this time?'

'Her father lost to him on the gaming tables. His entire patrimony. And then took his life for the shame of it.'

'Well, it seems Lord Fulsham has outdone himself on this occasion. The scandal was talked of in the club, and I was slightly acquainted with Fitzjames.' His eyes were intent on her face. 'I am puzzled, Miss Leigh; what have I to do with this sorry tale, apart from offering fellow sympathy?' Ivor Asprey's laconic response suggested he was bored with the conversation.

Wishing to get to the point of her enquiry before he stalked off, Angelica continued in a rush, 'I just wondered if you knew any gamester who could play more skilfully than Lord Fulsham?' She looked at him anxiously but was surprised when her words elicited a sharp laugh.

'Why, pray? Do you seriously think a seasoned gambler would risk all to win back a stranger's property, only to restore it without fee or favour?'

Angelica bristled. 'Well, I would if I could play, and was allowed within the sacred portals of White's or Brooks's to do so.' Her eyes flashed with feeling. 'Some heinous injustices need redress, indeed with neither fee nor favour.'

'What an admirable woman of parts you are, Miss Leigh. Not just the tragic, trusting Ophelia but a stout-hearted Maid Marian too, taking from the rich to restore justice to the poor.' His tone had turned more amused. 'Methinks you have an excessively idealistic view of human nature.'

'Well, I know someone who could play the shameless lord at dice, and win,' Angelica said with defiance, thinking of Mr Breville and hoping she was not wrong.

'I'm most gratified to hear that, Miss Marian. Thankfully, you won't be needing my help then.' Ivor Asprey took his daughter's hand and as he walked towards the door, turned to salute her in farewell. Angelica thought his haughty expression was lightened with a rather self-satisfied smile.

4

THE TIGHTROPE SHE WALKS

Angelica had never been more pleased to see Mr Brunner's large figure waiting for her and Mary around the back of the theatre, ready to take them home. She was still feeling cold and exhaustion had begun to steal up on her. The curricle clattered over the cobbles through the busy night traffic of horses, carriages and carts and deposited the two young women at the front steps of Mr Breville's house in Berkeley Square. Martin opened the door looking slightly the worse for wear. His wig had been abandoned and his short grey hair was ruffled as if he had been asleep. 'My dears!' he greeted them cheerily with a blast of alcohol on his breath. 'Come in quickly. It's cold and late.' He whisked off their cloaks and after bidding them goodnight disappeared into the kitchen offices at the back.

After a perfunctory wash, Angelica tumbled into her feather bed and fell into a deep sleep. The morning dawned dull and misty. The light barely penetrated the heavy curtains at the window and Angelica lay wondering why she felt strangely leaden and fatigued. In moments of physical weakness her natural lightness of spirit drifted away and she was left with the memory of fear and insecurity that marked her childhood. Before her mother had met Mr Breville they had lived a precarious existence, never certain whether the roof over their heads was safe or they could afford their next meal. Amabel Leigh was forced to earn what money she could beyond the pittance paid by the goldsmith for whom she worked. This meant trading on her beauty and charm to keep herself and her daughter alive. Luckily, she could rely on the attentions of the rich men who came to the shop and did not have to recourse to the street, but even so, she and her young daughter were open to unexpected dangers that scared the young child.

In the warmth of her bed, Angelica curled into a foetal position. The sound of the birds carolling in the trees outside her window lifted her spirits a little by reminding her of the wider world in which she now had a place and of her good fortune to be living under the aegis of Mr Breville, with some opportunities to direct her own life. The heaviness in her chest would improve, she told herself, once she rose and had eaten a little breakfast.

With an effort, she climbed out of bed and walked to pull back the curtains and gaze out on the gardens in the Square. She consciously breathed in the cold air. Immediately it made her cough, hurting her chest. The light was beginning to gild the new pale leaves on the plane trees as the sun burned through the mist. She could just see specks of colour where drifts of daffodils were coming into bloom and her heart began to beat optimistically once more.

She met her mother and Edward Breville at the breakfast table. Amabel Leigh looked up, her face flushed with excitement. 'Dearest, I'm glad to see you. As you know, we're leaving for Paris in two days' time. You say you're happy in the house with just the servants?'

'Of course, Mama. The production of *Hamlet* closes at the end of the week and I can concentrate on learning my part in *The Child of Nature*. You're back in three weeks. I'll manage very well.'

Mrs Leigh then peered into her daughter's face. 'You look very pale, are you ill?'

'No, Mama, just tired. The play is quite gruelling.'

Edward Breville had sat down with *The Sporting Magazine* and a second cup of coffee. He worked so hard Angelica seldom saw him at breakfast and it was amusing to hear him chuckling over various racing reports and other titbits of news. He caught Angelica's eye. 'You know that Irish beauty, Lady Cahir? She's been causing trouble in the Odéon Théâtre in Paris.'

Both women looked at him, curious to hear more. He continued to read, 'Apparently ladies and their cavaliers in neighbouring boxes complained at her continual talk through the production. Her ladyship brooked no rebuke and an officer was called to enforce her silence.' He looked at his mistress with a twinkle. 'She then addressed the audience from her box, "I come from a land of liberty to a country I supposed to be free! This treatment is worse than if the Bastille still existed!" The crowd erupted with cheers and she sat down triumphant, now privileged to talk as much as she pleases.' He slapped his thigh and emitted a hearty laugh. 'I like a spirited beauty!'

'I didn't know Lady Cahir was famous for more than her appearance. She came to see our production but was no noisier than the rest,' Angelica said with a smile.

Mr Breville put his hand on her mother's arm and said indulgently, 'My experience has taught me that for a woman, beauty is the trump card in life, and Irish beauty is double trumps.'

Amabel Leigh had risen to her feet and shook her head, then with a pout looked back at Mr Breville as she turned for the door. 'I must check with Cook what she needs to order to keep you fed, my dear,' she said over her shoulder.

Angelica realised she had Mr Breville to herself for a rare moment and decided to exercise her own charm and beauty on him. 'Sir, do you still play at Hazard?'

He looked at her with amusement. 'No, my dear. I have better things to do with my time. Why do you ask?'

'Do you know Lord Fulsham?'

'I have come across him at The Daffy. He likes spending time with the Fancy, trading boxing cant in the tap room.'

'Have you played him at dice?' Angelica was reluctant to abandon her increasingly implausible idea for the salvation of Isobel Fitzjames's future.

'I have. But my dear, I don't play any more now I have my business to run.'

She took his arm and smiled. 'As you are one of the best calculators of odds, I thought you would be the only person to beat Lord Fulsham at Hazard and win back my friend's family estates.'

His good-natured face looked surprised. 'This sounds somewhat of a fancy, Angelica. Which friend is this?'

'Isobel Fitzjames. I'm sure you've heard the scandal.'

'I have indeed. But I consider her father to be as much at fault as Lord Fulsham, ye know.' Edward Breville folded the paper, uncrossed his legs and stood up. He put a hand on her shoulder. 'It's an admirable mission of yours, Angelica, but it's buffle-headed to expect someone to risk all to win all. Particularly so, to ask anyone to do that for a stranger.'

Angelica hung her head, aware of the truth of his words: there was no answer to the injustice. 'I know, sir. I just feel for my friend and fear the destruction of her hopes.'

As someone who had created success from less than nothing, Edward Breville was more robust about unexpected reversals of fortune, especially through weakness or stupidity. He had his own life as a guide to how spectacularly the phoenix could rise. But as a man he did not appreciate how much more difficult it was for a woman to break free from the constraints of her circumstances. Angelica remained seated and as tiredness overcame her she found her eyes inexorably closing and with her head on her hand she fell asleep.

She awoke with a start. She was expecting Isobel Fitzjames at three for a stroll in Green Park before she had to prepare to leave for the theatre again that evening. Angelica had not the energy to change into her walking dress but slowly climbed the stairs to select the warmest pelisse to wear over the top of her morning gown of blue checked cambric muslin. Angelica was feeling the cold and wanted to be properly wrapped up. She slipped the garment on and was disappointed at how pale she appeared. A bracing walk would soon bring colour back to her cheeks, she reasoned, as she descended the stairs to greet her friend.

Isobel Fitzjames and her maid were let into the hall by a smiling Martin, who had taken quite a shine to this young, hesitant woman. He saw everyone in theatrical terms and so had cast her as more truly an Ophelia figure, ill-used by fate. Miss Angelica, he considered far too spirited and courageous for tragic Ophelia, and much more a Beatrice, from his favourite play, *Much Ado About Nothing*.

Angelica put out her hand in welcome. The young woman before her seemed low spirited but her clothes sparkled with distinction. Her pelisse of purple broadcloth was dramatically embellished with braided scallops and bows edging the collar and down the front opening. On her head was a matching bonnet decorated with braid and bows with silk flowers at the crown, the brim lined in pale lilac silk, setting off her colouring and features to great advantage.

'Good afternoon, Miss Isobel. Shall we step out or would you prefer a dish of tea first?'

'Oh, Miss Angelica, it seems spring has arrived, let's take advantage of it.' Mary emerged from the domestic quarters at the back of the house and greeted Miss Fitzjames's maid. All four young women descended the front steps and turned south towards Berkeley Street heading for Piccadilly and the Park. They crossed the busy thoroughfare and entered Green Park near the Queen's Basin where the water glinted in the sun.

'I'm surprised to see it so busy.' Angelica looked at the fashionable crowd promenading down the Queen's Walk. Men and a few stylish women were on horseback while curricles and phaetons harnessed up to teams of glossy horses drove sedately through the throng. Mostly people were on foot, strolling, hailing friends, standing in small groups in circles of sunlight between the trees, catching up on the latest gossip.

'It certainly lifts the heart. All the colour and gaiety.' Isobel Fitzjames barely managed a smile.

Angelica turned to look more closely at her friend, and said with some concern, 'Are your spirits very much in need of lifting?'

Miss Fitzjames met her eyes with a slight frown. 'I left my stepmother talking business with Lord Fulsham. I couldn't bear to be in the same house as them both.' In a rush of sisterly feeling, Angelica took her gloved hand in hers and squeezed it fleetingly. She wished she had something consoling to say.

At that moment they were approaching Earl Spencer's imposing town house, eight pillars across and dominating the eastern border of Green Park, its Portland stone bright in the afternoon light. People were streaming down the imposing flight of steps and onto the grass. Two handsome young men stood at the top, shading their eyes against the sun as they surveyed the milling crowd.

'Oh, Miss Angelica, look! Aren't those your friends?' Isobel Fitzjames's voice grew animated.

Angelica recognised Lord Latimer and Dante Locke just as they too saw her and waved, beginning to weave their way towards them through the promenaders.

'Oh, Miss Leigh. What a treat to find you here after the dullest afternoon.' Lord Latimer grasped her hand, his amused eyes gazing into hers. He turned to her companion and murmured, 'And it's Miss Fitzjames, if I remember rightly.' She too had the benefit of his charm and her face relaxed and looked almost merry.

'It's good to meet you again, my lord. And Mr Locke.' Angelica proffered her hand to the young man who was standing slightly to one side, with an abstracted expression on his face.

'Oh, Dante's been unsettled by the execrable poetry we've been exposed to at the Earl's assembly.' Charles Latimer laughed. 'He objected to the new Poet Laureate being there.'

'I don't disapprove of his early work. I do deplore, however, Mr Southey's apostasy in turning from fire-eating radical to supporter and supplicant of a corrupt government.' Dante Locke glowered into the middle distance as he muttered, ''Tis unconscionable that poets should dishonour the Muse by accepting the Crown's lucre.'

'Come, come, Mr Locke. Surely a poet has to eat too? He cannot live on ambrosia alone.' Angelica spoke in jest as Lord Latimer took her hand and tucked it into his arm.

They were walking together, the maids trailing behind, when Lord Latimer expostulated, 'We're so in need of a restorative drink. Rather than go to St James's may we repair instead to Berkeley Square with you?'

Angelica squeezed his arm companionably. 'Of course. I'm feeling rather fatigued and would be happy to turn for home.'

Charles Latimer peered into her face with a worried frown. 'I must say, Miss Leigh, you look a trifle peaky. Not your usual self.'

'Talk about my health is tedious, my lord. Do tell us what you were doing at the Spencers' this afternoon.'

'It's all my uncle's doing. The old Earl is a friend of Ivor's and a leading light of the dull tribe of Whigs.'

'At least he's not a Tory,' Dante Locke said sulkily. Most young hotheads blamed every ill on a government in power too long.

Angelica turned with a wry smile. 'So what did Mr Asprey think would be to your benefit?'

'Oh, Spencer's very proud of his extensive library and has regular meetings at his showy mansion when ancient texts are read out to an admiring audience. All raging bibliomaniacs, I fear.'

Dante Locke, walking with Isobel Fitzjames on his arm, interceded, 'And don't forget the music, Charlie. Some second-rate Handel songs sung by a querulous, elderly castrato. Despite being Italian, he made the afternoon unendurable.'

Angelica could not hide her curiosity. 'You have yet to tell me, Lord Latimer, what your uncle hoped you would gain by this afternoon's diversion.'

'Diversion is the word. Under orders from Mama no doubt, he was attempting to counter the wastrel occupations of young noblemen and turn my interests to something more worthy.' He snorted with derision. 'Society has become so monumentally insufferable for anyone with spirit or heart. 'Tis formed of two mighty tribes – the bores and the bored!'

Angelica said with a laugh, 'And you of course are neither.' She understood exactly the Duchess and her brother's intention. They had hoped to distract the son and heir from the company of actresses and gamesters, and the dangers of racing other wild bloods in curricles on the public highway. 'And did your concerned relations' plan succeed?' she asked mischievously.

Dante Locke glowered and took up the plaint, 'Miss Leigh, there was nothing there to attract a red-blooded young Tartar. Now if you or Miss Fitzjames had graced the gathering we might have had a sparkier time.' He brought Isobel Fitzjames's gloved hand to his lips and cast her a dark glance through lowered lashes. Angelica smiled. She was very close in age to these young men but had already lived a more varied life and felt much the older and wiser.

The bright afternoon was fast retreating as a thunderous dark cloud loomed up from the west. 'Luckily, we're home before the deluge,' Angelica said as she led the way up the steps of number seven, Berkeley Square.

Martin opened the door with a low bow and addressed her in his sonorous voice, 'Mrs Leigh asked me to let you know she's out shopping.' As he took the pelisses and bonnets, his eyes appraised the two young men who had turned up unexpectedly with his young mistress. 'Well, Miss Angelica, didn't pick these out of the gutter, did ye!' he said appreciatively.

Lord Latimer looked astonished at Martin's familiarity, verging on insolence. His mother ran a very formal ducal household in Grosvenor Square where servants glided about their duties without comment and never intruded or drew attention to themselves. Angelica replied in an amused voice, 'Tush, Martin! Would you bring some ale and ratafia to the drawing room, if you please?' She led the way up the grand serpentine stairs. Taking Charles Latimer's arm she explained, 'I'm so sorry, my lord. My mother's butler has a thespian way about him. It seems you can extract the man from the theatre but not the theatre from the man.'

'Well, he's very lucky to have your mama rather than mine as his employer.' He gave a grim smile. As they entered the drawing room, all eyes were immediately drawn to the glowing Lawrence portrait above the fireplace. 'And is this your mama?' Lord Latimer stood looking up into the sitter's inviting gaze.

Angelica smiled. 'It is indeed. The artist is quite the virtuoso, isn't he? Mama is almost as beautiful as her portrait.'

'I hope Mr Lawrence will be persuaded to immortalise you, my dear Miss Leigh,' he said as he impulsively grasped her hand. 'You need no flattery in paint but it would take an artist of his genius to capture your beauty, your colouring.' At that moment, Martin entered with a tray laden with a decanter and jug of ale and Angelica gently extricated herself. She offered the glasses of liquor to the company and indicated that they should sit down.

Dante Locke was in sympathetic conversation with Miss Fitzjames and so Angelica turned to sit beside Lord Latimer opposite the fire. 'This is a handsome room,' he said appreciatively, looking towards the three full-length windows across the grand façade of the house, reflecting an ominously darkening sky. Mrs Leigh had expressed her extravagant tastes by having the walls hung in primrose yellow silk which brought a lustrous sunniness to the space, regardless of the weather outside. They both looked at the dark head of Mr Locke bent solicitously towards Miss Fitzjames, her face unusually alive with feeling.

In a quiet voice, Lord Latimer said, 'The tragedy of her father and the Fitzjames family is all over the clubs, you know.'

'So I hear. I had hoped that a friend might win the estates back from Lord Fulsham.'

Charles Latimer laughed out loud. 'I presume there are no takers in this fancy?'

Angelica hushed his levity in front of Miss Fitzjames. In a low voice she explained, 'It's like seeking a unicorn in a hedge. The man I had in mind, whose house this is, said my head's in the clouds if I think any gamester would risk all to restore a stranger's patrimony.'

'Truly spoke, indeed. And Fulsham's such a skilled player there's only one person I know to match 'im.' Angelica looked at him, knowing just who he meant. 'But he's long given up the devil's bones; instead, he's become a serious, prosy type more interested in plying the laws of the land.'

'I find it hard to believe your uncle used to be such a gambler.'

Lord Latimer put his head in his hands in a show of mock dismay. 'You wouldn't recognise him now if you'd known him in his wild youth. Drinking, brawling, gaming.' He dropped his voice to a conspiratorial whisper. 'The gambling and miscellaneous harlotry meant he had already fought two duels by the time he was twenty-four. Even marriage to the beauteous Mrs Asprey, and cousin Elinor's birth, did not tame his ways.' He straightened his back and gazed into the distance. 'Aunt Emma's death completely felled him. It changed him into the unsmiling paragon you see today.'

Dante Locke looked across at his friend and gently remonstrated, 'Truly, Charles, you ride Mr Asprey rough. We need trusty Trojans like him in government. More useful than gamblers, rogues and fools like the rest of 'em!' As a poet, he felt it was his duty to be as radical as Lord Byron, and as much in thrall to freedom and revolution as the hothead Mr Shelley, whose privately printed epic, Queen Mab, had been lent to him at the university, firing his blood.

Lord Latimer turned back to Angelica and said under his breath, 'Dante and I met at school. He should never have been sent to Eton though. It's the home of bullies and brawlers and a devilish place for a poet. He suffered much.'

'But my lord, surely you're neither bully nor brawler?'

'Oh, I'm handy enough with my fists to have got by.' He gave a self-satisfied smile.

A great rumble of thunder rattled the windows, a flash of lightning illuminating the room with uncanny brightness. Angelica shivered; she was overcome with cold and tiredness and said, 'How I wish I could just stay here tonight and not have to go to the theatre.'

All eyes were turned sympathetically towards her. Charles Latimer, his face stricken, murmured under his breath, 'This is why I want to take you away from all this. Just wait until the summer.' He gazed into her eyes with intense feeling, his hand tracing a slow figure of eight on her palm. Angelica shivered, not entirely due to the approaching storm. She met his passionate gaze again and was taken aback by a prickle of excitement at the possibility of being loved by a man. Had she underestimated Lord Latimer's feelings for her, and hers for him? Or was it just that she was feeling weak and increasingly ill and longed to relinquish the self-sufficiency she had cultivated since she was a child?

Angelica stood up and straightened her shoulders. 'It's actually a profession I'm proud of and love. I only have two more nights before this production comes to a close. Then I can rest for a while.'

Isobel Fitzjames rushed forward and took her hands. 'Dear Miss Angelica, I wish I could be of more help to you. You have been so encouraging to me. I would particularly like to be in the audience for your last night tomorrow, but Mrs Fitzjames thinks the theatre beneath contempt.' The young woman's face was immediately suffused with embarrassment at her unconsidered words. She stammered, 'I don't mean what you do...'

With a tired smile, Angelica squeezed her hand. 'I assure you, my dear, your words do not offend me. I know how cheaply the *haut ton* hold my profession. I just try to live in a way that proves them mistaken.' She turned to the young men. 'Delightful as your company is, gentlemen, I fear I must prepare for my performance tonight.' They all glanced out at the rain sheeting out of a leaden sky. 'Martin can lend you and Miss Fitzjames a selection of our large umbrellas.'

She led the party down the stairs and as coats and hats, pelisses and bonnets were donned and Miss Fitzjames's maid was called from the kitchens, Martin handed out umbrellas. The young men bowed in farewell, Lord Latimer bringing Angelica's hand swiftly to his lips.

Isobel Fitzjames gave her a shy, fleeting hug. 'It's such heart's ease to be in the company of you and your friends. Thank you, Miss Angelica.'

'Come on, Miss Fitzjames, I know you live just round the corner; we'll escort you and your maid home.' Lord Latimer took her gloved hand and they dashed out into the storm.

* * *

The night's performance had been lacklustre. Everyone was tired at the end of a gruelling run and were conserving their energies for the final night. The torrential rain had not ceased and the audience too seemed more subdued than usual, the smell from the pit more pungent. Angelica hardly knew how she got through the ordeal. When she and Mary arrived home she was faced with a house in uproar. Martin was harassed, organising the numerous bandboxes and portmanteaus of clothes and accessories that Mrs Leigh had packed for her trip to Paris. The hallway was barely passable. Martin wrung his hands with a tragic expression on his face. 'Ah, Miss Angelica, your mama and the master are leaving early in the morning. Such a to-do! Where is there space for any more?' He scurried off into the kitchens to refresh himself with another ale.

Angelica wearily climbed the stairs to find her mother in her room. The bed was piled with dresses, chemises and bonnets. 'Mama, surely you've packed enough?' Angelica said as she sank onto the sofa between the windows.

Amabel Leigh was flushed with excitement as she held a turquoise pelisse against her face and gazed at her reflection in the looking-glass. 'Do you think this colour becomes me?'

'Mama, most things become you. But you'll be buying more clothes once you are there.' Angelica sighed; she was so bone weary she longed for bed.

Her mother cast the pelisse onto the bed and looked at her with concern. 'You look a trifle *fatiguée*, my dear. I don't want you ill while I'm away.'

'Oh, Mama. After tomorrow night I can rest and I'll be fine. You are not to worry.' She smiled and stood up. 'But I think I'll go to bed now.'

Mrs Leigh peered at her daughter and said fretfully, 'I cannot bear to see you so lacklustre and hollow-eyed.'

Angelica hugged her mother, kissing her on the cheek. 'Mama, you are to go to Paris with Mr Breville and enjoy yourself. You'll soon be back and I will be full of spirit again.'

* * *

After a restless night, Angelica crawled late from her bed. The birds in Berkeley Square gardens were not singing as insistently as at dawn and the delivery carts were still rumbling over the cobbles, the tradesmen's harsh cries floating up to her window. She dressed with little care, dragged a comb through her mane of hair and piled it haphazardly on her head. She intended to spend the morning on the sofa reading.

There were not many books in Mr Breville's house but Mrs Leigh had insisted on buying her own copy of the sensationally successful novel, *The Heroine,* and had enjoyed it so much she had recommended it to her daughter. Angelica remembered her mother chuckling over the tale and felt this was just what she needed to lift her spirits. Her breathing was laboured as she climbed the stairs and went into Mrs Leigh's bedroom where she sat with relief on the bed. Clothes were still scattered everywhere and the under-maid was slowly folding, hanging and putting away.

'Sara, I'm looking for a book Mama has been reading called *The Heroine*. It's three volumes in green calf covers.' Both women turned to the tables beside the bed where pots and bottles of lotion were lined up with a swansdown puff, fine scissors from the etui case and a small hand mirror in a silver frame. Angelica was interested to see that in pride of place was the White Imperial Powder she had given her mother from the cosmetical stores at the theatre, together with small bottles of Milk of Roses, Pear's Almond Bloom and a blue glass pot of zinc oxide. Angelica opened one of the bottles to sniff the contents and the scent of jasmine and roses drifted into the room. Glancing at the floor, she glimpsed the corner of a volume half obscured by the bedclothes. 'This might be it. I hope it's volume one.'

Angelica took the book to the sofa at the window in the morning room. She opened it to find the title page inscribed in Mr Breville's bold hand. *To my own dear Heroine, with Warmest Esteem.* The author was a poet born in County Cork and she was sure that had been part of the attraction for her mother. Despite the common disparagement of the Irish, Amabel Leigh was proud of her forebears. Angelica was quickly drawn into the story by the bright, witty character of Cherry, a young woman determined to live as the star of her own gothic novel, bemoaning her unsuitable name, preferring Cherubina.

As Angelica turned the page, a folded piece of paper fluttered to the floor. She picked it up and, with an uneasy feeling that she was intruding, opened it. She read in a hand she did not recognise:

My Bella,

I long to see you again. After all these years can you forgive me?

I will be in the country for a few days. England means nothing to me but that you and young Angel are there. And the sea is nothing but that which separates me from those I love. Don't tell anyone I am to return to those shores.

Yours ever, P

There was no date and Angelica wondered if it was a recent note, or one her mother had kept for sentimental reasons. It made her feel unsettled. Who was it who needed forgiveness, and what needed forgiving? The paper was not yellowed enough to have come from her father who had died more than fifteen years ago. But the writer seemed to have affection for 'Angel' who could only be herself. She realised she had never asked her father's given name, she knew him just as Mr Leigh. But if not him, who? In this troubled frame of mind she returned to the book. She had never before encountered such a brightness of tone in any fictional character and was soon engrossed, feeling her spirits revive.

One passage was heavily underlined, she presumed by her mother. 'Have I not far greater merit in getting a husband by sentiment, adventure and melancholy, than by dressing, gadding, dancing and singing?'

Angelica laughed out loud. So that was why her mother was always impressing on her the need to curb her lightness of spirit and amusement at the world. Heroines of gothic novels had to suffer and languish and certainly did not laugh. She could never be such an enervated heroine and so obviously would never attract the right kind of husband. Angelica read on, diverted. But her eyes started to flutter and finally close. She dozed in a fitful sleep to be woken by Mary with just ten minutes to get herself ready. Then both women bundled into the chaise and Mr Brunner delivered them to Covent Garden Theatre for the last performance of the run.

* * *

The last night of *Hamlet* had brought all of Angelica's and Mr Kean's admirers to the performance. The pit was rowdier than usual with alcohol and food liberally consumed throughout the evening and missiles rained down from the upper boxes. Before the lights were dimmed Angelica walked to the side of the stage and through a slight gap in the curtain, glimpsed one of the larger boxes filled with young bucks. Among them, she recognised Lord Latimer and Dante Locke, and the faces of a couple of other young men she had previously met. She could see glasses and bottles of champagne glinting in the low light and knew they had already begun drinking.

In a quick perusal of the auditorium, another of the more expensive boxes close to the stage was very noticeable for the colourful ladies in bold dresses and rouged lips who laughed, leaning over the front and waving, accompanied by Lord Rackham and an older crowd of dissolute rakes and dandies who sought their sport at the theatre, local bordellos and gentlemen's clubs.

All eyes, however, were drawn to the Royal Box, where the well-upholstered, red-faced Prince Regent was holding court surrounded by overdressed cronies and a couple of exquisite young women, expertly coquetting with their fans and casting provocative glances at the tumultuous scene below, where many a gaze and bawdy comment was directed their way. The Prince was unpopular and as the night wore on and more alcohol was imbibed, the ribald comments became more markedly addressed to him. Angelica knew it would be a noisy night.

Mary helped dress her one last time in the heavy brocade dress, adjusting the wig to show a suitable expanse of pale forehead. Angelica's cheeks had lost whatever colour they had and did not need such a liberal dusting of the white powder but extra rouge on her cheeks and lips ensured her appearance was not entirely spectral. She knew that to get through this final performance would take all her willpower. Her chest was heavy and tight, her voice breathy, and she was afraid she would be ambushed by a fit of coughing.

Angelica was so cold she asked Mary to collect her an early cup of hot chocolate from Mistress Pastow just to fortify her a little. She was sitting pensively in the chair in front of the speckled looking-glass when a slight knock at the door roused her and she looked up to see the manager slide into the room. David Dunbar had the unhealthy pallor of a man who lived by night and an insinuating manner that made Angelica bridle at the best of times. Now feeling weakened, she could barely summon the energy to protect her spirit from his baleful presence. 'How now, Mr Dunbar?' she queried in a quiet voice.

'You don't look too prime, Miss Leigh,' he said, peering at her with anxiety in his eyes. But the concern was not for her health but for his box office receipts. 'You're not going to cry off this last moment?'

'Never fear, Mr Dunbar. I'm a professional. I'll get through it.'

'And you're willing to be my lead actress in *The Child of Nature*?'

'I am. But I thought you were going to give the role to a more complaisant actress.' Angelica could not stop herself from reminding him of his threat.

David Dunbar was proof against embarrassment but his brow clouded with irritation for a moment, before saying with an airy dismissal, 'I don't know what ye mean. It was always your part in my plan.'

Angelica was watching him closely and knew he had something else to impart. 'Are you troubled by anything, Mr Dunbar? I'm sure you did not come here to enquire about my well-being.'

He paused by the door, his puffy features animated with the possibility of gossip. 'Well, Miss Leigh, you had a visitor earlier. A gentleman from France.'

Angelica met his slippery glance. 'Is this gentleman still here?' she asked neutrally.

'No. That was the suspicious thing. He seemed most agitated and when he heard a door slam in the distance he jumped, made his excuses and left.'

'Did he give you his name?' When the manager shook his head, she sighed. 'Perhaps you can tell me something more of this gentleman's business with me?' Angelica knew no one in France, but was aware she was known by repute to some Parisian theatregoers.

'He seemed very keen to see you but would not wait. He asked me where you lodged and of course I couldn't tell him. I did mention, though, you lived under your mother's roof in Mayfair, so he knew you were a woman of good reputation.'

Angelica was curious, despite her misgivings about men who vexed her with odd fancies about her own person or the characters she played. 'What did this gentleman look like?'

David Dunbar realised Angelica was even more in the dark about this stranger than he; with no juicy gossip to be had, he was impatient to go. In an off-hand way he said, 'Oh, more years than me. Hair with white streaks, once good face, now that of a rakehell. Irish I think but dressed as a Frenchified coxcomb, rings on his fingers and red heels on his shoes!' he said with some disdain.

The idea of this elderly fop amused her. 'Well, I thank you, Mr Dunbar. I have never met such a man before in my life. Perhaps he's just flying a kite?' A sudden coughing fit seized her and Mr Dunbar beat a hasty retreat. At this moment, Mary returned from Mistress Pastow's with the bowl of steaming chocolate and milk. 'Thank you, this will revive me.' She warmed her hands on the bowl, sat back in her chair and closed her eyes.

Angelica could hear the hubbub of the audience even in her small dressing room. She walked to the wings. The noise only lessened for a while when the clanking ghost appeared. The appearance of Mr Kean, however, never failed to silence them with his sheer force of personality and the power and beauty of his voice, although Prince Hamlet, the character he played with such energy and pathos, was one who invited a running commentary from the unmannerly wits in the drunken pit.

Angelica steeled herself for her entry onto the stage. Again, the sight of her hushed the general chatter but the plight of Ophelia always incited cries of advice and admonition, especially from the women. She summoned her energy; it was hard to keep the dramatic focus and convey the emotional heart of her character when there were so many distractions off-stage. Hamlet cursing Ophelia with the dismissive, 'Get thee to a nunnery, go!' riled up an already volatile crowd who knew the bawdy meaning of 'nunnery'. Ophelia's confused and heart-broken response, 'O, what a noble mind is here o'erthrown!' was lost in the jeers.

Angelica felt she was swimming through a storm that cast wave after tumultuous wave against her. The energy she had always relied on to pull her through and command the stage was failing. Even Mr Kean's compelling presence and sonorous voice did not quite quell the restive audience. Angelica returned to her dressing room to change for her final scene, already aware she was subsiding into some sickness beyond her will to resist. Her cheeks, now free of white powder, flamed with fever. Although she was relieved to relinquish the weight of the eighteenth-century gown, she could hardly bear the chill of wearing just her chemise with the ordeal of immersion to come. She gritted her teeth as she walked back to the wings, wrapped in a woollen cloak for warmth.

Her distracted appearance on stage, distraught and singing in a plaintive voice, silenced the audience at last. There was always the shock in seeing a young woman so undone and Ophelia, embodied by Angelica, had enjoyed the greatest popular sympathy of any of Shakespeare's characters in this play. The audience was hushed and as she slipped shivering into the tank of water, a great shout went up from the pit and an intoxicated young man sprang across the shoulders of the musicians in the orchestra and clambered onto the stage.

The pit erupted in catcalls and exhortations as he attempted to get to Angelica and save her from her watery death. There was consternation too from the boxes where Lord Latimer, unbeknownst to Angelica, vaulted over the front of his and rapidly made his way to the stage, intent on a heroic defence of his beloved. The attendants who were in the process of retrieving Ophelia from the stream to carry her away were distracted and let Angelica slip once more into the chilly water. They attempted to chase the interloper away with the broken papier mâché limb of the willow, while Lord Latimer's chivalric defence was blocked as he was brusquely ushered back onto the other side of the stage.

For what seemed like an age, Angelica lay submerged except for her face, close to losing consciousness. The chill had entered her bones and it was almost impossible to stop her teeth chattering. She felt she should just stand up and quietly slip away but was paralysed into inaction. Eventually the stage hands had bundled the intoxicated man out into the street and returned to their task. But the audience was too excited now to settle and the attendants carried Angelica's dripping, seemingly lifeless, body off with little sense of tragic ceremony.

Concerned for her mistress, Mary was waiting with another bowl of hot chocolate laced with brandy to warm her. Mr Dunbar had demanded that for the last night everyone should take a bow at the very end, so Angelica was not allowed to go home early to bed. Mary helped her into the heavy dress again. Her wet hair was coiled up under the wig, the damp intensifying the musky smell, and her skin, no longer hectically flushed, had turned almost blue. Rouge was quickly slathered on to make her seem closer to life than death and Angelica dragged herself back to the wings of the stage to await their final curtain call.

She turned to the two clowns who waited with her, distressed by the continuing hubbub of the crowd, and said in anguish, 'How can they so dishonour this? The poetry of Mr Kean's performance brings tears to my eyes. It is so tragic it wrings my heart.'

At the front of the stage, Hamlet's dying words were spoken in a voice of awful majesty, 'O, I die, Horatio. The potent poison quite o'er-crows my spirit.' The chatter in the pit and upper boxes continued.

The taller clown, the elderly actor, Ned Perkins, gave her a painted smile. 'Don't go worrying yourself, Miss Angelly, they are but fools and knaves who fill the benches. They have not the soul for this.'

Then with an unspoken recognition that something momentous was happening on stage, the auditorium grew quiet as Hamlet collapsed in his death throes to gasp out his last words, 'The rest is silence.' After the sound of a gunshot marking the end of the play, Angelica trooped on stage with the other characters and all the actors were met by good-humoured applause and cheering. Flowers thrown from the boxes scattered onto the stage at Angelica's feet. The stamping started and the chanting for Mr Kean and Miss Leigh brought the two together to walk to the front and bow low, in recognition of the audience's appreciation. Angelica could see Lord Latimer standing, clapping vigorously and noticed that the Royal Box was empty.

She did not know how she managed to get back to her dressing room. Mary had just whisked the damp wig off her head and removed the dress and wrapped her in her cloak when there was a soft rap at the door. 'Don't let anyone in, Mary.' Angelica was gasping for breath.

'It's Lord Latimer and Mr Locke, Miss Leigh,' the young woman turned and whispered to her mistress. With a weary hand Angelica indicated they could enter. She stood up to greet her well-wishers and fainted in Lord Latimer's arms.

His lordship immediately took charge. Still supporting Angelica, he ordered Mary to get Brunner and the chaise pulled up outside as quickly as possible. As Angelica regained consciousness she demurred at finding herself cradled against his coat, 'My lord, do let me sit a while.' Her voice was weak and she could barely speak but Dante Locke pulled the chair up and his friend lowered her with care.

Other admirers were queueing at the door and Lord Latimer went into the corridor to explain that Miss Leigh was indisposed, a statement that elicited some jealous muttering and sceptical looks as the disappointed sloped away. The two young men, with Brunner's help, half-carried Angelica into the chaise and climbed in opposite her and Mary. Lord Latimer's face was stricken as he watched her rest her head against the squab cushion, struggling to breathe.

When they arrived back at Berkeley Square, all three men carried her into the house where Martin greeted them with a squawk, 'What has become of Miss Angelica? She looks as sick as a horse.' Angelica was overcome with a paroxysm of coughing that brought tears to her eyes. Thrown into a panic, Martin gabbled, 'Lawks, a-mercy! That's a churchyard cough if ever I heard one.'

'Martin, don't be so melodramatic.' Angelica managed the firmest voice she could. 'I just need some sleep and I'll be fine.'

All eyes were on her pale, strained face then Lord Latimer walked forward and said authoritatively, 'Mary, please make sure Miss Leigh sleeps propped upright on a bank of pillows to help her breathe.'

Angelica took his hand for reassurance, and managed a wan smile. 'You seem very knowledgeable about such things?' She gazed up into his worried face.

'I am. My aunt Emma had inflamed lungs and it was the only way she could rest.'

'Was your aunt Emma Mrs Asprey?' When Charles Latimer nodded, Angelica for the first time felt fear about the seriousness of her condition. 'But, my lord, was that the cause of her death?'

He did not answer or look at her but, taking his friend's arm, saluted Angelica and turned smartly on his heel. Over his shoulder he said, 'Mary, look after Miss Leigh. I'll be back early tomorrow.' The two young bucks left the house and Mary and Martin helped Angelica up the stairs to her bedchamber.

5

BETWEEN DEATH AND LIFE

Angelica spent the night in a hallucinatory state pursued by half-waking dreams of suffocation and loss, running through wet sand in search of something, someone, somewhere. She was aware of Mary looming over her, urging her to sip some liquid, chafing her hands, banking up the fire, the flames throwing eerie shadows on the wall, creatures stalking the room beside her. She lay in a diffuse state of panic; it was difficult to breathe, her back and ribs hurt from the coughing that racked her body. The closer she was to upright the easier it was to catch her breath but her feverish restlessness was laced with fear. A deep fatigue rooted her to the bed.

Night blurred into morning and as Mary drew the curtains the light hurt her eyes. 'What's wrong with me, Mary?' Angelica called weakly from the bed.

'I don't know, Miss, but Martin's sent the boy for Mrs Leigh's quack so we'll know soon enough.'

Angelica could only manage a whisper. 'I'm sure he's not a quack.'

'Well, Cook has sent up this bowl of hot water with bay and thyme sprigs to ease your breathing.' She cleared the table by Angelica's bed and set it down with care, aromatic steam rising in the cold air. 'She asks, could you manage some broth?'

Angelica shook her head and then, overcome with her own feebleness, only had energy enough to close her eyes. Hours seemed to pass punctuated by her coughing. Hot and yet shivery, she heard a moan which could only have been hers. Mary placed a cold towel on her forehead. Angelica's hair was wet and heavy and had been plaited loosely to keep it off her face while she struggled for each breath.

Through a delirious haze she was aware of the dark presence of her mother's doctor, Hapwood, looming over her bed. He took her pulse and peered down her throat with a solemn expression on his face, then asked if he could listen to her chest. When she nodded and pulled her chemise down to expose her breastbone he put his ear to her skin and began to thrum on her ribcage in an attempt to listen to the resonance. Even in the stupor of fever, Angelica recoiled from this unexpected intimacy with a stranger who smelt of camphor and hair oil, and was relieved when he straightened up. Dr Hapwood shook his head, before bidding farewell and leaving the room.

In the absence of Angelica's mother, Martin had assumed the role of *pater familias* and it was to him Dr Hapwood gave the news that he would return to bleed the patient. 'The fever in her blood needs to be released,' he said with authority. His confidence in the extent of his knowledge and competence was not clouded by the merest quiver of humility or doubt.

Approaching Berkeley Square, Lord Latimer arrived at the front steps of number seven just as Isobel Fitzjames and her maid were at the front door. They walked into the house together to be greeted by Martin's stricken face. 'How is Miss Leigh?' Lord Latimer asked in an urgent voice before he had even removed his hat and coat.

'Not good, my lord.'

'What has happened?' He grasped Martin's arm in alarm.

'The young mistress is in a fever.'

'That dog just leaving, was he the quack, Hapwood?' Lord Latimer asked, his lip curling.

Martin was already distraught about the health of his young mistress and overwhelmed with responsibility for her; his frayed nerves were close to breaking and the arrogance of this young nobleman was the last straw. He snapped, 'Dr Hapwood is trained in a noble profession.'

Lord Latimer snorted. 'He killed my aunt Emma. It doesn't take much skill or training for that!'

This was too much for Martin who lost any semblance of deference to his betters. 'So my lord is trained in the medical arts too? Not content with being the beneficiary of a noble line, whose honour he has done little to earn?' he said with theatrical scorn.

Charles Latimer whirled round as if to strike the old actor, but restrained himself and instead said with cold disdain, 'If we were of equal rank I would call you out for such insolence.'

At this point Isobel Fitzjames stepped between them and said in her meek way, 'Gentlemen, I know it is Miss Leigh's health that concerns all of us most pressingly. Mr Martin, may I go and see how she is?'

Martin nodded and pointed up the stairs. 'Mary is there with her.' He then led Lord Latimer through to the library and asked him if he could offer him something to drink.

'Brandy would do the trick,' his lordship answered in a distracted way, then in an attempt at making some amends added, 'You look like you could do with a quaff yourself.'

'Thank you, my lord, but I don't tipple while working.' Martin's manner was stiff and correct. Lord Latimer was left alone, staring into the distance, thinking. Death was more present to him than it was to most of the young swells he counted as friends. He recalled how his father's injuries at Alexandria had not much affected him, a boy of barely seven, to whom the Duke was a stranger. But nearly sixteen years later the death of his aunt Emma, a young mother and loved by all, had shaken his sense of security in the natural order of things. 'To have this play out again.' He spoke out loud with a sense of dread as he walked to the window to gaze on a sky darkening before his eyes. With Mrs Leigh in Paris and Martin panicking, Lord Latimer was aware of an unfamiliar weight of responsibility settling on his shoulders.

The library door burst open and Miss Fitzjames dashed into the room, a distraught look in her eyes. She flew to Lord Latimer's side and grasped his hand in an uncharacteristically emotional gesture. For a moment she could not speak.

'How is Miss Leigh?' He caught her by the elbow and turned her to face him, the intensity of his manner demanding answers.

She took a deep breath. 'She barely knew me, my lord. She's so feverish, the doctor is returning to bleed her this afternoon. It reminded me of how my mother...' Her voice faded away as she clutched at his hand.

Lord Latimer extricated himself from her grip and paced to the window again, his mind in turmoil. He turned and said with quiet despair, 'That quacksalver Hapwood attended my aunt in her illness. All he does is bleed his patients and collect the lucre. And he bled her to death.'

Isobel Fitzjames was by his side in an instant. 'But he's an eminent doctor, Lord Latimer. We can't go against his advice.'

'Not while Miss Leigh is in this house, ruled over by the craven-hearted Martin.'

'You cannot expect servants to counter medical nostrums.'

'That is exactly why I owe it to Miss Leigh and my concern for her that I remove her to a house where she can be properly treated.'

'But she cannot go anywhere else, surely?' Isobel Fitzjames's voice faltered.

'Dammit! I have to get Miss Leigh away to save her life. I cannot allow her to be mistreated by a man who has already destroyed someone else I loved.'

'But how? Where?' Miss Fitzjames wrung her hands.

Lord Latimer was speaking quietly, almost to himself, as his mind worked through the possibilities. 'Certainly my mama would not even open the door to Miss Leigh. Her name cannot be mentioned in her presence. But I think I know where I could take her.' He smiled for the first time since he had entered the house.

'Where my lord? Where could Miss Angelica go until her mother returns?'

'My uncle, Mr Asprey,' Charles Latimer said with a certainty he did not feel.

She gasped, 'No! How can he agree? He a widower without a wife to protect his and Miss Leigh's reputation?'

'I don't see why he should not. Miss Leigh's maid will go with her. Uncle Ivor has a mansion with so many rooms and even more servants. There's a governess too, Miss Stafford, a sensible good woman, who could take charge of an invalid's care.'

Miss Fitzjames still looked doubtful but Lord Latimer now had the bit between his teeth. With renewed vigour he walked to the door. 'I will send a note to your address to let you know if my plan comes about and where you may be able to visit Miss Leigh. Good afternoon, Miss Fitzjames. *Adieu!*' He was quickly out of the door and down the front steps heading towards St James's Square.

Lord Latimer walked fast, his redingote billowing behind him as he strode down Berkeley Street, barely aware of the laughter of children with their nurses in the Square gardens. A pretty young woman wearing a veiled hat and riding a striking bay hunter, accompanied by her liveried groom, coquettishly glanced his way, appraising this tall young man, whose stylish clothing declared his wealth and breeding. But Lord Latimer was oblivious to her interest. His footsteps did not falter, determined as he was to see his uncle before he set off for the Houses of Parliament.

As he turned left into Piccadilly he was still lost in thought, working out the argument he would make for this unconventional arrangement. He crossed the busy thoroughfare to turn into the quieter St James's Street where gentlemen on horseback, driving their carriages or on foot were busy visiting their tailors, and entering their clubs for the dice and card games that never ceased. Several friends and acquaintances hailed the popular young lord but he was in no mood for casual dalliance and merely tipped his hat in salute. They gazed after his fast-receding figure and shook their heads nonplussed; what business could be so urgent that he would pass the seductive bow window of his club, with the promise of pleasure, and not falter?

Lord Latimer reached the leafy grandeur of St James's Square and for the first time slowed his step. There was an impressive ducal carriage slowly circling the central garden. For a moment he feared it was his mama's Arlington equipage but then sighed with relief when he realised it was another duchess on her way home from a social call at the Castleton mansion next door. He sprinted up the front steps of number four and Mr Goodall opened the front door with aplomb.

On sight of his master's scapegrace nephew the butler bowed low, exaggerating his usual punctilio in an attempt at instilling more of the propriety of things on the feckless younger generation. He took Lord Latimer's hat and coat and in response to the young man's impatience left him standing in the hall while he walked with deliberate pace to the library door, behind which Mr Asprey was at work.

Goodall knocked softly and asked in the kind of discreet voice that meant no visitor could hear a word, 'Are you at home to Lord Latimer, sir?'

The young lord had been pacing the black and white marble floor counting the squares as he did as a child, but felt an unexpected calm descend as he was ushered at last into the library. Even though his uncle was forbidding and chilly in manner, the young man always felt safe when he placed a problem in his hands. He remained standing as the door was quietly closed behind him and watched Ivor Asprey finish writing a sentence, deliberately putting his quill down on the blotter on his large oak desk. Only then did he look up to appraise his nephew, his deep blue eyes seeming to miss little.

'Well, my lord? To what do I owe this unexpected pleasure? Another scrape? More gambling debts?' he drawled, a wry look on his face.

Lord Latimer read this softening of his uncle's usual mien as a good sign. He flung himself into the chair by the fire and noticed the decanter of brandy and glasses glinting on the console table.

'If you need anything to drink, Charles, you'll have to help yourself. Don't expect me to leap up to wait on you.' Mr Asprey had turned his chair to face him. 'And you could pour me one too,' he added with a faint smile. 'I suspect I'm going to need fortification.'

Confidence rose in Lord Latimer's breast as he handed a glass to his uncle and sat down again, warming his own between his hands. 'Sir, I have a particular favour to ask of you.' He met Ivor Asprey's narrowing eyes with a steadfast gaze. 'I have come from Miss Leigh's house and she is feverish with what appears to be a serious influenza which threatens to become pleuritic.'

His uncle looked down into his glass and after a few seconds murmured, 'I'm sorry to hear that. But what is it to do with me?'

Lord Latimer could not maintain his calm and said in a rush of emotion, 'I'm so afraid, sir, that she will die as Aunt Emma did.' He hung his head, regretting mentioning the painful subject of Mr Asprey's wife, but his anxiety and panic at the thought of losing another young woman too soon drove him on. 'Miss Leigh has to live. She is evidence that goodness is no mere word and happiness more than a dream.'

Ivor Asprey ignored the young man's hyperbole and asked in a cool voice, 'What makes you think she will not live?'

'Because she's being treated by that blackguard, Hapwood.' His words were bitter. 'And that quack's returning this afternoon to bleed her!' There was a catch in his voice.

His uncle gave an involuntary shudder. The grief of watching his wife grow weaker and paler, her suffering increasing daily and he unable to salve it, had been almost more than he could bear and he recoiled from any reminder of his powerlessness to save her. 'I still don't see what you expect me to do.' His tone was harsh. 'Miss Leigh has parents, has she not?'

'That's just my concern. Her father is long dead, as you know, and her mother's in Paris. Miss Leigh is in the care of servants who have not the authority to gainsay her mother's physician.'

Ivor Asprey's austere face showed a dawning consternation. 'Don't tell me, young buck, that you intend taking the invalid to lodge with your mother?' He seemed both aghast and amused by the idea.

'Of course not! You know I cannot even mention her name in Grosvenor Square.'

Ivor Asprey's eyes narrowed. 'I presume you have not yet foresworn the beauteous actress?'

'No! I have not! You know I love her and intend to marry her.' Irritated by the levity he detected in his uncle's voice, Lord Latimer glowered.

'Ah, but does Miss Leigh know that? And has she agreed?' He crossed his long legs, his free foot swinging, as he watched the emotions play out on his nephew's handsome face.

Charles Latimer sprang to his feet in agitation. 'This banter is beside the point. I have to save her life and I can only do that with your help. Can I bring her and her maid here? Until her mother returns.' He extended his hands towards his uncle.

'What! You're madder than a hare, my lord. I'm a public figure whose probity is of concern. The seriousness of the issues I wish to reform cannot be deflected by scandal.' Exasperated, Ivor Asprey also jumped to his feet and the two men stood facing each other.

'Your house is large enough for her not to be seen by anyone. Miss Stafford is a competent and discreet woman who could take charge of her care. And you have the authority to resist the bleeding quack and his nostrums.'

'I can see you've got it all worked out. I commend you, young man, this must be the first time you've taken responsibility for anyone – oh! But I forgot, it's not you but me who will be taking responsibility for Miss Leigh and her survival!'

Lord Latimer grasped his uncle's hands and made as if to hug him. 'Does that mean I can bring her here?' he said, beaming, a weight shifting from him.

'No, it does not. I owe Miss Leigh nothing. I owe you something, 'tis true, but not this, to boldly flout your mother's wishes and to risk everything I value in my life.'

'But would you have her death on your conscience?'

'My conscience is already heavy; nothing could make that burden worse.'

'But you know what it is to care for someone with inflammation of the lungs.'

Ivor Asprey turned away, his face expressing all the sorrow of the last five years. With a sigh that seemed to come from the depths, he capitulated. 'What does Miss Leigh think of this plan of yours? She may not be happy to be parcelled up by you and delivered to my abode.'

Charles Latimer grasped his uncle's arm in relief and gratitude. 'She doesn't know. She did not even recognise one of her friends, Miss Fitzjames.'

'Ah, I've heard about Miss Fitzjames and her predicament.' His uncle then turned businesslike. 'You have to make sure Miss Leigh gives her consent. I do not wish her kidnapped. Most importantly, everything must be done discreetly. I have two important bills on Catholic emancipation and child labour to shepherd through Parliament. Any scandal attached to my name will jeopardise this.'

'I do understand.' He grasped his uncle's hand again. 'My mother won't know anything and I'll ask Martin, Miss Leigh's factotum, to have the family servants swear their silence.'

'I'll speak to Miss Stafford and the housekeeper will make up some rooms for Miss Leigh and her maid – Mary, isn't it? – at the back of the house.'

'Thank you, sir. Thank you. This has relieved me so. You will be the saviour of Miss Leigh.' His lordship's voice was thick with emotion.

'I only hope that will prove the case. If Miss Leigh agrees, bring her tonight when I am at Westminster. But come through the mews and the garden.'

* * *

Angelica was woken from fitful sleep by her maid who asked if she was willing to see Miss Fitzjames. She struggled to sit up. 'Is she downstairs already?' She could not manage the simple question without breaking in the middle to gasp for breath.

'She is, Miss Angelica. But may I tidy you first?' Mary did not wait for a reply but unplaited her mistress's hair and drew a comb carefully through the tangled curls. With the cloth that lay half-submerged in the bowl of herb-strewn water by the bed, she washed Angelica's feverish cheeks and passed it to her to clean her hands. 'Now, let's replace your chemise with a fresh one?' In response to Angelica's faint nod Mary whisked the damp, crumpled one off over her mistress's head and slipped on the fresh cool lawn.

Miss Fitzjames entered the room tentatively. She tiptoed to Angelica's bedside and took her proffered hand. 'Oh Miss Angelica, how are you feeling?'

'I would feel better if I could breathe,' Angelica whispered between gasps.

The fact she was recognised eased Isobel Fitzjames's worst anxiety and she squeezed the pale hand that lay in hers, saying, 'This is why I am here. Lord Latimer is concerned for your health and wants you to be cared for by a doctor other than Mr Hapwood. If you are willing, he's organised for you and Mary to stay at his uncle's house in St James's. Until you are better or your mother has returned.'

A fit of coughing shattered the peace of the room and eventually Angelica lay back pale and exhausted on her pillows. 'I feel incapable of thought, Miss Isobel. What do you and Mary think I should do?' She gazed across at her maid who had withdrawn to fold clothes by the window.

Mary returned to her mistress's side, her face stiff with concern. 'I would prefer your care was not in the hands of Mr Hapwood,' was all she said.

Miss Fitzjames was more expansive. 'I think Lord Latimer has your best interests at heart. He seems very exercised by Mr Hapwood's propensity for bleeding his patients. That was the physician who treated his aunt.'

Angelica's eyes were closed, but she murmured, 'Who subsequently died, depriving her child of her mother.' The effort of speech tired her out.

'Shall I tell Lord Latimer that you agree?' Her friend's voice was gentle. Angelica nodded.

As the light faded, she was wrapped in two cloaks, the hood of one pulled over her head for warmth and disguise. Fur-lined ankle boots were laced and tied and she slipped her hands into an enormous fur muff, its warmth and softness radiating a sense of comfort and safety. Together, Mary and Martin helped her down the stairs where Miss Fitzjames and Lord Latimer waited in the hall. It was the first time he had seen Angelica since coming to her aid at the theatre and he was shocked at how pale and weak she seemed.

He had hired a Hackney coach to travel incognito and all four of them squeezed into the mean interior. Angelica's luggage was heaved onto the back by Martin who was overcome with emotion in his farewell. Poking his head through the window he said, with a catch in his voice, 'Miss Angelica, you have been the sunshine in our lives. I pray to the Blessed Mary and all the Saints you come back to us restored. And soon.' She lifted her head and met his eyes, which were welling with tears that streaked the sooty powder on his lashes, adding a clownish pathos to his face.

'Remember, Martin, you tell no one where Miss Leigh has gone.' Lord Latimer's voice was stern.

The uncomfortable journey did not last long and under cover of darkness Angelica was soon half-carried from the mews through the gardens into the Asprey house via the back door. She gazed at the stone staircase curving upwards just as a tall young woman dressed in a grey checked dress descended, her hand outstretched. 'Miss Leigh, I'm Miss Stafford, Elinor Asprey's governess. I'm pleased to welcome you.' Mr Asprey's nephew was a frequent visitor and she inclined her head in greeting while he stepped forward to introduce Isobel Fitzjames. The Hackney was still waiting and both of them bade farewell. Lord Latimer handed Miss Fitzjames and her maid into the coach to return home while he turned to walk the few paces to St James's and his club.

Angelica was coughing again and barely had the breath to climb the stairs but once Mary had settled her into bed she could close her eyes at last. The house was hushed and seemed to run like clockwork. Illness had made Angelica particularly sensitive to her surroundings. The room was warm and she lay supported by pillows, listening to the unfamiliar sounds around her. She imagined that all the inhabitants of this well-organised household were held in a benign hand, and for the first time in her life she felt herself safe. The soft hooting of an owl outside her window added to the sense of peace. Although her sleep was broken with fits of coughing, she no longer felt afraid and could drift off into a more restorative sleep than she had had for days.

The morning brought Miss Stafford into her room. She was carrying a bowl and a towel which she placed on the table beside Angelica. 'Good morning, Miss Leigh. How was your night?'

Angelica struggled to sit up. Through pauses to gasp for air she said, 'Good morning, Miss Stafford. It's hard to know as I seem to slip in and out of sleep. But I do feel more rested.'

'It's your coughing that I'm here to address.' There was a calm competence about this young woman with her pleasing oval face and kind brown eyes. 'I have been taught by Mr Asprey a technique of gentle drumming on your back which will help bring up the mucus trapped in your lungs.'

Angelica looked surprised and Miss Stafford explained, 'I'll make a bank of your pillows and if you can lie forward so I can reach your back you'll find that it will make you cough. Here's a spittoon for you to spit in.' She placed the bowl next to Angelica's head as she began to rhythmically rap on her back with cupped hands. Angelica felt the vibration spread through her torso; her lungs which had seemed so heavy and solid began to give up some of the phlegm. She coughed and spat and coughed some more.

After about fifteen minutes Miss Stafford stopped, rearranged the pillows and settled Angelica again. She smiled. 'That was quite productive. I'm pleased.' Mary brought in a bowl of coffee for them both and Miss Stafford sat at Angelica's bedside while the patient closed her eyes, exhausted by the procedure.

Catching her breath, Angelica asked, 'Was this technique used on Mrs Asprey?'

Miss Stafford's face was serious. 'Sadly not. A Swiss doctor Mr Asprey contacted told him about it. But it was too late to save his wife's life.' She looked across at Angelica's pale face and put her hand on her arm. 'Don't concern yourself with the past. You will get better. That is why Lord Latimer brought you here.'

'But how did he get Mr Asprey to agree?'

Miss Stafford let out a little laugh. 'That young man can be an irresistible force.'

'It sounds rather like the mountain meeting Mahomet.' Angelica tried to laugh but was overtaken by a gasping cough.

'Indeed, they're as self-willed as each other, but I reckon Mr Asprey has the upper hand.' Her expression softened. 'He's not as harsh as he appears, Miss Leigh. Perhaps he did not want to think you might be treated by Dr Hapwood as he had treated Mrs Asprey.' She noticed Angelica sink back against the pillows and close her eyes. 'I will see you again before night time. Rest now.'

Miss Stafford walked down the stairs to collect her charge for the day's teaching and found Ivor Asprey sitting with his daughter in the morning room.

The child jumped to her feet. 'How is Miss Leigh? Papa's just told me she's ill upstairs. And it's a secret. But I'm so excited she's here. Can I see her?'

Miss Stafford took her hand. 'Not yet, my dear.'

Ivor Asprey looked up from *The Times*. 'Tell me, Miss Stafford, how is the invalid?' His light-hearted tone of voice belied the anxiety in his face.

Miss Stafford sat down and she too looked serious. 'I don't think she's over the worst.'

'That's concerning,' he said almost to himself then remembered his daughter and made an effort to sound more positive. 'I'm sure your care will secure her health. Come to me for anything you may need, Miss Stafford.' He folded his paper and got to his feet, bending to kiss his daughter on the cheek.

Elinor Asprey had been bursting to find out more and as her father departed turned to her governess. 'Miss Stafford, does she look like Ophelia?'

'Well, Miss Leigh is very pale and beautiful but cannot speak without gasping for breath or coughing, so she's not really up to playing Ophelia at present, I fear.'

Clutching Miss Stafford's arm, the young girl looked scared. 'She's not got Mama's disease, has she?'

The young woman shared with Mr Asprey's secretary, Nicholas Digby, an idealistic liberalism and she did not believe in shielding children from the truth. She took her pupil's hand and said simply, 'Your mama had an inflammation in her lungs. A kind of pleuritic fever overtook her which she was too weakened to withstand. Miss Leigh may have the same condition but she is stronger and your Papa and I will do all we can to help her get better.'

'Oh, please. I can't bear it if she dies too.' The girl buried her curly head in her governess's lap.

Miss Stafford lifted Elinor's chin and met her blue eyes with her reassuringly calm gaze. 'We must do all we can and hope for the best. Now to your lessons, my dear. You have the Kings and Queens of England to recite.'

Upstairs, Mary continued to minister to her mistress who seemed to slip in and out of consciousness. It was her job to keep the room warm and to make sure Angelica drank liquid throughout the day: a little broth, some watered milk and honeyed whisky that made her cough but helped her to sleep. Angelica's earlier panic had subsided although she still felt deathly weak and each breath was a labour. There was a peacefulness in the house that her mother's lacked. Angelica could close her eyes and give up the weight of responsibility she had felt since she was a child.

There was a rap on the front door of number four that barely penetrated her drowsing state. Goodall walked at a stately pace from the back of the house and opened it to a figure of dramatic appearance. Before him stood a man in middle age, tall and dressed in the French manner, his coat a little too exaggerated in the shoulder, the pantaloons tighter and embellished with ribbons at the knee. His hair was a striking russet streaked with white, worn longer than current English fashion and tied back in the old-fashioned way in a queue. He removed his tricorne with a flourish.

Goodall's unperturbed face showed no surprise or curiosity. 'Good afternoon, sir. What can I do for you?'

'My name is Prosper Crowe. I am visiting from Paris and would like to have a word with your master.' Mr Crowe spoke with the distinctive ending of 'master' that suggested to Goodall he was more familiar with the French or Irish language than with English.

With cool formality, the butler asked the stranger to wait in the hall while he checked if his master was at home. Prosper Crowe was uncowed by the grandeur or this unenthusiastic reception and gazed at the palatial proportions of the house, noting with interest the grand staircase and the enormous chandelier that hung over the marble chequerboard floor. Hands behind his back, he strolled to gaze at an imposing portrait of a man in eighteenth-century court clothes, his face the image of aristocratic hauteur. '*Vive La Révolution,*' he muttered. '*À bas les aristos,*' and made as if to run his rapier through some unsuspecting member of the *ancien regime,* as Goodall glided back to his side.

'The master is busy but asks your business.'

'Would you tell him I've come about Miss Leigh.'

Goodall's eye gave an almost imperceptible twitch. He knew that all the Asprey servants had been sworn to secrecy about the young actress's presence but returned to the library to pass on in some trepidation this latest piece of news. Ivor Asprey was about to leave for Westminster and was busy collecting his governmental papers together when his butler knocked again and entered. His head rose and as Goodall spoke he looked piercingly at him. 'How does he know she's here?' The chill in his voice made his butler blanch.

'It won't have been from anyone in your employ, sir.'

'What does he look like?'

'A well-dressed pirate, sir.' Goodall immediately regretted speaking out of turn and apologised.

His employer raised his eyebrows. 'Very well, show him in.'

Prosper Crowe's self-confident swagger was checked for a moment when he faced Ivor Asprey. Perhaps here was a man who saw beneath the surface of things? He approached with his hand outstretched. 'Prosper Crowe, sir, just in from Paris.'

'How d'ye do? Ivor Asprey.' Mr Asprey gave a curt incline of his head as they shook hands.

'Oh, I know who you are,' Mr Crowe said with confidence. 'I approve of what you are trying to do for Catholic emancipation.' A little of his swagger had returned with his attempt at regaining the upper hand in this discourse.

'Well, you're the master of me, sir, for I have no idea who you are and what I can do for you.' Ivor Asprey spoke with asperity.

'My apologies. I am Angelica Leigh's father and I would like to see her.'

Ivor was completely dumbfounded by this news but maintained his impassive expression. Not only had he no idea how the whereabouts of Miss Leigh had been discovered but, more importantly, he had been told by his nephew that her father was a naval hero who had died sixteen years ago in Aboukir Bay. 'Have you any proof of this?'

The piratical man opposite him laughed. 'Look at my hair!' With a flamboyant gesture he brandished his queue where his hair was less streaked with white. It was indeed an unusually rich colour. 'Isn't Miss Leigh known for her beauty? And her Celtic colouring?'

Ivor Asprey was not as easily convinced. 'I think it is Miss Leigh's theatrical talent that marks her pre-eminence.'

'Come now, sir, we are both men of the world,' Prosper Crowe said with a conspiratorial smile. 'We both know it is her beauty. The world is full of fine actresses, on the stage and off, but only those who are beautiful gain fame and notoriety.'

Mr Asprey felt himself bridle. He had no desire to be philosophically associated with this eccentric gentleman who appeared to consider himself the equal of anyone. 'Forgive me, Mr Crowe, but I am late for a meeting in Westminster. Laws you may approve of nevertheless need to be debated.' He picked up his case with his papers.

The visitor put out his hand. 'Halt a while, sir. You have yet to tell me if my daughter is under this roof.'

'You have yet to prove to me who you say you are and until then I have no inkling as to who your daughter might be.' Ivor Asprey bowed and left the room. 'Goodall, please show Mr Crowe out,' he said peremptorily as he strode out of the front door and down the steps into the Square to head south. He would be late to the House of Commons. Walking fast, he was perturbed, distracted from the important issues that awaited him. Just a couple of weeks ago Miss Angelica Leigh was unknown to him, but now she had come to dominate his thoughts. She lay upstairs in his house suffering the same sort of alarming respiratory disease that had carried off his beloved Emma.

Responsibility for preserving the young actress's life had been thrust upon him, and he had become somehow complicit in keeping this disreputable piece of information from his sister's hearing. Ivor did not care to fall out with her but there was no safe way to impart to the Duchess the news that the young woman she abhorred as a future daughter-in-law was being nursed under his roof. Not least was his concern that his work as a radical lawmaker depended on his reputation remaining unimpeached. His equanimity had been further unsettled by this eccentric man bursting into his well-ordered life to claim he was Miss Leigh's father. What unforeseen consequences would come from this: no longer the dead hero but a rogue by the looks of him, and very much alive?

Ivor Asprey's pace did not slacken as he crossed St James's Park. The more he thought of the change in his peaceful regime at home the more uneasy he became. Since his fateful meeting with Angelica Leigh he felt his life slipping from his control. This unhappy reverie was broken by a familiar voice, 'Mr Asprey, sir!' He turned to see the smiling face of his secretary.

'Oh, Mr Digby, I'm indeed pleased to see you. When did you arrive?' He had sent the young man to the cotton mills of Manchester to gather individual experiences of children's lives there, to add force to his arguments in the House of Commons debate that evening.

So involved were Mr Asprey and his secretary in their conversation that they did not hear the approach of Lord Rackham who unexpectedly appeared walking beside them. 'I can see your hearts upon your sleeves, gentlemen, for daws like me to peck at,' he said with barely concealed disdain. 'I shall vote against you, you know.'

Ivor turned to look at him and felt again an inward recoil that surprised him after all this time. 'I would expect nothing less.'

He saluted his secretary who continued to walk on while Lord Rackham put a hand on Asprey's arm to hold him back.

'Sir, beware of being a traitor to your class. There are those who are born to servitude and those to rule. It's dangerous to tamper with God's design in the matter.'

'*When Adam delved and Eve span, who was then the Gentleman*? I think you'll find, my lord, that such social hierarchies were not God's intent.'

Lord Rackham gave a bitter laugh. 'Well, if you put yourselves on a par with the Peasants' Revolt then you truly are a traitor to your class.'

They walked on a few more paces in silence. As they approached the entrance to the Chapel of St Stephen's, Lord Rackham paused. 'I forgot. Do you happen to know where Miss Leigh may be?'

Ivor Asprey kept on walking and said in a cold voice, 'Is her whereabouts of concern to you?'

'I do have some interests there, 'tis true, but I'm aware your nephew has a dunderheaded scheme to marry her and wondered if they'd absconded together?'

Ivor Asprey stopped dead. 'My nephew's business is his own.' His contempt was ice cold.

'That may well be, but perhaps it's time to rein in your family, sir, exert some authority. We are both men of the world and we know that an actress is not a suitable wife for a gentleman. If that gentleman is heir to a dukedom, this is indubitably the case.'

A month ago, he would have agreed with this sentiment; after all, it was his sister's obstinate belief too, but something about Lord Rackham's sneering manner and his own growing awareness of the singular character of Angelica Leigh made Ivor Asprey affronted on her behalf. With barely controlled animosity he said, 'I suppose, in your scheme of things, an actress is only fit to become a gentleman's mistress?'

'Exactly, my dear sir. Why would your nephew throw himself away on a woman he could set up in a house in Mayfair? It's the established order of things that matters, wouldn't you say?' His voice drawled with cynical ennui.

Ivor Asprey's fists clenched. Why did this man still provoke such violent feelings in him, he wondered, as he restrained himself from clouting that scornful smile on his lordship's face? Instead he bade him farewell with a brief bow as he turned towards his office.

* * *

It was close to midnight, all the arguments had been paraded in the Commons, at times emotional anecdotes meeting mulish resistance, but with a demand for more evidence the vote was postponed to the following week. The Members of Parliament were filing out of the chamber, discussing whether to head home or to St James's and their clubs. Mr Asprey was tired and considering relaxing at Brooks's for an hour or so when he saw Nicholas Digby shouldering his way through the surging crowd. 'Sir!' he called out and waved an urgent hand.

As he came closer, Ivor noticed how his secretary's usually genial face was contorted with anxiety. 'What is it, Nicholas?'

'You're needed at home. Miss Stafford is concerned about Miss Leigh. She seems to be failing fast.'

Ivor Asprey collected his coat and hat from his office and the two men walked quickly from the building. 'I have a Hackney waiting, sir.'

'Have you called the doctor?'

'He's already been. Says there's little to be done. He left some oil of poppy but to be used sparingly.'

The coach drew up outside the Asprey house and as they entered they found Miss Stafford coming down the stairs, her face pale, stray strands of hair loosened from her bun. 'Oh, thank goodness you've come.'

Distracted by anxiety, she grasped Nicholas Digby's hand with unexpected emotion.

Fear made Ivor Asprey throw the usual conventions to the wind as he sprinted up the stairs. Knocking quietly on Angelica's door he was let in by an ashen-faced Mary who wordlessly led him to the bed. Angelica lay very still and white, her eyes closed, her breath quick and shallow and with an alarming rattling sound coming from her chest. Horrified, Ivor felt his heart constrict. For a moment he was back at his wife's bedside, gazing on her almost lifeless form.

Determined not to be so helpless this time, he turned to Mary. 'The room needs to be warmer, bank up the fire. And then ask Cook for two bowls of boiling water. We need steam.'

Miss Stafford had entered the room behind him. 'I didn't know whether to continue with the pummelling of her back. She seems so frail.'

'Yes, it's essential. Her lungs are slowly drowning in mucus. We have to get her coughing, I'm afraid, brutal as that may seem.' He leant over Angelica and softly called her name, taking her hand. She did not respond. He turned to Miss Stafford. 'Please help me roll her onto her left side.'

In the desperation of the hour, Ivor Asprey ignored the impropriety of handling the young woman's body so intimately, and quickly turned her, pulling her right leg up and bending it at the knee to stabilise her on the bed. Miss Stafford worked beside him, brushing Angelica's hair from her face and pulling her chemise down over her hips to protect her modesty.

Ivor's face was set with anxiety. 'I need to be able to drum on her back to get to the right lung first. Get the spittoon.'

Angelica's eyes had fluttered open with alarm. She put a hand out to grasp his. 'Don't worry, Miss Leigh, this is just to help your breathing. Trust me.' She coughed and Miss Stafford wiped her mouth. She groaned and closed her eyes as Ivor knelt on the bed in front of her and leaned over to try the Swiss doctor's suggestion about how to release mucus in inflamed lungs. He cupped his hands and started to pummel her thin back. He was aware how fine-boned she was and was careful to moderate his action. He paused in the drumming when she started to cough.

'Spit it out into this, Miss Leigh,' Miss Stafford said, holding out the spittoon and wiping her mouth again with a handkerchief.

Mary had brought in the bowls of boiled water and set them steaming on the table. The fire was blazing and the room very warm. Ivor Asprey paused to strip off his coat and roll up his shirt sleeves. While he and Sarah Stafford worked to relieve the congestion in their patient's lungs, Angelica lay in a semi-foetal position, her body reverberating with the rhythmic percussion on her back. The coughing seemed more productive and Miss Stafford's concerned face swam in and out of view as she proffered the spittoon and wiped her lips each time. Mr Asprey continued to gently pummel her ribs. He had loosened his cravat and his fine linen shirt was damp with sweat. Only occasionally in the theatre had Angelica ever been this close to a stranger.

Illness had brought all kinds of indignities, but also heightened her senses. The doctor who smelt of stale camphor had laid his ear to her chest and made her recoil. Now it was Mr Asprey kneeling beside her, smelling of a sweet masculine warmth, leaning over her hip as he drummed on her back. His shirt was becoming untucked; it was so intimate a scene and with the bizarre clarity of a dream, Angelica thought if she were to put out a hand she could touch his breeches stretched tight over the muscle of his thigh and draw his vitality through her fingertips. In her physically depleted state he embodied strength, competence, safety and she knew that, despite how scandalous such intimacy would seem to the world, for her it was this house and this care that meant she could cling to life, and live. Her ribs were beginning to feel bruised by the insistent thrumming, her lungs hurt as she coughed, exhaustion overwhelmed her and she closed her eyes.

Angelica was so weak she could do nothing but struggle for breath but there was solace in having little energy for anything else. Others had taken responsibility for her and for everything around her. She had regressed to a state where only the most basic elements of life needed her attention. She was aware of the comforting sound of the hooting owl in the tree beyond her window and in a half-dream waited for the answering call from the other side of the mews.

By the time Ivor Asprey and Miss Stafford had finished their ministrations, Angelica longed to sleep for a week. They rolled her gently onto her back, propped up on pillows. Mary was asked to replenish the steaming bowls of water through the night and keep the room warm with a well-fed fire. 'Let me know if there's any change for the worse, whatever the time.' Ivor addressed both Mary and Miss Stafford. They stood looking down on the fragile figure in the bed. Angelica's beauty had always been striking for her vitality and brilliance of colouring but now, so pale and enervated, she seemed more like a Renaissance painting of a saint and this sense of death so close chilled them all. Ivor Asprey picked up his coat and turned on his heel to disappear down the stairs to the library, his face white with fatigue and foreboding.

* * *

Angelica slept better than she had in days. Her breath was calmer and less rasping. Fevered dreams had receded and let her rest. She awoke to find the small face of Elinor Asprey leaning over her. As she opened her eyes the young girl sprang back with an apology. 'Oh Miss Leigh, forgive me. But I was so worried about you. You are better, aren't you?'

Angelica struggled to sit up. She was touched by the child's sweet concern. 'I think I may be a bit better. My breathing is easier.' She took a gasping breath. 'Your papa and Miss Stafford were treating me last night with the percussive method. It might have worked.' Such a long series of words exhausted her and she lay back.

'Am I tiring you?' Elinor asked.

'No. Don't go. It's good to have some company.' She paused again. 'Just talk to me. I may not be able to say much in reply.'

The girl seemed to be pleased to have some company herself. She settled into the window seat. 'I shouldn't be here. Miss Stafford and Papa think I'm reading in the nursery. I'm meant to be translating *Aesop's Fables* from Latin. It's hard. I was showing Papa how good I was last week and translated *The Fox and the Crow*.'

Angelica smiled and nodded, her eyes still closed as Elinor Asprey continued, 'It means those who love to be flattered will eventually be punished when it's too late to repent. My papa laughed and said he hoped I wasn't thinking of him and I said no. Mr Digby had said he was proof against all flattery.'

'That's good to know,' Angelica murmured quietly, then started another fit of coughing. Elinor sprang forward and grabbed the linen handkerchief on the table beside the bed to offer to her. The girl was gazing at her earnestly. When Angelica was settled again she said shyly, 'Miss Leigh, do you think that there are some people who know what is best for other people?'

'Very seldom do others know what is best for us.'

'Well, I think I know that Lady Linus is not good for my papa.'

The words were so emphatic, Angelica opened her eyes to meet the angry blue ones, pricked with tears. She put out a hand to take the girl's in hers. 'I'm sure your papa knows what is good for him, and for you.'

'No he doesn't. He works so hard, he doesn't have time to think. And my Aunt Arlington keeps on telling him I need a mother. Well, I don't!' She stamped her foot in exasperation. 'I have Papa and Miss Stafford. I don't want Lady Snooty Fox poking her nose into our life.'

'He may be lonely and may find Lady Linus congenial company,' Angelica said, pausing for breath as she spoke. 'He may even care for her.' Her voice died away.

'I know he doesn't. He loved Mama who was sweet and warm. How can he love someone so cold?' Elinor's expression was anguished. She noticed Angelica's pale face and was suddenly apologetic. 'Oh, Miss Leigh, you're not well enough to hear my complaints. I'm sorry. I should go.'

Angelica squeezed her hand. 'It will all work out, I'm sure.'

'But I do know what's good for people, Miss Leigh.' Her blue eyes, so like her father's, met Angelica's with defiance. 'I think Miss Stafford should marry Mr Digby. She loves him, you know.' She dropped her head and then muttered, 'And I really hope you marry my cousin, Charlie, and then you'll be a duchess when my horrid Aunt Arlington dies.'

'Miss Elinor! You shouldn't speak so of your aunt, you know.'

'I don't see why not. She's so interfering and she doesn't care for me, so why should I care for her? Why does someone good like Mama die when the horridest people still live?' Her mulish expression changed to one of mischief. 'I'd so like it if you were part of my family. Please will you marry Lord Latimer?'

Angelica was overwhelmed with fatigue but did not want to dismiss the child and her fears. 'Lord Latimer hasn't asked me to marry him.' She took a breath. 'I think it may be just a passing fancy.'

'You see, Miss Leigh, you think you know better than he does!' The girl giggled with a sense of triumph.

Angelica managed a small smile. 'Perhaps we suffer from the same pretensions?' She longed for rest and suggested Elinor could run an errand. 'Before you go back to your books, could you ask Mary if she can bring me some broth?' She sank back on her pillows. 'I'm feeling quite hungry.'

'Of course.' Elinor Asprey turned at the door. 'I know Lord Latimer is coming to see how you are this morning.' She left giving Angelica a cheeky smile over her shoulder.

6

THE PRODIGAL'S GIFTS

After the alarums of the night, Angelica recovered more quickly than the doctor expected. Carefully nursed by Mary and Miss Stafford, she was soon recuperating downstairs. She spent the mornings in bed and the afternoons reading in Mr Asprey's library, a time when he was at the House of Commons and so would not be put out by her presence. After a few days of this regimen she was strong enough to receive Lord Latimer and Isobel Fitzjames. They had arrived at the appointed hour of three and were shown by Goodall into the small sitting room at the front of the house. Here a fire burned, keeping the room unnaturally warm. Still weak and pale, Angelica sat on the sofa looking ethereal in a sprigged lilac gown with a primrose yellow spencer which made her red-gold hair all the more striking.

Charles Latimer entered the room in a rush, his face flushed with emotion. Taking her hand, he pressed it fervently. 'Oh, Miss Leigh, thank God! I have been out of my mind with worry about you.' He brought her hand to his lips before sitting beside her on the sofa. 'Been haunted by Mrs Asprey's fate and determined it would not be yours.'

Isobel Asprey settled on Angelica's other side, slipping her arm through hers. 'Lord Latimer and I came each day to enquire about your health. Mr Brunner, your mother's man, has also been here on the same mission. This house was so hushed it was alarming. What a mercy to see you so recovered.' Her delicate face, usually veiled with sorrow as befitted a gothic heroine, was bright and no longer seemed burdened with care.

Lord Latimer too, seemed light-hearted and relieved. 'I was afraid if you had stayed under the authority of your mother's physician I might never see you again.'

Angelica turned to them and said, 'I have to thank you for my renewed health. Your persuasive powers, Lord Latimer, brought me here and your uncle and Miss Stafford have practised this new treatment with great effect. My back must be bruised but my lungs are much better. I can both breathe and talk!'

'I think we need to celebrate.' Lord Latimer had sprung up and was pacing the floor. 'I have an exciting suggestion to put to you. Will you be properly restored in three weeks' time?' His hazel eyes sparkled with mischief.

'I should hope so. I'm already learning my lines for the next play.' Angelica lifted the manuscript of *The Child of Nature* from the floor, her part underlined in wavy pen.

His voice dropped conspiratorially. 'Mama has organised a ball to celebrate my coming of age. She's asked to use Uncle Ivor's house on the river at Hampton as it's closer to London than ours.'

Angelica looked at him askance. 'There's no possibility you can escort me to that, Lord Latimer.'

'Aha! But there is. I've told Mama I want a masquerade ball. So no one will know it's you. Miss Fitzjames has already decided to go as Columbine so I thought I could be Harlequin.'

'And I suppose you think I should be Pierrot?' Angelica laughed. 'It's far too dangerous, my lord! Also I would be impersonating a male character in trousers. If I was found out, scandal would be heaped upon scandal.'

'No, no. I thought you could be the Faery Queen. If you powder your hair the colour would not give you away. And of course you'll be wearing a mask. No one would know it was you. Please come, Miss Leigh. There's no joy unless you're there.'

Angelica leant back on the sofa, suddenly overtaken with fatigue. 'As I feel at the moment, my heart quails. But when the time comes I may well be strong enough. But how will you explain this Faery Queen to your eagle-eyed mama?'

'Don't worry, I'll work out something clever and water tight. Don't forget she's only ever seen you on stage. She won't suspect a thing.'

Isobel Asprey stood up too. 'You look in need of rest, Miss Angelica.'

Lord Latimer grasped Miss Fitzjames by the arm. 'Before we go, don't forget your remarkable good news!' Angelica looked up with a question in her eyes.

Her friend could not stop herself beaming. 'It's the most extraordinary turn of fortune. Some well-wisher sent me the deeds for the Fitzjames House in Berkeley Square. This was part of the family fortune lost by my father to Lord Fulsham.'

This piece of news startled Angelica. 'That is wonderful. How extraordinary.' She stood up to take both Miss Fitzjames's hands in hers. 'Could Lord Fulsham have taken pity on your plight?' Her mind was in turmoil with questions and fragments of theories.

'Oh no. It wasn't him. He was fretting and fuming when he arrived to tell Mrs Fitzjames. He lost at Hazard it seems, something so rare, he was quite discomposed. But no one knows who his challenger was, as they were gaming in a private club where everyone is sworn to discretion. The Honour of Gentlemen.'

Lord Latimer interrupted, 'The remarkable thing: the deeds are made out in Miss Fitzjames's name, so her stepmother cannot dispossess her. And most of her father's bonds were part of the bet, so she will have income too. She will be independent.'

'Oh, such good news.' Angelica clasped her friend in a hug. 'Does this now bestow some freedom on you? To marry if and where you will, and to live as you choose?'

Isobel Fitzjames looked shy and glanced at Lord Latimer. 'I only heard this news yesterday and I haven't thought of the full meaning of the change in my prospects. I'm freed from the imperative to marry Lord Fulsham to restore the family fortunes, 'tis true.'

Angelica accompanied them to the hall and having bade them farewell returned to the sofa. She felt so deathly tired she lay full length and fell asleep.

* * *

The young visitors had been gone for barely an hour when Goodall was summoned once more by a peremptory rap on the front door. The man he considered an Irish pirate stood there, with all the swagger of Punch. Goodall did not like him any the better on second acquaintance. 'Could you let Miss Leigh know I'm here to see her?' Without being expressly invited into the hall, Prosper Crowe sauntered in and put his hat and elaborate Frenchified coat into Goodall's reluctant hands.

'The master's not here,' he said icily.

'I know that, my man! He's at Parliament doing what his constituents elected him to do. And I hope he gets round to Catholic emancipation too!'

'I wouldn't know 'bout any of that, sir.' Goodall's manner was lofty. As a proud butler, he did not appreciate being called 'my man' by someone as apparently disreputable as this visitor.

'Never mind. I would like to see Miss Leigh, I presume she is here?' The butler knew that the last time this person called, his master had sent him off after only a few minutes' curt conversation and so went in search of Miss Stafford to ask her what he should do.

Miss Stafford approached from the back of the house and inclined her head with courtesy. 'Good afternoon, Mr Crowe. May I help you?' She drew him to the far reaches of the hallway where their conversation was less likely to be overheard.

'Yes, indeed I hope you can.' Prosper Crowe's hybrid of a French-Irish accent became more marked as he set out to charm this good-looking young woman. He bowed elaborately low and met her surprised gaze with a twinkle. His looks were familiar; the russet hair and lively green eyes reminded Miss Stafford of Angelica's striking looks. He continued in his engaging way, 'Here from Paris for a few days. I'm Angelica Leigh's father. Mr Asprey asked me to return with proof, and here it is!' He flourished a letter from his coat pocket. 'Her mother wrote to me about our daughter when I was in France. And the girl was about sixteen.'

Miss Stafford did not know that Lord Latimer had confided to his uncle that Angelica's father was a naval hero killed in a sea battle some fifteen years before; she thought it unremarkable that this exotic stranger would want to see his daughter. 'She's still recuperating. I shall see if she's well enough. Please wait here, Mr Crowe?'

She entered the small sitting room just as Angelica was waking. Struggling to sit up, Angelica put out her hands. 'Miss Stafford, I'm sorry I fell asleep. It's so warm by the fire.'

'Rest is good for you, Miss Leigh.' She straightened the cushions on the sofa. 'You have a special visitor. Are you feeling able to receive him?'

Despite her weakness, Angelica felt a jolt of excitement. 'Special? Who could it be?'

'Your father, just over from Paris and keen to see you!' Miss Stafford's voice betrayed some of her own excitement. She was quite unprepared for the shriek and Angelica's hand grasping hers.

'No! You must be mistaken. No, no. no.' She put her face in her hands as her shoulders shook.

Miss Stafford sat down beside her, concern and incomprehension etched on her face. 'What is it, Miss Leigh? I can always send him away.'

'It's just my father is dead. He was killed at sea when I was five years old.'

'Could you be mistaken, my dear?' Miss Stafford's voice was quiet as she put her arm round Angelica's thin shoulders.

'Why do you ask? Does he look like me?'

'He does. And he has a letter from Mrs Leigh referring to you, written only five years ago.'

'What does this mean?' Angelica's tear-stained face was anguished. 'Is he an imposter? And if so, why?' It was all too much for her to process. It seemed so unexpected, so unlikely. But then the alternative was equally unsettling. 'I can't bear to think my mother and father have been lying to me all these years.'

'I can always ask him to come back tomorrow. But if you want to see him and ask for yourself, I will stay to chaperone you.'

Angelica nodded. Her heart was beating fast, and questions and emotions filled her mind in a confused mix of shock, anger, disbelief and hope. As Prosper Crowe entered the room, she knew immediately he was related to her, but how? He looked delighted to see her and completely lacking in embarrassment or remorse. In his hand was a letter, the handwriting distinctively her mother's, which confirmed an alternative story to the one of her tragic, fatherless childhood.

Confusion and dismay at the duplicity of both her parents overcame Angelica and she flew at him, powered by a rush of anger. 'How could you? After all these years? How could you have let me believe I had no father?' He caught her in his arms as she beat against his chest. 'You left Mama and me to live in penury. She prostituted her honour so we could eat. I was hungry and afraid most nights. How could you?' He tightened his hug so her hands flailed, powerless. She sobbed, gasping for breath.

Prosper Crowe grasped both her arms and held her away from him, a warm smile on his face, as if the words Angelica had thrown at him had barely penetrated his self-regard and unruffled good humour. 'Oh, me darlin' angel child! Let me look at ye! What a beauty, so like me own sainted mammy, God rest her soul.'

'It is shameful to forsake your family!' She glared at him. But the emotion drained her strength and she staggered, her knees buckling. In an instant, Miss Stafford was by her side and Prosper Crowe put his arm around her back to hold her upright.

'Come and sit down, me darlin'. It don't do, y'know, to get in such a state.' He and Miss Stafford settled Angelica back on the sofa and Mr Crowe poured a glass of brandy from the decanter on the sideboard and pressed it into her hand. 'I do owe ye an explanation, I know.' He poured a glass for himself and offered one to Miss Stafford who demurred.

Angelica put her head back and closed her eyes. Barely able to speak, she asked in a small voice, 'Why did you and Mama think it a good idea to let me think I had no father?'

'Because I had fled into exile. You see, I faced prison, even death.'

'But you still owed me the truth that you were alive.' At first it was the deception that had troubled her most but into her spinning thoughts fear intruded. 'What had you done? What could carry the death sentence?' Physically exhausted though she was, Angelica's mind was reeling with shock and dismay.

For the first time, Mr Crowe's optimistic manner was partly deflated. 'I was in serious debt,' he muttered, not meeting her eye. But then, taking a large gulp of brandy, his liveliness returned. 'From nothing, I then created a gaming club in Paris for gentlemen, the Dionysius in Rue Richelieu. Just next door to the famous gunsmiths, Jean le Page, which proved useful with so many customers wanting to blow their brains out. Or somebody else's.' He let out a snort of laughter. 'Not called Hazard for nothing, ye know.' His pride in what he had achieved was evident.

'But why not share some of your good fortune with your family? It would have made all the difference.'

'In order to escape notice by the English authorities I'd to live as if dead to everyone I had ever known.'

'If it's so dangerous for you to be here, why risk everything now?'

'My darlin' daughter was such a success as Ophelia, her fame reached Paris and I needed to see her, regardless of the danger.'

If Angelica had the energy she would have railed against him for choosing to see her only once she was famous and therefore more interesting to him, but she was too exhausted. It struck her uneasy mind that she had not been formally introduced and did not even know her father's name. Was he a Leigh too? 'Pray, what is your name, sir?'

'Prosper Crowe.'

She was taken aback. It sounded so unlikely. 'No, your real name.' Angelica had to understand who her father really was. After all the deception, she needed that piece of information at least.

'I cannot tell ye that. Still a warrant for my arrest.'

'But how can I know you if you're still masquerading as someone else?' A sob escaped Angelica. She accepted this swashbuckling stranger was her father but feared how untrustworthy, how elusive he remained, somehow slipping through her fingers still.

'I'll be able to see ye again before I return to France. I want to give your mama something I owe you both, so will wait to see her next week when she returns.'

'But where are you staying, if I need to contact you?'

'I have befriended Mr Brunner. His maternal family is from the same village in Ireland as mine and he suggested a fellow Irishman who runs the Red Cockerel in Grafton Street. It takes me back to the old days.'

'I don't think you should go to Berkeley Square. It's not my mother's house, it's Mr Breville's. And he's a decent hardworking gentleman who shouldn't be compromised.' Angelica felt suddenly protective of the man who had behaved more like a father to her than her own ever could.

Prosper Crowe seemed to sense something of this disparity in parental responsibility and with a dramatic gesture he pulled from his pocket a blue velvet pouch. He tossed this into Angelica's lap. 'I want you to have this.'

She looked up at him as she slipped her hand into the bag. Her fingers met cold, hard, facetted stone. Slowly she drew out a necklace of sparkling clear stones, set as a rivière in silver and gold. It coiled in her hands as if alive and she gasped at its coruscating beauty.

'It's your grandmother's necklace,' her father said with dramatic emphasis. 'Her most precious possession.' For a fleeting moment, Angelica wondered if her histrionic talents had come directly from him, and the thought was not entirely comfortable. 'Look at the clasp,' he said.

She gazed at a clasp set in blue stones with the initials ABC picked out in green; were they emeralds, she wondered?

'Those are her initials, Angelica Boyle Crowe,' he said with some satisfaction.

She gasped. It touched her deeply to think she had been named after this grandmother. Looking down at the necklace sparkling in her lap, her scepticism about him softened. 'I've never had a sense of family, or in fact any real jewellery, only glass and coral beads. Is it really for me?'

'For whom else should it be but my beautiful daughter?' He picked up her hand with the necklace entwined in her fingers and flashing her the most beguiling smile, kissed her palm.

His charm and Angelica's delight in the gift did not quell her sense of outraged unease. 'I still don't understand what has brought you back at this time?' she asked him with a frown.

'Because I thought it was about time my daughter knew who her father was. I was successful at last and I would not embarrass her. She could be proud of me, as I am of her.'

'But why didn't you just write and warn me first that my dead hero of a father was in fact alive, and manifestly less heroic?'

He frowned. It disconcerted him when his charm did not sweep all reservations before him. He recognised he was a rogue but considered everyone else to be so too, just more the hypocrite that hid their villainy from plain sight. Very soon his liveliness had returned. 'I also wanted to deliver to your mother some of the currency I owe you both for all these years of absence. In gold coins. I couldn't entrust a courier with that.'

Miss Stafford had been discreetly reading a book in the window seat but she rose to her feet and walked over. 'I apologise, Mr Crowe, but I'm responsible for Miss Leigh's recuperation and I fear she is tiring. It's been a busy day with visitors. Perhaps you could continue this conversation tomorrow?'

Angelica put out a hand to touch hers. 'Thank you. I'm tired, 'tis true.'

Prosper Crowe bowed. 'Indeed. I shall be honoured to come tomorrow.' He cocked a questioning eyebrow at Angelica, then smiled. 'A strong Irish girl like me daughter needs fresh air. Might I accompany ye for a short promenade in St James's Park at noon?'

Angelica nodded, feeling somehow bamboozled by the force of his personality. As the front door closed behind him, Elinor Asprey came skipping down the stairs, her face bright with excitement. Hair flying, she cannoned into Miss Stafford who was leaving the small sitting room where Angelica lay back on the sofa. 'Now where are you going, Elinor?' Miss Stafford asked as she caught her by the arm.

'I wanted to see Miss Leigh. Might I?'

'Not now, my dear. She's fatigued by too many visitors and I've left her to rest.'

'Oh, please, Miss Stafford. I've finished all my work. Even my arithmetic. I've got something important to ask her.'

A wan voice came from the room. 'I'm very happy to see Miss Asprey for a short while. Do let her in.' Angelica had slipped the necklace back into its velvet pouch, unwilling to advertise its presence.

Miss Stafford stood aside for her charge. 'Just for five minutes.'

Elinor approached the invalid with care, her eyes wide. Angelica patted the sofa beside her; she liked this girl's independence and bright curiosity, which Miss Stafford's advanced ideas as a teacher seemed to foster. 'Miss Leigh, is your father a pirate?'

Despite her tiredness, Angelica chuckled. 'No! What makes you think that?'

'Well, he looks just like one, with his hair and his tricorne hat. And I heard Goodall describe him to my father as a pirate.'

'No. He runs a gaming club in Paris.'

'Oh, how exciting! I wish I had such a papa.'

Emotion rose in Angelica's breast and she drew herself up, turning to face the young girl. 'Miss Elinor, your papa cares for you and is always there to be relied upon. My father has been absent all my life, even when my mother and I were close to starving. He allowed me to think he was dead. That is not exciting, I assure you.'

Elinor hung her head. 'I know. And I am sorry. I just wish my papa didn't work so hard. I wish I could do more things with him.'

'It's hard for you.' Angelica put an arm round the girl's shoulders. 'But at least your father is intent on making people's lives better. Mine, I'm afraid, just preys on their weaknesses.'

Elinor looked into Angelica's face with an earnest expression in her blue eyes. 'How can that be, Miss Leigh?'

'Because he panders to the worst appetites of gluttony, drunkenness and greed. Gambling destroys so many lives.'

'But Papa gambles at Hazard.'

'I think he used to but has given it up. Most men of means can be reckless when they're young.'

'Like cousin Charlie?'

'Indeed, but your cousin seems to think that your papa has become very sober and upstanding since he became a Member of Parliament and responsible for your upbringing. So you do not need to worry about that.'

Angelica smiled as the girl lifted her face to kiss her on the cheek. 'Oh, Miss Leigh. I so like you being in our house. May I come and read with you in the library tomorrow?'

'If your school work is done, of course. But I'll soon be returning to my mother's home. I won't be here much longer now I am well.'

Elinor's expressive face displayed every emotion. Angelica noticed a puzzlement in her eyes as she said, 'Will you be going to Charlie's masquerade party at Papa's house?'

'It's the Duchess of Arlington's ball for her son and she wouldn't choose to have me attend.'

'She's told me I can't come as I'm too young. But that can't be her excuse for you?' she said mischievously. 'Lord Latimer cares for you and has told me once he's attained his majority he intends to marry you.'

Angelica frowned. 'He really ought not to talk so carelessly.'

'But it would bring happiness. You'd be part of my family.'

'Oh my dear, I would very much like to be part of your family. But I don't think it's realistic, you know?' She had taken the child's hand.

'Why is Aunt Edwina set against you, Miss Leigh?'

'It's complicated. Actresses like me aren't expected to marry into your world.'

The girl's brow wrinkled. 'So Lady Linus is the sort of woman to marry men like my father and cousin Charlie?'

'That's the way it is,' Angelica said with a wry smile. She sighed. 'I think I'll really have to go back to bed, Miss Elinor.'

'Of course. But I don't understand the world. You're much kinder, wiser and more beautiful than anybody I've seen.' The force of her feeling had made the young girl spring to her feet, just as Miss Stafford re-entered the room. Together they helped Angelica up from the sofa.

Miss Stafford handed the velvet jewellery pouch to Angelica. 'Don't forget this, Miss Leigh.'

Quick-eyed, Elinor had noticed the transaction. 'What's in that?'

Angelica smiled. 'Perhaps I'll show you some day.' When she was alone in her room she withdrew the necklace from the bag and fixed the clasp round her neck. Gazing at her reflection in the looking-glass, she gasped at its beauty. The necklace seemed to gather every scintilla in the room and intensify it into a flashing, flowing river of light that added luminosity to her own face. She put her hands to her throat and cradled the stones. 'My grandmother's most treasured possession and I will treasure it.' Could they be diamonds, she wondered, but the value was of little consequence; it was the connection with family that touched her spirit. From feeling alone in the world with only her mother to call her own, she now knew she had a family, flawed and unknown, but family none the less.

* * *

The morning dawned bright and fresh with the kind of pellucid light that comes after a night of rain. After being so ill, Angelica's first walk in the fresh air was something to look forward to. She dressed in her favourite sky-blue twill gown with the long sleeves that kept her warm, and threw her fur-edged tippet over her shoulders. Mary was surprised to see her up but deftly arranged her abundant hair into a loose bun. Then on a whim, she added a yellow silk camellia that gave her mistress an exotic appearance for the usual morning pursuits.

Angelica descended the stairs and made her way for the first time to the breakfast room. She entered without a sound and was surprised to see Ivor Asprey still there; he usually breakfasted early before riding his hunter in the Park. She stood uncertainly at the threshold watching him, absorbed in a paper he held in one hand. There was a bowl of steaming coffee by his elbow as his long fingers turned a page of what looked like a handwritten report. His dark head was bowed as he read. She noticed how fine the line was between his cheekbones and his aquiline nose, and his hair, still slightly damp from his morning ablutions and curling over his high white collar, seemed darker than she remembered. She could only have stood there for a half minute or so, seeing him as if for the first time, when he looked up, surprised. His deep eyes softened as he smiled, languidly uncrossed his legs and rose to his feet.

'My dear Miss Leigh, what a pleasure to see you up and looking so much better than when I last saw you.'

Angelica blushed at being reminded of the dire state from which his speedy intervention had saved her. But she had put from her mind the thought of how improper it had been for him to see her in such disarray. 'I haven't been able to thank you, Mr Asprey, for saving my life.'

'Come and sit down. I don't think you were on the brink of quite such a crisis but you were not at all well, 'tis true. I am just pleased I could do something to help you, which I could not do for my wife.'

Angelica sat down while he poured her some coffee and offered her a plate of sweet pastries. He sat beside her and seemed to be seeing her for the first time too. Her large green eyes had a clear sparkling candour as they met his. The sun burnished her hair with an aureole of light and he noticed the frivolous camellia and smiled. 'I must say, Miss Leigh, you do look particularly well. Why, there's even some colour in your cheek.'

They sat for a few minutes in easy silence drinking their coffee, when he turned again to her. 'I hear from my daughter that a pirate father came to visit you?'

Angelica glanced at him, anxiety creasing her brow. 'Indeed, I was very shocked as I thought he was dead.'

'That must have been shocking indeed.'

'And I was angry. Mrs Leigh and I lived in penury and fear for much of my early life.'

'I am sorry to hear that. As you know, my work in Parliament is concerned with safeguarding children from exploitation. Sadly it thrives where there's poverty and desperation.'

'This is what I told Miss Elinor. That you were a far better papa than mine.'

He let out a gust of laughter that took Angelica by surprise. Usually so cool and controlled, this had obviously amused him and she saw a glimpse of the carefree spirit his nephew missed so much, and mourned. Still chuckling, he said, 'I presume you were having to promote my virtues against the more evident attractions of a pirate?'

She too laughed. 'Yes, indeed. But your daughter's a clever, affectionate child and she immediately recognised how lucky she is.'

'And how unlucky you are?'

Angelica dropped her eyes from his sympathetic but piercing gaze. 'It is indeed difficult to accept I was lied to all those years when I would have been grateful for a father. That he did not care for us. But I suppose as a debtor in exile he could not risk returning?'

'You are too charitable, Miss Leigh. Everyone has a choice, even in the most unpromising circumstances.' Mr Asprey's face was stern and his lips set in an uncompromising line. He abruptly changed the subject. 'Tell me, are you employed in another play?'

'I am. I shall be Amanthis in a silly play adapted from the French by Mrs Inchbald. You'd think she'd have known better.'

'Why? What's it called?'

'*The Child of Nature* and I am indeed this paragon. A girl, beautiful but ignorant of the world and carefully cloistered, nurtured to please only men. Indeed only one man.'

'It sounds provoking indeed to any young woman of sense and sensibility.' He smiled. 'I think even my fanciful Elinor might jib at that bit.'

'Ah, but she's still romantic enough about her papa to like the ending.' She met his eyes, smiling. 'Amanthis gives up her chance of happiness and a new life with the nobleman she loves, to live a vagabond life caring for her father who turns up unexpectedly, telling her he's destitute.'

He laughed again. 'I don't think Miss Stafford would allow her to think that a good idea! That young woman has very radical ideas, you know, about the rights of women. She and my secretary are great followers of Mr Godwin. My sister and Lady Linus think it's all dangerous nonsense and I should expel these revolutionaries within my walls!'

'Oh, no! Miss Stafford is a wonderful young woman. She cared for me so well. And Miss Elinor loves her.'

'Do not fear. I am enough in thrall to my daughter not to do anything so rash as to evict someone she loves.'

Angelica met his eyes and neither of them could look away, caught in a timeless moment of recognition. She felt her cheeks colour, she knew not why. Breaking the spell, she looked down at her hands then gathered her courage and said quietly, 'She longs to see more of you, you know.'

A flash of irritation or guilt creased his brow. He looked as if he was about to say something bitter but when he did speak it was to say, 'She's very attached to you, Miss Leigh. She chatters about you whenever I see her. Thinks you the kindest, most beautiful creature that ever walked this earth. I would appreciate it if you did not encourage her into the theatrical profession. I have other plans for her.'

Angelica gasped. She felt his words sting like a slap across her face. She had thought him so relaxed and companionable that she had been lulled into forgetting that they were not social equals and his attitude towards her profession was almost as dismissive as his sister's. She could not forget that the first time she met him he had attempted to buy her off, to prevent her marrying his nephew and sullying the family's noble blood.

She got to her feet, her cheeks flushed. 'I can assure you, Mr Asprey, I would never dream of influencing your daughter. If she were mine, I too would not want her entering my profession. Do you think I'm happy being leered at, having lewd comments shouted at me from the pit, being propositioned by rakes and stupefied sots, and treated as public property by any man who can pay the shilling for a theatre ticket?' She paused to catch her breath and continued in a quieter voice, 'It is exhausting. I promise you, she will get no encouragement from me.' She walked rapidly to the door.

But Ivor Asprey was quicker. He seemed to spring from his chair with one athletic move and barred her way. He grasped her hand. 'Forgive me, Miss Leigh. That was insufferably rude of me. Of course your kindness and charm can only do Elinor good. She is lonely, I know. It's just that no other woman in her life, be it her aunt or' – he paused – 'any friend of mine, can measure up to her idea of you.'

Angelica bowed stiffly. 'I will endeavour to be less kind and charming to her then. I'm thinking of returning to my mother's house tomorrow, anyway, now that your and Miss Stafford's generosity has returned me to health.'

'Please don't go prematurely on my account. It has been most pleasant to have you in the house. The place seems lighter and happy again. And Elinor, who is my every joy, seems to be happier too.' His eyes, usually of the deepest, coldest blue seemed to have become brighter and warmer as he still held her hand in his. Angelica gently extracted it and felt a dull sadness well up at the thought of the gulf between them. It was hard to be treated as an outsider when for the first time she had met people with whom she longed to belong.

At least she could reassure herself that there were good things she could do in this world she was not allowed to join. The question that had been bothering her came to mind as she met his quizzical gaze. 'Mr Asprey, there's something troubling me.' Clutching her hands together with anxiety at her presumption, she swallowed hard and asked, 'I wondered if you had decided to play Hazard again?'

He met her intent gaze with a startled expression that quickly softened into amusement. 'Why so, Miss Leigh? I know I told you I no longer gambled. But now and again, for the sake of old times or in a good cause, I might rattle the bones. Why such supposition? Is my behaviour to be interrogated, now?'

'I apologise for my effrontery.' Angelica was suddenly aware of how rude and arrogant she had been in first giving him advice about his daughter and then quizzing him on his gambling habits. She looked up to find Mr Asprey still waiting for further explanation. She knew she had to pursue her question to the end and in a rush of words she continued, 'Miss Fitzjames has had her ill-fortune turned to the good by a well-wisher. Your skill, it is rumoured, matches Lord Fulsham's and as the only other gamester who could challenge either of you is out of the country, I was left wondering about you.'

'You seem to add detecting to your many other skills, Miss Leigh. Is there no end to your talents? But I'm afraid I will have to leave you wondering.' He bowed and stood aside to allow her to pass.

* * *

As the clock in the hall chimed twelve, Goodall opened the front door to Mr Crowe's knock. He was dressed more soberly in dark coat and breeches, his tricorne hat replaced with a conventional curly-brimmed beaver worn low. His distinctive auburn hair was almost obscured by hat, high collar and scarf. Angelica had been waiting with some excitement and more than a ripple of anxiety. There was so much she wanted to discover about her father and his life leading up to this unexpected arrival in her life.

Despite the bright breezy warmth of the spring day, she was dressed in her wool pelisse, made from fine broadcloth and trimmed with fur; soft kid boots ensured her feet were warm and the most fetching Leghorn straw bonnet of blue framed her face and kept her unruly hair in check. Prosper Crowe grinned at the sight of her. 'Hardly believe me daughter has grown into such a beauty,' he said, chuckling as he tucked her hand companionably into his arm.

It was not evident to anyone that this was father and daughter out walking and so Mary accompanied them, to keep up appearances. The small party turned south towards St James's Park. Angelica was grateful to be out in the air and sunlight again. There had been many a moment in the last weeks when she could not imagine ever being well again and yet here she was, strolling with someone long dead to her, someone she had believed for all her adult life to be at the bottom of the sea, his bones picked clean by the fishes. She glanced up at Mr Crowe. His height and profile were striking, even though he looked as if he was in disguise. She wondered just how much danger he would be in if apprehended before he could escape back to France. A tremor of fear went through her.

'My dear, do you think you could make an old man happy and call me Papa?'

His voice startled her from her thoughts and the words took her aback. She didn't think of this exotic stranger as a 'papa', let alone the more formal 'father'. Her mother's protector, Mr Breville, was closer to that ideal with his easy, avuncular manner. Brunner even, had shown more concern and care than her true father had, or possibly ever would. She looked up to meet his smiling eyes, as green as her own, and stuttered, 'I'm not sure, sir. I don't feel I know you yet. I don't even know your true name.'

Mr Crowe chuckled again. 'Takes time, me dear. Two more days for you to know me better. You're always welcome in Paris, ye know. Come and preside over my gaming tables. Your presence would make it the most fashionable and frequented club in the whole city!'

Turning as soon as they could off busy Piccadilly, they relaxed as they strolled on the grass amongst the avenues of trees. Angelica felt her chest expand for the first time as she breathed in deep the cleaner air. The cold made her cough but that merely cleared her chest further. The birdsong too was so much sweeter now that the sound of carriage wheels and shouts of the carters had receded in the distance.

Angelica knew she was truly on the mend and tomorrow would return to Mr Breville's and her mother's house. She felt her familiar lightness of spirit return. Grasping Prosper Crowe's arm in a spontaneous expression of joy at being alive, she said, 'Tell me about your club.'

'Well, as you know, it's called the Dionysius in Rue Richelieu, one of the best addresses in Paris. I have a master chef and offer dining and the best champagne and brandy.' He was on the favourite topic of his success and she listened with mixed feelings.

'Is this the policy of gaming clubs, to get the clientele half-cut before they approach the tables?'

'What a cynical thought, daughter of mine! All the best clubs offer the pleasures of fine food and wine. But a particular clever ploy of mine is to allow the young men who serve wine to the gamesters to lend money too. When a gentleman has cleared out his ready coin he does not have to stop gambling to collect more.'

'That sounds immoral, but hazardous for the house too.'

'Ah no. It's productive of immense profit, for sure. If the borrower should win, he usually refunds the loan before leaving the room; and if unsuccessful, it remains for him to repay the waiters as "a debt of *honour*". I will, of course, cover any outstanding waiters' loans. Lending money to a losing gamester is like filling a leaky vessel. There is no end.'

'Surely then, this will hasten their ruin?' Angelica was aghast, thinking of Isobel Fitzjames's father and the family tragedy that had ensued.

Prosper Crowe seemed unconcerned by any individual tragedies but instead chose to concentrate his thoughts on what a successful business he had built on this easy-loan principle. Oblivious to Angelica's recoil, he explained, 'There is a disposition in gamesters to pursue a run of ill luck, a sort of frenzy and spirit of revenge to regain what they feel unjustly deprived of.'

He gazed down at Angelica's sceptical face. 'What I do is within the law. It's just the psychology of men that allows me to profit. Let a man win, and the gratification renders him incapable of leaving the tables.' He shook his head in disbelief. 'If he retires, it's only to come again, so that he must lose the more he plays. Not edifying, I agree, but human and luckily to my benefit. I should engrave Ovid's aperçu over the door: *Quo plus sunt potae, plus sitiuntur aquae.* You drink but then are forever thirsty.'

'Terrible to consider it was ever thus.' It distressed her to think of the thousands of lives that had been ruined by this addiction.

'Don't exercise yourself, darlin' with the cares of others. Can't take on the troubles of the world.'

'Perhaps not, but we shouldn't set out to profit from them.' She had turned to face him with a darkened brow.

'Come, come, Angelica. Let's turn to something cheerier. Your next play. Tell me about it.'

'It's called *The Child of Nature*,' Angelica said in a subdued voice.

Prosper Crowe's buoyancy was undiminished. 'I saw a production in

Paris, in French of course, by Genlis. As you can imagine, I approve of the primacy of the father in his daughter's affections.'

Being reminded of the plot irritated Angelica and she abruptly stopped walking to turn and look Prosper Crowe in the eye. 'Yes. Mama and I thought it a farrago of nonsense. It doesn't surprise me it's based on a French play. Probably a popinjay of a playwright, a negligent father himself indulging fond fantasies of reconciliation.'

'Woah there, Miss High and Mighty! The original author's a woman, the Comtesse de Genlis.'

'Well, then shame on her!' Her irritation dissolved with the absurdity of it all and they both laughed. Just at that point they were interrupted by two young men cantering through the trees towards them. Lord Latimer dismounted before his horse had come to a proper halt and he ran forward to grasp Angelica's hands. 'Oh, Miss Leigh. I'm consoled to see you out taking the air.' With fervid emotion he gazed into her eyes. 'And looking so well too.'

Prosper Crowe had been watching this display of affection with interest. Lord Latimer only then realised Angelica was walking not only with Mary but also with a striking gentleman of middle years. Was this the prodigal father his uncle had warned him had returned from his watery grave? 'I beg pardon, sir. I was just gratified to see Miss Leigh restored to health.' He bowed.

Angelica stepped forward with a smile. 'Lord Latimer, may I introduce Mr Crowe to you. He's my father, visiting from France for a few days. Sir, these are my friends, Lord Latimer and Dante Locke, a poet you know.' She indicated the young man still mounted on his black stallion, his dark hair worn long and dishevelled, his pallid face unsmiling.

'How d'ye do?' Prosper Crowe's Irish-French lilt was pronounced as he set out to charm this new audience. Dante Locke then dismounted and wandered over, his horse's reins looped over his arm. To no one in particular, he addressed the air, 'My art cannot flourish in this stifling country. Like Lord Byron, I must flee these indifferent shores to find fame with the infidels. What hot-blooded poet can write of soft hills and daffodils when there are tales of Greece, wild Syria and the barbarous Albanese?' He looked pained at the thought he had been deprived of such an exotic muse.

Prosper Crowe shook his hand in greeting. 'Mr Locke, come to Paris by all means, but beyond that I fear the Plague is driving back your compatriots on their Grand Tours.' He dropped his voice. 'I assume you've been reading "The Giaour"? Now that Napoleon's war is ended, Paris is full of young Englishmen set on romantic adventures in the Orient. That damned poetic lord has a lot to answer for.'

'But to stay in England is to sentence oneself to a desert of ennui.'

'Wouldn't know 'bout that. Certainly Paris'll chase off any ennui.' Prosper Crowe laughed in his bluff way. They continued to expand their differing views on Byron's works while Lord Latimer, leading his horse, offered his arm to Angelica. Lord Latimer sensed this unexpected resurrection of her father was not an unshadowed joy for Miss Leigh.

'This dramatic turn in affairs must be quite an alteration for you, Miss Leigh?'

She took his arm with gratitude. 'You're right, my lord. I think I'm still recovering from the shock. I feel disinclined to overlook his or my mother's deception.'

'You will always have my sympathy, you know.' He squeezed her hand.

'I think I should be heading back to St James's Square; I'm beginning to tire.' Even her voice was losing its force.

'Of course. You must be careful.' Lord Latimer leant in closer. 'Especially as I am determined you will accompany me to my masquerade ball.' He whispered this, his lips almost touching her ear. Angelica sensed his warm breath on her neck and the unexpected intimacy took her by surprise and made her heart skip a beat.

'I fear that it is unnecessarily provoking to your mother. And uncle.' She smiled at him, suddenly shy.

But the spirited young man swept aside any reservations. 'They will never know. It will add to my fun.'

'I'm not so sure it will to mine.'

'Oh Miss Leigh, it's not like you to be a marplot. You're usually the most lively of companions in every lark.'

Angelica was not feeling particularly larky. However, despite her mother's view that a joyful spirit militated against her advancement in highest society, she knew her temperament had always carried her through every kind of difficulty and obstacle and was grateful as her health recovered to feel hope bubbling again. The thought that she would have occasion to wear her grandmother's beautiful necklace as a kind of protection and validation made the adventure appear rather more appealing. She smiled up into Lord Latimer's handsome face and said, 'As long as Isobel Fitzjames is also coming?'

'Of course. And Dante too. And I don't know if my wicked uncle and sour-eyed Lady Linus will be there. It all depends on what stage his bill on child labour might have reached in Parliament.'

They were just about to leave the Park when Angelica pulled him slightly away from the party and dropped her own voice. 'Talking about your wicked uncle, could he in fact be a fairy godfather?'

Lord Latimer returned her mischievous gaze. 'How so, milady?'

'Could Miss Fitzjames's benefactor have been Mr Asprey?'

His lordship looked startled. 'You mean returned to the gaming tables to do a good turn for a stranger?'

'Hush! I don't want this bruited abroad. Mr Crowe runs a gaming house in Paris.'

'Well, if my uncle has risked everything to play Hazard against that libertine, Lord Fulsham, he's more reckless and foolhardy than I would ever have imagined! Damn me!' He ran a hand through his hair. 'That would mean he'd returned to his old ways. He's become so worthy and high-minded, I really don't think it's possible.'

They walked on a few more steps before Angelica noticed a familiar horseman approaching at speed. Only when he was about to canter past did the rider rein his horse in sharply. She looked up into the lean face of Cato Rackham, his eyes gleaming at the sight of her. 'My dear Miss Leigh,' he purred. 'I am relieved to see you so well. You disappeared from your mother's house and stories of your demise were rife. To where can you have been spirited away, I wonder?'

'Thank you for your concern, Lord Rackham. I am much recovered.' He had dismounted and she offered her gloved hand as his eyes flickered over her person appraisingly.

'When can we enjoy once more your presence in the theatre?'

'The new play opens in a month, I believe.' She dropped her eyes, embarrassed by the expression in his.

Cato Rackham then surveyed the rest of the party, and bowed his head briefly in greeting. 'Mr Locke, Lord Latimer, good day.' His eyes settled on Prosper Crowe who had pulled his hat a little lower and his scarf up, half obscuring his face. 'Good day to you, sir. Do we know each other?' His piercing gaze was on her father's face.

Angelica turned back to Lord Rackham and said, 'My lord, may I introduce a friend from France, Mr Prosper Crowe. Mr Crowe, this is Lord Rackham.'

Both men bowed while Lord Rackham looked from Mr Crowe's face to Angelica's, a peculiar expression in his eyes. 'I must be mistaken in thinking we have met. Forgive me. When do you return to your homeland?'

'In a couple of days when I have concluded my business obligations here.' Prosper Crowe spoke in a strange, neutral voice, all his natural lilt gone.

Cato Rackham turned to address Angelica. 'Miss Leigh, I will call on you at your mother's house. It has just occurred to me I might have a proposition that will interest you.' With that, he swung into the saddle and cantered back through the trees.

Something about this interaction disturbed Angelica's equanimity. There seemed to be a hidden threat behind Lord Rackham's words. She always found his rakish demeanour unsettling but her father's reaction to him gave her cause for further anxiety. They were both rogues, but of a quite different stripe. Was it just that each recognised the disreputableness in the other? She took her father's arm as they strolled up the incline towards St James's Square, walking slightly ahead of the young men and Mary.

Prosper Crowe smiled down at Angelica with a certain sly admiration. 'I had not realised my beautiful daughter had caught the eye of the young lord. He's the son and heir to a dukedom, if I'm not mistaken. Who'd have thought my little angel could become the duchess of a noble line, endowed with great estates!'

She bridled under his presumption and avaricious glee. 'Sir! I do not expect this at all. Lord Latimer is a charming young man, but I am an actress and his family would oppose any such liaison.'

'That may still be true in France, despite *La Révolution*, but here actresses are perfectly acceptable as wives of the aristocracy. You should not be shy on that account.'

'Mr Crowe, I hardly need your advice on such matters!' Angelica could not keep the anger from her voice.

He laughed. His complete lack of shame made him difficult to reprove. As they reached the shiny door of number four, Angelica turned to him and offered her hand. 'Thank you for accompanying me on my first walk for a long time. It has done me much good. I now know I am well enough to return to my mother's house tomorrow.'

Mr Crowe bowed. 'I will call on you and Mrs Leigh in the next few days. I have much to say to her, not least to commend her on our daughter.' He bowed again before walking off, pulling his hat further over his brow.

Lord Latimer and Dante Locke also took their leave. Bowing over Angelica's hand, his lordship said, 'Miss Leigh, I too will call on you at home. We have much to discuss.' His expression was full of portent.

Revived by his breezy conversation with her father about the vagaries of Continental travel, Dante Locke also clasped Angelica's hand and held it to his breast, his dark eyes lustrous in his pale face. With a soft lisping voice he intoned,

> 'Adieu, fair thing! Without upbraiding I fair would take a
> decent leave;
> thy beauty still survives unfading, and undeceived, may
> long deceive.'

Angelica gave a mock curtsey. 'Why thank you, Mr Locke. Is that you or Lord Byron speaking?'

The young man smiled. 'How could I say it better?' Angelica and Mary left the men standing on the pavement as they walked up the front steps and entered the warmth of the Asprey house.

* * *

It was late afternoon by the time Angelica descended the stairs from her room to read in the library, as she had promised Elinor she would do. She noticed a note on the central table in Ivor Asprey's distinctive hand, next to a small pile of three leather volumes.

If you need something more edifying to the soul to read – Mr Scott's Waverley. Lord B recommended the novel to me when I met him at Lady Melbourne's, the best he had read for years, he said, better than all the 'feminine trash'. I suspect in his severe judgement your play might belong in that category.

That made her laugh. She sat down on the sofa and began to read. With the force of both the author's imagination and her own she was almost at once swept into the heart of Jacobite Scotland. So engrossed was she that she jumped with a gasp when the door was flung open and Elinor Asprey dashed into the room with a cry and threw herself on Angelica's breast.

'What's the matter?' She tried to lift the sobbing girl's face, but she was hiccoughing between the sobs and could not utter a coherent sentence. 'Calm down, my dear, then tell me what's troubling you so.'

In between gasps and blowing her nose, the girl stuttered out in woeful tones, 'I've angered Miss Stafford and I'm afraid she'll leave me.'

'I'm sure she won't leave.' Angelica was patting her thin back.

With her eyes rimmed red with crying, Elinor piteously said, 'You see, I asked her to marry Mr Digby. I so want her to be happy and stay with me forever. But she was cross and said I was very presumptuous.' Her voice faded with a gasp. 'And that I had disappointed her.'

'I'm sure her displeasure is fleeting. She will not take lasting offence, you know.' Angelica's heart was touched by the child's distress. She too had been presumptuous in her interfering comments to Elinor's father and felt ashamed and wished to reassure the girl, and in a way reassure herself too.

'Mama left me a letter she wrote before she died. She said I have a gift for knowing what will make people happy. She told me to always have courage and be kind.' She hung her head, overcome by the memory. 'I try not to interfere and tell people what I think, but I do know Miss Stafford and Mr Digby would be happy together.'

'I'm sure you're right. But it's better to leave people to discover these things for themselves.'

'I think Miss Stafford knows already. Perhaps it's Mr Digby who doesn't realise happiness is there for him to take.' She sobbed again. 'I shouldn't have said anything, I know.'

'You should also read less romantic literature.' Angelica smiled.

Elinor's sense of humour came to her aid and she giggled through the tears. 'At least I haven't told Papa what I think about Lady Linus.' She spontaneously threw her arms around Angelica, who gave a surprised laugh. 'You see, I can be kind and have courage. I did hold my tongue!'

'Well, that is a good thing at least.' There was a knock at the door and Miss Stafford entered. She walked across to the sofa.

'Good afternoon, Miss Leigh. I'm glad to see you so restored.' She smiled and then turned to her charge. 'Elinor, I am sorry for my sharp tongue. I know your presumption comes from a truly kind heart.'

Elinor Asprey stood before her governess and said with contrition in her voice, 'I apologise, Miss Stafford, for speaking of matters that don't concern me.'

Sarah Stafford put a hand on her shoulder. 'I can see why you should think my future does concern you. I can assure you that I won't be leaving this house while you need me.'

The young girl gave her a quick hug and then sat down, a doleful expression clouding her face. 'But Miss Leigh is leaving to go home tomorrow. We shall all miss her.'

Angelica looked from one to the other. 'Ah, but Berkeley Square is not very far away. You and Miss Stafford can come and see me for tea.'

Miss Stafford had put another log on the fire and picked up a shawl from the back of the sofa and put it over Angelica's knees. 'Above all, you must keep warm, Miss Leigh.' She then put out a hand for her charge. 'Come now, my dear. Mr Digby is waiting to have supper with you and me, so we must bid Miss Leigh goodnight.'

Angelica was touched by the child. She had something brave and passionate-hearted in her nature that reminded her of herself when young. She would miss her too. She opened the first volume of *Waverley* again and before too long the warmth in the room, the crackle of the fire and the failing evening light made her eyes close and sleep come, the book still open in her lap. Not even a maid entering quietly to light the candelabra on the table beside her woke her. She was on the Scottish moors on some undeclared adventure; despite the wildness and the wind she was warm and secure. She could see a mighty stag on the distant crag and had to get to his side, but knew not how to cross the valley.

* * *

Ivor Asprey left Parliament early. He walked up from Westminster, tired and cold, and found himself longing for his chair by the fire and a glass of warming brandy in his hand. Entering through his familiar front door, he gave his hat and coat to Goodall. 'Where's my daughter?'

'She's with Miss Stafford having her supper.'

'Good, I'll see her later.' He walked through the hall towards the library and opened the door. The room was warm and welcoming with a well-established fire burning in the grate. His chair awaited him, the decanter of brandy glinting in the firelight, but the atmosphere was changed. On the sofa a woman slept like some young goddess, or Ophelia, so still, so beautiful and unexpected. For a shocking instant he wondered if she was dead and started forward. Then he noticed the colour in her cheeks, the rise and fall of her breast, and was consoled. Her Botticellian hair had come partly undone and curled round her face and over one shoulder and her shawl had slipped to the floor, revealing her neat feet and ankles. She looked completely at home.

With a jolt of his heart Mr Asprey realised how much he missed having a woman in his life, how much he would miss Angelica Leigh. He had grown accustomed to her presence, even if she herself was mostly unseen, but the light-heartedness and grace that had newly settled on his household could only be due to her.

He walked quietly to her side and picked up the shawl to drape across her prone figure. As he straightened it under her chin, Angelica's eyes flew open. Still lost in her dream, they were soft and unfocussed. But then she met his intense blue gaze and in an involuntary movement raised her hand to gently touch his face with a finger as if to see if he was real.

It was a moment of being in which time stood still. This mystical connection only lasted seconds and it was Angelica who was the first to break the spell. She sat up with a start and straightened her skirts. 'Oh! Mr Asprey, forgive me. I must have fallen asleep.' As colour rushed into her cheeks, she continued, 'I was dreaming of a great stag on the Scottish moors.' She tried to smooth her hair and twist it back into a bun.

He watched her with an inscrutable expression. 'I can't think of a nicer dream,' he said in his equable way. 'But shall I call in Mary to chaperone you?'

Angelica was about to stand up. 'No, no, I should be on my way.'

Ivor walked towards the fire. 'May I pour you a brandy? I am in great need of a glass myself.'

Angelica hesitated, then smiled and took the proffered glass.

She sat down again. 'How is the bill progressing?'

He sank into his chair, sighed and closed his eyes as he stretched his legs towards the fire. 'I'm afraid there are too many vested interests. It's frustrating progress. But I have to keep hammering on the door until it begins to open. Just a chink will do.' They sat, sipping their brandy and gazing into the fire, both aware of a vibrating energy in the space between them.

'I might not see you tomorrow when I leave but I do want to thank you for your care and that of Miss Stafford's. I don't know how I would have managed alone in Berkeley Square.'

He was looking at her over the rim of his glass. 'It has been our privilege. You will be missed.'

The tension of their unexpected intimacy eased, replaced by easy silences filled with their own thoughts. Angelica was thinking of her father and the complexity of feelings still to be unravelled. She met Mr Asprey's eyes, narrow and watchful in the flickering light. 'I was walking in St James's Park with my father when Lord Latimer and Dante Locke rode up and joined us.'

He shook his head. 'Those young dandies need an occupation to better employ that excess energy.'

'Well, Mr Locke is writing poetry. He thinks he needs an oriental adventure to inspire him.' Ivor Asprey sighed, a long-suffering expression on his face. She continued, 'Your nephew said you'd offered your country house for his party, as it's closer to London than his own family seat.'

'Cloudberry Court is an easy coach ride from Mayfair.' He seemed less than enthusiastic. 'He's a spoilt boy and can be very persuasive.' He was gazing into the fire and Angelica wondered if he was thinking of how Lord Latimer had pressed him into taking her in against his better judgment. He looked up with a rueful expression. 'It is my sister's ball, I'm afraid, I'm just offering use of my house. I have no say over her guest list.' Their eyes met and the meaning of his words was clear.

Angelica nodded. 'I do realise that the Duchess of Arlington is unlikely to extend a welcome to me, or women like me, at her son's party.'

He put out a hand but did not touch her. 'Miss Leigh, I may have treated you with scant respect when I first met you. I apologise. I have grown to esteem you greatly and am sorry for my old prejudices and discourtesy.'

'I understand that a careful mother wants the best for her only son.'

'A prideful mother!' His exasperation burst forth and he drained his glass and looked for a moment as if he was about to fling it into the fire. After a while his sanguine manner had returned and he said, almost to himself, 'Who can know what's for the best?' He leant across to pour himself another glass of golden liquid and then drained it in one draught.

Angelica rose to her feet. She folded the shawl and picked up the first volume of *Waverley*. 'May I borrow this?'

He was standing beside her, turning the book over in his hands, his thumb stroking the gilded, banded spine. 'Of course. Come back for the other two volumes when you need them.'

'I wish you restful sleep, Mr Asprey.'

'Do you not require dinner?'

Angelica shook her head. 'Thank you, but no. I'm tired. I've a busy day tomorrow.'

'I hope you sleep well too, Miss Leigh. And fare thee well. In all your endeavours.' His face was serious in the candlelight as he escorted her to the door. Just as she turned to go, he caught her hand, turned it over, unfurling her fingers, and then pressed her palm fleetingly to his lips. Taken unawares by the intimacy of the gesture, Angelica felt a prickle of excitement and her eyes widened. With a small intake of breath she said, 'Mr Asprey!' Then, as he released her hand, added, 'I must go.'

Ivor Asprey too was surprised by his uncharacteristic action. He was troubled by the cracks appearing in his hard-won control, and resisted what was stirring in his heart. This was the young woman his nephew loved and wished to marry and he felt some shock at trespassing into that emotional terrain. With what mysterious magic had she unsettled his life and sent a tremor through his family? He watched Angelica climb the stairs then returned to his favourite room that now seemed bereft.

7

MUST LIFE MIMIC ART?

The following morning the Asprey mansion bustled with activity as the master of the house left soon after breakfast for his weekly shooting practice at Manton's Gallery in nearby Davies Street. Angelica and Mary packed, making ready to return to Berkeley Square, and Elinor Asprey and Miss Stafford attempted to conjugate some irregular Latin verbs in the schoolroom. The girl's attention, however, was elsewhere; she listened for the sound of the family chaise arriving at the front of the house to convey Angelica home. Hearing the wheels rumble over the cobbles, she leapt from her chair to run down the stairs and bid Angelica a tearful farewell.

The coachman had just stowed away the last of the portmanteaus when Elinor noticed a coach, large as a ship, sway into St James's Square from the direction of Pall Mall. It was distinctive both for its size and the large gold crest on the door. 'Quick, Quick! Miss Leigh,' she cried, 'the Duchess is about to visit. Don't let her see you here!'

Shyly leaning into Angelica for a last embrace, she watched her new-found friend and her maid bundle themselves into the Asprey chaise and the horses spring away, turning smartly out of the Square at Charles Street, thus avoiding the approaching ducal carriage. Elinor then bounded back inside the house and found Miss Stafford standing in the hall. 'Aunt

Edwina is about to arrive. She'll have some scold for me, I'm sure. Pray tell her I'm indisposed.'

Miss Stafford caught her arm and said severely, 'Elinor, you know I can't tell your aunt untruths. Find your courage, my dear, and your good manners. She's probably hoping to see her brother and won't be concerned with you.'

'She pokes her nose into everything,' her charge muttered.

Goodall answered the knock of the liveried footman. The Duchess herself, in a striking pelisse of dark blue bombazine, sailed into the hall. She was a tall woman with a large upholstered bosom and her appearance was made all the more imposing by a turban in matching blue, with a purple ostrich feather bobbing at the crown. Lady Linus's willowy figure followed her, her fine symmetrical face set off by an up-to-the-moment Parisian redingote with its tight bodice and flaring skirt. Pale grey eyes flickered over Miss Stafford and her charge as she managed a fleeting smile.

'Good morning, Miss Stafford, Elinor, I'd like to see my brother.' The Duchess of Arlington's conversation tended to be a series of statements and orders.

Miss Stafford gave a slight curtsey. 'Good morning, your Grace, and Lady Linus. I'm afraid you've just missed Mr Asprey. But may I get you some refreshment?' She led them into the small sitting room, followed by a subdued Elinor.

'We're shopping for various costumes for the masquerade at Cloudberry Court. I do enjoy a masquerade. It reminds me of my youth.' For a moment the Duchess's face lost its imperious cast and she looked almost mischievous, but soon resumed her manner of exasperation at the intransigence of the world, not least her brother's. 'I wondered if Ivor needed me to pick up anything. He's so provoking. He says he has too much work to come.'

Elinor Asprey sat down on one of the upright chairs and folded her hands in her lap. On tenterhooks she watched the two women, aware it was the time to practise her good manners to please Miss Stafford. 'What might you choose to go as, Lady Linus?' she asked in a polite voice.

'Oh Elinor, unlike her Grace, I don't really approve of disguise. But if I were to attend, I think I might go as Hypatia of Alexandria. And carry an astrolabe.'

'But wasn't she cruelly murdered?' The girl looked questioningly at Miss Stafford.

The Duchess of Arlington's bosom swelled as she tutted, 'Young girls should not know about such things. Miss Stafford, I trust she hasn't learnt this under your tutelage.'

Elinor was quick to protect her governess. 'No, Ma'am, I read about Hypatia in a book in Papa's library.'

'And which book might that be, Elinor?' Her aunt's smirk revealed her disbelief in her niece's explanation.

'Monsieur Voltaire's *Philosophical Dictionary*.' She could not erase from her voice the faint lilt of triumph.

'Surely your father does not allow you free run of his library?' The Duchess's handsome face creased with a frown.

Lady Linus appeared to want to change the mood and produced a small book from her reticule. 'Elinor, I think this would be helpful to your education, written by Mr Gisborne, a man of God.' She opened it with care. 'It's on the duties of young women and how best to conduct themselves, indeed most useful in guiding our way.'

Elinor sat, uncertain as to what was to come. Miss Stafford had left to ask Cook to make tea for the visitors and the girl felt exposed. The Duchess settled back in her chair, with an expression composed for an improving sermon. Portia Linus leant forward, her pale eyes shining with evangelical zeal.

'I'm going to read you my favourite passage. If you listen carefully, you can imagine Curate Gisborne bestowing on you the benefit of his thoughts and prayers.' She turned to the bookmark and began in reverential tones, 'Where is to be found the most amiable tendencies and affections implanted in human nature, of modesty, of delicacy, of sympathising sensibility, of prompt and active benevolence, of warmth and tenderness of attachment; whither should we at once turn our eyes?' She paused for dramatic effect and looked towards Elinor Asprey's bewildered face, as if expecting some kind of answer. She then continued with emphasis, 'To the *sister,* to the *daughter*, to the *wife*. These endowments form the glory of the female sex.' She closed the book with a smart clap.

There was a self-satisfied smile on both women's faces, as if they assumed these glories for themselves, but they looked at the girl with an air of expectancy. Elinor wondered what she was meant to say or do, other than applaud and answered in a puzzled voice, 'I am a daughter, but I have no sister and do not want to be a wife.'

'Stuff and nonsense, my dear! What else is there for a young woman to do with her life?' Edwina Arlington did not have much patience with missish ideas of independence or romance.

'Well, I thought I'd like to be an actress.'

These simple words fell like a capital sentence on the room. The sense of shock and outrage rolled towards Elinor like a wave and she looked round anxiously for her governess. Miss Stafford had just re-entered carrying a tray with a tea pot and bowls and a plate of macaroons. She was just in time to hear the Duchess of Arlington's stentorian tones. 'Elinor! No girl from a family like ours can even consider such a thing. What are you thinking?'

'It's just that I like the idea of being someone else, the imagination and feeling...' Her voice trailed off.

'No, no, Elinor. Such women are beneath society's consideration. The sensibilities you mention lead to unsteadiness of mind, a fondness for frivolity and dissipation of the energies with trifles.' Miss Stafford had moved to stand beside her charge under this rhetorical onslaught from her aunt. So exercised was the Duchess that she drew herself up to her full height and started pacing the room. 'An excess of sensibility leads to rejection of graver studies, and an unreasonable regard for superficial wit and meretricious accomplishments.'

She turned with a swish of her stiff skirts and continued in the most withering tones, 'Actresses embody this excess of sensibility with their thirst for admiration and applause, full of vanity and affectation. As long as I breathe you will never become an actress, my girl!'

Miss Stafford broke in, 'Might I pour you some tea, your Grace?' The Duchess sat down heavily, her face pink with emotion. Lady Linus was the still centre of this storm, a cooler, more intellectual woman who fixed her eyes on the young girl and asked, 'Elinor, is there a particular person you are thinking of when you say you'd like to become an actress?'

The girl sensed her governess stiffen beside her. Danger lurked and she realised she had to be careful never to mention Angelica's name. She glanced round the room and her gaze alighted on the book their guest had brought with her, left on the floor and half-hidden by the sofa. 'No one in particular. But I have been reading *The Heroine* and it has made me think about other ways of living.' She sensed Miss Stafford relax and she hoped she had navigated her way well enough through this storm.

Her aunt harrumphed again. 'Your reading habits give me a great deal of concern. I shall have to speak to your father. Miss Stafford, surely you should be checking on the suitability of the girl's reading matter? Her mind is at a tender stage and has to be marshalled within the bounds of ladylike virtues.' Miss Stafford had poured the tea and put a bowl and saucer on the table beside the Duchess, together with the plate of macaroons. This broke her Grace's concentration and she started to drink the hot perfumed liquor.

'Lady Linus, do have a macaroon. They are rather fine. Did Cook make them, Miss Stafford?' She passed the plate to her companion, who appeared deep in thought.

'She did indeed.' Miss Stafford gave her ward a meaningful look.

Elinor Asprey took this lull in the inquisition of her moral education as a chance to escape. She stood up and curtseyed to her aunt and Portia Linus. 'Forgive me, Aunt Arlington, Lady Linus, I have to return to my Latin composition. I bid you farewell.' She bobbed and left the room as quickly as decorum allowed.

'That girl needs a mother,' the Duchess said, brushing a crumb from her lap.

'I could not agree more, m'lady. Women are the moral centre of any family. If Elinor had a mother there would be none of this nonsense about becoming an actress!'

The Duchess nodded. 'Well said, my dear. You know my sentiments on the matter.' She helped herself to another macaroon.

* * *

Angelica and Mary disembarked at Mr Breville's house in Berkeley Square. Martin was overjoyed to see them. He had not had time to put on his wig and so greeted them with his grey hair spiky and dishevelled. 'Oh my dears! I feared I'd seen the last of you, Miss Angelica.' As he took her hand with a theatrical bow, he intoned in his deep baritone voice, *'Death lies on her like an untimely frost. Upon the sweetest flower of the field.'*

'Oh tush, Martin! You can see I am well recovered; frost lies not on this flower of the field. Indeed it's good to be home.'

Mr Brunner also emerged from the kitchens to greet her. He strode forward, smiling, and grasped her hands. 'Miss Angelica, welcome home. It is a pleasure to see you so well. I called on that Mr Asprey's house to check on your progress, but I am delighted to see you at last.'

'It is a pleasure to be home with you all too.' She took off her bonnet and said to Brunner, 'I think I must take Storm out for a ride this afternoon. Would you check that Robert can get her saddled up and accompany me?'

His battered old face was wreathed with concern. 'Don't overtire yourself, Miss Angelica. You're only just back from the shores of the Styx.'

'I can't have you enacting a dying scene over me too. Martin's already read the last rites.' She gave him a wry smile and he laughed his big belly laugh.

Angelica joined Mary unpacking clothes in her bedroom. It was strange to be back. She felt she had voyaged to a different world of illness and peered over the precipice. Her recuperation was a kind of rebirth, nurtured in a household that she felt was akin to family, but in a way she had never known before. Until now, family meant her mother and herself, then later, the kindly Mr Breville and their fond but motley servants.

In Mr Asprey's house she had been much in the company of Miss Stafford and Elinor Asprey which gave her the sense of sisterhood for which she had longed all her life and in part created with the closeness of her relationship with Mary, her maid. Mr Asprey's secretary, Nicholas Digby, had added his own intellectual zest, reading with Miss Stafford in the evenings while Angelica dreamed by the fire. He was also the arbiter in discussions on Latin meanings, and explained in pithy fragments conversations with his employer about social justice. That employer, so influential yet elusive, set the tone in the house of competence and generosity of spirit.

However, the few times she had seen Mr Asprey, Angelica was aware of a barely contained fervour that could flare without warning. Was this the reckless energy that Lord Latimer recalled as characteristic of his uncle's youth? The thought that he was not quite what he seemed made him mysterious to her, and somehow thrilling.

Angelica sat on her bed while Mary busied herself. It interested her to think of his character, as she would analyse the dramatis personae in a play. To believe Lord Latimer, his uncle was at heart a carefree and pleasure-seeking rebel tragically shackled by grief and responsibility, constrained by 'propriety's cold comfortless rules', as he damned them. The young man mourned the hero-uncle he had once known. But Angelica had seen something daredevil in Mr Asprey, and emotional too, despite his support of the proscriptions of a society that excluded her. But then there were those moments of deepest connection between them she could not explain. Fleeting but unforgettable: could this be the heart of love?

Mary had finished folding and putting away her clothes and turned a searching gaze on her mistress. 'It won't be long before m'lord will come calling.' Having been the focus of other young men's romantic desires, Angelica had learned the ardent beam of their affections would pass in time, but Charles Latimer had surprised her by being more steadfast in his passion. She enjoyed his company, his light-hearted approach to life and the quickening of her animal spirits when he was near. His wealth and status added a certain frisson too; what woman, with a desire to make a mark on the world, would think it negligible to be offered the chance to become a duchess? But Lord Latimer was so young; would his love last – and could she love him?

Her reflections were interrupted by Mary carrying her best riding dress for the afternoon's expedition together with an expensive riding hat, a modified version of a man's silk top hat with two curling pheasant feathers and broad silk ribbon to tie under the chin. Mary seemed determined to show her mistress off to greatest advantage. To have Angelica elevated by marriage to Lord Latimer would add status to her position too. Lady's maid to a countess, about to become a duchess, had far greater social cachet than maid and dresser to an actress, however celebrated. Nevertheless, Mary was uneasy. In as casual a voice as she could muster, she said, 'I wonder if Miss

Fitzjames will accompany Lord Latimer? Recently they seem as peas in a pod.'

She turned to see Angelica reclining on the bed, her eyes half-closed. 'I'm sorry. All of a sudden I'm so tired. I think I'll rest for an hour or so before riding Storm out.' As Mary passed her bed, Angelica took her hand. 'I haven't thanked you properly, Mary, for all your care of me. I don't think I would have come through without you.'

'Oh, you're stronger than you think, Miss Angelica,' she said as she left, closing the door behind her.

It was four in the afternoon before Robert, the Breville groom, brought the striking grey mare, saddled and gleaming, to the front of the house. Angelica emerged into the late afternoon light looking like a French fashion plate in her emerald green habit with the black military frogging that emphasised her shape so well. Her black hat with its flirtatious curls of feather set off the vibrancy of her hair and her fine fair skin. Robert cupped his hands to make a step to give her a lift into the saddle and she sprang up lightly and settled herself sideways, arranging her heavy skirts to sweep down over her leg lodged in the stirrup. Cutting a dash in the saddle was one of the more rarefied skills for young ladies who wished to catch the masculine eye.

Angelica and Robert rode at a sedate pace towards Hyde Park. They headed for Stanhope Gate which gave them almost immediate access to the Serpentine and the shelter of the ancient oak trees leading to the King's Drive. It was still sunny and the air was crisp as they trotted then cantered along the well-worn trails that criss-crossed the Park. There were a number of horsemen and women and many curricles and phaetons and the occasional barouche taking the air. Riders and drivers and their passengers saluted friends and acquaintances, stopping for a while to exchange greetings and gossip.

Angelica was aware that her horse could never pass unnoticed in any gathering and there were occasions when she regretted choosing such a beautiful and flashy mount, but having glimpsed Storm, how could she have chosen any other? Robert, riding behind her, could see that it was not just Storm's striking looks that drew so many appraising glances. They cantered through the trees bordering Oxford Street and had just reached the turnpike building when Angelica was hailed by a rider on a large black horse.

'Good afternoon, Lord Rackham.' She bowed her head politely, determined not to show how much his sudden appearance unsettled her.

'What a delightful surprise, Miss Leigh.' He doffed his hat. 'May I join you for a while?' Angelica nodded but her spirits faltered. Lord Rackham had so many hidden motives and she was uneasy knowing she was somehow implicated in some dark plan. They trotted on together, commenting politely on the weather and the passing scene. She was disconcerted to see how well he looked in the saddle. What a pity, she thought, that his character was so disreputable, for he was highborn and a good-looking man; he could have been sought after rather than feared and avoided as a cynical rake.

As they approached a copse of trees he suggested they walk a while. Before Robert could help her down, Lord Rackham had sprung athletically from his horse and stood with his hand up to help Angelica dismount. She unhooked her right leg from the pommel and slipped down Storm's side to be caught round the waist in Lord Rackham's firm grip. His fingers pressed into her flesh, warm and hard through the cloth of her jacket. Once on the ground she stepped sideways to escape his grasp. He led her towards the trees with Robert following with Storm, at a discreet distance.

'Miss Leigh, I have been meaning to talk to you since meeting your intriguing companion, Mr Crowe.' There was an expression in his eyes that made her heart miss a beat. 'I thought it uncanny how alike you both were. Could you perhaps be related?'

'Indeed we are.' Angelica attempted a light-hearted tone of voice.

'Father and daughter?' His eyes were on her face with the cool intensity of an interrogator set on delivering his *coup de grâce*. She nodded, her spirits plunging.

'I presume that is a mixed blessing?' He did not take his eyes from her face. 'You see, Miss Leigh, I did, in fact, recognise him. He has a memorable look and I do not forget a face. I know him as something more troubling than merely your father.'

For Angelica, who had yet to discover much about Prosper Crowe herself, even his true name, these words filled her with dread. She said as evenly as she could, 'I cannot comprehend what you could possibly mean, my lord.'

'There is an arrest warrant for your father, still outstanding.'

His words were clipped and they shocked her like a splash of cold water. He had discovered this fact, what else did he know that he would surely use against her in some way? Her chest tightened. 'I realise this, Lord Rackham. But he is about to return to France and will soon be beyond English jurisdiction.'

'Not so easily, my dear. In Parliament I am in charge of excise and guarding our coastline and he won't be able to leave unmolested by the law.'

Angelica felt the colour drain from her face, the strength from her limbs. She hated the fact she had to steady herself against his lordship's proffered arm. 'How can this be? He has not been in this land for fifteen years or so.'

'I'm afraid some crimes are too heinous to be erased by time.'

Panic rose in her breast. 'But it was only debt. He did not take anyone's life.'

Lord Rackham did not answer but watched her trying to compose herself. He placed his other hand on her arm. 'There is a solution very satisfactory to me, and to which I hope you might agree.'

Angelica met his eyes. All her acting skills were needed now to appear calm and assured despite the turmoil of her thoughts. What had her father done? How little she knew him but yet could not bear to think of him imprisoned. A dread thought gripped her; was it even worse? That it was the gibbet that he had escaped when fleeing to France? She wished she was leading Storm and could lean against her for strength instead. 'What could that solution be, Lord Rackham?'

He took a step towards her and looked down into her face with eyes that had grown dark and hungry. 'A young woman in your profession with such beauty as yours understands the relationship between such as you and a man like me.' When she did not respond he continued, 'If you come to my house in Curzon Street by three tomorrow then I will call off the Water-guard and Excise men who patrol the coastline and ports. Your father will then have unimpeded passage back to France.'

Angelica could feel his breath on her cheek. She was astounded that he felt he could talk so to her. It was a measure of his scant respect for her. Meeting his eyes she asked, 'I presume this is not an offer of marriage, Lord Rackham?'

He turned away from her gaze with a harsh laugh. 'You're no foolish young miss. And almost as versed in the ways of the world as am I. It should come as no surprise that men like me do not marry women like you.' He looked back at her with a feral smile that showed his teeth. Without a modicum of embarrassment or shame he set out his terms. 'However, I will set you up with your own household. You may continue your work in the theatre if you wish and have your own friends, within reason. In return, you accompany me to a few select soirées and entertain me at home.'

Angelica had sensed this was always what Lord Rackham had had in mind since he'd first started visiting her at the theatre. But now he held her father's life in his hands he had an inducement to make her comply with his wishes. She could not risk enraging him with a hasty dismissal and had to think fast. 'So, Lord Rackham, I have until tomorrow afternoon to accept your offer?'

'Indeed. Think carefully, Miss Leigh, I consider it a generous offer. I think you too will come to find it most satisfactory. I look forward to sharing some tea with you at Rackham House. Number twenty-eight Curzon, opposite the gardens of Chesterfield House.'

'And you will guarantee my father would not be apprehended at any port?'

'Of course. What is the use in having power if one doesn't use it to one's own advantage?' He took her gloved hand and pressed her fingers. Glancing up, she saw his face unexpectedly lightened by a sly humour. 'Your beauty is compelling, Miss Leigh. I am under your spell and will not be able to rest until I can claim you as mine.' He still had hold of her hand and deftly unbuttoned her glove and slipped it from her fingers. Looking down at her hand, he slowly put it to his lips and held it there. Angelica shuddered and he sighed. 'You won't regret our association, I promise you.'

So close to recoiling with a cry, Angelica nevertheless maintained a certain dignity as she turned to walk over to Robert, who gave her a lift into the saddle. She replaced her glove while a kind of shame washed over her. No gentleman would treat a young woman of his own class in such a way. She looked up. Lord Rackham was already mounted on his steed. He raised his hat in greeting before wheeling his horse around and cantering away through the trees.

Turning to Robert, Angelica said with some urgency, 'I have to get home to talk to Mr Brunner.' It was all she could think of. How to get her father out of the country and to safety.

* * *

Mr Brunner listened to Angelica with concern. She omitted to tell him about the bargain that hung over her, only that Prosper Crowe had to find a way of escaping the country when the excise men were on the alert along the coast. 'I think we will either need a crafty smuggler, unknown to the authorities, or some alternative private boat that sails from one of the unfrequented coves on the southern coast.' Since Lord Latimer's precipitate behaviour to save Angelica's life, Mr Brunner had discovered a new respect for the young nobleman. No longer such a spoilt, over-privileged wastrel, he considered him now a worthy colleague in any enterprise. His pugilist face cleared with the thought. 'The only person I know who might have such a yacht is that young lordly friend of yours. Dashing young blades like him are often given boats as playthings when they turn eighteen.'

Angelica was agitated, pacing the hallway, her mind full of contrary scenarios about how best to proceed. This suggestion seemed as good a place to start as any. 'Would you take a note to Lord Latimer at Arlington House in Grosvenor Square? I cannot call myself. It wouldn't do to have his mother get word of such a scandal, my person is scandal enough for her.' She did not add how it would delight the Duchess to have her father's disgrace as even more reason to make Angelica *persona non grata*.

Mr Brunner returned, breathless with the deflating news that Lord Latimer was at the racing at Newmarket and not to return until the morrow. Angelica's sense of resolve gave way to urgent anxiety. The only other competent men she knew were Mr Asprey and his secretary, Nicholas Digby. She determined to get a Hackney carriage to Westminster Hall and hope for an audience with one or the other of them before Parliament's late sitting began. Her tiredness forgotten, she called into the kitchens for Mary.

Still wearing her riding habit, Angelica reached for her blue cloak whose hood usefully covered her hair. She did not want her presence advertised to Mr Asprey's colleagues and enemies; it would be mortifying to bring embarrassment or discredit down on his head while he was engaged in promoting such important legislation.

Mr Brunner hailed a cab and the two women climbed in as it set off south to Westminster. Although it was possible for ordinary tourists to visit areas of the ancient Hall, this was the first time Angelica had seen it and she was amazed at the size and age of the building with its crumbling headless figures in the niches in the wall. The Hackney carriage slowly approached the elegant colonnade that marked Speaker's House where she could gain entry to the House of Commons. As they walked through the cloister a constable in uniform greeted her and asked her business.

'Could you tell Mr Asprey there is a lady to see him?' Angelica had disguised her distinctive hair by pulling up her hood and did not wish to give her name. The constable looked at her sharply but seemed satisfied she was not about to cause any trouble. He left the two women in the spacious lobby waiting by a great Russian stove that emitted so much heat the vast stone building seemed almost cosy.

At the sound of footsteps, Angelica looked up to see Nicholas Digby striding towards them, the tails of his dark coat flying. When he was almost upon them his face broke into a warm smile. 'Ah, Miss Leigh, Mary! I wondered who this mysterious "lady" could be. I hope nothing has happened?' His eyes were concerned as he took her hand in greeting.

Angelica did not reply but said instead, 'I hope I'm not interrupting anything too important.'

'Mr Asprey has some time before he goes into the committee meeting.' He led the way back up the corridor and through a green and white painted door into an office overflowing with books and papers. He indicated a chair for Mary and then led Angelica into the inner sanctum where Ivor Asprey sat at a desk, his quill poised. The light slanted in through the gothic window and his dark figure intent on a letter in his hand was burnished with the warm glow of late afternoon sun. As Mr Digby knocked he looked up, abstracted.

Angelica had thrown back her hood and the same sunlight caught her hair, seeming to set it aflame. His eyes met hers with a look of open surprise but then concern made him rise and come towards her. 'To what do I owe this pleasure, Miss Leigh? I hope nothing is amiss?' Nicholas Digby had withdrawn back to the outer room where he addressed the pile of correspondence.

With Mary next door, Angelica found herself alone with Mr Asprey. She was unexpectedly shy. 'I apologise for bringing my trouble to your door, but Lord Latimer is at the races, my mother and Mr Breville are in Paris until tomorrow and I could think of no one else competent to deal with a conundrum as urgent as this.'

'You intrigue me, Miss Leigh. You seem to specialise in knotty problems that you seek help to unravel.' He was smiling and Angelica felt herself blush at the thought of her previous presumption in asking him to return to his gambling ways to help her friend.

'I promise not to make a habit of it, Mr Asprey. But this time I am confounded as to what to do.'

He motioned to a chair and they sat with their backs warmed by the sun. 'I was riding in Hyde Park and met Lord Rackham by chance. He told me he had recognised my father and knew him for a felon who had escaped justice when he left for France.'

Ivor's eyes narrowed. 'I presume he has some damnable plan to turn this to his advantage?'

'He's in charge of the Waterguard and Excise men who patrol the ports and the coast and he said he had issued a command to apprehend him.'

'I knew he was vengeful but didn't think he was personally so full of malice. I fear he's up to something.'

She dropped her head. She knew she would have to tell Mr Asprey everything but was ashamed of the bargain Lord Rackham had offered her. 'He would only allow my father to leave if I agreed to meet him tomorrow afternoon and consent to become his...' Angelica hesitated, finding it hard to say the word, but Mr Asprey understood full well, interrupting her with an explosive exclamation as he leapt to his feet.

'The devil he will! I knew Cato Rackham was without principle but didn't expect him to stoop so low.' He was pacing, his blue eyes colder and harder than Angelica had ever seen before. 'Goddammit! I should call him out for this. Avenge your honour and rid the world of his malignancy!' he stormed. 'I have long abhorred him. An old wound for sure, but hatred is by far the most enduring pleasure.' He stopped in front of Angelica, his hair disordered and eyes blazing. 'I cannot allow Rackham to ruin another young woman's life. To prey on someone as defenceless as you. By God! I'll have to call him out.'

In panic, Angelica too sprang to her feet. 'No! No. Just think of the scandal. Two parliamentarians fighting over an actress! Your reputation would be sullied, the ridicule, the satirists and lampooners would have a heyday!'

Her reason did not mollify his outrage as he continued his pacing. 'How dare Rackham treat you so!' Despite her own fear and distress, Angelica was surprised at how gratifying it was to have Mr Asprey so exercised on her behalf. No one had ever before shown such concern for her reputation and welfare. She was even more taken aback when he grasped her hands and said with feeling, 'I and my family have also treated you ill. I apologise and want you to know I will not stand in your way should you choose to accept my nephew's hand in marriage. I consider him a lucky man if you should have him.' He turned away, moved by emotions Angelica could not fathom. She too found herself confused by her heart. She should have felt delight at having his blessing for her union with his nephew but instead felt a hollowness settle in the pit of her stomach. But she had no time to think. Mr Asprey had returned to pacing.

Angelica watched him, astonished at how this usually self-contained man seemed energised by his own boldness and struggled to regain his usual cool, businesslike demeanour. Turning back to his desk, Ivor Asprey said in an emphatic voice, 'This is all for the future. We have now to get your father away to France tomorrow.'

'But your name cannot be linked to a criminal escaping justice. I believe my father is a debtor whose sentence is still outstanding. You have to remain beyond reproach.'

He was serious. 'You seem overconcerned with my reputation, Miss Leigh. I do have the redoubtable Mr Digby, you know. But you're right, it is scandal indeed for a member of His Majesty's Government to assist in an evasion of the law, but it is also a scandal that another member of that same Government is prepared to blackmail you for his own libidinous ends.' He came to stand beside her, his body tense with muscular energy. 'It's occurred to me, I have a friend who moors his yacht in a hidden cove on his land that runs to the sea, near Cuckmere Haven in Sussex. I can send a courier now to alert him to make ready his captain and crew. We'll have to get your father there tomorrow at the latest.'

'Mr Asprey, this shouldn't be your problem, it's mine. I am ashamed to involve you at all.' Angelica met his gaze and noticed the liveliness in his eyes which had replaced his usual cool regard.

His young reckless self was in the ascendant again. 'It would be a plea-sure to frustrate the devilish plans of Lord Rackham.' He took her hand. 'And having already been involved in saving your life, Miss Leigh, I'm not about to abandon that life to a villain like Cato Rackham.' His eyes were so intense and alive Angelica found it hard to look away, her emotions in tumult. No longer was Mr Asprey the self-controlled patrician that she held in some awe; now this youthful, devil-may-care side of him energetically matched her warm impulsive heart.

Ivor Asprey strode to the door, calling for Nicholas Digby. 'Could you discover the whereabouts of Miss Leigh's father, Mr Crowe? He'll be in a tavern or club where Miss Leigh cannot enter. Please ask him to visit her at Berkeley Square. Impress on him the urgency.'

Angelica followed him to the door and collected Mary from her seat by the window. 'I don't know how to thank you, Mr Asprey, or you too, Mr Digby.' She bowed.

'Thank us when we've completed our task. I'm hoping we can outwit Lord Rackham and the authorities, but we're running out of time.'

Angelica pulled the hood of her cloak over her hair and she and Mary hurried out, escorted by Nicholas Digby who hailed a Hackney carriage to take them back to Berkeley Square.

Now that she had time to think, Angelica began to worry. After an hour had passed she started to walk from the window to the fireplace and back; her father should be here by now. Afraid that Nicholas Digby had been unable to locate him, she felt desperation begin to rise; she must see him;

he had to leave London at dawn the following day to stand a chance of evading the border and customs defence forces and there were questions she still needed to ask him.

As the light was failing and the candles were lit, there was a loud rap on the front door. Angelica jumped and ran to the window. A smart curricle and a pair of black horses were pulled up outside. The door into the small sitting room opened and Martin's rouged face appeared. 'Lord Latimer to see you, Miss Angelica. Shall I show him in?'

She nodded and her heart skipped a beat as Charles Latimer came through the door, dusty and dishevelled from his drive back from Newmarket. She ran towards him and clasped his hands. 'Oh my lord, how good to see you. I'm so worried about my father.'

He held onto her hands and pulled her close, his eyes dark. Angelica gave a little gasp. Although they were the same age, it had become a habit to dismiss him as merely a susceptible boy; now she saw him for the first time as a man. His hair was windblown, his face grimy from the road and she was disconcerted to find him so attractive. With some shame, Angelica wondered if her equanimity had been so shaken by her close brush with death, followed by the arrival of her father and his uncertain fate, that her febrile emotions alighted on any likely recipient. Now Mr Asprey's blessing on her union with his nephew merely increased her confusion. To find herself within such a short time attracted to two men, so differing in age and experience, made her mistrust her heart.

Just at that moment the door opened and Mary slipped into the room to sit quietly in the window seat. For all his theatrical unconventionality, Martin was as protective of Angelica as a mother hen and had summoned Mary from the kitchens as chaperone.

Angelica pulled her hands away and stepped back. 'I sent for you at Grosvenor Square, but you had left for Newmarket. I did not know what to do for the best.'

Lord Latimer threw himself into the chair by the fire and stretched out his legs in their dusty boots. 'Why? What has happened to distress you so?'

'Do you remember meeting Lord Rackham by chance in the Park as we walked there with my father?'

'I do, indeed. His lordship always disturbs the air he passes through.'

'Apparently, he recognised my father. He told me as his arrest warrant is still active he has given orders to the coastal patrol and the ports to prevent him boarding any ship to France.' She was disinclined to add the shaming caveat that he would only call off the law if she was compliant with his desire to set her up as his mistress.

Forgetting his fatigue after the day's drive, Lord Latimer was on his feet, his fists clenched. 'Goddamn the man! Apologies, Miss Leigh, no wonder he's called Black Cat, he works his mischief wherever he goes. What's to be done?'

'When I couldn't find you, I went to your uncle for help.'

Lord Latimer's whole manner relaxed again. 'Wisest thing to do. The most capable and trustworthy man I know to get anyone out of a scrape. Lord knows he's rescued me many a time. As long as he wasn't nose in the air and riding his high horse.'

Despite her anxiety, Angelica laughed. 'No indeed. He was most accommodating. I'm just waiting to see my father. To say goodbye. Mr Asprey's secretary will accompany him in your uncle's fast chaise to a secret yacht owned by a friend.'

Lord Latimer slapped his thigh in mirth. 'He was accommodating, was he! That's a first. Miss Leigh, you've been weaving your witchy wiles!' He looked up at her with mischief in his eyes, the thrill of this pending adventure exciting his boyish spirit. 'He's thinking of Porky's yacht, beautiful sloop moored in a smugglers' cove. Well I never. And my uncle a lawmaker too, breaking the law! He's playing with fire. Must think very highly of you, Miss Leigh.'

'That was exactly my concern. For his reputation. He owes me nothing and yet his generosity humbles me.' She glanced up to see Lord Latimer's eyes on her face, a speculative gleam making her wonder exactly what thoughts so animated his handsome countenance.

'Well, it strikes me I did you a favour being out of town. There's no doubt my good old uncle has come up with a better plan than I could have done.' At that point there was another rap on the front door and Angelica held her breath, desperate that it should be her father at last.

Prosper Crowe burst into the room, wild-eyed and a little the worse for drink. She started forward. 'Mr Crowe, Papa!'

With a cry, he grasped her to his chest. 'Ah, thank ye, Mary mother of God! Now facing disgrace and possible death, me daughter acknowledges me.' His voice turned mournful. 'Mr Digby has told me I have to flee once it's light.'

Angelica struggled to disengage herself from his embrace and motioned to Lord Latimer. 'You recall meeting my friend?'

'Yes indeed. Hoping he will become more than a friend.' His eyes were bleary and unfocussed as he smiled in Lord Latimer's direction.

'Papa! Hush. Do not speak thus!' She felt her colour rise with embarrassment.

'Don't be a scold. You're too beautiful – more suited to being a duchess.'

Angelica shook his arm. 'You are in your cups, Papa! Stop talking like a spoony drunk.'

'So now you use the language of the street.'

Her anger flared with memories of poverty and fear in her childhood. 'Yes! Your neglect of Mama and me meant we lived on the street. I know far worse language than that!'

Lord Latimer was standing beside her and took her hand. 'Miss Leigh, I know you have important matters to discuss with your father. I am tired and should go home to change. It's been a long day.' He bowed over her hand, saluted Prosper Crowe and turned for the door. 'I can see myself out.' Mary followed him and at the door turned with a frowning glance at Angelica.

Angelica remembered that the dangers of the present mattered more than the resentments of the past. She turned to Prosper Crowe. 'Mr Digby has told you what he wants you to do?'

He sank into a chair. 'Yes. Very good of your friend, Mr Asprey. I had brought over from Paris a box of gold Napoléons for you and your mother but I'll take one to pay for my passage.'

Angelica knelt by his side and said with some emotion, 'Papa, unless I come to Paris, this may be the last time we see each other. It'll be too dangerous for you to return to England.'

He hung his head. 'I'm sorry to have been such a poor father. I cannot make the lost years better but I want to share some of my good fortune in business with your mother. The gold is in a strongbox in the hall. Perhaps some amends for the past?' He looked at her, sadness suffusing his face; for the first time since the shock of his return from the dead, Angelica's heart was touched.

She hugged his knees. 'Oh Papa, it is uncanny how like our story is to the play I am about to perform.'

The Child of Nature is bad enough in the theatre, not meant to be as life, ye know.' He chuckled. 'I am hounded from my country, 'tis true, my life may well hang in the balance, but I don't expect ye to follow me into exile.' He kissed the top of her head. 'I just ask that ye live life as ye wish. Perhaps even live it as a member of the nobility!' he added with a smirk.

'"*Oh, my father! To be your comfort in a state like this, would be my happiness.*" I've just been learning my lines in the last act.'

'Then Papa applies the thumbscrews, does he not?'

'Yes, my theatrical father answers, "*I see my fate, and submit to it. My child, live happy, and forget me as often as you can. Receive my blessing, and my last farewell*". Then he elaborates upon his own suffering and his expectations of the daughter he has neglected. As you remember, she's a dupe and, despite "*dying of despair*", agrees to sacrifice her happiness for his!' They laughed, their heads together, close for the first time in their lives, just at the point they were to part.

He sat back and looked serious. Emotion had sobered him up and he was focussed. 'Proud of ye, Angelica. More than I ever hoped for a daughter of mine. And all credit to Mrs Leigh.' He held her close. 'All I can say is forgive me. There's always a warm welcome for me daughter in Paris, whenever she should choose to come. The theatre is reviving and your beauty will secure a place at the very heart, if ye should ever want it.'

'Oh, Papa. I'm sad that we have to part. For many years I longed for a father and now I have one he has to go.'

'But we will write. And when you marry perhaps I can come one last time, in disguise?'

'The pity of it. But at least I have my grandmother's necklace to remind me of family. Thank you so much for that.' She hugged him again.

His face lost its humour and he said in a serious voice, 'It may be valuable, you know. Not paste but diamonds. Don't flash it about.'

Angelica smiled. 'I don't mind how valuable or not it is. I think it beautiful. And to know your mother's love for it somehow imbues the stones too; her love will combine in them with mine.'

Prosper Crowe rose to his feet. 'Must be going. I have to pack and get some sleep before rising with the birds.'

Angelica reached up to touch his silvered auburn hair, tied back in the old romantic way. 'You must also travel in some disguise. Powder that hair, Papa. Like me, you are too easily identified.' They embraced and then walked into the hall. Martin was not in evidence and it was Angelica who offered her father his coat and helped him into it, then passed over his jaunty tricorne hat. She looked at him, still a fine figure of a man, and stood on tiptoe to kiss him on the cheek. He motioned to a small pirate's chest, wooden and brass-bound, which was pushed under the console table, put a finger to his lips and winked.

Prosper Crowe took Angelica in his arms. 'Darlin' daughter, take care of yerself and choose yer path in life well. I approve of both the gentlemen who love ye.'

Still in his large embrace, Angelica gasped, taken aback by his words. 'I don't know which gentlemen you mean, Papa.' She coloured and gazed up into his face with puzzlement. He surely did not know Lord Rackham?

Disengaging from her father's hug, she clutched his hand, but he chatted on, his Franco-Irish lilt more marked than ever. 'Well, it's obvious to a fond father that there's the young blood with every advantage and then the admirable sobersides, who is not quite as sober as he seems.' He cast her a knowing grin as he tipped his hat. 'Both strike me as eminently fitted to claim you as their prize.'

'But Papa...'

'We'll meet again, Angelica. Adieu!' and with a wave he sped down the front steps and into the night.

She sighed, her heart full of the turmoil of loss and dread and the confusions of love. Her father's last riposte made her realise he meant Lord Latimer and Ivor Asprey. Of course, it would have struck Mr Crowe that only love would make such an eminent politician risk his career and repu-tation as he had done. However, Angelica believed what propelled this honourable man into such reckless behaviour was not his feelings for her but the exhilaration of being reunited with his lost youth. Grief and responsibility had so tamped down the well-spring of his nature and now some latch had slipped and this new energy flowed into his parched soul and he was revived. She was too tired to try and unravel the meaning of it all and after the alarums of the day, Angelica thought longingly of bed. Mary obviously had something to say to her too, but it could wait until the morning.

8

SHE SHALL GO TO THE BALL

When Edward Breville and Amabel Leigh returned from Paris there was even more commotion in Berkeley Square than when they had departed a month before. Trunks of fine china, fabric, gowns and every luxurious accessory from shawls to bonnets, gilded boxes and pretty ceramic ornaments were unloaded from the great coach they had hired to convey them from Dover to London. Angelica flew into her mother's arms. 'Welcome home, Mama. I'm so pleased to see you.'

'Oh, how glad I am to be back!' Mrs Leigh had flopped onto the sofa in the drawing room while servants bustled to convey the luggage to her bedroom.

Angelica gazed at her mother, struck by how elegant she looked in pink and grey striped satin, and youthful too, with excitement sparkling in her eyes. 'It seems a most successful trip.' She laughed.

'Truly divine. Paris is recovering fast from the war. All the elegant shops and restaurants are open. C'est ravissant.' She patted the sofa. 'Come and tell me about what's been happening to you.'

Angelica took a deep breath. 'I don't know where to begin. My cold turned into an inflammation of the lungs. I thought I was dying, but am much better now.'

Her mother grasped her shoulders and hugged her fleetingly. 'Oh my darling. I should have been here. Did Martin and Mary manage?' Her eyes were full of concern.

Angelica did not want to have to go into the whole story at this point as she had much more important news to impart. 'Then Mama, the most extraordinary thing. My father turned up unheralded. I could not have been more shocked. And angry.' She had moved away from her mother's side and looked back at her with a searching look. Amabel Leigh's hand flew to her face. She grew pale and for a while could not speak. Angelica continued, 'How could you and he have thought it a good idea to have me believe he was dead?'

Mrs Leigh reached out for her, her voice breathless. 'Angelica, it was a time of terrible fear. His life was in real danger. He had to get away and probably never return so we thought it less painful for you to think he had died.' Her face was contorted with the memory.

'But what had he done, Mama, that was so terrible? I thought it was just debt.'

'Is that what he told you?'

'He evaded my question and also wouldn't tell me his real name.'

'Well, his name is Peter Crowley. What is he calling himself now?' Her voice sounded wary.

'Prosper Crowe. In fact, he was hoping to see you but early this morning was dashing for the coast to evade the law once again.'

Amabel Leigh held her head in her hands. 'He seems no better now than he ever was.'

'Well, he has managed to make a success of his life in Paris. Running a gentlemen's gaming club feeding off the gullible. I told him we could have done with some support from him when we were starving.' Angelica walked to the window and said in a sorrowful voice, 'Mama, I feel I cannot trust you any more to tell me the truth.'

Her mother cried out in distress, 'Oh my dear. I did not know what to do for the best. You were my only concern. The fact he was a criminal and exiled in disgrace was something I could not bear. So I told you he was a hero who had died fighting for Lord Nelson. You *can* trust me, I assure you on my life!' Her voice rose with emotion.

'Well, in a belated gesture he brought with him a small chest of gold Napoléons as a long-owed debt to us both.'

'What? Where?'

'It's under the hall table. I haven't looked inside. On his past behaviour, it may well be full of brass.'

At this point Mr Breville entered the room looking weary. 'Angelica, my dear.' He approached her with his arms wide. 'We have had the most successful trip. I am delighted with the range of porcelain ordered for the business, and at most gratifying prices, thanks to the suppressant effects of the war.' He turned to his mistress. 'Amabel, my dear, have you shown Angelica our present for her?'

Mrs Leigh jumped up, grateful to have a reason to change the subject to something cheerier than her shortcomings as a parent. 'It is so charming.' She tripped up the stairs to her suite of rooms where the trunks were being unpacked, disgorging a riot of colour. Angelica heard the rustle of silk as she returned. Her mother was holding in her arms the most beautiful evening dress she had ever seen. It seemed a rippling constellation of stars.

She gasped. 'Mama! Mr Breville. Is this for me?' Mrs Leigh handed over the gown of inky blue overlaid with silver organza lace. It shimmered in the light as if constantly moving. 'I've never seen anything as lovely, even in a French fashion plate.' She held it against her body and twirled with delight. 'I'll wear it tomorrow to the masquerade ball to celebrate Lord Latimer's majority.'

Mrs Leigh grasped her hand. 'Oh, this is exciting. I'm delighted you have such an auspicious occasion to wear it.'

'Yes, I'm going as the Fairy Queen. How better to impersonate such a magical creature.'

'It's a masquerade?' her mother enquired, an excited expression on her face. When Angelica nodded, she continued, 'I have just the thing. An exquisite Venetian mask I bought from this special *modiste* in the Rue Saint-Honoré.' She dashed upstairs again and came down with a navy-blue silk mask embellished with paste jewels on the temples and cheekbones and a cockade of silver feathers on one eyebrow.

'Oh Mama! That just sets the look perfectly.' Angelica kissed her mother's cheek and took Mr Breville's hand. 'Thank you both for such lovely presents. My friend, Miss Fitzjames, and I will be leaving with our maids tomorrow afternoon. I hope you are happy, Mr Breville, that I've asked Robert if he will harness your team of four to the fast chaise. We will return the following day.'

'Of course, my dear. What is mine is yours.' He bowed with a benign smile.

Angelica looked down again at the evening gown she still had clasped to her bosom. She knew she would draw all eyes in this sparkling dress and it would be all the more imperative to protect her identity. This elegant mask would do much to disguise her face.

There was a knock and Martin entered with a letter on his silver salver. He bowed elaborately and proffered it to Angelica. It was written in a childish hand and she smiled. Martin straightened up and said, 'The Asprey footman is waiting in the hall, Miss Angelica. Is there a reply?'

She opened it and read a letter written in various coloured inks, her name surrounded by a drawing of a bower of forget-me-nots.

Dear Miss Leigh,

 I miss you So Much. The house is Awful Dull without you and Papa is back to Silence and Work with his Breakfast. Miss Stafford has some errands to run in Bond Street and said, if You agreed, I could visit for an Hour tomorrow afternoon. So hopeful I can see you.

 Your Friend, Elinor

Angelica smiled and said, 'Martin, thank you. Please tell the messenger that one hour after noon would suit me well.'

'Who is this, dearest?' Her mother's face was full of curiosity.

'It's Lord Latimer's cousin. A clever charming girl I've grown to know and like.' This was gratifying news to her mother. The more her daughter was courted and embraced by Lord Latimer's family the better. Angelica turned for the door. 'Mary and I must get my clothes ready for the party and prepare our packing.'

She walked up the stairs, suddenly weary and with a sense of foreboding she could not quite place. As she entered her room and lay down on the bed she heard the clock in the hall chime three times, and her hand clutched her throat. This was the hour Lord Rackham expected her. This was the hour when she would have chosen her father's safety over her own happiness. Her visceral recoil from such a bargain did not quieten the sense of guilt that had she been a true daughter, then filial love and duty would have propelled her into Lord Rackham's arms. Angelica thought of the new production planned for the theatre, in which her part as the heroine, Amanthis, was held up as the model of female virtue. But that moral probity depended on self-sacrifice, something Angelica was not prepared to do.

She lay on her bed thinking of how her contempt for Lord Rackham's offer would rouse a vengeful rage in his breast; gripped with sudden fear, she was desperate to know if her father had managed to escape these shores. She recalled the despairing words in the script she had just learnt and would have to utter on stage as the young heroine realised the personal cost of her bargain:

Terrible – what have I done? What promised? – Oh, Heaven! I am sinking under a weight of misery – a chilliness seizes me – my strength is nearly gone.

Yet shame had meant she had not confided to anyone, except Mr Asprey, the humiliating bargain she had been offered. Nothing could have made her feel more keenly how far she was from being accepted by the highest society in which Lord Latimer, his mother, Dante Locke and Mr Asprey belonged. Lord Rackham's offer would never even have been whispered to a woman of their class and the fact he was so brazen underlined the degraded status in which her profession was held, in which she was held. This thought filled her with a sense of hopelessness.

But for what did she hope? Angelica clasped her hands together and sent an unspoken prayer that her father had evaded the excise men and was already at sea. She added a prayer for love and acceptance for herself, but it was Mr Asprey's dark austere face rather than Lord Latimer's handsome, mischievous one, that arrived in her mind's eye. Like young Elinor, Angelica prided herself on knowing what was best for others, but was quite confounded by the powerful emotions at play in her own heart.

She drifted off to sleep and was woken by Mary, shaking her shoulder and saying with some urgency, 'Miss Angelica, Lord Latimer and Mr Locke are downstairs, in the library. Will you see them?' Angelica rose from her bed in a hurry, tidied her hair as best she could, and ran down the stairs. She entered the library to be confronted by a tableau of bored young blades, leaning on either side of the mantlepiece in elegant disarray. Martin hurried Mary in as chaperone behind her.

'Ah, Miss Leigh, our apologies for dropping by uninvited.' Charles Latimer took her proffered hand and bowed.

Dante Locke said with a rueful expression, 'I told Charlie this was not the thing to do. Spring ourselves on you uninvited. More than a trifle *infra dig*, I thought.'

'Dammit, Dante, 'tis not like you to be so stuffy. I wanted a few words with Miss Leigh before we meet again at the ball tomorrow.'

'May I call for some refreshments?'

'Thank you, but this whisky will do well enough.' Lord Latimer gestured to the decanter and glasses on the console table. With a nod from Angelica he poured out a glass for himself and his friend. 'My formidable mama is snuffling the air like a bloodhound, I'm afraid. She's suspicious that I'll smuggle you, or any number of unsuitable inamoratas, into the ball so Dante is going to pay you more court than I may.' He took a gulp of liquor. 'I hope, Miss Leigh, you'll appreciate this is just a politic design. I'll manage to snatch at least two dances with you without alerting the old termagant.' He gave a mirthless laugh.

Angelica was rather taken aback at being lumped together in his speech with other 'unsuitable inamoratas' but she knew Lord Latimer spoke some-times with little thought. She smiled equably. 'Well, Miss Fitzjames and I are travelling together tomorrow afternoon, so we'll see you both there. I shall be delighted to dance with Mr Locke, if he can bear to be monopo-lised by me.'

Mr Locke bowed low. 'I shall be honoured to partner you. You will know me as the Pierrot in blue. My tailor has excelled himself.'

Angelica laughed. 'I'll be the Fairy Queen. With Lord Latimer as Harlequin and Miss Fitzjames as Columbine, we'll be a veritable *commedia dell'arte*; perhaps we can entertain the company?' She then grasped his lord-ship's hand. 'I trust no one will recognise me, Lord Latimer. I could not bear to be shamed by your mama or bring trouble down on your head.'

'Oh, Mama is already wont to ring a peal over me for every transgression. You are not to fear. Dante and I and Miss Fitzjames will be there to protect you.' He was light-hearted. 'After all, it's my party tomorrow and for once I can insist on having my way.' He led Angelica to the window, away from the corner where Mary sat with some darning, and in a low voice enquired, 'I suppose no news of your father?'

Angelica turned anxious eyes to meet his face. 'No. I wouldn't expect to hear until tomorrow. But I am concerned.'

'What kind of heinous crime, I wonder, could Mr Crowe have committed that the shades of Newgate threaten after all these years?'

Angelica found his bluntness distressing but could only agree this was an underlying fear of hers too. 'Perhaps his debt was to some noble personage who is disinclined to mercy?'

'But you can put your mind at ease, Miss Leigh. Any enterprise involving my uncle and his secretary stands the best chance of success. Individually they're impressive, together they're invincible.'

Angelica gave a wan smile. 'I so hope you're right.' They walked back into the centre of the room where Dante Locke was inscribing in a note-book the latest couplets that had come to mind.

'Come on, Dante, time to leave Miss Leigh in peace.' Lord Latimer slapped his friend on the shoulder.

Angelica walked with them to the door. 'I have your niece visiting with Miss Stafford tomorrow,' she said with a smile.

'She barely stops chattering about you, you know.' Lord Latimer tossed the words over his shoulder as he turned, and with Dante Locke, ran down the front steps into the Square.

* * *

Angelica spent the following morning with her mother. Amabel Leigh was in the highest spirits showing her daughter all the treasures she had gleaned from the Parisian modistes and other grateful shopkeepers keen to see the tourists return to the city. As she twirled in an ermine-lined pelisse of silver-grey velvet, Angelica watched her from the bed, troubled by every kind of question.

Martin and Robert, the groom, had struggled up the stairs with the brass-bound chest left in the hall by her father. When the men had gone, Amabel opened it and they both gasped at the sight of so many gold coins; running them through their hands made it seem truly like they had stumbled upon pirate's treasure. 'Mama, how did my father earn his living and why is there still a warrant out for his arrest?'

Amabel did not welcome any questioning of her past. 'I never asked much. I knew he owed people money and possibly robbed people too, but you see, Angelica, I was so grateful to him for picking me off the streets and giving me a home. And then you came along and were my only care.'

'Do you think we can believe that these gold coins truly are his profits from his club?'

'Who knows? But he always had a way about him so I wouldn't be surprised if he's made a success of something that demanded a certain braggadocio and flair.'

'Oh Mama, I'm so afraid of what we don't know about him.' Angelica's head sank under the weight of anxiety. 'I am so ashamed to have implicated a good man in his nefarious deeds.' She looked up to search her mother's face, hoping for some further elucidation, then expostulated, 'And we still don't know if he is safely on his way to France!'

'He has the luck of the devil, my dear, and his welfare is not your responsibility.'

'But what if I could have done more to save him?'

Amabel Leigh had cast off the beautiful fur-lined pelisse and slipped into a military-style spencer with plush burgundy tassels that became her wonderfully well. She grasped her daughter's hand and her eyes turned gimlet sharp. 'What do you mean, Angelica? What more could you have done?'

Angelica turned away. She could not even confide in her mother the shameful bargain offered her by Lord Rackham, in part because she wondered if her immediate dismissal of it was due to some excess of pride in herself. The thought of where her duty lay continued to trouble her.

There was something else she had not told her mother which concerned her too. 'Mama, did you ever meet my father's mother?'

'No. Why?'

'Well, he gave me a very beautiful necklace he said had belonged to her.'

'That's quite possible, my dear. I believe he came from Irish gentry stock. A family with land near Cork.' Angelica was unhappy that she had omitted to tell her mother details while being so critical of her for the same omissions. Somehow Prosper Crowe, or Peter Crowley, or whoever he was, seemed to contaminate others with his secrecies and lies. And what about Mr Asprey and his probity? Her creeping sense of anxiety and shame suffused everything.

'Oh Mama, everything he touches he threatens to spoil.' Her voice was despairing.

'You see why we were better off without him,' her mother responded with some satisfaction.

Angelica turned away. 'I must go and prepare for tonight's ball. Miss Elinor Asprey is dropping in for an hour or so.'

* * *

There was a knock on the door which was opened by Martin to find Miss Stafford and Elinor Asprey, dressed in a blue dress with a ruffled collar under a matching pelisse, and a jaunty straw bonnet tied haphazardly over her brown curls. 'Good afternoon, ladies.' Martin, in full theatrical make-up, was delighted to welcome to his domain this handsome woman and bright-faced child. He bowed low.

Angelica came running down the stairs to greet them. 'Good afternoon, Miss Stafford. And Miss Elinor, what a pleasure to see you.' She took their hands. 'May I offer you some tea to drink?'

Miss Stafford smiled and shook her head. 'I've an appointment at two, so cannot stay. But, Elinor, I'll be back to pick you up in an hour.' Her charge was watching Martin and had her hand over her mouth, stifling a giggle. Appreciative of any audience, Martin was practising his Irish jig down the corridor to the kitchens, his feet flashing as he danced away and then back carrying a glass of lemonade, perfectly still, on a tray.

He bowed theatrically and placed it on the hall table then offered to take Miss Asprey's pelisse. 'Thank you, sir.' She bobbed a quick curtsey.

'Come upstairs, Miss Elinor. Mary's helping me dress.' Angelica led the way with Elinor beside her and Martin following with the tray.

As they passed, Mrs Leigh bustled out of the drawing room and Elinor was introduced to her. Angelica's mother was still euphoric from her travels and was at her most effusive. Taking the girl's hand she led her into the room, picked up a handful of French bon-bons and slipped them into Miss Asprey's pocket, then kissed her on the forehead. 'You'll be a beauty when you're grown.'

When Elinor was shown into Angelica's bed chamber she was ushered to the window seat and Martin proffered the glass of lemonade with a flourish. She bowed her head in thanks. Angelica sat at her dressing table. 'Well, how are you, Miss Elinor?' She cocked an amused eyebrow as Mary started to brush out her long hair.

'I'm missing you, and Mary too.' The girl took a sip of her drink. 'Your house is so much more fun than mine.'

'When I stayed with you I thought your house was so peaceful and secure. You see, we all want the opposite of what we have.' Angelica had stood up so Mary could remove her day dress. She stood in her chemise with her pretty French stays laced over the bodice.

'Miss Leigh, are you getting dressed for Cousin Charlie's ball tonight?'

'I am, but it's a secret between us. I can only go because I'm going in disguise.' Angelica gave the girl a mischievous smile.

'I don't think Papa is going. Lady Linus certainly is not. I heard her tell Miss Stafford she disapproves of the behaviour encouraged by the wearing of masks. People thinking themselves anonymous and free from censure leads to all kinds of wickedness.'

'So Mr Asprey trusts his sister and nephew to treat his house well in his absence?' Angelica's voice was teasing but disappointment made her heart lose some of its buoyancy. She heard the clock on the Grosvenor Chapel strike two and shivered at the passage of time. How fervently she hoped that Mr Digby had been successful in the escape plan for her rascally father.

Her anxious reverie was broken by Elinor's voice. 'Miss Leigh, what costume are you wearing tonight?' Angelica turned to meet her candid gaze.

'I shall be the Fairy Queen wearing a fairy dress brought back from Paris by my mama.' Mary had brought it out from the dressing room and in the afternoon sun it seemed to dance, a smoky blue with scintillas of silvery light.

The girl sighed. 'Oh, that's beautiful. You shall be the belle of them all.'

Mary slipped the gown over her mistress's head and Angelica stood before them transfigured. She marvelled at how a beautifully made dress could make you feel so alluring and, judging by the expressions on the faces of the two young women in the room, transform your appearance too. After a moment, Mary became businesslike again. 'Now, sit down, Miss Angelica. I must disguise your hair and pin it in a style that suits.'

Elinor Asprey had finished her lemonade and walked to stand beside Mary to watch her dressing Angelica's hair with blue powder. 'You will look like a creature from a fairy world.' The young girl seemed transfixed. 'Lady Linus says that disguise is the work of the devil. What can she mean? When you are acting a part, Miss Leigh, you are pretending to be someone else, are you not?'

Angelica met her eyes in the looking-glass. Her question had been serious and needed a considered reply. 'Yes, that's true. But pretending to be other than you are to entertain is very different perhaps from what Lady Linus may dislike. Have you spoken to Miss Stafford? Might she suggest Lady Linus is referring to Lucifer, disguising himself as the serpent in the Garden of Eden?'

'I think Lady Linus is a serpent disguising herself as a good woman in order to marry my father.' The girl's face in the mirror had turned mulish.

Angelica swivelled in her seat to face her. 'Elinor! That's a very disobliging thing to say. Why so?'

The young girl hung her head. 'I'm sorry, Miss Leigh. That was not kind but it's just that she's affectionate and helpful when she's with him. But when he's not there she's so prosy and opinionated in her fancied judgement. She disapproves of so much that is fun.'

Angelica took her hand. 'Are you very upset about the idea of your father marrying her?'

'Yes. I will have to run away if she comes to live in our house.'

'Oh, Miss Elinor, I do understand. It all looks so bleak when you feel you have no sway over your own life. But you must trust your father to know what's right for him, and for you too. Have you spoken to him at all about your worries?'

'No. He's working so hard I barely see him. When you were living with us, I sometimes heard him laugh. I even heard him whistling while he was getting dressed one morning. All this has gone. Now it's only frowns and silence.'

'He's trying to shepherd very difficult reforms through Parliament, you know. He might just be burdened with that. Things will get better.'

Elinor threw her arms around Angelica and buried her face in the bodice of her beautiful dress, muttering, 'I wish you'd marry him, Miss Leigh. You'd make us all so happy.'

Angelica was shocked. She lifted the girl's face and met those troubled blue eyes. 'Come now, my dear. You know your father's reputation is of utmost importance in his work. I'm afraid as an actress I'm not an ideal wife for him. Your father cannot afford to give his enemies ammunition to use against him.'

Elinor Asprey's head drooped and a tear splashed onto Angelica's hand. Her heart was touched by this lonely, sensitive girl. 'You and I will always be friends and you can come and see me any time, you know. I'm sure your father would never object to that.'

'If he marries Lady Linus I want to come and live with you.' Elinor's voice had become determined.

'Let's see what happens. I'm sure it won't be as bad as you imagine.' But Angelica found her heart clutched by the thought of Mr Asprey marrying. Why? she wondered, when all good sense suggested he could not be hers. She was shocked by the possessiveness that overbore all her pragmatic knowledge of how the world was ordered. If she could not marry him, she did not want him marrying anyone else. She felt her face flush with shame and confusion at the selfish thought.

Mary had been working on Angelica's hair and had plaited and pinned it into a romantic confection of waves and curls, her natural bright colour obscured beneath an ethereal bluish tint. 'You do, in fact, look a picture, Miss Angelica.' Mary stood back and admired her mistress and her own handiwork.

Elinor gasped, her eyes wide. 'You look like a goddess from the night sky,' the young girl said, suddenly overcome with shyness. 'How can anyone be so beautiful?'

For the first time, Angelica looked closely at herself in the mirror and did not recognise the vision gazing back at her. The dress was cut low over her pale breasts, the neckline edged in silver filigree lace. The blue-grey satin fell from a high waist and the overlay of silver gauzy lace created an illusion of shifting starlight. The Parisian modistes had perfected a way of slightly stiffening the hem so it stood out from her ankles and rippled when she moved. Angelica was delighted with her reflection and gratified by how her blue-tinged hair obscured her identity. She walked through to the dressing room and picked up the Venetian mask, put it on and re-entered the room. Elinor clapped and laughed at the sight of her. Angelica was gratified that no one at the Duchess of Arlington's party would recognise her, of that she was sure.

They heard the knock on the front door and Martin's voice greeting Miss Stafford. Elinor rose reluctantly from her perch on the window seat and Angelica removed her mask to accompany her down the stairs to her governess.

Looking up from the hall, Miss Stafford's serene face also registered a look of wonder at the ethereal vision that led her charge down the stairs. 'Miss Leigh!' she said with a gasp. 'You look wondrous. I would not have recognised you.'

Angelica came forward and took her hand. 'It has been so good to see you and Miss Elinor again. Thank you for accompanying her. We can spend longer together next time when we both have more time.'

The girl shyly gave Angelica a quick hug. 'Don't crush that lovely dress, my dear,' Miss Stafford said with concern.

'It doesn't matter. I think the silver thread in it makes it quite robust.' Angelica was reassuring as she hugged the child back.

'Enjoy the ball, Miss Leigh,' Elinor Asprey said and Angelica put her finger to her lips with a mischievous wink.

* * *

It was mid-afternoon when Angelica threw on her cloak to protect her striking dress and hide her blue hair, and she and Mary were handed into Mr Breville's best chaise. They were staying the night at Cloudberry Court and leaving before the household was up the following morning. Their portmanteaus of luggage had been stowed at the back by Robert, now sitting on the box beside the coachman who set the horses' heads north, towards Grosvenor Square. They entered through Charles Street and the grand Square with its gardens opened out in front of them. The trees in full leaf cast a fitful shade over the neat flower beds already bright with calendula and geranium.

This was the first time that Angelica had seen the Fitzjames mansion that had been restored to her friend after the mysterious gambler had extracted it from Lord Fulsham's grasp. The house was the central one on the east side, with pillars above the ground floor extending to the attics. As the carriage drew up outside the grand portico, Angelica gazed out on the embodiment of the difference between their stations in life. She could never own a house like this with all the privilege that accompanied it and for the first time realised how much freedom wealth brought in its train. Perhaps, due to her intervention and the reckless gamble of Mr Asprey – she felt sure now it *was* him – Miss Fitzjames could live her life as she chose. With an uncharacteristic wistfulness, Angelica realised such precious liberty could not be hers.

Robert knocked on the door and Miss Fitzjames emerged with her maid carrying a portmanteau. She waved, and descended the steps wearing her cloak, with just a glimpse of a floaty pale dress which Angelica surmised was her costume as Columbine. Both young women were handed in, with Isobel sitting beside Angelica, their maids on the seat opposite with their backs to the horses.

'Good afternoon, Miss Angelica.' Miss Fitzjames took her hand. 'You look beautiful indeed.' The front of Angelica's cloak had opened to reveal the skirt of the dress and she had removed her hood for the journey so her hair was displayed in all its silvery-blue intricacy.

Isobel Fitzjames had also thrown back her hood and her glossy brown hair was ringleted and curled in a charming confection of controlled disarray. She opened her cloak and revealed the pretty small bodice embroidered with traceries of green vine and lilac columbine flowers interspersed with embroidered butterflies and bees.

'Your gown is lovely too. What an adventure this will be. But you do know, Miss Isobel, my identity cannot be revealed to anyone.'

Her friend was wide-eyed. Her sensibility was such that the idea of a beautiful heroine's clandestine entry into the enemy stronghold compelled her imagination with its potential for tragedy. 'You must be so careful, Miss Angelica. Dangers lurk when and where we least expect them.'

Angelica's spirits were more naturally buoyant and she had never thrilled to the idea of the suffering gothic heroine of so many popular novels, nevertheless, since her father had entered her life, a small trickle of unease had become her constant companion. She still did not know if he was safe, neither did she know how much others had been implicated in his unlawful doings.

Isobel Fitzjames looked at Angelica's unadorned neck and décolletage and fingered her own necklace, a festoon of natural pearls with garnets. 'Miss Angelica, does the Fairy Queen wear any jewellery of any kind? If you'd like something of mine, I have a fleur-de-lis of blue topaz that would look very fine with your hair.'

Angelica smiled. 'That's very kind, Miss Isobel. I do have my grandmother's necklace in my reticule. I thought I would only put it on when we arrived.' She extracted the velvet pouch and slipped her fingers in to withdraw a small section of the sparkling river of stones. Isobel's eyes widened and Angelica returned the pouch to her reticule. 'It's the only family heirloom I have and I'm surprised how much it means to me to have something my grandmother loved.'

'Yes indeed. These pearls were my mother's and I feel especially close to her when I wear them.' Angelica noticed how the melancholy settled on her friend's face once more. 'I miss her so much, you see. It's clear I will never stop missing her. Now I'm orphaned it is my mother's loss I feel most keenly.'

Angelica put her hand on her arm in sisterly feeling. Much as her own mother's attitudes and priorities grated, she knew that she always had someone who would protect her against any detractor. Even the advent of her father, trailing clouds of deceit and danger as he did, meant Angelica did not feel quite so alone in the world.

Both young women looked out of the window to see the road to Richmond winding off between the trees on their right. The comfortable sway of the coach had sent both of their maids to sleep. In about an hour they would arrive at Cloudberry Court and the thought made Angelica's heart start to beat a little faster. Mary and Isobel Fitzjames's maid had fallen asleep, lulled by the sway of the luxurious coach on its well-oiled springs. Isobel grasped Angelica's hand, a shadow of unease clouding her face. 'Forgive my presumption, but you once told me you thought Lord Latimer did not really care for you as he professed to do. Is this your opinion still?'

Angelica was surprised by the question, and her friend's expression of anxiety and embarrassment gave her pause for thought. She attempted to answer her honestly. 'Well, I used to think that it was just a young man's passing fancy, but I have been gratified by how enduring and loyal his attentions have proved to be.'

They both fell silent with their own thoughts, then Isobel Fitzjames, still troubled, said shyly, 'I think Lord Latimer is a fine and honest gentleman. More admirable than anyone I have ever met. And I will be forever grateful for the part he played in ensuring my inheritance returned to me.'

Angelica turned her great green eyes to meet her friend's flushed face. 'Do you know who challenged Lord Fulsham then?'

'No, not for certain. But Lord Latimer knows who my benefactor is and I'm sure it's his intervention which caused the miracle to happen.' Angelica felt a strange longing to talk to Mr Asprey again as, however certain she felt of his involvement, she so wished for confirmation. Indeed she found it hard to contemplate how much she had imposed on this proud and private man, how much she owed him. She recognised her own pride too. She had achieved a certain control over her life but was now disconcerted at how much her heart seemed to be focussed on the last man she would have chosen to love, or should have chosen to love. But this was one secret she had to keep from the world and certainly from Ivor Asprey himself.

Sitting beside her friend, Angelica realised that Isobel Fitzjames had feelings for Lord Latimer that perhaps she did not. Certainly she found his attraction to her exciting and her youthful spirit responded to his, but he and Dante Locke were more like the brothers for whom she had longed. She took her friend's hand and lowered her voice so not to wake the maids, 'Miss Isobel, I am pleased if you and Lord Latimer have grown close. I have no claims on him. He is indeed a fine young man, and you are both the best of friends to me.' There were sudden tears in Miss Fitzjames's eyes as she looked away but her hand sought Angelica's and gave it a light squeeze of thanks.

Confused as her feelings were, Angelica knew she could not stand in the way of her friend's happiness but that did not prevent a small knot of envy at how settled Isobel Fitzjames's life had unexpectedly become with her inheritance restored to her and the chance of to unite herself with one of the great ducal families of England, with all the advantages of title and estates.

The days were lengthening into high summer and there were still streaks of light in the sky as the Breville coach joined the stream of carriages full of brightly plumed guests that turned off the main road and into the drive of Cloudberry Court. Trundling down through an avenue of large spreading chestnut trees, their chaise turned a corner and the house was revealed at last. Angelica could not suppress a gasp.

Before them was a Palladian mansion, stone-built, impressive, regular in its tall windows, twenty across, with alternating pilasters. Angelica and Isobel Fitzjames clasped each other's hands in excited anticipation. Angelica recovered her grandmother's necklace and asked her friend to attach the clasp at the back of her neck. The young woman then sat back and admired the sight. 'Are those diamonds? They set your gown and your skin off to perfection. You will be the beauty of the night.' Both women put on their long satin gloves and their masks, and were handed out of the carriage by Robert. They joined the crowd of fellow bucks and beauties, none of whom they recognised in their costumes and masks, and were swept forward on an excited, chattering tide of guests.

As the young women entered through the great double doors, Angelica was overwhelmed by the splendour that greeted her. Awash with candle-light from thousands of candles in chandeliers and candelabra, the wide hallway led to the ballroom. This extended across the back of the house with a series of arched doors to the orangery, with the parterre and gardens beyond. The strains of an orchestra drifted on the air, mingling with the sounds of chatter and laughter.

Mary and the Fitzjames maid had remained in the coach as it was driven round to the mews and stables on the far side of the house and here the luggage was unloaded and a housekeeper greeted them to show them to their mistresses' allotted rooms. Meanwhile in the grand hall Angelica and Isobel relinquished their cloaks to the footman and were suddenly revealed in all their glory. Each young woman gazed with admiration at the other.

'Miss Isobel, you are a vision of pastoral beauty. Like a painting by Fragonard, with just a swing needed to complete the fantasy.' Angelica laughed in appreciation of what a picture her friend presented.

Isobel Fitzjames was naturally less expressive but even she let out a little cry of delight at the sight of Angelica in her Parisian gown of silvery, starry gauze over smoky blue satin, the magnificent necklace sparkling at her throat, and the Venetian mask a work of art in itself. Angelica caught sight of herself in the vast rococo looking-glass that lined one wall of the hall and she could hardly believe the image of romance and seduction that confronted her. Most gratifying of all, she knew that no one would recognise her for the flame-haired actress who, as Ophelia, had taken the theatre world by storm. She glanced around the crowd, hoping to see Lord Latimer or Dante Locke, and instead noticed the formidable Duchess of Arlington standing at the entrance to the ballroom, greeting her guests. She realised she had first to run that particular gauntlet.

The young women moved forward with the swell of the crowd and as they approached their hostess they saw she had not deigned to dress up or don a mask but was wearing a cherry-red evening dress, with the famous Arlington ruby necklace nestling in her ample décolletage. Angelica felt her anxiety rise. She extracted her fan from her reticule as extra protection and, as she was introduced as the Fairy Queen and her companion as Columbine, she fluttered it, trusting in its power of distraction. Both young women bowed in greeting while Lady Arlington's fierce blue eyes appraised them so intently Angelica feared her mask would melt away under that penetrating gaze.

With relief, Angelica moved into the magnificent ballroom and gasped in wonder. The vast ceiling was painted as an evening sky with a rosy sunset suffusing the clouds, fires burned in the five mighty grates and massed candles lit the kaleidoscopic throng of every kind of fantasy and extravagance. A nymph in a dress of silk leaves barely covering her body drifted past, hanging on the arm of a satyr, complete with horns and boots fashioned to look like cloven hooves. Angelica was disconcerted; everyone was disguised and masked and therefore unrecognisable but there was also a sinister sense that their very humanity had been subsumed by something more primitive.

She was longing for a familiar sight to settle her nerves when out of the throng emerged the tall shapely figure of a man she did recognise; Lord Latimer in breeches patterned in harlequin diamonds, his jacket close-fitted and a surprising yellow. His black mask could not obscure his unruly brown hair and glittering, mischievous eyes. Beside him his friend, Mr Locke, cut a differently striking aspect, dressed as he had promised in blue as a Pierrot, in so far as he had a blue floppy ruff, loose pantaloons under one of his tailor's immaculate jackets created not in broadcloth but blue satin. This aberration of his craft, Angelica thought, may well have made the fastidious creator shudder.

So relieved was Angelica to see them she wanted to rush forward to grasp their arms but, aware of the proximity of the Duchess, restrained herself. Lord Latimer took Miss Fitzjames's hand and bowed low while Dante Locke brought Angelica's to his lips with an elegant turn of his wrist. The young women laid their gloved hands on the gentlemen's proffered arms and walked with them to the furthest point of the ballroom.

Here, Lord Latimer turned to Angelica, his face flushed with excitement. 'You are the belle of my ball. Elinor told me privately you would be and she was right. You look astonishing, Miss Leigh. Quite takes my breath away, I hardly feel worthy of you.' Then he turned to her friend. 'And you, my Columbine, how lucky any Harlequin would be to have you in his arms. I hope you will honour me with the first dance?' The orchestra struck up. He smiled and said, 'I have requested we have mostly quadrilles and waltzes, despite Mama's objections, but it's my ball and I'm tired of the reels and cotillions of her youth.'

They made up a set for the opening quadrille. There was excitement in the room as this was a new version of the cotillion of their parents' day and most dancers in the room had been practising the intricate steps for the balls of the new Season. Angelica and Isobel Fitzjames stood opposite Lord Latimer and Dante Locke while two other couples joined them to make up the rectangle formation. The music started and, as they danced into the centre in pairs to twirl then exchange partners, Angelica found herself dancing opposite a young man dressed as Pan in a revealing pair of gold tights with golden wings on the temples of his mask.

When it came to the twirl, he slipped his arm insistently around her waist, pulling her closer to his body than propriety allowed. He swung her around and then released her rather late so she had to skip to her next position facing Lord Latimer to repeat the same movement, but in a more decorous way. The young Pan's eyes were on Angelica throughout and it made her uneasy. When the music came to a flourishing halt the couples wandered over to an adjoining room where refreshments were available. Lord Latimer and Mr Locke went in search of ratafia and lemonade for the women, ale for themselves.

Angelica met Isobel Fitzjames's eyes and they laughed. 'This is the most beautiful ball I have ever been to,' her friend was breathless.

Angelica's enthusiasm was more guarded. 'It's only the second I've attended and it's much grander than the first. I don't know that I care for the fact everyone is anonymous, except to their intimates. It makes me nervous.' The clandestine nature of her own presence added to her unease.

'I know. I saw that young Pan paying you too much attention. Could he have recognised you?' Isobel Fitzjames looked across at Angelica. 'I thought it presumptuous of him. You look far too imperious and beautiful for any young whippersnapper to think he had a chance of intimacy.'

Angelica glanced at her, surprised at such emphatic talk. Perhaps her usual diffidence was retreating as she realised just what power she held in her hands, now she was independently wealthy and beholden to no one. The men returned with their drinks and Lord Latimer was congratulated on the excellence of the orchestra and the beauty of the house. 'Ah, as you know, the house, sadly, is not mine. The Arlington pile is in the distant wilds of Derbyshire and is dark and ruinously ancient with none of the conveniences of Uncle Ivor's luxurious lair.'

'Is he here?' Angelica heard herself ask the question that was on her mind but she had not meant to voice.

'I think he's working. Anyway, that reproachful puss who, dammit, is determined to become my aunt, thoroughly disapproves of such licentiousness.' He then looked to where his mother was holding court at the far side of the room. Despite being such a stickler for propriety, the Duchess, with her weakness for the wild masquerade balls of her youth, had not needed too much persuasion to host this one. Lord Latimer took his friend's arm. 'Talking of a different kind of termagant, I have to pay respects to Mama and dance with her friend's wall-eyed daughter. Come on, Dante, you can offer your respects to the Duchess and then we're free for the night.' They set off together. The harlequin lord said over his shoulder, 'We'll be back for the dance after that. Let's hope it's a waltz.'

At that moment a young man dressed as a hussar asked Isobel Fitz-james if she would join the reel that was about to start. She looked across at Angelica who smiled and said, 'I'm happy to sit this one out.' She turned her back on the merry throng of dancers and gazed out on the dark garden lit by flaming torches making little inroad into the inky night. Her thoughts were with her father, wondering if he was safe but also straying to the absent honourable Member of Parliament who unexpectedly had become the key to so much in her life.

Angelica felt a hand on her elbow. 'Do I know you, oh beauteous queen?' Startled, she turned. Already tense, she shuddered at finding the winged mask of Pan leaning in towards her face and could smell the ale heavy on his breath.

She pulled her arm away. 'No, sir, you must be mistaken.'

'Come now, madam, I know you're Lady Fenton and we know each other very well indeed. Don't trifle with me.'

Angelica recognised the name of a famous aristocratic coquette and she was suddenly angered at the presumption of the young man. She had suffered as an actress from just this kind of *lèse-majesté* from privileged young men who thought any woman should be grateful for their attentions. She whirled round to face him. 'Sir, I am not Lady Fenton and, even should I be, I think she and I deserve more respect than you are currently displaying. You are a gentleman after all.'

He leaned closer and there was an air of menace in his stance. Angelica noticed his dark eyes were bloodshot and his hair more dishevelled than fashion dictated. She hoped he would just go away. He was obviously in his cups and with his face so close to hers he hissed, his noisome breath assaulting her with spittle, 'You may not be Lady Fenton, but you are no better than that high-flyin' harlot.' He grasped her wrist. 'Dressed like that you have little cause for complaint if you attract attention from a red-blooded blade like me. Flaunting your beauty comes at a price.' He bent his head as if to kiss her and quick as a flash her other hand flew up to slap him. He blazed, 'God damn you!' and with that profanity turned and stalked off, a slightly ridiculous figure in his sagging gold tights.

Angelica was shaken by the encounter. She was reluctant to think that perhaps Lady Linus had a point about masquerades inviting licentious behaviour. She certainly had long thought that beauty was both a gift and a curse. She walked from the ballroom into the orangery where the scent of orange blossom was thrilling. Some of the foreboding she had felt dispersed in the scented air. Taking deep breaths restored her spirits.

She stretched up to touch a small orange hanging just beyond her fingertips and saw a hand from behind her reach up to pull the branch closer. She turned, her heart speeding. Was this another importuning young man? With a sob of relief she looked up into the face of Ivor Asprey. He was dressed in a dark coat but had changed his trousers for pale knee breeches in deference to the formality of the ball, and had donned a plain black mask, but his stature and intense blue eyes were unmistakeable to her. Excitement radiated outwards from her heart.

'Oh, Mr Asprey! I'm so pleased to see you.' She had this overwhelming desire to be enclosed in his arms but with more decorum grasped his hand.

'I am gratified that my presence causes you such pleasure, Miss Leigh. I came especially to give you some news.'

'Yes, yes! I've been on tenterhooks since leaving your office two days ago.'

'This is a secret only you and I can know.' He paused for the import to sink in. 'I am pleased to tell you your father has safely disembarked in France.' A sense of relief so overcame her she felt her knees buckle. He caught her by both elbows and led her to a bench. 'Sit here and restore yourself. I know what a strain this must have been for you.'

'Oh, I have been much concerned. And guilty that I have implicated you too in something so dangerous.'

Ivor Asprey sat beside her. 'We will not speak of it again. I have many enemies in Parliament who are against my reforms and I do not want to give them any ammunition.' He had crossed his legs and looked down at his dancing shoes. 'But know this, Miss Leigh, I would do anything to help you and you are never to hesitate in coming to me should the occasion arise.' He spoke in a low voice that was nevertheless emphatic with feeling.

Angelica looked at him, so upright and honourable and yet offering his help to her in any enterprise and she was pierced to the heart. In that moment she had the confirmation she'd sought; it was he who had risked his own reputation and fortune to gamble against Lord Fulsham, because she had asked him. It was he who had saved her father, because she had asked him. Gratitude and love washed over her in a wave that threatened to sink her. She put her gloved hand on his; they sat there saying nothing but feeling everything.

Angelica turned to him, wishing she could tear off their masks and see each other's faces free of disguise. But she could not risk the exposure, for his sake and her own. Shyly she asked, 'How did you recognise me? I thought I was proof against anyone's detection.'

In a voice that started light and amused then grew more emotional, he said, 'Miss Leigh, I'd know you anywhere. You could shear off your hair, grime your face with cinders and tear your dress to rags, I would still know it was you.'

Angelica had been holding her breath in disbelief and hope. Her heart was beating out its rhythm, 'Can this be? Can this be?' her mind whirling. *Is this how it's always been from the moment I first saw him, imperious in my dressing room? So different from the men who usually congregated there, supplicants for my favours?*

He was watching her and she barely managed to say, 'How so, Mr Asprey?'

He took both her hands and turned to face her. 'By those witching green eyes, and the particular way you walk. You forget I've had to endure

two performances of *Hamlet* when most of your delectable self is revealed
to your audience.' His smile had some of the roguery of his reckless youth.

This broke the tension between them. 'Just when I thought you were
being uncharacteristically charming, you remind me of being dishabille on
stage.' She laughed.

Then the thought of her disreputable profession quelled her ecstatic
spirit, how it disqualified her from the life of acceptance and belonging for
which she had begun to yearn. Her head sank with recognition of society's
prescriptions.

Sensing Angelica's loss of heart, Mr Asprey put a finger under her chin and
lifted her face. 'You are so lovely, even with that ridiculous blue hair. I'm very
close to breaking all the rules of gentlemanly etiquette and kissing you, Miss
Leigh.' He closed his eyes as if summoning his strength of resistance. 'Knowing
you has broken the constraints on my wilder self, but if I'm to get anything
done in this world I have to rein in that undisciplined youth.' He smiled and in
a businesslike manner took Angelica's hand and tucked it into his arm. 'Come,
I think we shouldn't give any cause for gossip. Would you honour me by being
my partner in the next dance? I think I can hear the strains of a waltz.'

They emerged from the orangery to the dazzling show of dancers
pairing off and readying for the first waltz of the evening. This was still a
new and daring dance and the excitement in the room was palpable. Angelica's heart was hammering so hard she feared her whole body vibrated. Mr
Asprey took her in his arms as the music swung into the one-two-three,
one-two-three. Although there was the required gap between their bodies
as they danced in a straight line, when he led her into a turn he pulled her
closer to his hip so that they moved fluidly as one. It was thrilling to feel his
warmth radiating through her dress, the strength of his shoulders rippling
under her hand, the muscle in his waist contracting as he whirled her into
a spin; Angelica feared she would swoon if his arms were not holding her
close. They did not speak. She glanced up into his face and met his blue
eyes that had softened and deepened, his pupils large and black.

As the music came to an end they stood for a moment, unwilling to
separate. He dropped his head and whispered in her ear, 'You so enchant
my senses, Miss Leigh, you make me reckless. You are my nephew's

intended inamorata and not mine to claim.' They both looked across at where Dante Locke and Lord Latimer were laughing with Miss Fitzjames.

'I think his fever for me may have passed,' Angelica said without emotion. She realised now how Mary had been trying to warn her about the growing closeness between her two friends. 'While I was ill, he and Miss Fitzjames were united in concern and saw much of each other.'

'And how do you feel about that, Miss Leigh?'

'I have never really succumbed to that conceit. I just objected to being told by you and his mother that I was not worthy to be his bride.'

'You are a proud and ardent woman. When I first met you and saw your spirit it was the beginning of my restless sleep.'

'While you have had the temerity to ask me about my romantic life, may I ask you about Lady Linus?'

His face clouded. 'I have been remiss. Working such long hours, I didn't address her belief that she mattered more to me than she did. This is my fault and guilt.'

'Your daughter told me she would run away from home if you married her.'

He laughed. 'And I suppose she was determined I should marry you?'

'That might have been part of her plan.' Angelica coloured. 'Of course I told her that being an actress quite disqualified me.'

'I don't think that's for you to decide, Miss Leigh.' Mr Asprey surreptitiously slipped off her glove and kissed the naked palm of her hand.

This caught Angelica quite unawares. He had done it before with the same electrifying effect. She shivered with a sharp intake of breath. 'Mr Asprey!'

'Yes, Miss Leigh?' He looked up with a question in his eyes. 'You must know by now just how dangerous I find your beauty.' Angelica looked away, uncertain if Mr Asprey would only ever offer her an arrangement like Lord Rackham's, or indeed the more benign protection Mr Breville extended to her mother. He was immediately serious again. 'Now I must leave you with your friends while I go and pay court to my sister.'

They walked up to Lord Latimer whose eyes widened at sight of his uncle. 'You're here! I thought you had too much work to do, saving the factory tots from wicked mill-owners. But you couldn't keep away from a good party, could you, Uncle?'

The orchestra struck up again and a merry Scottish reel drew everyone back to the dance floor once more. The prancing, leaping, clapping and laughing had become more exaggerated as the night wore on and alcohol lubricated the young men and high spirits loosened the young women's manners and decorum. Angelica was faltering with tiredness after such an emotional evening and admired the tireless energy of the dancers and musicians as they played on into the dawn. Mr Asprey had disappeared to see to some problem in the stables and Mr Locke, Lord Latimer and Isobel Fitzjames went in search of food when Angelica began to think longingly of bed. She turned towards the orangery to await their return when a tall, imposing woman of middle years approached her.

'Madam, wait a moment!' Her voice was peremptory. Angelica turned to be confronted by a woman dressed as Queen Elizabeth in a great lace ruff and an elaborate pearl-embellished mask hiding most of her creased powdery face. Her eyes glittered.

'That's a very fine necklace,' she said in a voice that was accusatory rather than conversational.

Angelica put a hand to her throat. 'I thank you, madam. It's my grand-mother's. I'm very lucky to have it.'

'I don't think luck has much to do with it. Or your grandmother, if it comes to that.' The stranger did not take her eyes off the stones. 'I am certain it is mine.' Her voice rose in indignation. 'Look at the clasp! I think you'll find my initials in emeralds and sapphires.'

Angelica felt panic rise in her throat. This was worse than anything she had feared or even imagined. Her hands flew protectively to cover the neck-lace as she stuttered, 'My father gave it to me. It was his mother's.'

The lady's outraged voice had summoned a small crowd and embold-ened by her audience she put out a hand and in one deft tug wrenched the necklace from Angelica's throat. She held it aloft triumphantly. 'Look! My monogram on the clasp. This was stolen from me at gunpoint on the highway between Newbury and Hungerford some twelve years ago.'

A cold horror crept up Angelica's spine. Had her father lied to her yet again and the necklace was not his to give? An even more heinous thought

assailed her, that her father had been that highwayman, armed and dangerous, a crime that carried the death sentence. Perhaps he was even involved
in a murder? With a cry she extricated herself from the accusing crowd and
ran across the parterre where knots of people were conversing, coquetting
and playing at love. Soon she felt the grass under her feet and the dark
gardens stretched before her, the torches burning low. She could not bear
the shame of being accused of theft; she dare not yet face what this revealed
about her father.

Angelica could not go back into the house. Her friends were eating in
the dining room, Mary was below stairs with the rest of the servants, Mr
Asprey was busy elsewhere and she shuddered at the thought of placing in
his lap once again any further scandal attached to her name. She just
wanted to get home.

Tearing off her mask she ran towards the stables, intent on finding
Robert. He was her trusty groom, discreet and capable. He would help her
now and she could go to ground like a wounded animal and wait for any
hue and cry to pass.

9

THE END OF THE DREAM

The horses had been settled for the night and the sweet scent of hay and their warm flesh greeted her as Angelica entered the yard. Where would she find Robert, she wondered? The Breville carriage was unmistakeable as were the four bays that had pulled it there, standing still and asleep in their stables. 'Robert,' Angelica called softly. 'Robert!'

A tousled head popped out from the loft above the horses. 'Miss Angelica, what're ye doing here?' His head disappeared and he emerged from the back of the stables, tucking his shirt hurriedly into his breeches. 'Miss Angelica. Ye up to snuff, miss?' His honest nut-brown face was wreathed in concern.

'I'm sorry to wake you, Robert, but I have to get home. I wondered if you could saddle me one of Mr Asprey's hacks?'

'No, I could not. Ye can't ride home on these roads. 'Tis madness. A lass alone!' He was so aghast, Angelica felt sorry for causing him such distress. 'I'll take ye back in the carriage then return for Miss Fitzjames and the maids.'

'No, Robert. There isn't time. You know I'm a good horsewoman. It will only take me about four hours.' An inspired thought then came to her. 'And I will travel as a youth. As long as I can borrow a set of your clothes. Would that be possible?'

'Only got me livery. 'Spose ye could have that,' he said reluctantly. 'I'm not a brawny man but they'll still be way too big.'

'I'm sure they'll do. I just need to disguise that I'm a woman then I'll be safe.'

'I don't like it, miss. What to tell the master when he asks me what the devil I was thinking, letting you go?'

'You just say that unless you planted me a facer, knocking me stone cold, there was no way to stop me.'

'Well, Miss Angelica, I'll tell ye this. Ye always were a headstrong lass, ever since you were a slip of a gal.' He disappeared into the stable and returned with his breeches and braided jacket, his boots and a braided top hat.

Angelica had been gazing to the east and pointed out that dawn was not far off. She joined the horses so she could dress in her borrowed livery. It was a struggle to undo the buttons down the back of her ballgown but luckily her stays were French and unlaced at the side.

'Robert, I just need some string for a belt to keep these breeches up, else I'll be an embarrassment to you and myself.' Despite being heartsick she could not but be amused at how she must appear. Her spirits lifted at the thought that she would grasp her destiny once again. When she arrived home she could think what to do next and find her way through the flood of emotions after this one startling and portentous night.

Robert woke Mr Asprey's head groom and asked which mount would be most appropriate to borrow. He pointed out a chestnut horse and said, 'This is Meg. She's a sweet-tempered mare with the stamina for the ride.' Robert saddled her and led her out of the stable.

Angelica had folded up her precious dress along with her chemise and stays, placing her dancing shoes and the Venetian mask in a separate pile. Robert's eyes widened at the sight of his mistress dressed in his oversized livery, the baggy breeches tied with string. His brimmed hat just about hid her hair, still unnaturally blue and coiffed but untidy, with tendrils escaping from the pins. To his eyes she did not look like a groom, not even like a youth, but the livery and hat hid most of the incongruities of her appearance. He offered his hand for Angelica's booted foot then tossed her up into the saddle.

Meg was a handsome mare. Robert relayed the groom's warning, 'She's not a galloper, mind, doesn't care for hard riding but is a reliable and willing hack.'

Angelica felt liberated to be dressed in man's clothes, able to ride astride and travel with little chance of notice. The jacket and breeches were far too big for her but they were warm and as long as she was in the saddle their capaciousness did not matter. She waved at Robert. 'Don't forget to give my clothes and the message to Mary. It's very important you tell her I have had to go home. And please tell Miss Fitzjames and Lord Latimer, so they don't worry.' For some reason she did not want to let Mr Asprey know, so embarrassed was she by the whole debacle happening in his house, within sight of his prideful family.

'I saw Milord and Miss Fitzjames in the garden, miss, and they didn't seem to be worrying about anybody much.' When he saw Angelica's frowning face he regretted his levity. He knew that servants, however bawdy and disrespectful their talk about their masters when they were relaxing with their own, were always discreet when talking to others about their betters. 'Sorry, miss.'

'Oh, don't worry now, Robert,' Angelica said impatiently. 'It's far more important that you deliver my messages. And please give Mary my clothes.' She looked at the lightening sky. 'I think it's just about clear enough to see.'

'Take care, Miss Angelica. The road is well signposted. It's a main thoroughfare all the way to Hyde Park Corner.' In an afterthought he added, 'Do ye want me barker?'

Angelica recoiled. The thought of her father using a pistol to threaten his victims on the highway was terrible enough. She did not want to have anything to do with firearms and violence and vigorously shook her head. Robert put his hand in his pocket and pulled out some coins. 'Take these, miss. Ye'll need them for the tolls.'

'Thank you, Robert, for everything. You have helped me more than you can know.' She saluted him and turned the horse's head towards the east. The air was chilly and the early light hazy and grey, but Angelica felt her spirits lift at the thought of the open road before her and no scandal to follow yet on her heels. She encouraged Meg into a trot as they headed off up the drive.

The avenue of chestnut trees offered a dense shade but their large candelabra of flowers just coming into bloom glowed like foam on the sea. A ghostly barn owl skimmed the parkland on its way home after hunting. Early dawn was the margin between nocturnal animals ready for sleep and those who lived by the light. The newly roused birds were in full-throated song and as Angelica rode on up the hill a small herd of red deer set off towards a copse, startling a leash of hares. To be alone with such wealth of wildlife was balm to her soul. Her tiredness fell away. Meg too seemed energised by the prospect of new horizons and her ears were pricked forward, her nostrils savouring the fresh morning air.

As they approached the road, Angelica was relieved to see the grand wrought iron gates to Cloudberry Court were still open from the previous evening's revelry. They trotted through and joined the intermittent early traffic of lone horsemen, occasional carriages and country carts fully laden with vegetables, firewood or flowers on their way to the city. Meg was an amiable ride. To pace her, Angelica slowed her to a walk as they approached Hampton village green where a few children were already sailing their makeshift boats on the pond and skimming stones before the dame school opened for lessons.

An hour passed fast enough but the light did not brighten much and the threat of rain made the air ominous and heavy. The excitement at the beginning of her journey had given Angelica a surge of energy that was quickly dispersed by her underlying sense of shame and fatigue. As she tired, her mind returned to the humiliation of her necklace and how it changed everything. What a fool she had been to believe anything her father told her. How naïve to think those lovely diamonds could have belonged to her family and could ever have been hers. In this mood of self-reproach Angelica's mind then turned to Mr Asprey. In the thrill of that unexpected intimacy with him she had forgotten for a few hours the social gulf between them, she had believed that happiness with an honourable man she loved would be possible, openly declared rather than secretive and irregular, set up in a house in Albemarle Street. How deluded she had been. Now she faced the fact that such hopes were mere romantic dreams dissolving in the unforgiving light of day. With a bleak pragmatism Angelica knew she had to accept her place as the daughter of a criminal, possibly even a murderer, tainted by blood and outlawed by her profession from the best society. Energy drained from her as her shoulders slumped and she had to fight to keep her eyes from closing in sleep.

* * *

Back at Cloudberry Court, it was past dawn and the ball had come to an end, the musicians and revellers drifting away. The visiting valets and maids, dozing by the great kitchen hearth and in the adjoining servant's parlour, awaited the call from upstairs, from their masters and mistresses in need of help with undressing and getting ready for bed. Mary had been roused from fitful dreams by Robert with Angelica's message. She hurried from the kitchens and by the time she could find Lord Latimer he was so mauled, as she reported back with a snigger, he could barely understand what she was saying. Miss Fitzjames was with him and she grasped that Angelica had not retired to bed early, as they had thought, but been called away. She too was tired and did not question Mary further as to why and how.

The revellers, most befuddled with drink, bade their goodnights and stumbled up the grand staircase to their rooms. The sickle moon still hung in a sky that was pale and grey and threatening rain, but no one in the house was concerned with the view from their windows. Exhaustion could no longer be resisted as the servants barely had time to strip off their masters' and mistresses' ball clothes before pleasure-sated bodies collapsed into bed.

By five o'clock in the morning all the bedroom doors were finally closed, the floorboards ceased creaking and the house settled at last into relative peace. Only one person was still awake. Mr Asprey was in his library reading his favourite poem of Goldsmith's. The mellifluous heroic couplets of *The Traveller* and the poet's humane view of society never failed to settle any tumult in his breast.

Since the death of his wife, grief and guilt had cauterised his heart. In Ivor Asprey's life, work and a concern for the greater good took the place of romantic love, but he did hold his precious daughter close to his heart; for her he would give the world. Having abandoned his youth to the pursuit of risk and pleasure, the unexpected tragedy of Emma's death had meant coquettes like the Countess of Hilperton and worthy women like Lady Linus barely altered his stoical expectations of love. He would follow his appetites when necessary, and do his duty by remarrying, but he would never make himself vulnerable again to such regret and despair. Self-control and equanimity had become the mainspring that kept him productive and sane.

Yet, since he had met Angelica Leigh his usually disciplined spirit had been shaken to the core. She was the focus of his nephew's attention and he had no thought of her as anything other than an inconvenient diversion, of which the headstrong boy would eventually tire. But that was before he met her and was disturbed to find a character and beauty deeper and more seductive than the usual light-skirt he had expected. But still he resisted. Miss Leigh was socially beyond the pale. His mind repeated the words, *She was not for him to covet.*

Ivor kicked the last log smouldering in the grate, hoping to coax a bit more warmth from the fire, but could not wrench his mind from the memory of the young actress brought mortally ill to his door. From that point his icy control began to melt. Her suffering broke through his heart's reserve and he was haunted by the thought of her clinging to life. Despite the impropriety, he could not help checking on this young woman every night while she slept, with Mary beside her on a truckle bed.

Miss Leigh's pale beauty and fragility as she struggled for breath, for life, touched him to the core. Most nights she was unaware of his presence but occasionally her eyelids would flutter and her eyes would rest on his face, and she smiled and sometimes reached for his hand as if still in a dream. At moments like these he felt a timeless connection that in the light of day he still tried to deny; he could not allow his mind to recognise how deeply her presence in his house, under his protection, affected him.

She was not for him to covet. The leather-bound book lay open, his hand upon it but his heart was beating with a strange skip in its rhythm. This tantalising young woman's own feelings were still a mystery to him. Was this what it was to go slowly mad he wondered, as his vaunted self-control slipped from his grasp? The devil take it! The wild appetites of his youth threatened to assert themselves again. Just hours ago, he had been over-

come with the impulse to abandon himself to the passions of old, to take
Angelica Leigh in his arms, not in the decorum of a waltz but with the force
of urgent desire. Long forgotten, barely acknowledged, how it had throbbed
insistent in his veins.

Ivor Asprey forced his thoughts back to the poem in his lap. He had to
regain his equilibrium to be useful for anything. He was alarmed at the
thought of returning to the anarchic emotions of old, but even the
measured philosophical poetry of Mr Goldsmith had become full of different, more dangerous meaning. The barren solitariness of his life seemed
now undeniable as he read words he had read so many times before
without this jolt of recognition.

> *My fortune leads to traverse realms alone,*
> *And find no spot at all the world my own.*

He stirred restlessly, the fire was almost out and he was dog-tired but
unwilling to relinquish himself to bed and sleep. Goldsmith seemed to
continue to mock his choice to live a cerebral life committed to public duty.

> *Vain, very vain, my weary search to find*
> *That bliss which only centres in the mind:*
> *Why have I strayed from pleasure and repose,*
> *To seek a good each government bestows?*

Sadness rose in him like a tide at the thought of love lost. But also the
realisation of the love he had denied. He determined to see Miss Leigh on
the morrow before she left for home. There was so much to ask, so much to
say. He followed the poem to its end and there was the message he had
chosen all these years to ignore:

> *How small, of all that human hearts endure,*
> *That part which laws or kings can cure!*
> *Still to ourselves in every place consign'd,*
> *Our own felicity we make or find:*
> *With secret cause, which no loud storms annoy,*

Glides the smooth current of domestic joy.

How he longed for that smooth current of domestic joy. How long he had deluded himself that he could live as an island without it. Ivor closed the book, blew out the candles and headed up the stairs to bed. Dawn was already spilling its cold grey light through the east window on the landing. He walked past the sleeping guests, aware his house was full of strangers, but when he came upon one room, its door still wide open, nobody occupying the great canopied bed, he paused. Across the foot of it lay a sparkling dress fit for a Fairy Queen.

His heart missed a beat. Where was Miss Leigh if not in her bed? A new horror gripped him; surely she would not have compromised her honour and gone to his nephew's bed? The shock was almost physical then mixed with a seeping shame that he could ever have thought such of her. Even as he suppressed the idea, a darker emotion of rage and jealousy contracted his heart. This black energy had propelled him when young into deadly challenges and he could not allow himself to revisit such reckless and bloody times. But neither could he fully suppress this primal possessiveness that gripped him, this chilling fear of loss.

He walked silently to Lord Latimer's room, across the main landing from his own. He listened at the door and could only hear the noisy breathing of someone who had overindulged in wine and brandy. Slowly he turned the door handle, half-dreading what he might find. Ivor Asprey stood at the threshold gazing at the great bed before him.

His handsome young nephew was sprawled across the cover still wearing his linen shirt and little else, his arm flung out, his face turned towards the window, his body in intoxicated sleep, and entirely alone. Relief flooded through his tired mind, soon followed by consternation. Where was Miss Leigh? He could not go to bed without knowing she was safe. He decided to visit the servants' quarters where the young kitchen lad slept by the hearth to feed the fire through the night.

As Mr Asprey entered the warm room a boy of about fourteen sprang to his feet. 'Don't get up, Jake.' He held up his hand. 'I just need to know if you recall seeing one of my guests, the lady dressed as the Fairy Queen?'

The lad sat down again, rubbing the sleep from his eyes. 'No sir. So

many prime articles and hurly-burly romps, couldn't tell the difference.
Heard the clop of a prancer's hooves, though, just as light broke.'

'Thank you, Jake.' He strode out to the stables beyond the house. All
seemed quiet. Horses sleeping, the grooms too in their cots above them. He
walked to the small house where his head groom, Rocky, had his own quarters. Knocking quietly, he called his name.

The door opened to reveal the familiar weather-beaten face but with
sleep-tousled hair. 'Oh, sir! What's the trouble?' Rocky was hurriedly
pulling on his breeches.

'Did a horse and rider leave early this morning?'

'Yes. Robert, the Breville groom. Asked to borrow one of your hacks. I
didn't want to bother ye so said he could take Meg.'

'And did you see who rode off on the mare?'

'Only saw a cove in Breville livery. I thought he'd be needed back in
town for some reason. Didn't enquire further.'

'Was this rider alone?'

'Yessir. Shall I fetch Robert?'

'If you please, Rocky. And harness the two bays to my curricle.'

The wise face looked concerned. 'Don't look to me like you've had
much sleep, sir. Shall I accompany ye?'

'No, I'll be fine. I just need some more useful clothes. I'll be back in ten
minutes. If I can see the Breville groom then?'

* * *

The early summer sun was already over the horizon when Ivor Asprey set
off up the drive. The clouds hung low and the damp air was heavy, the light
dull and diffuse. Usually he would like nothing better than setting out with
his favourite prancers for a drive where no one could make demands on
him. It was a rare enough respite. But he was anxious and lack of sleep
made his emotions more volatile than he liked. He joined the traffic on the
main road. The Breville groom had told him Miss Leigh was the mystery
rider. Although he knew she had about two hours' advantage he could not
stop himself from scanning the horses ahead, expecting one of the riders to
be her.

Ivor knew he could drive his bays at quite a pace for a mile or so before slackening them off to rest. He had paid a great deal for this beautiful pair, buying them from a friend embarrassed by gambling debts. Despite his exhaustion he could not deny the exhilaration in travelling at speed, over-taking every cart and carriage on the highway. His youthful spirit had been awoken by Angelica Leigh and for a short while he could give it its head.

After half an hour he reined his horses in from a canter to a trot. The exhilaration had dispersed and fatigue and exasperation at the reason for this wild goose chase seeped into his soul. What a headstrong woman to take off without a word! Responsible as he was for his guests, Miss Leigh had given him little choice but to hare off after her once she'd taken flight, with what cause he had yet to fully discover. Away from her he found himself longing to return to his old life of unruffled emotions and undi-luted work. But the unsettling presence of this enchantress seemed to disperse every good sense and rouse all the animal spirits of old.

As he entered the boundary of the village of Chiswick on the River Thames he noticed an oddly dressed figure standing rather forlorn, with his own chestnut horse beside her. All his new determination to close his heart again dissolved in the presence of her siren self.

* * *

Angelica's low mood seemed to have been transmitted to her horse. Her hands were slack on the reins as Meg stumbled occasionally in the ruts of the ill-kept road, her head down. Angelica was so nearly asleep she wondered if she ought to dismount and walk for a while, but before she could think any further Meg had stepped into a pothole and, caught off-balance, fallen to her knees. Half asleep and inattentive, Angelica was thrown off over her neck. Even in that split second she knew to protect her head and landed instead on a shoulder, saved from the full impact by the padding in her oversized jacket.

She scrambled unsteadily to her feet, picked up her hat that had tumbled to the ground and quickly crammed it back over her increasingly unruly hair. She was shocked, but unaware as yet of any pain. Meg, however, was not so fortunate. As the horse struggled to stand, it was immediately clear that her knees were grazed and bruised. Angelica led her to the verge, watching her gait closely. She walked unevenly and was stiff. Angelica ran her hand from knee to fetlock and as the horse trembled under her touch she realised she was lame and could not be ridden any further. She dropped Meg's reins to allow her to crop the grass and she herself sat down to think what best to do.

Her right shoulder had begun to throb. She slipped a hand gingerly inside her jacket and ran her fingers along her collarbone to her shoulder joint to see if anything felt broken or out of shape. She was so tired she just wanted to lie back on the grassy knoll in the shade of a lime tree and give herself up to sleep, but she knew that would not get her home; instead, both horse and rider would have to limp on as best they could for the six miles or so to Berkeley Square.

Wearily, Angelica got to her feet. She collected Meg's reins in her left hand and coaxed her away from the grass. They began walking, along with the motley collection of pedestrians heading for London and work in the glass and metal foundries, the workshops, market gardens and midden pits that served a growing metropolis. She plodded on in the footsteps of a laundrywoman carrying laundered sheets in a bag on her back.

By now it was close to six o'clock in the morning and Angelica esti- mated she would not be home for another two hours. She was sorry to have left in such a hurry with only enough money for the tolls, for hunger was joining with fatigue and the pain of her shoulder to make her feel nauseous and slightly unsteady on her feet. They were overtaken by a cart carrying loaves and pastries to deliver to the gentry and the smell of new-baked bread that wafted in its wake almost made her swoon. Angelica rubbed her temples in an attempt to keep awake and was shocked to see her hand with a smear of blood. She must have grazed her face when she hit the ground.

The road began to follow the River Thames and the fresher air and endless activity of every size and type of boat on this great watery thor- oughfare helped distract her. Meg also seemed to have perked up. She was still lame and her right knee and fetlock appeared swollen but she walked beside Angelica gazing with her upon the mighty river and the mudlarks who collected what bounty they could scavenge from the water's edge. As a bedraggled Angelica and her lame horse approached the village of

Chiswick, she saw a wooden signpost for St Nicholas Church and stopped for a moment to survey the ancient tower.

* * *

Angelica was aware of the scrunch of wheels very close as a curricle pulled up beside her. She noticed first the beauty of the matched bays, then looked up to see a familiar figure leap from the driving seat. Surprise and relief drained the last shreds of energy from her. 'Mr Asprey, what are you doing here?' She leant against Meg for support.

He was by her side looking weary. 'I might ask you the same thing, Miss Leigh?'

Hardly believing he had arrived when most needed, it nevertheless shamed her that it was becoming a habit, but at that moment it was one for which she was profoundly grateful. Relief swamped more uncomfortable emotions, for she had sworn to herself she would not involve him any more in the scandals of her life. Angelica looked up to meet his enquiring gaze. 'I had to get home quickly and could not wait until morning,' she muttered in some embarrassment. 'But you didn't have to follow me.'

'You wonder why I'm here, foregoing sleep to embark on a wild goose chase to try and find you? If a guest goes missing from my house in the middle of the night it would be remiss not to investigate further, would you not agree?'

His stern line of questioning was abandoned as he noticed with consternation the damage to her face. 'What has happened to you? You look like you've been brawling. This isn't why you left is it?' Ivor took both her elbows so he could examine the damage more closely. Angelica winced and cried out. He let go of her in an instant. 'What's injured?' His voice was urgent.

'I don't know. Meg stumbled in a pothole and I came off her back. I don't think I've done any serious damage to my shoulder.'

He gazed down the road and said in a voice that brooked no demur, 'The Burlington Arms is just a hundred yards further. We can get some refreshment and the horse some care. I know the grooms there, they'll look after Meg until Rocky sends someone to collect her.' Mr Asprey tied the reins to the back of his curricle and, aware that Angelica could not use her right arm to pull herself up, placed his hands round her waist and lifted her into the seat with great care. He then sprang up beside her.

Glancing at his face, Angelica noticed a curl of amusement round his mouth. Without turning towards her he said, 'You look the most disreputable groom I have ever seen. Your nose is grazed, your forehead raw and that unlikely blue hair is coming undone. Your livery is so ill-fitting it's practically falling off. What self-respecting groom would be seen in public like that?' He laughed. 'I wonder what damage it does to *my* reputation being seen in such company!'

Angelica hung her head; little did Mr Asprey know how close he had come to the truth. When he discovered the reason for her flight from the ball she feared he would realise he certainly shouldn't be seen with her in polite society anywhere. With some mischief in his voice he said, 'If it's not too indelicate to ask, how do you keep those capacious breeches from falling down?'

'It's very indelicate of you to even notice I'm so improperly dressed. It's shaming indeed to reveal my legs to you or any man.' Despite the desperateness of her situation Angelica could not prevent her own sense of humour from breaking through.

'Come, come, Miss Leigh. Such modesty is misplaced when I and half of London have already seen you in a sodden chemise carried lifeless from the stage.'

'You are ungentlemanly, sir, to continue to remind me. That was Ophelia you saw, not Angelica Leigh.'

He chuckled. 'Forgive me, but it was undeniably the corporeal form of a very beautiful actress called Miss Angelica Leigh.' He was still amused when he drove the curricle into the courtyard behind the Burlington Arms. Ostlers sloped forward to take the horses' heads and glanced with some curiosity at the unusual personage sitting beside the driver they knew well. Ivor Asprey was brusque. 'Can you ask Jim to see to my horse, Meg? She's lame having fallen on her knees on the highway.' He jumped to the ground and walked to Angelica's side of the carriage. 'Give me your left hand and I'll lift you down. I don't want any more damage done to that shoulder.'

Tiredness had sapped her strength and she could barely stand. As she slipped to the ground with Mr Asprey's arm round her waist, Angelica almost crumpled when her legs had to take her weight. He held her to his chest while she steadied herself. The ostlers were watching this performance with some bemusement. They knew Mr Asprey as a gentleman truly up to the mark, a top sawyer who knew his horses and dealt well with everyone. But this strange burlesque of a groom looked half-cut and as if he'd come off worst in a brawl – he was not even dressed in Asprey livery.

Angelica was aware of their interest and disengaged herself from her rescuer's arms. 'We're causing comment, Mr Asprey.'

'I really couldn't care a damn.' Angelica looked at him with surprise. 'And yes I will curse in front of you now you have given up your privileges as a woman.'

'I think you should be more concerned about your reputation, sir.'

'I doubt any of the men here know or care what I do.'

'But you cannot know who else might be interested. Lord Rackham for instance.' Angelica realised how the nagging pain of her shoulder and the nausea of sleeplessness made her emotions fragile; she shuddered at the memory of the predatory lord.

'You need some food. Come.' Mr Asprey led the way into the inn where he was greeted like an old friend and immediately shown to a private parlour at the back. There was a fire and Angelica sank with relief onto the bench by the table. 'Would you like some hot chocolate to restore you, Miss Leigh? And some rolls and ham and cheese?'

She could only nod and her head sank to her hand. Mr Asprey sat opposite her. 'Before you can sleep we have to investigate this injury and whether I have to get my surgeon to see you.' He asked Angelica to extend her right arm and see how high she could lift it. When she gasped at the pain he took her hand and gently lifted it higher, then back behind her, before rotating it with care.

She was wincing, clenching her jaw trying not to cry out, but he looked pleased. 'At least your shoulder isn't broken or dislocated. Good. Now to check your collarbone.' He put his hand on the front of the coat but the wool fabric was so thick and the embellishment of braid made it impossible to feel her bone beneath.

'Miss Leigh, I've had some experience with boxing injuries, would you permit me to check your collarbone and shoulder properly?' When she nodded he undid the top fastening and slipped a hand in under the heavy wool cloth. In a businesslike manner, he ran his fingers gently along her collarbone until he reached her shoulder. His cool sure touch made her shiver. Their faces were so close she had to turn away. His eyes were thoughtful as he concentrated on the progress of his two fingers and thumb inching back along the bone. He closed the coat fastening and said with satisfaction, 'Nothing broken, thank goodness. You'll live.'

Then Ivor Asprey's eyes caught her gaze and his cool grave efficiency faltered and a spark of more unruly energy flickered between them. Angelica held her breath, her eyes wide. At that moment the inn keeper bustled in carrying a tray with a tankard of ale and a bowl of hot chocolate, together with a plate of meat, cheese and bread. The connection was broken and Angelica closed her eyes for a second. When she glanced at the food on the table she realised how famished she was and started to eat a roll stuffed with a lump of hard yellow cheese. Something so modest had last tasted so good when she was a hungry child back in Rupert Street.

They both sat in silence for a minute of two, Ivor watching Angelica over the top of his ale glass. 'Now you're a little revived with food, I'd be grateful for some explanation as to why at dawn I was propelled onto the highroad instead of heading for my bed.' He sat back and crossed his legs, brushing the dust of the journey from his immaculate top boots. Angelica noticed the lines of fatigue etched across his brow.

'I didn't expect anyone to follow me.'

'Well, having saved you from a deadly bout of influenza I wasn't about to let you break your neck on the King's highway. Come, Miss Leigh, you're prevaricating. What caused you to flee?'

'I don't want to involve you in any more of my scandals.'

'I'm already involved,' he said in a droll manner, stretching his legs towards the fire.

Angelica realised she could not maintain her latest resolution to keep her shame to herself, and especially from Mr Asprey, without seeming petulant. In a hesitant voice she began to tell her sorry tale. 'In the last hours of the ball I was waiting for my friends to return from supper. A tall imposing lady dressed as the Great Queen bore down on me.'

'Ah, the Countess of Bellingham, the formidable Alfreda. The Barton-Craig family dominates the northern Marches. Your father should have chosen more carefully.'

Angelica looked startled. 'How do you know my father's involved?'

'If there's trouble it tends to be traced back to him, would you not agree?'

'But neither you nor Lord Latimer were there to see my ruin.'

''Tis true, but then nothing much escapes me, Miss Leigh. My staff accuse me of being omniscient.' He smiled as if reminding himself of something amusing. 'But ruin it cannot be. Fine actress as you are, I've never thought you melodramatic.' He cocked an eyebrow at her, awaiting still an explanation.

The food had revived Angelica and she felt vestiges of her old spirits return. Mr Asprey was looking rather insufferably smug she thought, as she said, 'If you're such a prodigal of knowledge then you don't need me to elaborate on what happened next.'

He stirred the fire with his boot. 'Did it involve, by chance, an ancestral necklace?'

Angelica closed her eyes in an attempt at warding off the memory of her mortification. 'Yes,' she said quietly. 'I thought it was my grandmother's and I loved it.'

'Instead it was the Countess's and she claimed it had been stolen from her at pistol point on the highroad.' His voice was quiet and grim.

How could he know? She looked at him, shocked. He waved his hand as if it was of no consequence. 'You knew about my father's criminality and yet you seem untroubled?'

To her amazement he was nonchalant. 'I've never subscribed to the idea that a father's sins should be visited on his child.'

'Well, I could not be as sanguine. I had no answer to the Countess and was utterly humiliated. My father had lied to me yet again and for all I knew was not only a highwayman but possibly a murderer too. Do you see why I didn't want to involve you again? Do you see how shamed I am by my blood?' Angelica wrung her hands in anguish. Her beautiful face was grey with tiredness and scarred by her rude meeting with the road. Her hair was well and truly unravelling in front of Mr Asprey's eyes. She looked like an urchin wearing oversized hand-me-down clothes of the most incongruous kind.

He took her hand and said quietly, 'Rest assured, Miss Leigh, I don't believe anyone recognised you. And your father may be a villain but he's not a murderer.'

'How can you be so sure?' Her green eyes filled with tears she was too tired to resist.

He offered her his linen handkerchief. 'Before I was willing to risk my reputation in getting involved in his precipitous return to France, I had to know who exactly he was and of what he had been accused.'

Angelica grasped his arm urgently. 'And who is he? What has he done? No one has told me the full truth yet. I've been so afraid it's too terrible to mention.'

Ivor Asprey's face was serious as he finished his ale.

'Your father is Peter Crowley, called for much of his criminal life, "Red Crowley", on account of his hair. He was a notorious highwayman but known more for his audacity and wit than his violence.'

'Oh no, I feared it must be so.' Angelica's face was stricken. 'How was he caught?'

'Like all flash scape-gallows he tried his luck one time too many. On Hounslow Heath he held up the coach of Lord Dunster, a crack shot himself. The old Earl shot the horse from under your father, and winged his arm.'

Angelica's heart plummeted. Her hands covered her face. 'Was he sentenced to... hang?' The word was so awful she barely managed to articulate it.

Ivor's voice was neutral. 'He wasn't sentenced. He escaped from Tyburn a week before his trial and managed to get to France before the authorities were alerted.'

'And you risked your reputation to help him escape this second time? Why?'

'Because an irresistible young woman I had come to admire tickled my vanity in thinking I could.' His expression was hard to fathom and Angelica was uncertain if he was serious. Then he added, 'However, that young woman seems to have disappeared.' As he continued, she knew he was teasing her. 'It strikes me, Miss Leigh, that it's fortunate you cannot see yourself as others see you.'

She could not suppress a giggle and put a hand to her hair. 'I must look a fright.'

'You do indeed. More frightful than any woman I have had the misfortune to know.' He grew serious again and his eyes intense. 'I commend you, though, for your lack of vanity. Unlike most beautiful women, you seem to be blessed with the luxury of knowing you look delightful in whatever state you're found. Or perhaps it's just a natural insouciance?'

Angelica felt herself colouring. 'It's not like you, Mr Asprey, to be so philosophical and flattering.'

'I'm afraid your advent in my life has made me do many things which are not like me at all. I have to apologise for my behaviour last night. I realise I was not quite gentlemanly. I forgot myself. I forgot for a moment you were my nephew's intended and I should not have presumed on your good nature, as I did.'

'You did not presume on me at all. And I suspect that our initial diagnoses of the situation are proved right. Lord Latimer's attentions have moved on to Miss Fitzjames, a much more suitable young woman.'

She glanced up to meet his gaze as he said, 'I know you have suspected this and in part accept it but I hope you have no regrets?'

Angelica's tiredness meant she had not the energy to dissemble. 'I cannot deny as he persisted in his attention I began to see him in a more affectionate light. And I cannot deny the advantages of becoming a duchess were not lost on me. But Mr Asprey, I knew we could never marry. The gulf between us was too great. And it is hard to have a prominent family like yours set against one.'

'You know I changed my mind on that,' he said with wry tenderness.

'Yes, but you were right. Shakespeare was right. Do you remember quoting Laertes back to me? Hamlet's will is not his own, for he himself is subject to his birth... And therefore must his choice be circumscribed?'

'That was before I knew you for who you are. I was wrong.'

'Society would disagree with you, especially now my blood is proved so tainted.' Her spirit was subdued by the events of the night. 'Perhaps Lord

Rackham is right, after all. I'm only fit for a gentleman's mistress; if I'm fortunate he will be rich and keep me for a while.'

Ivor Asprey started with shock at her indelicacy and the sense of defeat in her manner. 'Miss Leigh, you are not yourself. I would never hope to hear you speak like this. You're just fatigued. Let's get you home to sleep.' He rose to his feet, offering his hand.

They set off again in the curricle. Angelica was pale with emotion and tiredness and he glanced at her with concern. 'You look burnt to the socket, Miss Leigh. We'll be in Berkeley Square in just about an hour. Try not to fall asleep. I don't want you slipping off the seat.' He spread a blanket over her knees.

Angelica concentrated on watching the passing show. Traffic was now much more congested as the day advanced and they approached London. She could smell the woodsmoke in the air. The sun too was making a wan attempt at penetrating the milky sky. Mr Asprey's gloved hands holding the reins caught her attention, and she marvelled at his unshowy skill in weaving his horses through the throng without slackening speed. Despite her determination not to rely any further on his competence she relinquished her watchfulness, aware that at last she was in safe hands.

As Angelica relaxed, she gradually lost her struggle to remain awake and her eyelids fluttered closed. Her head tipped sideways onto Mr Asprey's shoulder as she gave herself up to blessed sleep. He looked down in consternation. She was so slight and her clothes so heavy and ill-fitting she could easily slip off the seat. The only recourse was to hold onto her by placing his left arm around her shoulders and drive the rest of the way with only his right hand to control his horses.

* * *

Martin opened the door and his eyes registered shock and panic. 'What's befallen you, Miss Angelica? A devil-ridden ramshackle! Your damaged beauty! And why in groom's toggery?'

Angelica was too tired to respond and Mr Asprey stepped forward. 'Is it Martin?' He gazed on the clown-like face of a middle-aged man wringing his hands in distress, and smiled. 'Miss Leigh is in need of sleep. Mary will be back later.'

At that moment Mr Brunner emerged from the back of the house, his battered old face revealing little surprise at the bizarre sight of his dishevelled young mistress in oversized livery. 'Miss Angelica.' He greeted her and nodded at Mr Asprey. 'Good morning, sir.' He recognised her companion from the times he had visited the Asprey mansion to enquire about his mistress's health. 'Mrs Leigh is out but when she returns I'll tell her you are home.'

Angelica turned to Mr Asprey and offered her hand. 'Thank you, for arriving just as I needed help.'

He bowed, saying formally, 'It is my honour, Miss Leigh. Perhaps I may take you for a drive in Green Park tomorrow afternoon?'

Angelica resisted her heart's cry, *yes, yes, yes.* Instead she smiled and answered with regret, 'I'm afraid rehearsals start for my next play. As I'm the "Child of Nature" herself I'll have to practice female perfection and passivity.'

'I can see just how much of a trial that will be for you,' Ivor Asprey said with a smile, and turned to go.

* * *

Angelica quickly divested herself of Robert's clothes and slipped into bed to give herself up at last to sleep. In the middle of the afternoon she was woken by Mary, gently shaking her shoulder. 'Miss Angelica, Miss Angelica. I'm sorry to trouble you but we've just arrived home from Cloudberry. We were so worried about you.' She then noticed Angelica's grazed face. 'Lawks! What has befallen you, Miss?' Then not waiting for an answer continued in an urgent voice, 'Miss Fitzjames is downstairs in a state. Can you see her?'

Angelica dragged herself back to consciousness and climbed out of bed. Her hair was a mess and Mary immediately began brushing out the blue powder to return it to its natural golden state. 'Mary, I fell off a horse. Hence my disreputable look.' She had not the energy for further explanation and clambered into a morning dress of oyster pink jaconet. Glancing at herself in the looking-glass, she was surprised at her pallor and how the graze on her forehead was already scabbing over. She pinched her cheeks and set off down the stairs.

Isobel Fitzjames was looking even worse than Angelica felt. Her eyes were red-rimmed and her face stiff with constrained emotion. 'Oh, Miss Angelica, your face! What has happened? I'm so glad to see you. I've been so concerned about why you left so precipitously.' She dashed to her friend's side and almost sank to her knees.

'Come and sit down. You look done-up. Do you need some refreshment?'

'No, no.' She was agitated. 'I have something so troubling on my mind.'

Angelica leaned forward with concern. 'Why? What has happened?'

The young woman seemed almost speechless with distress. 'I'm so afraid you left in such a hurry because I'd betrayed you so shabbily,' she whispered. 'I feel ashamed at how I've treated you, my truest friend.' Her eyes were cast down and Angelica thought she may be silently crying.

'Nothing can be this bad, surely? Just tell me.' She took her hand.

With a sob she looked up to meet Angelica's sympathetic eyes. 'When I was friendless and frightened you gave me hope. I can't bear you to be kind now when I have repaid you so ill.'

Angelica was losing a little patience. 'Miss Isobel, we aren't in a novel now, or a Cheltenham tragedy,' she said briskly, then continued in a softer tone of voice, 'My dear, what can have caused you so much grief?'

Miss Fitzjames took a breath and blurted out, 'I think I love Lord Latimer.' Her hand flew to her mouth, her eyes wide, horrified at the import of what she had just said. What had been unspoken between the friends in the carriage was now clearly stated, and it shocked them both.

Angelica felt a jolt run through her at hearing the words make concrete something she had known tacitly and come to accept. She summoned her actress skills to hide her fleeting shock and be able to say with perfect equanimity and truth, 'My dear, this is not a betrayal, I assure you. Lord Latimer is not mine to claim. He's a friend, as are you and that will not change.' Angelica held the young woman's hand between both of hers as she looked into her eyes and asked, 'Does he return your feelings?' Isobel Fitzjames nodded, her face bleak.

'Well, that is a cause for happiness, surely?'

'It is if it doesn't hurt you.'

'As you can see, it doesn't upset me. You know I was never going to be a suitable wife for Lord Latimer. You're so much better placed and his whole family can rejoice with you.' Angelica knew this was reasonable and fair; it was the way of the world, and she felt a sisterly pleasure in Isobel Fitzjames's finding love, but her heart was pained by how hard it would prove for her to do the same.

Isobel coloured. 'Oh Miss Angelica, I've been so ashamed, and frightened that it was because of me you rode off into the night.'

'No, no. It was not you but something else that happened. So you can rest assured.'

With relief, Isobel threw her arms around her friend. 'Thank you, thank you. You've put my mind at ease. It's the first time I've felt happy since my father died.'

'Dear Isobel, you must be happy, because to find someone you love who loves you in return is rare enough. To have no barriers to your union is even more felicitous.'

At this point Martin knocked on the door. 'Lord Latimer to see you, Miss Angelica,' he said, his expressive face conveying some turbulence of emotion Angelica could not quite interpret.

'Show him in, thank you, Martin.' Lord Latimer usually entered every room with a certain swagger borne of an innate confidence as the son and heir of a dukedom and thousands of fertile English acres, but this time he appeared subdued. His gaze rested on Miss Fitzjames for a moment as he greeted both women and she was quick to gather her reticule and make her farewells. Angelica followed her to the hall where her maid was waiting. They hugged and she returned to meet Lord Latimer.

He took her hand and without saying a word they sat on the sofa together. Angelica was relieved that Mary had not been summoned by Martin to chaperone her as she wanted freedom to talk. 'Miss Fitzjames has told me about your feelings and hers and I have assured her I am happy for you both.' She was surprised at how formal her voice sounded.

He brought her hand to his lips. 'Miss Leigh, my admiration and affection for you are undiminished. Thank you for settling her mind. But I'm afraid mine is troubled.'

'How so, my lord?'

'My love for you is not easily quelled. You excite my senses. I've never known anyone as beautiful. Or desirable. I don't think I ever will.' His head bowed over her hand again. Angelica had always been surprised by his frankness but was afraid now of what indiscretion he might utter next. 'Miss Leigh, you will always be my first passion, like amaranth it will never fade.'

She placed her hand over his as he lifted his head and their eyes met, both pricking with tears. 'That means a great deal to me, Lord Latimer. But I know you and Miss Fitzjames are so well-suited you will be happy, and make your family happy.'

'You will always have a piece of my heart.' He pressed her hand against his coat. 'Dante thinks I've treated you as badly as Hamlet did Ophelia. But this was never my intention. While Miss Fitzjames and I were so concerned with your health, we grew closer. Then there came a moment when I realised I wanted to take care of her. I *needed* to take care of her. She seemed so vulnerable, like an orphaned bird in a storm in want of shelter and I could protect her.'

The salutary thought flashed into Angelica's mind that perhaps her mother was right all along; to have a blithe spirit and to live confidently in the world made a young woman less attractive as a wife than the gothic heroine of fiction, frightened, fainting and grateful for Sir Galahad. She extricated her hand from Lord Latimer's fervent grasp.

He looked at her with some of his old mischievous spirit. 'Did your Cinderella flight from the ball have anything to do with the Countess of Bellingham I saw leaving your side looking triumphant? I knew that dreadful termagant had been up to some devilish dos.'

'I'm afraid the devilment was entirely my father's doing.'

'So your battered face was not due to the Countess' ministration.' He chuckled.

'No, more an altercation with the road.'

'What with your father's escape and this, you've had to deal with so much upset, I'm sorry. I hope you know you can call on me any time. I'll do whatever you need me to do, Miss Leigh.'

'That is a consolation. I am embarrassed by how often I have turned to your uncle for help. I have sworn I will not again.'

'My dear Miss Leigh, please go on involving him in your troubles. He is so much more cheerful. Much more the man he used to be since you broke through his shell of propriety and restraint.'

Angelica looked at the young lord with startled eyes. 'Lord Latimer! You are funning now. You cannot suggest the scandals besetting me and bothering him have made him happier?'

'Well, something has. And I can assure you it's not that mistress of discord, Lady Linus, always trying to batten him down with her philosophy of denial.' He had stood up to take his farewell, serious again, his heart in his eyes. 'Miss Leigh, never doubt my affection for you.'

Angelica saw his eyes darken and he took a step towards her. There was a tension between them and she knew he wanted to kiss her but as a gentleman he would not even presume to brush her cheek. Instead, she took his hand and brought their entwined hands to her lips then passed them back for him to kiss. 'You are the best of friends. Thank you, Lord Latimer. You probably saved my life with your decisive action. And I wish you and Miss Fitzjames every happiness.' She led the way into the hall where Martin was hovering.

He handed over his lordship's coat and curly-brimmed hat and as the front door closed behind their guest, the theatrical butler grasped Angelica's hand. He drew her away into the alcove under the curve of the stair. 'Miss Angelica, there is so much chattering in the kitchens about last night!' His kohl-rimmed eyes were round with apprehension and his words tumbled out. 'Mary just returned with Robert and Miss Fitzjames and she was agog. The story in the servants' hall is that you were attacked by the Countess of Bellingham because her son danced with you! And Mary is afraid that Lord Latimer is paying his attentions now to Miss Fitzjames. You'd be the perfect duchess, I don't want to think of you not being married.'

Angelica laughed. 'Oh Martin, don't worry about me. I was not attacked for dancing with anyone's son. I'm not yet such a dangerous woman! But I appreciate your concern.' Martin readjusted his wig and his face relaxed. Angelica took his hand. 'Now tell me where Mary is. I'll explain it all to her. And apologise for worrying her so. We've got to prepare ourselves for rehearsals tomorrow. My new play opens in a week.'

The front door opened again and in a blast of cool air Angelica's mother blew in, resplendent in a pale blue satin pelisse with matching corded tassels as trim. Ever since her return from Paris, Mrs Leigh had looked a picture of health and elegance in her new outfits, her mood still elevated by her social success with Mr Breville, being wined and dined by the great porcelain manufacturers. Her own household was much enriched with a new dinner service by the Duc d'Angoulême's factory in Rue de Temple, decorated in pink and gilt swags and flowers, and two enormous faience vases to go either side of the mantlepiece in the drawing room, matching the Lawrence portrait for magnificence.

'Angelica! You're back. Come and tell me about the ball.' She kissed her daughter, then noticing her grazed forehead said, 'Oh Angelica! What now?' She divested herself of her pelisse and flung it over Martin's outstretched arm and tossed her bonnet onto the hall table. She led the way into the morning room and subsided onto the small sofa in the window. 'Come and sit, dearest.' She patted the primrose yellow satin beside her.

Angelica sat down reluctantly. There was so much to tell she did not know where to start, but it was such a litany of woe she was uncertain if she could even begin. She started with the innocuous. 'The ball was a beautiful affair and my dress was perfect. Thank you so much, Mama.'

'So?' Amabel Leigh said with an abstracted air. 'Did you dance with Lord Latimer?'

'I did. But Mama, you have to give up your ambitions to be the mother of a duchess.' Angelica smiled despite herself. 'It's as I'd always predicted. Lord Latimer's interests are now with a more suitable young woman.'

Angelica was surprised that her mother did not seem in the least cast down by the news. 'Dearest, I was about to suggest that you'd be far better suited as a French aristocrat's wife. Now the war is over and the nobility are returning to Paris I was struck by how *gentil* they are, how full of *joie de vivre*, a little short, perhaps, but they can charm the secrets from the moon.

Your lightness of spirit, I like to think it's Irish wit inherited from me, is not so appreciated by the English. Paris deserves you. I think you would make a fine *Comtesse!*'

Angelica leapt up. 'I have no time for any more matchmaking, Mama, and nothing would induce me to share a city with my perfidious father!'

'Oh la la!' Mrs Leigh trilled. 'I hope this means you no longer blame me for trying to shelter you from the knowledge of his existence.'

'I don't know what I think any more,' Angelica said bleakly. She bent and kissed her mother's rosy cheek, disappointed that she had not shown any curiosity about the healing scab on her face. She returned to her room to continue learning her lines for the morrow.

10

DESIRE AND PERIL

Angelica went to be bed early, desperate for sleep, and quickly sank into oblivion. In the early hours she awoke with a creeping uneasiness at the shift in the very foundations of her life. Everything was changing. She lay in the dim light, gazing at barely visible trails of jasmine and flickering dabs of colour from the tiny birds' wings on the chinoiserie wallpaper she loved so well. To her dismay her unruly heart ached not for a father or Lord Latimer but for an austere man who she feared had given up on the anarchy of love. Her mind retraced the previous night and the dawning of desire as she waltzed in Ivor Asprey's arms and she shuddered with the shame of what had then followed, altering her prospects of happiness for ever.

Angelica recoiled from the memory of the necklace she had worn with such ignorance and pride. Well, that pride had been truly punished. Once again she was that disregarded child in the cold room above the gold trader's in Rupert Street, and she curled into a ball, her hands tight round her knees. Her confidence and naturally vivid nature could be undermined too easily by the ghosts of the past and she had to struggle sometimes to leave the memories behind.

Mary entered with a bowl of hot chocolate which she placed on the table by the bed. She drew the curtains back on a grey day, washed with rain. 'Miss Angelica, you asked me to wake you at eight. I hope you slept well.'

Angelica stretched her limbs and yawned. She had to put on a good show as usual. 'Good morning, Mary. I feel almost restored.' She smiled. 'Although I'm not looking forward to rehearsals this afternoon. Have you read the play?'

'I have. Bird-witted part for you. Both women are sorry hussies, I agree, but 'twill be a success I'm sure, though that shrimp, Mr Kean, has turned down the Marquis of Alamanza.'

'Ah, it'll be the corpulent Mr Egerton instead. At least the young Count I'm meant to love will be played by Mr Jones, an altogether more amusing type.' Angelica climbed out of bed and mustered her spirits to meet the new day.

Awaiting her at breakfast was a note in a large looping hand in violet ink which Angelica immediately recognised as from Elinor Asprey. Sitting with a cup of coffee she read,

Dear Miss Leigh,
    I have some Important News to impart.

Here she had underlined the words and drawn a blue dove with a pink message in its beak. And a ghost of a red heart with an arrow. Angelica smiled as she sipped her coffee. The handwriting continued.

Miss Stafford is taking me to see Mr Barker's Panorama in Leicester Square this morning. If it Suits you she can Leave me with You for an Hour at 11 while she visits Hookham's.
    Please Say Yes.

This was underlined twice.

I also want to hear about the Ball.
    Your Elinor Asprey

She had obviously been practising her Elizabethan signature as the curlicues under her name had become even more elaborate than in the last message.

Angelica walked to the door and called Martin who drifted towards her from the back of the house. 'Is that young chit visiting us again?' he enquired, unconcerned at such unseemly overfamiliarity.

Angelica knew he had been charmed by the child when she last visited and laughed. 'Indeed it is her. I suppose that handwriting is rather distinctive.'

'As is the cascade of yellow stars she'd inscribed on the back.'

'Could you get this message round to the Asprey house in St James's Square?' Angelica took up a piece of writing paper from the drawer in the hall table and wrote, *Yes, indeed* in her own distinctive hand, folding it and adding Miss Asprey's name and address to the front.

She walked through to the library to pick up her script and study again her first entry onto the stage in Act II, the innocent 'Child' about to be introduced to a wider world than the benign imprisonment to which she had been subject. After a couple of hours there was a knock on the door and Martin announced the arrival of Miss Stafford and her pupil.

Elinor Asprey looked up at Angelica. 'Miss Leigh! Your face, what happened?'

'I just came off a horse, but it's healing fast. I'm surprised you noticed.' She took the girl's hand and came forward to take Miss Stafford's. 'I trust the Panorama lived up to its advertisements?'

'It was like magic, I thought I was flying like a bird over London.' Elinor jumped up and down with excitement.

Miss Stafford smiled. 'I have seen it before and it is very much worth the shilling entry. I recommend it, Miss Leigh. I have also promised Elinor that Mr Digby and I will bring her to see your performance when *The Child of Nature* opens.'

'I don't think any freethinking radical could possibly approve of it. But I hope you will be able to disabuse Miss Elinor of its pernicious moral!' Both women gave a conspiratorial chuckle as the girl looked from one face to the other.

Miss Stafford turned to go. 'I'll be back by noon if that suits you, Miss

Leigh?' Angelica walked with her to the door then returned to the library where Elinor's head was bent over her script.

The girl looked up. 'I wanted to see what made you and Miss Stafford laugh about me.'

'It's not about you, it was about what a ninny the young woman is whom I have to portray on stage. But much more important: what is your news?'

They sat together on the sofa in front of the fireplace. 'You know how I perceive what's best for those I love when sometimes they don't know so themselves?'

Angela nodded with a rueful smile. 'And you know how dangerous such certainty can prove to be.'

'I try not to exercise my conceits too often. But as I much desire Miss Stafford should marry Mr Digby and she desires it too, I had a plan. We were about to go to the Panorama two days ago. At the last moment I said I was feeling queasy and wanted to stay at home, they then had to go without me,' she said, triumphant at her ingenuity.

'And?'

'Well, Miss Stafford came back looking different. Molly, our kitchen cat, has the same satisfied smile when she's been licking the crust from Cook's bowl of curds.' The girl's elfin face was flushed with delight.

Angelica could not stop herself from laughing. Serious again, she said, 'You care a great deal for Miss Stafford, do you not?' Elinor nodded. 'You must trust that she and Mr Digby will manage their own affairs perfectly well without your help, you know.' Angelica's voice was kind as she took her hand. 'It can become quite a burden if you think everyone's happiness depends on you.'

The young girl was thoughtful for a moment and nodded, saying in a quiet voice, 'However hard I tried, I could not make my mama live.' Her whole body seemed to subside. Then her face brightened again. 'Tell me about the ball. Papa would not talk much at all. He seemed very tired when he went to his library this morning.'

Angelica felt another jab of guilt at the thought of how much trouble she had brought to his door. 'Your father's house looked beautiful with all the flowers and candles.'

'I think you looked beautiful in your dress and blue hair. Did you dance with Charlie?'

'Indeed, I did. And with Mr Locke who thought poets shouldn't dance but he did, as a favour to me.'

The girl's candid blue eyes gazed into Angelica's. 'Did you dance with Papa?'

'One dance.'

'And did you like it? He doesn't often dance.'

'Yes. Very much. He's a very good dancer.'

'When I asked him if he thought you looked beautiful he said, "very", that's all he would say.' Elinor turned away and added shyly, 'Miss Leigh, I know you think I shouldn't interfere but there's something I want even more than Miss Stafford getting married to Mr Digby.' She had clasped her hands together and her fingers were white with the force of her grip.

Angelica took her small interlaced hands between her own. 'And what is that, Miss Elinor?'

'I told Papa at breakfast this morning I wanted you for my new mama.'

Angelica gasped at such unexpected frankness, then felt a rush of affection for the motherless girl. She put her arms around her slight shoulders and kissed the top of her head. 'Anybody would be fortunate indeed to have you as a daughter.'

Elinor Asprey pulled herself away and said, tears pricking her eyes, 'I don't want just anybody, I want you.'

'I know. And I would be very happy to be your mama, but the world is complicated and our wishes can't always come true.' They sat together in silence, Angelica aware of the small frame and bird-like pulse under her hand. Her own heart was beating at the thought; above all she needed to know how his daughter's surprising confession had affected Mr Asprey. Assuming a nonchalance she did not feel, she asked, 'What did your papa say?'

'Nothing.' The girl hung her head for a moment then, lifting her gaze, she giggled. 'But he did smile. He hasn't smiled much since you left.'

Angelica could not stop herself smiling too; a small flame of hope ignited in her breast. They chattered on about music, piano practice, Angelica's new play and the desirability of learning Greek. Too soon, there was a knock at the door and Martin appeared. 'Miss Stafford for the young lady.'

'I'm sorry. I'm sooner than expected but Mr Digby's returning early from Westminster and needs me to research some of Mr Hume's writings.'

Elinor caught Angelica's eye who quelled the girl's knowing expression with a quick frown as she turned to greet Miss Stafford. 'Of course. We have had time enough for conversation and I shall look forward to meeting you all again when you come to see me in the new play.'

'What time do you start rehearsals, Miss Leigh?' Elinor Asprey asked.

'Just after three this afternoon.'

'And do you walk there?'

'Yes, if the weather's fine. It only takes half an hour. Why so many questions, Miss Asprey?' Angelica smiled down at her. 'Were you thinking of joining us?'

Miss Stafford intervened. 'I'm afraid her music master is due this afternoon. He's teaching Elinor the latest arrangement of some North Country dances.'

They entered the hall where Martin sprang forward, flourishing the young girl's pelisse like a matador's cape. Elinor giggled again and slipped her arms into the sleeves, then gave a quick curtsey to Angelica in farewell. Governess and charge tripped down the front steps and with a wave turned into the hazy sun to walk south to St James's Square.

* * *

With some deliberation, Angelica dressed in one of her best afternoon gowns. She was about to meet new members of the cast and even though her part seemed paltry after the demands of Ophelia, she wanted to look distinctive as the troupe's leading lady. Mary had put out her lilac and primrose yellow cambric muslin with the flattering high square neckline, the short bodice fastened at the front with satin-covered buttons. She slipped it over her head and as Mary buttoned it up she was pleased to see how the colours flattered her, making her eyes greener and hair more golden. The bodice was lilac and the skirt and long inner sleeves a light primrose with small lilac cuffs and silk primroses round the neck.

Sleep had restored colour to her cheeks and as Angelica caught sight of herself in the looking-glass in the hall she was surprised at how well she looked. She had dabbed some powder onto her healing graze and it was already receding. Gathering up her script she fastened her pelisse, placed her best Leghorn bonnet on her head and picked up her reticule. Mary contemplated her with an amused face. 'Miss Angelica, you're blooming again. Your heart is not broken?'

Mary and Angelica had spent their girlhoods together and Angelica recognised her maid's protectiveness when she had suspected Lord Latimer's affections were shifting elsewhere. Angelica grasped Mary's arm with a smile. 'Never fear, my heart's not even bruised.' They walked towards the door and she paused before saying, 'Although that's not quite true. Perhaps my vanity was puffed a little to have such an attractive young nobleman swear he was in love with me and for a while there was an answering perturbation in my heart. More shamefully, there was some vanity and delight in discomfiting my detractors by becoming a duchess!' She caught sight of herself in the looking-glass, a mischievous smile on her face. 'I am glad it did not come to pass.'

They stepped into the cool afternoon. The sun was still hazy as they set out on their brisk walk to Covent Garden. The green gardens of the Square were left behind as the two young women walked down Bruton Street and into the bustle of Bond Street. Once again, the sight of Angelica drew admiring glances from the young men lounging along the pavement, or driving their curricles slowly to show off their flashy horses. Angelica turned to Mary with a wry smile. 'In company like this, I can see the appeal of the veil. Anonymity is a boon, don't you think?'

'Well, Miss Angelica, I'm anonymous enough. It's you who draws all eyes, some of 'em impertinent, for sure. They're just piffling jack-a-dandies!' she added with disdain. They were about to turn off the fashionable thoroughfare into Burlington Gardens when a curricle, being driven rather fast, came to a halt beside them, the horses whinnying and stamping. Angelica recognised these beautiful bays immediately, then when Rocky took the horses' heads she knew Mr Asprey was the driver. An uncomfortable flashback of how he and the same horses had come to her aid on the highroad the day before made her flush. Here he was before her, tall in his driving coat, the capes blown back over a shoulder, his curly-brimmed beaver in his hands. 'Good afternoon, Miss Leigh, Mary. I'm glad I caught up with you.'

'Caught up with us, pray? How did you know where we would be?'

'I've already warned you, I'm omniscient.' He seemed in the most light-hearted of moods. He even chuckled.

'I think not omniscient, sir, just blessed with a spy in the family.'

He let out a bark of laughter. 'You know my daughter well, Miss Leigh. Anyway, may I hand you and Mary up and I'll drive you to the theatre?'

There was just room on the seat for them both but it meant Angelica was squeezed in tight against Mr Asprey. If she had tried to make an inch or so of space between them Mary would have been thrown off the bench by the first rut in the road.

'Spring 'em, Rocky,' Mr Asprey called to his groom who let the spirited horses free then leapt up behind as the curricle passed. Mary and Angelica put an arm around each other to steady themselves. She was acutely aware of the pressure of his thigh against hers, a sense they were almost joined at the hip. She could feel his muscles tense as he handled his mettlesome team through the busy traffic. 'First day of rehearsals?' He glanced down at her.

'Yes, indeed.'

Turning serious, his voice dropped so as not to be overheard by Rocky, perched behind them scanning the road ahead. 'I've had visits this morning from both my rapscallion nephew and Miss Fitzjames. They spoke of your generosity of spirit. I said I would not have expected less.' They were bowling through Leicester Square and Angelica peered through the trees at the Rotunda on the further northern corner where the famous Panorama paintings were exhibited. Ivor Asprey manoeuvred the horses into narrow Cranbourne Street and within moments they pulled up in front of the grand colonnaded façade of the theatre.

Rocky jumped to the ground and handed Mary down but Ivor put his hand on Angelica's and said, 'Could you spare me a minute or two?'

Angelica looked up, meeting his blue eyes with her own startled gaze. 'Of course. You delivered us early.' She turned to Mary and said, 'I'll join you before three.'

She sat, barely breathing, her thigh still tight against his. His gloved hand remained on hers in her lap when eventually he said, 'You have woken me to myself, Miss Leigh.' His voice was quiet and his eyes closely watching her face. 'I was as ashes where once I had been flame, but you have rekindled the fire in me. I fear I can no longer live without its warmth.'

'Mr Asprey, what are you saying?' Her heart was beating fast with a growing hope that he could love her, but there was confusion and despair too. Was he about to suggest some irregular arrangement instead, after all she had been told often enough it was all an actress could hope for.

Angelica watched him remove his glove and noticed with a pang his strong lean hand. He lifted her own gloved fingers and began to undo the tiny pearl buttons at the wrist. She held her breath, her whole being alert to this new feeling of almost unbearable anticipation. Slowly he withdrew her glove, one fingertip at a time and she felt a tremor of excitement gazing down at her small pale hand lying in his. Her breath became uneven as his hand enclosed hers.

Angelica was aware of nothing outside the envelope of their unspoken feeling. The market seethed around them as the morning traders packed up their goods into carts, and children and dogs scampered through the debris, scavenging any ruined produce that remained. The shouts and cries and rattling wheels barely penetrated her consciousness. Every nerve vibrated; she was only aware of the man who sat tensely beside her, the man who made her pulse throb in her throat and her spirit long to know him and be known, to love with every fibre of her being and find an answering passion in return.

Angelica turned her hand so she could interlace her fingers with his, filling her with a sense of intimacy and joy. Ivor Asprey looked down with a kind of wonder as if he too was only now allowing himself to believe and said, so quietly she wondered if she had heard aright, 'I'm laying my heart bare before you. I do not wish to armour it again against the world.' He met her eyes, his own soft with emotion. 'My heart has been so cold, neglected, shut away. I have never known true love for a woman before and now it overwhelms me with its irresistible force, like a tide rolling in to shore.' He brought her hand to his chest and murmured, 'Will you accept my poor, disregarded heart, Miss Leigh, hand in hand, heart on heart?'

The spell between them was broken by Mary's voice calling from the theatre door, 'Miss Angelica, Dummie Dunbar's kicking up. He wants you here now for the read-through.'

As Angelica shifted on the seat to move, Ivor kept her hand pressed to his heart, his eyes closed for a moment. 'May I call on you? I'm busy in Parliament all tomorrow with the critical stage of my child labour bill. May I come to you the following afternoon, at two?' She nodded, not trusting herself to speak.

Mr Asprey leapt to the ground to help Angelica down from his curricle. He had returned to his polite public demeanour. They inclined their heads to each other and she turned and walked away, removing her bonnet as she approached the stage door. The sun at last emerged through the low cloud and light lit her hair like a halo. He stood motionless long after he had watched her disappear into the dim doorway. His face was inscrutable but he held his ungloved hand to his face and breathed in the scent of her skin.

Angelica's heart was in turmoil. She knew she appeared distracted as the cast was introduced. She barely noticed the handsome Mr Jones who would play her love interest, the Count Valantia. Their manager, Dunbar, was as slippery as ever, always in search of a sensational aspect to add to the production. Could Miss Leigh, in the part of Amanthis, be surprised at her morning toilette, he mused out loud. No, she could not, Angelica insisted, grateful for the support of Mr Jones who was young and more of a purist about honouring the script. Angelica's success in *Hamlet* had given her a little more influence and she felt she could now resist Mr Dunbar's more meretricious ideas.

After a desultory read-through of the play in which everyone's energy seemed subdued, the cast was dismissed early. Angelica had asked Mr Brunner if he could pick them up in the carriage at five o'clock, still half an hour away. She turned to Mary and said, 'I can't bear to remain in this dingy room awaiting the hour, let's watch for Mr Brunner from the theatre steps.'

The Piazza was filled with activity and the young women observed with fascination and occasional alarm as the gamblers and drinkers started to spill onto the street. Women and girls congregated around the taverns and there was laughter and ribaldry. Children played in the dirt and chased each other and the stray dogs. Mary knew well the life of these homeless waifs, the camaraderie and the vulnerability, and it still made her shiver to think of how she had had to scrabble to survive before Mrs Leigh happened upon her that auspicious night.

She took Angelica's arm and pointed to a doorway by the theatre. 'It was there that your mother found me trying to sleep in an old fruit crate. She seemed such an angel and smelled so pretty.' Angelica knew the story of how her mother exerted her charms on Mr Breville and the grubby waif had been taken in to be trained as a maid for Angelica.

Mary still had hold of her arm. 'I was so hungry and dirty and will never forget that beautiful well-upholstered carriage. Then to arrive at a palace of luxury and warmth in Berkeley Square was like a fairytale.'

'You have been such a friend to me too, Mary. When you arrived at the house I no longer felt quite so alone. There was always someone who would fight for me. You are quite a fighter you know.' They laughed.

Angelica's eye was caught by a tall, dark figure emerging from a house on the corner of Southampton Street. The immaculate black coat and dark trousers made Lord Rackham such a striking presence amongst the colour and chaos of the market square. He strolled into the centre of the Piazza, greeting a few people on his way. Angelica tried to shrink back into the shadows of the theatre portico but too late as his keen eye caught hers and he walked towards her. 'My dear Miss Leigh, what a pleasure. After my disappointment last week too!'

'Good afternoon, Lord Rackham.' With the modicum of politeness necessary, she extended her hand.

He was standing too close to Angelica for her comfort when he murmured, 'It is indeed convenient to see you as I was about to send you a note requesting a meeting. I have some important information to convey to you that affects your friend's illustrious career.'

Angelica was taken aback by his words. 'Which friend might that be, Lord Rackham?' she asked coldly.

He snorted. 'Keep your ingenue act for the stage, my dear. You know full well who I mean. It seems you are quite intimate with the honourable Member of Parliament for Abingdon, that paladin of virtue.' His voice drawled with contempt. 'It is his career with which I am concerned.' He smiled like a fox, his eyes cold and only his teeth glinting between bared lips. 'Perhaps you will do me the honour, and bestow on your friend some critical benefit, by visiting me at my rooms in Parliament?'

Angelica felt something cold slither down her spine. What might he know of how she had implicated Mr Asprey? She met Lord Rackham's gaze and foreboding gripped her. She recognised what she found so disturbing was his blackness of soul. He knew himself a villain but so deep was his misanthropy he scorned the best of humankind as being mere hypocrites in the world, operating as cynically as himself. This profound lack of shame made Lord Rackham invulnerable. With a chilling intuition, Angelica knew he hated to be bested and would go to any extreme to achieve his ends.

She could not bear to maintain his gaze and lowered her eyes, saying, 'I consider Mr Asprey's work of national importance. If I can help his career I will attend your office tomorrow.'

Lord Rackham took her hand again. 'You're a sensible woman. I'll expect you at three, Miss Leigh. Don't let me down this time,' he said with a hint of menace. 'Come to the entrance and the Parliamentary officers will lead you to my rooms.'

Just at this moment, Mr Breville's curricle swung into view with the bulky figure of Mr Brunner sitting up in the driving seat. Angelica almost called out with relief at the reassuring sight. She waved and the curricle wheeled round to pull up at the steps. Lord Rackham tipped his hat and turning on his heel, melted into the crowd.

Angelica realised how tightly she had been holding herself together, for when she tried to walk down the steps the tension drained from her. 'Mary, take my arm would you?'

Mr Brunner had jumped down and was by Angelica's side in a trice. He handed her and Mary up into the curricle and turned the horses for home. Angelica was silent. Just a few hours before she had been surprised by hopeful joy in Ivor Asprey's company but how short-lived that had been. Since being apprehended by Lord Rackham, an inexpressible dread gripped her spirit and her buoyant heart was suddenly weighted with lead. She feared Lord Rackham as a formidable foe and had a growing sense of horror that somehow he could destroy the man she now knew she loved.

In her training as a maid, Mary had learned discretion and so had moved out of earshot as Lord Rackham engaged her mistress in conversation, but it was clear there was a struggle of wills between them, and the power was not with her mistress. She leaned across and said, 'Lord Rackham's a lone wolf, that's the trouble.'

'I know. This is what I fear. He is proof against affection and contempt. What can you do with a man like that?' By the time they had returned to Berkeley Square, Angelica's fatigue had crept into her bones and her heart lay heavy in her chest. Extremes of emotion drained what energy she had left. She sought out her mother in the drawing room.

Mrs Leigh sat in the window seat with her appointments' diary open in her lap. Since her return, not only did she have a new wardrobe, with the unmistakeable Parisian stamp of luxury and fine detail, but her pretty face was less disconsolate. Mr Breville seemed increasingly charmed by her and she was at her most outrageously coquettish with him as he gave her carte blanche with his fortune. There was a light-hearted harmony in the household.

Mrs Leigh glanced up as her daughter entered the room. 'How did the rehearsal go?'

'Rather dully.'

With Angelica's flat words her mother peered more closely. 'My dear, what's troubling you?'

'Nothing, Mama. I'm just tired. I think I'll go to bed early, and be better in the morning.'

'I have the answer. Something to cheer you.' She tapped her finger on her diary. 'Just two weeks until the Jubilee Celebration. I thought I'd hold our own Jubilee party. We'll start in Hyde Park. On the Serpentine there'll be re-enactments of Lord Nelson's victory on the Nile.'

Angelica knew excitement was already building. All the London parks would be given over to riotous fêtes for a couple of days. A national holiday had been declared and the theatre would be dark so Angelica had three full days' holiday to enjoy.

Mrs Leigh looked up from her diary. 'You went to bed last night quite indisposed, I want to know more of what's transpired. Come and sit down.' She patted the seat beside her.

'Oh, Mama, I don't want to go over it. Suffice to say that when I was ill, Lord Latimer and Miss Fitzjames grew closer and I think might well marry.'

Her mother's eyes flashed. 'What a sly jade! I didn't know it was she who was Lord Latimer's intended. And you a friend to her too.'

'You, of all people, should understand how the heart roams where it will. We cannot direct whom we love.' Angelica's voice tailed off as she thought of the thunderbolt that had struck her, with not much warning. How much easier if her heart had been stirred by a man of little conse-quence in the world. But it had settled on one of the most esteemed reforming politicians whose public behaviour had to be beyond reproach. Criminality, scandal and dishonour could not sully his door, but wherever she went Angelica feared all three followed like a shade.

She wished she could confide in her mother, but Mrs Leigh had grown up with such deprivation, she'd learned young to grasp what she could for herself with little concern for scruples. Angelica's childhood had been poor too, but thanks to her mother's willingness to work at any employment that came her way, she had been provided with sufficient food and shelter to enjoy the luxury of a conscience. She recognised the existence of a universal good beyond her own need; Mr Asprey, in his work to better the lives of factory chil-dren belonged in that rarefied place. Angelica feared her love for him could not be more ill-placed; her reputation was so clearly at odds with his.

In a moment of dejection, she wondered if perhaps her destiny, after all, was not love and marriage and social acceptance, but merely to be the companion of a rich man, subject to his whims, like Mama. Or perhaps more congenially, there was a chance that a resourceful woman like herself could continue to work and gain independence; she enjoyed her profession but being an actress would not be available to her for ever. However, Mr Breville planned to open a shop in Mayfair selling his finest imported French porcelain, perhaps she could help develop his empire?

'Mama.' Angelica's voice was thoughtful. 'Perhaps I won't marry. I could continue my acting, and then when Mr Breville opens his emporium...'

Her musing was cut short by her mother snapping her diary shut and springing to her feet in irritation. 'Angelica! Don't be tiresome.' She stamped her foot. 'What hoity-toity disregard for your greatest gift. God gave you such beauty, Angelica, so you could make your way in the world and unite with a noble family. Of course you will marry!' Amabel Leigh flounced to the window and looked out, disgruntled by the contrariness of her wilful daughter.

Angelica walked to her side, putting a hand on her arm. 'Mama, I know how tirelessly you've worked to care for me when times were hard, and I couldn't be more grateful that you and Mr Breville share your home with me.' She took a deep breath. 'But you of all people should know how my profession, and now my father's criminal past, disqualifies me from that life you'd hoped for me.'

Her mother turned with an anxious expression in her eyes. 'It's not like you to be so cast down. What has happened?'

Angelica was surprised to hear her own voice express what she thought she'd hidden in her heart. 'I love a man with whom I have no future.'

'Why? Is he already allianced?'

She had let the secret out and now continued warily, 'No, but he's a prominent lawmaker engaged in important work.'

'And?' Mrs Leigh waited for further explanation.

'Any elevation of me can only detract from his own probity.'

Natural shrewdness had propelled Mrs Leigh from the poverty of the street to the affluence of Berkeley Square and, putting an arm around her daughter's shoulders, she said in a confiding voice, 'My dear, men are the most susceptible of beings. Love will make them do all manner of things that the world might consider wrong-headed and foolish beyond measure. You have the charms to drive even the most sober man to distraction.'

Angelica pulled away impatiently. 'Mama, you don't understand. I wish to protect him from my reputation, the very last thing I want is to drive him to distraction!'

'High principles indeed, Angelica, but you must think of your future too. And you may have no choice in the matter.' She gave her daughter a knowing smile.

Since her chance meeting with Lord Rackham in the Piazza, Angelica could not escape a real foreboding; he was not called the Black Cat for nothing, and it seemed he was stalking her while out to trap Mr Asprey in his claws. This was something she could not confide to her mother for what exactly was there to confide? Tired already by the day's activity, Angelica turned to Mrs Leigh whose head was bent over her appointments' diary once more. 'Mama, I think I might go to bed early and face the morrow anew.'

'Before you go, can I mark you in for the Jubilee picnic? As you've seen, they're building that bridge and fireworks tower in St James's Park. It should be prodigious fine.'

'Yes, I accept with pleasure.' Angelica bowed. 'Goodnight, Mama.'

As she passed Martin in the hall he hailed her. 'Miss Angelica. A letter!' He slapped it on a silver salver and flourished it before her. Angelica opened it and read a hurried scrawl in Isobel Fitzjames's light hand, requesting an audience the following morning at eleven.

Angelica withdrew a piece of notepaper from the drawer in the table in the hall and wrote simply, *Yes, indeed*, and signed it with a cursive 'A'. 'Martin, can you see that delivered tonight to the Fitzjames house in Grosvenor Square? Thank you. Goodnight.' She barely had the energy to smile as she climbed the stairs to her rooms.

* * *

Despite her troubled mind, sleep would not be resisted. As Angelica sank into her feather bed she felt herself falling out of consciousness and into a dark starless universe of silence. She was woken to pale sun as Mary drew the curtains back on a fine day. For a moment she had forgotten the foreboding of what was to come. Her blithe spirit returned with a sense of how good it was to be alive and to hold her own future in her hands. She loved and was loved. Ivor Asprey's stern face softened with a rare sweet smile materialised in her mind's eye but then the dark form of Lord Rackham suddenly appeared with his wolfish look. Angelica broke the reverie by leaping out of bed.

Mary poked her head out of the dressing room where she was selecting the day's clothes. 'No rehearsals today, what do you like to wear?'

'Oh, my green muslin this morning. Miss Fitzjames is coming. And then to go to the Houses of Parliament to see Lord Rackham. I need my armour. Perhaps my emerald green pelisse over the matching silk.'

'Are you sure, Miss Angelica? That's a very fetching outfit,' Mary said with a sly look in her eyes.

'It is fetching, I know, but it's modest in colour and design and makes me feel at my imperious best; I fear I'm going to need all my strength.'

'You don't have to go, you know.' Mary's rough childhood had made her less accommodating and more cynical in her relationship with the world.

'I do. I fear he's hatching some dark plan to discredit Mr Asprey and ruin his parliamentary career.' As Angelica spoke a wild scheme entered her mind. Lord Rackham was a notorious high stakes gambler; she wondered if he was as financially embarrassed as many of his peers. Half of the chest of coins from her father was meant for her use, might he be susceptible to the sight of gold? It seemed so many men were. She determined to take as many coins as she could without drawing attention to herself. Maybe she could buy Lord Rackham's silence?

Angelica dressed hurriedly. Mary combed out her hair, freeing the tangles from the night. It tumbled down Angelica's back almost to her waist. Mary wove it into fine plaits and coiled them onto her head with tendrils soft round her face.

Angelica had just finished her last cup of coffee and strolled into the hall when there was a knock on the front door. Without waiting for Martin, she opened it to find Isobel Fitzjames on the doorstep, her face lively and flushed. She grasped Angelica's hand and followed her into the hall. 'Oh, Miss Angelica, do you mind if we walk to Hyde Park? Lord Latimer and Mr Locke are going to be there exercising their horses. They want to see us and I'd really like to meet them.' Her words tumbled out in excitement.

Angelica smiled. 'Of course. It's a lovely day and I could do with some fresh air to blow away the indolence of the night.' She ran upstairs for her pelisse and bonnet. 'I think we can leave our maids here, don't you agree?'

Within minutes, the young women were walking briskly up Davies Street towards Grosvenor Square and the gate into the Park. Isobel was light-hearted as she grasped Angelica's arm and said, 'My lord is taking me to see his mama and papa for a formal introduction tomorrow. You've met the Duke, can you tell me anything about him?'

'He's never recovered from his terrible injuries, at the Battle of Alexandria I believe. Certainly a good decade ago. He keeps to his rooms but is amiable and most exercised over his collection of snuff boxes and mulls.'

'Oh good, perhaps I can take him one of Papa's.' Her small face looked relieved.

'I think he would very much appreciate that.'

'And the Duchess?'

'Well...' Angelica hesitated. She did not wish to alarm her young friend who was easily frightened. 'She's got a reputation as a woman who is seldom gainsaid. The best person to ask is Lord Latimer; after all, she is his mother!' Angelica laughed.

'But he just talks in hyperbole. He calls her Madame Virago but I know he's funning. I saw her at the masquerade ball but she wouldn't have noticed me.' Her brow wrinkled with anxiety.

Angelica turned to face her. 'Miss Isobel, try not to be cowed. Lord Latimer has chosen you. He comes into his inheritance this summer. Eventually he and you will become the Duke and Duchess of Arlington and his mama will become the Dowager, and the power in the household then resides with you.' Just at that moment there was a flurry of hooves and Lord Latimer on his grey stallion, Pegasus, rode up, closely followed by Dante Locke on a handsome ebony steed. The young men jumped down, swept off their hats and strode towards the women, smiling, their reins in their hands. Angelica's breath was caught by how striking both were with the sun behind them, casting an aureole of light around Lord Latimer's head.

'Miss Leigh, Miss Fitzjames, the day is suddenly brighter.'

'Oh tush, my lord, don't waste your flattery on us,' Angelica remonstrated with a smile. She watched them tie their horses to a tree, the reins loose enough to allow them to crop the grass. Lord Latimer turned and took both Angelica's and Miss Fitzjames's hands, bestowing on them his mischievous, flirtatious smile. Dante Locke bowed to both young women, his face so set his dark good looks had grown unfamiliarly thunderous. He took Angelica's arm and folded it into his. He obviously wanted to talk to her privately and marched her off at the head of the party.

After walking a short while he said in a low voice, 'Miss Leigh, I have told Charlie that I think he has treated you most shabbily.'

Angelica patted his gloved hand with hers. 'No, no, Mr Locke. Lord Latimer owed me nothing.'

'But he owed something to *love!*' His voice was agitated. 'Love is not inconstant, to be taken lightly and altered on a whim.' They walked on, his head bowed. 'When I love it will be for ever, how can it be otherwise?'

'You are a poet. These things go deep for you. But Lord Latimer is not like you or me. He is born to great estate and as such his future is not entirely for him to decide.'

'But that is fetter-bound!'

'I doubt he sees it that way. I think he and Miss Fitzjames are very well-suited and we must be happy for them.'

'But how can he choose to marry another when he has once loved you?' So affected by emotion was Dante Locke that he stopped walking and swung around to face her, his dark eyes blazing. 'More beautiful than Ophelia and more ill-used! It hurts my soul.' Lord Latimer and Miss Fitzjames were deep in conversation and were fast approaching, unaware of the febrile nature of the discussion ahead.

Angelica took Dante Locke's arm again and urged him to walk on, saying under her breath, 'I do appreciate your concern for me, and for the integrity of love. Sometimes we don't really know our own hearts, and then suddenly we do.' Her voice had an odd catch in it and he turned, surprised to see her eyes shining, but troubled.

'Miss Leigh, do you mean you love another?'

'I have never loved anyone until now. But your poet's sensibility might not accept that love can be ill-placed, and sometimes sacrifice becomes the greater art.' Angelica realised just how willing she was to set aside her own desires in order to protect the man she loved.

There was a wildness in her look and he strove to console her. Pressing her hand to his face, he said with feeling, 'From when I first beheld you on stage I knew joy was a flame in you. It could not be snuffed out even in the worst of storms, burning ever stronger in the following calm.'

Angelica was touched by his fervour and it comforted her to think that he might be right. That the precious flame in her own spirit could never be extinguished however hard the circumstances. They had walked in a loop round the horses when Lord Latimer and Isobel Fitzjames joined them.

Lord Latimer's eyes were dancing as he took her aside. 'Oh, Miss Leigh, my niece is up to something. Has she been in contact? She seems to be full of mischief and I fear it involves you!'

'She came for a brief visit yesterday. She does think she has a particular talent for matchmaking. I have warned her about it.' Angelica laughed quietly and continued, 'But I don't think it involves me, more her beloved Miss Stafford.'

'Oh, that might explain it. She's certainly a most managing young miss. I deplore that the female line in my family seem to suffer from a surfeit of conceit and dogmatism. Do you know, she had the temerity to suggest I would look handsomer in a coat not so closely fitted. Can you believe it? As if she knows better than my very expensive tailor, toast of the well-togged *haut ton!*'

'She is a fanciful-minded girl and I do enjoy her company.'

'She is a bore about you, you know, and is forbidden to mention your name in my mother's company. Elinor is continuing her surreptitious campaign against my uncle's plan to marry Lady Linus with a dark insistence she'll run away from home and become an actress if he does.'

Angelica felt the shock of his words. She had forgotten about Lady Linus, and yet Lord Latimer implied that her place in the Asprey household was still taken for granted. His light-hearted talk had also reminded her of an actress's place in the order of things. With a wry smile she said, 'Ah, my profession is an effective warning against moral decay.'

Lord Latimer was quick to backtrack on his words. 'No, no, Miss Leigh, not by me nor by Elinor. And even my forbidding uncle seems to have softened his stance.'

Angelica decided it was time to go home and restore her spirits before she faced whatever ill Lord Rackham had in mind. 'Do not exercise yourself on the matter, my lord, but I will have to take my leave. I need to make a visit this afternoon.'

She turned to Miss Fitzjames. 'I hope I'm not cutting short your morning too.'

'Not at all.' She took her arm. 'I have an appointment with my dressmaker.' The young men bowed, kissed their fingers and turned back to their horses. '*Au revoir, mesdemoiselles.* We'll meet again.'

As the men mounted their horses and trotted into the sun, Isobel Fitz-james squeezed Angelica's arm in sympathy. 'I'm sure it's only the Duchess who holds such severe views.'

'Don't concern yourself, my dear, I've grown used to it and am no longer upset by the judgement of strangers.'

'So you've never met her?'

'No, I don't think she would have knowingly allowed me into her domain.' Angelica turned and gave her friend a smile that masked the frustration and hurt that still surprised her, despite her denials. 'Remember however, she did unwittingly share her air with me when we went to Lord Latimer's ball.' They walked on, chatting about the progress of Isobel Fitz-james's new evening dress, which was in the process of creation, and Angelica's enjoyment of Mr Asprey's copy of *Waverley*.

Gothic heroines had not lost their allure for Miss Fitzjames. 'I've been so alarmed reading *The Monastery of St Columb,*' she offered as they walked towards Berkeley Square.

'I've heard Miss Roche's powers to spin a story are failing, but not for you it seems? More amusing to me was something I've just finished reading. *The Heroine* mocks the ideal of the wilting gothic heroine.'

'Ah, but the author's a man. What does he know of the lives of women at the mercy of the masculine sex?'

Angelica remembered how recently Miss Fitzjames had been entirely in the toils of a cruel fate conjured by her father's ruinous actions and the controlling power of his beneficiary. 'Oh, Miss Isobel, I'm sorry. I had forgotten what you have suffered. But your mystery benefactor has given you back your freedom?'

They had reached the Breville mansion in Berkeley Square and collected Isobel Fitzjames's maid from the kitchens. As they parted, Isobel answered, 'I don't have his name but he truly saved my life,' she added with a catch of tragic emotion in her voice. They briefly hugged. 'You are the noblest of women,' she said, and suddenly shy turned away to walk with her maid the few hundred yards to Grosvenor Square.

* * *

For her ill-omened visit to the Houses of Parliament, Angelica dressed carefully in her high-necked walking dress with a matching pelisse, both in a fine emerald batiste that was sober while still managing to illuminate her dramatic colouring. She found her small portmanteau in her dressing room and crossed the landing to her mother's room. The chest of gold coins had been stowed in the wardrobe filled to overflowing with winter pelisses. There amongst all the folds of luxurious fabric Angelica found and opened the trunk, extracting one hundred coins, glistening gold in her hands. She folded them into a silk shawl to stop them clinking, put her copy of her script at the top to disguise her bounty and descended the stairs to collect Mary.

She had asked Mr Brunner to bring the town chaise round to the door for half past two. Angelica did not expect the interview to last very long and had asked him to wait for them. Her heart was fluttering as the carriage set off towards Piccadilly. Mary sat beside her and knew her mistress well enough to understand the ordeal she faced, demanding all her wits and courage. She said grimly, 'Miss Angelica, you don't have to agree to anything. Make him wait for an answer.'

The carriage wheeled round towards the entrance at Speaker's House. Once again Angelica looked at the sad state of the headless statues on the front of the building and the coats of arms, crumbling into decay. It was a bleak thought that the statues had been decapitated in the Civil War more than a hundred and fifty years before and there had been no restoration since. How unstable things suddenly seemed. She climbed out of the carriage and with Mary walked into the vast lobby, crowded with men coming and going, intent on business. A Parliamentary Officer met them and Angelica said she was expected by Lord Rackham.

After a confusing detour through the corridors, Angelica and Mary were shown into an outer office surprisingly free of books and papers, and the officer closed the door behind them. There was a console table with decanters of various liquors and a collection of glasses. A cold light fell from the small north window onto a blue sofa with a Kashmir shawl thrown across one arm. In the centre of the room was a card table with four chairs informally arranged as if the players had only just left the game.

Mary took one of the chairs and Angelica sat on the edge of the sofa and waited, her portmanteau of gold coins behind her skirts.

The door opened and Cato Rackham entered as panther-like as his soubriquet suggested. 'Miss Leigh,' he purred. 'Forgive my not being here to welcome you.'

She stood up and he took her gloved hand in his. He was tall and stood rather too close but the sofa prevented her from stepping back. His dark eyes were on her face and she was acutely aware of his physical presence. He seemed full of suppressed energy and the fragrant musky smell of his pomade filled her nostrils. She lifted her chin, hoping that she gave an impression of confidence.

'Come through,' he said abruptly and led her into his own office, closing the door smartly on Mary, leaving her to wait. Here Angelica noticed the enormous desk and wondered how it too could be so free of any evidence of work. When she had visited Mr Asprey's offices, most notable was the sense of industry, the piles of paper, the books open everywhere on tables, pieces of paper with scrawled notes, the sense that there was urgent work being done. Lord Rackham pulled out a chair for her and another for himself. Again he sat too close, their knees almost touching.

'Miss Leigh, perhaps you are unaware of how important a man's probity is when he decides to embark on an unpopular mission?' His voice drawled but his eyes were gimlet sharp as he noticed her almost imperceptible flinch. 'Your friend, Mr Asprey, is engaged in controversial work and needs all the support from his fellow Members in the House that he can muster. Preventing brats in the middens of Yorkshire from working in the mills until they are grown past ten years old is just taking profits from the system, you know.'

Angelica could hardly bear the tension of his unsettling presence, aware of an aggression tightly sheathed, but only just. 'I approve of Mr Asprey's work. Why are you making such a point of this, Lord Rackham?' She barely recognised her voice, so weak and quiet.

He had uncoiled his lean frame to walk to the window. Angelica watched, feeling the silence between them crackling with what was yet unsaid. He turned, the daylight catching his narrowed glance and making his eyes glitter. 'I am making this point because I know just how associating with you has compromised Mr Asprey.'

So febrile were her emotions, anger flared at these words, not least because she knew their truth. It was what she feared too. She stood up. 'Mr Asprey does not "associate" with me. I don't care for your insinuations!'

Lord Rackham was by her side in a flash. He grabbed her wrist. 'Don't play the innocent with me, Miss Leigh. I know he's the only reason your criminal father was able to avoid the law of this land, whose very laws he has sworn to uphold.'

Angelica accepted with a plunge of spirit that she was at every disadvantage; all he said was true, and it was entirely her fault that this disreputable libertine had any hold over the most admirable man she knew. 'What are you proposing, my lord?'

He still held her by the wrist and looked down into her troubled face. 'I'm glad you're such a perspicacious young woman. If you wish me to ignore these glaring faults in the estimable Mr Asprey, I think we may negotiate something advantageous to us all.' His thin smile met her defiant gaze. But his hand on her wrist could tell her heart was less stalwart than she attempted to appear and was beating out a more anxious rhythm.

Angelica pulled her arm away and walked to where her portmanteau sat on the floor beside her chair. 'Perhaps we may. I wondered if a charity of your choosing might be grateful for a donation?' She was shaking as she opened the bag and slipped her hand into the silken folds of the shawl, withdrawing a handful of glistening gold coin.

She did not have a chance. He was beside her before she could even turn around and pinned her arms from behind, his face close to hers, his words full of quiet menace. 'Now you try to bribe a member of His Majesty's Government? This alone could place you in the hell of Newgate, you sorry, stupid hussy!'

Angelica recoiled, realising how her single-minded pursuit of protecting Mr Asprey had blinded her to the danger of such behaviour as this.

Still holding her arms tight, Lord Rackham said in a voice that was smooth and urbane once more, 'My plan is much more diverting, you know. Recall my previous offer, to save your father from a hanging? So rudely flouted, indeed. I'm prepared to offer it again, to save Mr Asprey's precious, self-righteous skin.'

Angelica felt her colour rise and managed to wrench an arm free to whirl around and face him. 'Why the animus against Mr Asprey?'

'Don't care for a man who wears his virtue on his sleeve. We're all as wicked as each other, just some of us don't pretend to be otherwise. If he makes a show of his heart, I am happy to be the daw to peck it to destruction.'

Angelica felt the blood pound in her ears. 'What Mr Asprey means to do is of importance to our greater good. Children should be protected.'

She was thinking of Mr Brunner's experiences in the mills but was cut short by his lordship's dismissive snort. 'Spare me the piety, my dear!' He took her arm more gently this time. 'You already know how you quicken my blood. From the moment I first saw you as Ophelia, in a state of undress, my heart was snared. Your beauty haunts me. And to have you here with me, your spirit bold and defiant, I find it hard not to take you in my arms right now!'

Angelica felt the net closing in. 'Lord Rackham, what is it you propose?'

'You know very well what I propose, my dear. The house in Albemarle Street still awaits.'

Angelica could not control an involuntary shudder. 'My lord, what if I refuse your offer?'

'I will not hesitate to take what I know about both Asprey's activities and yours to the Serjeant at Arms right here, right now. The evidence is to be found in your portmanteau, after all.'

Angelica's heart was thumping and she tried to think how best to navigate this newly threatening sea where calling his bluff seemed as perilous an option for her as acceptance of her concubinage to him. 'When would you need my answer?' she asked, hoping for time to think.

'Now,' he drawled. 'I won't make that mistake again.'

Angelica clenched her hands so hard she felt her fingernails bite into her skin. 'Well then, yes, my lord. You leave me no alternative. On the proviso that you never again hint at anything that might harm Mr Asprey's reputation or career.'

'Very noble, Miss Leigh. You have been too long exposed to the dramatic arts, I fear.'

He advanced on her and pulled her close, his arms holding her tight to his chest. 'I think we can seal this bargain with a kiss?' Without waiting for an answer he tilted her chin upwards and pressed his lips hard on hers.

She recoiled. The smell of him, the alien feel of his skin, the hardness of his arms around her back, the fingers pinching her chin so she could not pull away. Breathing hard, he looked coldly into her eyes. 'Come now Miss Leigh, I'm sure you can do better than that. Surely you have done this before?'

Angelica had never been so physically intimate before with any man but was not about to give him the satisfaction of knowing this. Tentatively she slipped her arms round his neck and lifted her face to let him kiss her again, willing herself not to shrink away from his touch. She was an actress, she told herself, now she had to summon her skills to save the day. His mouth pressed down once more and prised open her lips with his as his hand slipped inside her pelisse to clamp her hips hard against his groin. He was breathing deeply and his eyes were half-closed. Angelica felt a combination of alarm and horror. Every cell of her body and every filament of spirit recoiled. She had to use the most iron-bound restraint not to cry out in protest. This was not the way she wished her first experience with a man to be, and this man was not one she could ever desire.

She realised, however, with great clarity that, although unwilling to sacrifice herself for her father's safety, she was more than willing to sacrifice everything for the man she loved. She pulled herself free. 'Lord Rackham, I have my maid and coachman waiting. I must be gone.'

'On your honour.' He smirked. 'I take it our deal is made. You will move into the house I have prepared with every comfort next Monday, and I will never mention to anyone the illegality of Mr Asprey's activities. He will continue freely to promulgate his perverse reforms with never a demur from me.'

Angelica nodded, then grabbed her portmanteau and walked quickly to the door. Lord Rackham opened it, his eyes so full of cupidity and triumph she gasped. He spoke in a firm matter-of-fact way. 'I will see you next Monday at eleven at number twenty-four, Albemarle.'

Angelica grasped Mary's hand and could not leave fast enough. They were back in the wide corridor by which they had come, but the Parliamentary Officer had led them here and they had not paid attention. How to find their way back to the lobby and escape?

Angelica led them in one direction past closed doors with no sign of the way out, feeling a rising panic in her chest as the sense of entrapment grew. 'Mary, do you recall the way we came?' she asked, her voice betraying her anxiety. Mary looked as perplexed as Angelica felt. Just as she was turning back to retrace her steps, Angelica saw a familiar figure striding towards her carrying a sheaf of papers. 'Oh, Mr Digby, I'm so glad to see you,' she cried and to his consternation almost fell into his arms.

'Miss Leigh. What are you doing here? Mary too. You look quite distraught.' He took Angelica's elbow and led her into his office. 'Sit down for a minute. Can I get either of you something to drink?'

He was standing before her, concern etched on his kindly face. 'Oh, I'm in so much trouble!' She didn't mean to confide in him but had not the energy to stop the words tumbling out.

'Would it help to tell me more?' he asked quietly.

She shook her head. 'There's no answer I'm afraid.'

'Well, if anyone knows what to do it will be Mr Asprey. He's back from his committee meeting in a minute or so.'

Angelica jumped to her feet. 'No, no! He must not know I've been here and in such a state.'

'What must he not know?' A deep amused voice cut through her panic. She turned to see Ivor Asprey walk into the room, carrying even more papers, which he put down on a desk. He stood there, tall and soberly dressed with a wry look of amusement on his face.

'Oh Mr Asprey.' Angelica took a step towards him, then stopped herself. She had made her bargain to save him and his career and he was the last person in whom she should confide. Recognising her distress, he took her arm and led her into his office, clearing some books from a chair so she could sit. Her head sank into her hands.

'Two brandies, please Mr Digby,' he called before closing the door. 'Now tell me, Miss Leigh, what has distressed you so.'

'I cannot. I really cannot.' Angelica's mind was racing. How could she possibly tell him what she had agreed to? He would forbid it and open himself to Lord Rackham's revenge. She was also frightened at what his wilder nature might do.

He drew up a chair next to her and she shrank away, afraid of Lord Rackham's contamination already on her skin. She could smell him still; perhaps Mr Asprey could too. His lean handsome face watched her with tenderness, his eyes bluer than she remembered. 'I don't want you to do anything you feel uncomfortable doing.' His words were so quiet and understanding tears sprang to her eyes. Mr Digby had brought in the brandy and she gulped a mouthful. The burning liquor hit her throat and made her cough. Ivor handed her his linen handkerchief.

'Does your distress involve me?' His words were neutral but they released a wave of emotion in her. She did not want to cry and could only nod.

'Why not share it? It may not be as bad as you think.'

'It is worse than you could imagine,' Angelica said in a small voice. She put out her hand for his. 'I so wanted my first kiss to be yours.' He gave her a startled look as she continued, 'But Lord Rackham kissed me and I feel defiled.'

Ivor Asprey leapt to his feet with a curse. 'The devil take that man as his own! And I will hasten him on his way.' He made as if he was about to leave and seek out the black lord.

'Oh no! My Asprey, please don't go. I need you here. Please!' He turned and with a puzzled face returned to stand beside her, his face troubled and a sense of outrage emanating from his person. She took a deep breath and said, 'Before I can say anything more I really wish you would kiss me to wipe my memory of Lord Rackham and allow me to start again.'

His face was shocked with a shifting combination of concern and tenderness. 'My dearest Miss Leigh, I cannot dishonour you so.'

'But I am already dishonoured and I need you to restore my honour. Please kiss me, Mr Asprey.' She had stood to face him and each took a step towards the other as if drawn together by an invisible thread. He took her hands and Angelica lifted her face, still stained with tears. This time she was overflowing with feeling and longing for his arms, for his lips.

'Miss Leigh, are you sure? I did not envisage our first kiss to be like this.'

He was smiling down at her, but he was troubled too. In the crook of his arm Angelica leant into him, excited yet consoled and murmured into his chest, 'I did not wish it this way either, but my wishes have been overborne.' Without another word, he bent his head and met her lips. Warm and soft and compelling, she felt her whole being flood with desire, focussed on this passionate meeting of their bodies at last. He smelled of heathery wool and fresh air and the brandy they had just drunk. She could feel his heart beating and her own slowed to match its steady rhythm. Stretching up on tiptoes, she slid her arms around his neck and held him as tightly as he held her and they kissed with a fervour she had only dreamed of. She abandoned herself to the moment, hardly knowing where her body and soul ended and his began.

When they eventually parted, he led her to the chair and sat beside her, still holding her hand. She felt the colour rise to her cheeks as she met his eyes full of amusement and desire. 'You do realise, Miss Leigh, that you've left me no alternative but to make an honest woman of you?'

Angelica gasped and dropped her gaze. Could he mean that? Was it a proposal of marriage after all? She was in such tumult, her voice had a catch of emotion she could not name. 'When you hear what I have to say, you may not think it.'

'Let me be the judge of that. Tell me now, what wickedness has transpired with that hell-born rake?'

Angelica's heart was in his hands and she knew she could not keep anything from him. She related her story and how she could not see any way to protect him from Lord Rackham's malevolence. Ivor Asprey was on his feet again, his softness replaced with white-hot anger. It alarmed her, but excited her too, to see this eminently cool, disciplined man so impassioned. 'So he's blackmailing you to prostitute yourself to save my reputation!'

'I first tried to offer him some gold coin!'

He turned sharply towards her, his hands raked through his hair, making him look quite wild. 'You tried to bribe a Member of His Majesty's Government? You're a dangerous woman and I can't let you out of my sight for a moment!'

'But what was I to do?'

'It is not your business!' His voice was emphatic. 'Did it ever occur to you that I would risk everything for you? What is my reputation if I cannot have the woman I love by my side?'

This was the first time he had actually said the words *the woman I love* and Angelica felt a lurch of happiness. She looked at him but could not speak. He was still pacing. She recognised the wild youth that his nephew had suggested was banished by guilt and grief. Angelica realised she was seeing the raw heart of the man, and it thrilled her. Ivor Asprey stopped pacing and a hard martial light in his eyes spelled danger. He said in a voice filled with emotion, 'There is only one way. Stay here, Miss Leigh.' And he strode out of the door, calling to Mr Digby as he passed his desk. 'I want you for my second.'

Angelica flew out of her chair and started to run after him. She was gripped with the worst dread of all, that the man she loved was about to risk everything and challenge Lord Rackham to a duel. Things were suddenly a great deal worse.

'Go back to Digby and Mary, Miss Leigh! This is no one's business but mine.' And he strode down the corridor to Lord Rackham's rooms.

'Mr Digby, we have to stop this!' she sobbed, terrified at the thought of losing him to death or exile. Mary had leapt to her side.

'Now, do sit down, Miss Leigh. This is really between the men. It's a matter of honour you see.' Nicholas Digby's voice was calm but emphatic.

'No! I don't see. What could be more important than life? Please will you stop them, Mr Digby? Please.'

His face was serious and drawn with anxiety. 'As Mr Asprey says, this is his business and his alone. As his second I have a duty to see if there is another way for honour to be satisfied, but I don't hold out much hope. This has been a long time coming.'

'Where will this take place?' Her face was full of anguish.

'I cannot tell you that, even if I knew. Women are to be kept from this business at all costs.'

'How can you say that, Mr Digby? You a radical, too! Mr Asprey and his work are far too important to be left to the chance of a bullet, his life hanging by a thread – and all to satisfy some outmoded concept of honour!'

'Miss Leigh, you do not understand. This is part of an ancient chivalric code. He is protecting the woman he loves and he is acting to maintain his own sense of honour in the face of unforgiveable provocation. Even a Godwinian as I am would do the same. It is men's business.'

Angelica picked up her portmanteau and, grabbing Mary's hand, dashed from the room. She must think what could be done. She could not bear to allow that her behaviour might be the cause of the greatest tragedy of all. There was only one thought in her mind. She had to stop this disaster from happening.

11

LOVE AND HONOUR

Angelica bundled Mary into the chaise and they subsided on the seat as Mr Brunner set off for home. Her mind was reeling with the events of the past hour but the overriding certainty was that she had to find a way of preventing the duel. She appeared unusually distrait and Mary grasped her hand in concern. 'Miss Angelica, do not distress yourself so. You must leave Mr Asprey and Mr Digby to work things out.'

'Oh, Mary! It's all my fault. If Mr Asprey has challenged Lord Rackham and asked Mr Digby to be his second, he's serious about it!' She heard her voice ending in a kind of wail.

Mary was more matter of fact in most things and she scoffed, 'Didn't think Mr Asprey such a cod's head but wouldn't put anything past that wicked lord.'

'But Mary, what can be done?'

'Nothing, Miss Angelica. Let them get satisfaction by taking a pop at each other, might shake up their jingle-brains if nothing else.'

'No, Mary! He cannot die. He has such important work to do. And... I love him!' It was the first time she had said it out loud.

Mary was unperturbed and merely nodded. 'It's no secret, Miss Angelica.'

Her mistress continued in a voice full of emotion, 'If he dies because of me I could not live with myself.'

'Miss Angelica, ye're not in a play now, don't blame yourself. Mr Asprey'll only do what he wishes, ye know.'

'Help me find a way of stopping this duel, Mary.' Angelica's green eyes were on her maid's face, knowing it was a vain request but she could not keep her anxiety to herself.

Mary's mobile face was furrowed with thought. 'Well,' she said warily, 'my cousin, Dan, I call him my cousin, he's as much a foundling as me, but now a Bow Street man. But the Bow Street officers need to know where the duel will take place, and when. They also need you to flash the blunt.'

Angelica remembered the gold coins in her portmanteau and said, 'There's no trouble with that. But how to discover the field of combat?' She gazed out of the window and realised they were travelling down Pall Mall, close to St James's Square. She stood up and banged on the chaise oof and Mr Brunner brought the horses to a halt by the side of the road. His reassuring face appeared at the window and she said, 'Apologies, Mr Brunner, but could you first of all take us to the Asprey house, in St James's Square?'

Within a minute or so she had scrambled out, leaving Mary to wait. 'I won't be a moment, I just hope Miss Stafford can meet me.' She ran up the front steps and rapped on the door.

It was opened by Goodall whose severe formality softened noticeably at the sight of her. 'Ah, Miss Leigh. What a pleasure to see you again.'

'Thank you, Mr Goodall, I have fond memories of my stay here under your care.'

He put out his hand to take her pelisse and bonnet but Angelica said in a voice still breathless, 'I'm not expected, I know, but is Miss Stafford available for callers by any chance?'

He nodded and showed Angelica into the morning room. She paced, aware of how wrong all this was. She was now involving Mr Asprey's employees but such was her desolation at the thought of losing him, of the nation losing him, she could not walk away with a shrug.

Sarah Stafford entered the room and Angelica took a step towards her and said with relief, 'Oh Miss Stafford! I'm so pleased that you are here.' She stretched out her hands. 'I apologise for coming unannounced but there is something of great moment for which I need your advice, if not your help.'

Miss Stafford appeared unruffled but her eyes were watchful. She suggested they sit. 'I've left Elinor writing about Queen Elizabeth and her pirates. I didn't tell her you were here as I thought it might be a private matter you wanted to discuss.'

'You're right. I'm in some despair as I don't know how best to proceed.'

'Why? What has happened?'

'Because of me, Mr Asprey has felt compelled to call Lord Rackham out. And he's asked Mr Digby to be his second.' Angelica had grasped Miss Stafford's hand as she spoke, only glancing up when she heard her measured response.

'This is a matter for them, Miss Leigh. Their honour is held so dear it can seem nonsensical to us, but I know Mr Asprey will not aim to kill.'

'That may be so, but we cannot know what Lord Rackham will do, so deep is his antipathy for his rival.'

Sarah Stafford reached for her hand as Angelica took a deep breath before confiding what lay heavily in her memory. 'Miss Stafford, I was eleven years old when an American gold trader who knew my mother told me of the duel that had just been fought in his country by a politician he considered the reforming hope for his people. I consider Mr Asprey a similarly important man for our country.'

'And what transpired in that case?'

'The man was a Mr Hamilton and he was shot and killed by his Vice President. All that promise, all the possibility of reform, snuffed out by one bullet. And all to redress an imagined slur. The American gold trader had tears in his eyes as he told me and I feel now as full of foreboding about Mr Asprey's fate.'

Miss Stafford sat quite still, her head bowed. 'I can understand your agitation. I now share it too. Not only will the country be the poorer but I could not bear Elinor to lose her only parent. What do you suggest we do?'

Angelica leaned forward, a small hope rising in her heart as she grasped both of Miss Stafford's hands. 'Oh, thank goodness you too see the necessity of action, however irregular. My maid, Mary, has a friend who's a Bow Street officer and I have the money they require to investigate. We just need to know where and at what time the combat is due to take place.' Miss Stafford nodded. 'I hoped that you might find that out from Mr Digby?' Angelica added with some shyness. She was asking a great deal but she also knew that Miss Stafford loved Elinor Asprey like a daughter and would do anything to save her any more anguish.

Just at that moment, the girl's pale face peered round the door. Her blue eyes lit up with an irresistible merriment. 'Miss Leigh! Miss Stafford didn't tell me you were here.' She danced into the room and curtseyed, then impulsively grasped Angelica's hand. 'I've finished my essay on the Queen's pirates and was thinking I could go for a walk with Miss Stafford. But you are here! This is beyond my hopes.'

Angelica laughed; the girl brought out all her own light-heartedness and joy in life. 'Well, I only dropped by for a moment and must be going. But perhaps we could meet for a walk next week?'

She offered her hand to Miss Stafford who took it and met her eyes with a meaningful look. 'I'll send a note of time and place later this evening,' she murmured as all three walked into the hall.

'Oh, Miss Leigh, I so want to see you. I have more news to tell you.' Elinor's eyes sparkled with the import of what she had to share and Angelica met Miss Stafford's eyes and saw she was blushing, her fine face suffused with happiness. Angelica took her hand and squeezed it. 'Congratulations,' she mouthed over the girl's head.

As Angelica climbed back into the chaise she leant her head back on the squab cushions and closed her eyes, suddenly very weary.

'Well?' Mary's voice cut through her reverie.

'Miss Stafford is as concerned about her young charge having her father killed. If she can, she will find out the details and let me know. I am asking her to betray the confidence of the man she loves. It is so impudent of me.' She paused with the import of what was at stake. 'But Mary, I don't need to tell you how discreet we have to be.'

They continued in silence with just the clip-clopping of the horses' hooves on the cobbles and the occasional shouts of drivers and carters as they passed. Angelica was aware of the enormity of what she intended to do, of what tragedy might transpire if she didn't succeed. She had always been brave but now that she had been overtaken by this fierce love for Ivor Asprey she felt unsettled and vulnerable. Only with her mind more tranquil now she had a plan, was Angelica able to appreciate at last that he seemed to love her in return and, miraculously, appeared quite unconcerned by her dubious family and sullied reputation. But underlying her unexpected ecstasy was a throbbing fear that clutched her heart; even love such as theirs could be destroyed in one fell act.

As they entered the house in Berkeley Square, Martin sprang forward with excitement, straightening his wig and struggling into his frock coat. 'The mistress would welcome your presence in the drawing room,' he said mock-formally as he took Angelica's bonnet and pelisse. Turning to Mary, he continued, 'Mrs Leigh is giving us all the day off for the Jubilee celebrations, so we can see the balloon ascent, battle enactments and fireworks.' He linked his arm in hers and danced her down the corridor to the kitchens at the back.

Angelica mounted the stairs to find her mother sitting on the sofa between the windows, various handwritten lists strewn around her. She looked up as her daughter entered the room. 'My dear, I'm having such fun organising our party for the Jubilee. I'm giving the servants the day off. Martin's threatening to leap over the moon with joy.'

Angelica could not even begin to confide the day's momentous events to her. Their sensibilities were so different it took energy she did not presently possess to argue her point of view against Mrs Leigh's pragmatic eye for the main chance. However, she had to explain about the gold. 'Mama, this morning I took a hundred coins from the chest Mr Crowe brought from France.'

Her mother barely looked up from her notes as she said, 'I consider that bounty for you. Mr Breville is more than generous to me. I hope you spend it wisely, my dear.'

'Oh Mama, thank you.' Angelica dashed to her side and embraced her. 'That's very kind of you.'

Amabel Leigh kissed her cheek and laughed. 'It's the least that your papa owes you and it's Neddy you have to thank. It's Mr Breville's generosity that makes mine possible.'

'Well I am. I think him the perfect companion for you.'

Her mother looked up, a smile on her lips and a coquettish tilt to her head. 'And I indeed am the perfect companion for him.'

'Indeed. When is he back from the Staffordshire potteries?'

'Oh, tomorrow, I hope. It's a long journey home.'

Angelica sat down again and took up her book. It consoled her that the smooth leather binding of Mr Asprey's *Waverley* had been handled by his hands too.

As they were going in to dinner, Martin arrived, flourishing a silver salver with a note at its centre. Bowing deeply he said, 'All very havey-cavey, Miss Angelica. Some scruffy young whelp delivered it and dashed off before I could speak.'

Full of trepidation, she unfolded the paper. There in Miss Stafford's elegant hand she read:

Chalk Farm Tavern, tomorrow at dawn, half past the hour of four

She stuffed the paper into her pocket and took her mother's arm. 'I'm sorry to leave you to dine alone, Mama, but there's something I have to do.' Before Mrs Leigh could remonstrate with her, Angelica dashed from the room to find her maid. Within minutes, Mary was tying her bonnet in the hall while Angelica slipped into her pelisse, grasped her bonnet and the portmanteau she had stowed under the hallway table.

'Mary, it's still light for a couple of hours. I hope you're happy to walk? We involve fewer people in our deeds.'

She nodded. 'Bow Street Magistrates is just next door to the theatre. And I think cousin Dan is one of the officers on duty tonight. I'll be glad to see him.' They set off towards Piccadilly; Angelica had chosen one of her larger brimmed bonnets and tucked her flaming hair out of sight so she was less recognisable.

As they walked quickly past the male preserves of St James's on their right, Angelica was reminded again of just how shocking the enterprise was she had embarked upon. If she were to invade the exclusive portals of one of the august gentlemen's clubs of the area it would be as nothing compared to her effrontery in interfering in the sacred matter of masculine honour. To disrupt a duel was outrageous but this was just what she intended to do. And in order to do so, she and Mary had to enter the Bow Street Magistrates where the only women to darken their doors were drunks, thieves and bawds. Young ladies, even on the margins of polite society like Angelica, were expected to keep well away from the contamination of the underbelly of London life.

They walked on past Albany where it was rumoured Lord Byron had just moved into Lord Althorp's set, with his talking macaw, and was living the life of a Regency dandy. Mary peered into the courtyard of the great building. 'I saw the poetic lord once at the theatre, talking to that buffle-headed whore, Susan Boyce. She did seem very taken with him in his midnight blue opera cloak.'

Angelica laughed. 'Mary! You shouldn't talk so.'

'Why not? 'Tis saucy ninnies like her who bring your profession into disrepute, giving licence to hell-hounds like Rackham.'

'Come now, Mary. You may be right about Lord Rackham, but Mr Kean considers Lord B's interest in the theatre more artistic than carnal. He calls him the most discerning of critics – methinks largely because he rates Mr Kean so highly.' The women chuckled. Soon they were at Leicester Square and Angelica offered to carry the portmanteau which she feared had become quite heavy in Mary's hand. As they rounded the corner of Russell Street, they saw an officer of the Horse Patrol in his distinctive red waistcoat standing outside the door to the Magistrate's Office. An idea came to Angelica that she could offer a donation to this newly founded body of law enforcement; that way it would not appear to be a blatant bribe.

The man stood aside in some surprise as Angelica and Mary entered the building. At the desk sat another officer writing in a ledger. He looked up, bored, then seeing Angelica, her beauty barely obscured by the size of her bonnet, leapt to his feet. 'Miss, what may I do for you?' Mary stepped forward and asked if Dan Pellini was on duty. The officer nodded and looked at them both with curiosity. 'He's down with a felon in the cells. I'll fetch him. Who shall I say?'

'His cousin, Mary Summer, but he'll just know me as Mary.' As the man disappeared into the back of the building, she turned to Angelica. 'I only became Mary Summer once your mother plucked me from the streets. The season was summer, so that became my name.'

A tall, raw-boned young man entered the room, smart in his uniform, his curly chestnut hair waxed into a neat helmet that befitted the seriousness of his job. 'Mary, 'tis good to see ye.' He came forward with his hands out and took one of hers.

'Dan, it is too.' Mary turned to Angelica. 'Miss Leigh, this is Dan Pellini, my childhood companion. Dan, this is my mistress, Miss Leigh..' Both bowed as Mary continued, 'I'm glad to see you, and doing so well.'

The first officer was watching this exchange with interest. Angelica touched Mr Pellini's sleeve. 'Sir, may we tell you our business?' He nodded and walked to the further corner of the room and opened a door.

'This is our interview room.' He gestured for them to enter a small dingy space lit by one high window, grimed with dust and soot, the threads of cobwebs hanging with trapped dead flies. 'Sit down, ladies.'

Angelica pulled Miss Stafford's note from her pocket and smoothed it. Looking at Dan Pellini she said with serious intent, 'This is a most sensitive matter and I really wish you to guarantee confidentiality with everything I say, as well as any action you may agree to do.'

'Well, that depends, miss.' He was wary.

Angelica lifted the portmanteau onto the table between them and opened it up. She removed a handful of gold coins. 'I am very anxious to pay the Bow Street officers properly for their professional efforts, especially to support the Horse Patrol.'

Dan Pellini's manner became more focussed and grave. 'Tell me the problem and I will abide by your strictures on privacy and confidentiality.'

Angelica pushed the piece of paper with the place and time of the duel across the table to him. 'Two eminent lawmakers are determined on a matter of honour, the field of combat, as you see, is Chalk Farm.'

'We don't care to interfere with gentlemen and their private business, miss. Nobs and bigwigs are a law unto themselves.' He shifted uneasily in his seat.

'That may well be, but as you know it is against the law to conduct such business. I am merely asking you to fulfil your duty and disperse the combatants before any lethal action takes place.' She let the coins slip through her fingers, a glistening, clinking stream of gold. His eyes were irresistibly drawn to the sight. 'But you must assure me that there will be no reporting of this either officially or to the scribblers of Grub Street. Nor mention of the names of the principals involved.'

Mr Pellini ruminated for a second of two, his wide good-humoured face wrinkled with the puzzle of how best to proceed. Seeming to have made a decision, he met Angelica's piercing gaze. 'I could take three officers with me and log it in the duty roster as investigating an armed affray. That way no names need be mentioned.'

Angelica leapt up and grasped his hand. 'I am so grateful to you, Mr Pellini. Have you a container into which I can put the fifty spankers I have for your trouble?'

He pulled a cloth bag out of the drawer in the desk, as if ready for just such a transaction, and Angelica counted out the fifty Louis she had agreed as recompense enough. She looked into his face, her eyes searching his. 'I can trust you, Mr Pellini, to conduct this with discretion. No names. No arrests. Just disruption through your presence?'

Mary grasped her cousin's arm and said with fervour, 'Thank you, Dan, I know we can trust you. I always could.' And they clutched at each other's hands with the memory of their shared street life as children and how they had protected each other in the feral back alleys of Covent Garden.

'Come and see me again, Mary,' he said, his eyes crinkling into a smile.

The women left the building in a hurry, just as two raggedy ruffians were being manhandled through the door, stinking of ale and with blood pouring from the head of one. Angelica took her maid's arm. 'Mary, I'm exhausted. Let's hail a Hackney cab to take us home.'

'You look worn thin. With another rehearsal tomorrow afternoon, you must rest.' They heard the sound of horses' hooves as a cab drew up to deliver a couple to the theatre and Mary stepped forward to catch the coachman's eye. They climbed into the evil-smelling interior, the straw dirty on the floor, the seats greasy with years of grime. They were grateful to be back in Berkeley Square within fifteen minutes.

'Thank you, Mary. It was a stroke of luck that your cousin Dan was there and able to help. All I can do now is pray.'

* * *

Angelica slept deeply and without dreams. At dawn she awoke with a start and lay there wondering why her heart was racing. She felt weighed down with nameless dread. The birdsong seemed louder than usual, with a note of alarm in the sweet notes that carolled from the throats of robins, thrushes and blackbirds hopping in the bushes in the Square. She sat up, suddenly aware of what the hour meant. Was her agitation and the heaviness of spirit a portent of what was to come, or had already been? She crept from her bed, not wishing to wake the household, and stood at the window holding back the curtain so she could look out on the gardens below. The new rising sun could just be seen through an early mist which wreathed through the trees. Chalk Farm was on higher land; would it be even more obscured by gauzy ribbons of cloud, she wondered, or had the sun burnt through to brighten the fields?

Cold and tired, Angelica knew she could no longer sleep but crawled back into bed to warm her toes and shoulders. Despite the knot of anxiety in the pit of her stomach, her mind was in flight with the astounding knowledge – *the man I love loves me, and whatever happens that will always be, for how can love so elemental turn to hatred, or indifference, and die?* But did Fate hear her happy cry, she wondered, and place a warning band across her heart? She was not yet safe in his arms but there could never be another man for her. She knew this now and the certainty gave her strength; nothing could deprive her of this joy, not even death. She held this truth close while she waited for news.

Despite the early hour, Angelica decided to get dressed and slipped into her everyday blue calico with a pale-yellow braided spencer over the bodice for warmth. She went down to breakfast before her mother had risen from bed. Restless, she picked up the script that was growing onerous to her as increasingly she jibbed at the play's assumption that complete innocence could exist while in real life she was dealing with momentous matters of life and death. She paced to the front window and back, not certain what news she expected and from whom. Would Miss Stafford send her a note that Mr Asprey was at breakfast, as cool as a cucumber, as if nothing had transpired?

Her emotions were growing increasingly frayed when close to eleven o'clock she heard a sharp rap on the door. Martin opened it to a man so forbidding and austere in manner that his natural ebullience deserted him. A crestfallen face peered round the door of the morning room where Angelica stood tensely by the fireplace, her script tossed aside. 'A gentleman to see you, Miss Angelica.'

She sprang forward, her face suffused with joy. It could only be him. She swept into the hall. 'Mr Asprey, you are well?' Her joyful words died on her lips as she saw how white and grim he looked.

He met her bright face with a frosty hauteur and bowed stiffly. 'Would you do me the honour, Miss Leigh, of accompanying me to Hyde Park for a drive?'

'Yes, of course.' With a sinking heart Angelica climbed the stairs to her rooms to collect her pelisse and bonnet, which she crammed on her head with little concern for the effect. Martin opened the front door for them; even his demeanour was subdued.

Without saying a word, Mr Asprey handed Angelica into his curricle. Noticing he was without his groom, Angelica enquired, 'No Rocky?'

'No. I don't care to catechise your character in front of the servants,' was the cold response. He had not turned to meet her gaze and drove his horses off towards Grosvenor Street. Angelica glanced at his profile, so distinguished, so beloved to her, but set now so adamantine that not even a muscle twitched on his jaw. Eventually he pulled his horses up under a distant copse near the Tyburn turnpike. Angelica felt she was heading to as uncompromising a demise as all the criminals who had been brought to Tyburn gallows before her.

At last Ivor Asprey spoke, his voice quiet but compressed with fury. 'Miss Leigh, Lord Rackham and I were threatened with arrest this morning. The Bow Street officers said an unknown young woman had tipped them off. Pray tell me, if that was you?'

Angelica was confronted with the humiliation her actions had brought down on a proud man's head. She could only look away, her own face ashen.

'What makes you think you have the right to interfere in matters of *my* honour when I had expressly warned you to leave my business to me?' He was almost hissing in self-righteous affront.

Angelica looked down at her hands which were clasped tight together in her lap. 'I just could not contemplate losing you.'

'This is not about you and what you cannot bear. This is my life and my honour – and so, forgive me if I'm wrong – *my business*! How can I ever trust you again?'

Angelica's emotions were so raw she felt her outrage flare. 'I beg to differ. It's not just about you, Mr Asprey. What about your daughter who has no mother and only you in the world?'

'I don't need you to remind me of my duty to Elinor!' His anger had turned from cold to hot. 'I love her more than life itself.'

'But not more than your honour, sir.' Angelica's voice was dismissive.

'This is not something I would expect you to understand.' He grasped her shoulders and turned her to face him. She was surprised to see such a wild light in his eyes.

'Well, no, Mr Asprey, I don't understand. Was it not me who Lord Rackham dishonoured, not you?'

'In dishonouring you so, he dishonoured me.' There were pinpoints of colour on his cheekbones.

'How so? Am I your sister? Your wife? No, sir, you have no claims of blood or loyalty to me.'

In one athletic movement he jumped from the platform of his curricle to the grass and paced, raking his hand thorough his hair, growing wilder in his looks as he walked restlessly away, then back. 'You have made your business my business from the moment I first met you. You have ruined my peace of mind, risked my reputation. For you I have risked everything!' He held his head in his hands.

Angelica could not listen any longer to this litany of the woes she had brought to his door. She scrambled down from the seat, catching her bonnet ribbon in the wheel which tore it from her head. She knew her hair was coming undone and she probably looked a sight but she could not care less as she faced a far more distressing state of affairs. The accusation that she had brought such ruination to his life was almost too much to bear, for she knew it was in large part true.

She turned on him with indignation. 'It was *you* who burst uninvited into my life, on a mission to bribe me to give up the presumption that I, a *déclassé* woman, an *actress,* could ever consider marrying into your high-crested family. It is *you* who ruined my life!' She was looking so tempestuous, her eyes flashing, her glorious hair in disarray that he felt his anger give way to surprise, admiration and then to an overwhelming desire to take her in his arms.

'Miss Leigh, such a fighting wench! Take care or we'll frighten the horses.' He caught her arm. 'Come here.' In one deft movement he folded her against his chest and planted a passionate kiss on her lips. For a moment she succumbed to the thrilling insistence of his body, then recalled the ambivalence in their relationship. Was his interest in her no more permanent than Lord Rackham's, who wanted her as a mistress under his control? In which case she was damned if she would be lulled into acquiescence. She struggled free and pushed him away.

'Have a care, sir! While I asked you to kiss me once, that does not mean you can kiss me whenever the impulse takes you!'

He bowed. 'We have both behaved badly and I apologise.' His words were contrite but there was amusement in his eyes.

She felt she should show an equal grace but struggled to contain her ire. 'Mr Asprey. I accept I have compromised you on more than one occasion, and I apologise. But I repeat, it was not I who first sought you out.'

'No, I blame my managing sister. Devilish interfering woman!'

'So the disasters of your life are due to two interfering women, and you have no part in the debacle? That is not very noble, sir, let alone honourable. Where is your precious honour now?'

'Madam, you more truly belong in the Courts of Law and are wasted on the stage,' he drawled, his cold demeanour once more in ascendance.

Ever-present was the spectre of Lord Rackham and Angelica needed to know how she stood. 'Pray tell me the current condition with Lord Rackham?'

Ivor Asprey's brow darkened. 'He will not hold you to your bargain. I extracted that promise from him. One good that came from your *unconscionable* interference is that Rackham was eager to keep his name from the constables' despatches, or worse still, the ribald lampooners in the press. So I paid off the Runners to stop their mouths – and to silence Lord Rackham's too.'

Angelica felt relief flood her body. She said in a faint voice, 'So I don't have to accede to Lord Rackham's demands?'

Mr Asprey was at her side in an instant, grasping her by the arms to shake her. 'No, you provoking miss! You should never have agreed to such a wicked plan. My reputation is for me to mind; how many times do I have to tell you, *it's not your business.*' His voice rose with exasperation.

'And how many times do I have to tell you that your daughter, your friends and your concern for working children matter too? How can it be just about you and your honour!'

He spun away from her and paced to the edge of the copse and back, his face dark with conflicting emotions. 'I don't like what I've become. These last years I determined to gain equilibrium and control over my heart, my life. But meeting you has broken my bounds. Now I'm unmoored and at sea. You are a danger to me and I to myself.'

Angelica realised this was what she feared most, that no amount of love could outweigh the detriment of an ill-starred union. Somehow all had become unstable and fraught with peril. Her voice was quiet and forlorn when she answered, 'I too don't like what I've become. Before, I was blithe-spirited, now anxiety and fear of loss stalk my days. I don't wish to feel so bereft again.' Ivor Asprey could not know the scars of her childhood; for her, insecurity recalled a time when every hope seemed beyond reach, and uncertainty and suffering were familiar companions. 'Mr Asprey, please could you take me home?'

In a subdued mood, he handed Angelica up into the curricle and walked round to spring up into the driving seat beside her. He turned his horses and they proceeded towards Grosvenor Gate in silence. The horses trotted through the grand Square where the Duchess of Arlington's mansion sat in imposing splendour. Soon they reached Angelica's home. Neither of them moved. 'Why so quiet, Miss Leigh?'

Angelica turned to meet his quizzical gaze. 'You say I have ruined your life, Mr Asprey. Perhaps marriage to a suitable woman will begin to restore the equilibrium you miss?'

His face, no longer amused, had turned guarded and cold. 'Can it be, Miss Leigh, that you know me better than I know myself? I hardly need your opinion on whether or whom I should marry. I get enough unwarranted advice already from my sister and daughter.' He sprang to the ground to offer his hand to her.

Angelica had managed to cram her bonnet back on her unruly hair but had not bothered with the ribbons. Ivor Asprey helped her to the ground and they stood facing each other, seeming as if strangers. He looked at her beautiful face, the sparkle gone, and in a distracted manner picked up her bonnet ribbons and tied them in a bow to one side of her chin. His fingers inadvertently brushed her cheek and she trembled at his touch. In a quiet voice he said, 'I'm sorry it has come to this. But how can I trust you again?' He turned away, anguish etched on his face.

Stifling a sob, Angelica dashed up the front steps and into the house. Martin watched her run up the stairs to her room and shook his head. He knew at first sighting of Mr Asprey this morning that he was no bringer of light. He watched the curricle disappear around the Square, a solitary figure holding the reins of a magnificent pair of high-stepping matched bays, then he shut the door.

12

BONFIRE OF PROPRIETIES

The next few days passed for Angelica in uncharacteristic gloom. She went to her rehearsals, increasingly disenchanted with the part of Amanthis, a silly girl if ever there was one, and the production, which Mr Dunbar was attempting to inject with shock and sensation. Her own mood was in stark contrast to the excitement in the city as everyone prepared for the biggest party of the century. One hundred years of the Hanoverian kings combined with the euphoria of peace at last after the signing of the Treaty of Paris and the banishment of the Emperor Napoleon Bonaparte. The exhilaration included a celebration of the sixteen-year-anniversary of Admiral Nelson's remarkable victory in the Battle of the Nile and a naval battle enactment was planned for the Serpentine in Hyde Park.

On their walks through St James's Park, Angelica and Isobel Fitzjames watched the building of the great bridge and pagoda designed by the Regent's favourite architect, Mr Nash. It was such a magnificent construction it seemed an extravagance as the backdrop for a firework display in a country impoverished by so many years of war, but no such consideration quelled the excitement of the people. Miss Fitzjames was full of her own excitement. 'The Duchess has given her blessing,' she said shyly. 'Lord Latimer and I will be married in the spring.'

'Oh Miss Isobel, this is wonderful news. Are you happy?' Angelica grasped her hands and met her eyes.

She blushed. 'Yes, very happy. I could not believe I could be so. When I first met you, I was close to despair. The great grey Thames seemed a preferable destination to Lord Fulsham's bed.' Her face clouded with the memory, then coloured, embarrassed by her own frankness. She hugged Angelica with uncharacteristic fervour. 'But look how life can surprise with bliss. It will with you too, Miss Angelica, I know so.'

Angelica had never felt so far herself from marital happiness and changed the subject. 'Are you and Lord Latimer attending any of the Jubilee spectaculars next week?'

'We're joining the Duchess's picnic in Hyde Park to watch the naval battle on the Serpentine and then making our way down to St James's to see the fireworks.'

'I'll be in Hyde Park too for Mama's picnic. The firework display is sure to be a spectacular end to the evening.'

Miss Fitzjames turned to look closely at Angelica. 'You don't seem to be your usual self. Are you unwell?'

Angelica looked away. 'I think I'm just fatigued. Perhaps not quite recovered from my illness.'

They arrived back at Berkeley Square and Miss Fitzjames collected her maid and walked on to her mansion in Grosvenor Square, restored to her by Mr Asprey, having returned to the gaming tables once more. Angelica shuddered at what she had asked from this honourable man. What a blind and self-centred woman she had been – worse even than the spoilt and unworldly character she so objected to in her latest play. She hung her head with shame at the thought of how she had imposed on him time and again, and how he had never let her down, whatever the cost to himself.

What Angelica could not know was that Ivor Asprey was himself rattled by how she had released some suppressed energy that had awoken him to the power of love united with desire. It was an unruly force he thought he had banished from his life for ever, but now it crackled within, resistant to restraint. For a man who had come to pride himself on his control and authority in the world, it was alarming to find he longed to embrace this more vivid life. How dangerous love could be to all the settled virtues he had sought: what enchantment had Miss Leigh cast over him?

* * *

The day of the Jubilee celebrations dawned clear and warm. It was a national holiday and rehearsals at the theatre had been cancelled even though *The Child of Nature* was two days from its first night. The sunny streets were filled early with roistering crowds who were already drinking and full of the pleasure of the day, heading towards the royal parks for a variety of extravaganzas. Angelica was happy to join her mother and Mr Breville at the picnic in Hyde Park but as the sun began to set the promise of an enactment of the Battle on the Nile drew all revellers to the Serpentine. There, replica boats, fully rigged and magnificent in their massed number, floated peacefully on the green water. The ducks and waterfowl paddled around unconcerned by these vast interlopers, and dogs and children gambolled in the shallows.

Crowds of revellers ate and drank at the water's edge, waiting for the mock battle to begin. Emerging out of the surge of spectators, Angelica saw the tall figure of Lord Latimer with Isobel Fitzjames on his arm and Dante Locke beside him. She made her excuses to her mother and joined her friends. 'Miss Leigh!' His lordship waved and the small group threaded their way through the crowd to meet her.

Isobel Fitzjames and Dante Locke grasped a hand each and they led her back to their space at the water's edge. Lord Latimer gazed down at her and chuckled. 'We have had such goings on in Uncle Ivor's house. Has Elinor not told you yet?'

Angelica met his gaze with a smile. 'No, she's coming to tea next week. But she did seem to be bursting to tell me something. I have an idea what it might be.'

Dante Locke frowned. 'Charlie, don't gossip; fools may prattle and the knave betray but you're a friend!'

'Oh don't be such a prosy fellow!' He laughed and turned to Angelica. 'There are lovebirds in the trees of St James's Square. The blue-stocking governess and Uncle's topping secretary are getting rivetted. Elinor is over the moon. Thinks she contrived it all.'

'I thought that might be it. Happy news, indeed. I know your niece has wished for this to happen.' Angelica felt a pang at all the conjugal happiness that surrounded her. Then his lordship continued, 'Oh, and Ivor's fault-finding Lady—'

At that point the battle enactment began with an enormous explosion which made the crowd scream in alarm; birds took off from the water in panicked flight and the dogs barked. A mighty cheer went up as a ship keeled over, spilling 'French' sailors into the water amid large plumes of black smoke.

Angelica felt the mayhem depicted at sea mirrored the turbulence in her heart as she wondered what Lord Latimer had been about to say, dreading he was to tell her of the overdue engagement of Mr Asprey and Portia Linus. But no one could be heard above the cacophony of the cheering crowds and the series of bangs and explosions as boats blew up and enemy sailors splashed about in the Serpentine before dying noisily on the shore. She dared not ask him to elaborate and so, left with her own thoughts, determined if Mr Asprey could not be hers she would never marry but instead commit herself to an independent life, earning her living in commerce alongside Mr Breville.

As the Battle of the Nile began to fizzle out with boats lying like beached whales, and sodden sailors shivering on the grass, the friends walked towards St James's Park where the firework display, the crowning spectacle of the day, was expected to begin. Together with a motley crowd consisting of members of the *haut ton* and the hoi-polloi, they headed south; aristocratic privilege and beauty rubbed shoulders with the poorest of London, the urchins, pickpockets, card sharps and thieves. Everyone was in the highest spirits, most lubricated by alcohol of every kind.

It was again possible to hear each other speak and Angelica caught Lord Latimer's sleeve and gathered her courage to ask the question that had been consuming her. 'You were about to say about Lady Linus and your uncle.'

'Well, it's not quite about them, it's more that Portia Linus has found a more worthy subject for her campaign of moral reform.'

'What do you mean?' Angelica could not allow her hope to rise.

'She's given up waiting for Uncle Ivor to propose and is now seen about town with a reprobate in far greater need of salvation.'

'What can you mean, my lord? Don't speak in riddles.'

'Yes, Charlie, really bad form. You're tattling like a fishwife.' Dante Locke was known for being high-minded about such things.

'Oh all right then. She's set her cap at a gambling lord, Abercrombie, who just happens to be dripping in lard, but I think it's the possibility of reform that she finds even more attractive than his twenty thousand a year. Poor devil!'

An effervescent joy rose in Angelica's breast. But she suppressed the laughter in her voice as she asked with feigned nonchalance, 'What does Mr Asprey say about this state of affairs?'

'Oh, he's so morose these days, he barely speaks and has become an even duller dog than he was before.'

Isobel Fitzjames chided him gently. 'My lord, that is not fair. He's shepherding his controversial child labour bill through Parliament. He's preoccupied with higher things.'

'That may be, but I think he needs to be taken in hand by a know-it-all chit whom he loves and who loves him.' He looked across mischievously at Angelica who coloured at his words and gave him a startled glare. Was it so obvious to everyone, she wondered, and then was overwhelmed once more with her longing for it to be true. Miss Fitzjames and Dante Locke both protested at his indiscretion but he continued, 'As you can see, I've been talking to my cousin, Elinor, whose matchmaking plans have turned elsewhere.'

They were just entering St James's Park with a crush of people round the gates as Angelica slipped her arm into Dante's. Handel, played by a distant orchestra, drifted on the breeze and she felt her heart lift with the music in airy celebration. 'Miss Isobel and I have been watching the building of the bridge and pagoda over the Canal in St James's Park. It's a most impressive construction.'

'You can see it clearly from here.' Lord Latimer pointed to the top of the pagoda already lit up with lanterns above the trees. Angelica felt her own excitement rise. It looked so majestic and yet strange, like a deity arrived from a foreign land. It was dark now as they joined the revellers lining the Canal side, with a band playing a rousing march. The first fireworks were set off and everyone's head craned back to watch the spangles of stars exploding into the night sky. A great sigh went up from the crowd. Deafening salvos of crackling light lit up the dark as more fireworks were set off, popping and sizzling against the shadowy trees. Scintillas of flame rained down on them all, extinguishing as they fell to earth.

Wishing to see the bridge and pagoda from a better vantage point, Lord Latimer led the way to the beginning of the construction where it spanned the Canal. They marvelled at how gaily the pagoda was painted, hanging with gas lanterns and towering above them, the centre point of a firework display emitting comets of streaking light and cascading stars.

But the light seemed to no longer be in intermittent flashes. Tongues of flames and billowing smoke were issuing from the top of the building, flickering and curling round the wooden tower. There were more cheers as people thought this was some further dramatic display but then pieces of burning wood began to break off and fall to the ground and Angelica realised the whole pagoda was going up in flames.

'Lord Latimer, we should move away,' she said, pulling on his arm. But at that moment she heard her name called and looking back along the bridge, she saw Elinor Asprey in her party dress waving in excitement. She seemed to break free of Miss Stafford's hand and set off towards Angelica. In horror, Angelica watched the child brilliantly illuminated by the conflagration as she ran across the bridge.

'No! No, Elinor! Go back, go back!' she cried. But the girl ran on, an eager smile on her face, just as a large block of blazing wood fell at her feet and instantly set her dress alight. The crowd screamed but Angelica sprang forward and reached her first. She wrapped the skirts of her pelisse tight around the child, stifling the flames of her burning dress, and gathering Elinor into her arms, she promptly jumped into the Canal.

The cold water made her gasp. It was not deep and there were barges and other boats along the water's length. She looked down into the girl's shocked face. 'Are you all right?' she asked but before there was an answer Angelica found herself grasped in a steely grip.

'Come, this is the best way to get out.' She looked round into the

ashen face of Ivor Asprey. He had grasped his daughter under one arm
and locked his other around Angelica's waist. They waded to the Canal
edge where Lord Latimer and Miss Stafford helped pull them out.
Angelica and Elinor sat on the ground as Ivor peeled back the singed
fabric of the pelisse and examined his daughter's legs. Her dress was in
charred ribbons and her skin was blistered but unbroken. She was whim-
pering as she clutched at her father and Angelica. He encircled them
both, his head bent between theirs as he whispered, 'Oh, my darlings, my
darlings. Thank God you're safe.' Behind them the whole pagoda was in
flames and lighting up the sky with a sulphurous yellow. There was
confusion as people dashed from the scene and others came to stare.
Someone tried to pump water from the Canal to douse the lower flames,
but all in vain.

'Thank you, thank you.' Ivor took both Angelica's hands, his face full of
anguish at the thought of what he might have lost.

Angelica took off her sodden pelisse, her teeth chattering, and Lord
Latimer stripped off his coat and offered it to her to wear. Miss Stafford
removed her pelisse and wrapped her charge in the warm dry fabric. 'We
must dress those blisters with honey and goose fat. You saved any deeper
burns by precipitously leaping into the water, Miss Leigh,' she said in her
calm voice.

Ivor had already divested himself of his coat and emptied his boots of
water before putting them back on and was left wearing just his linen shirt
and breeches, all soaked to the skin. 'Quickly, I must get you home and into
the dry.' Mr Digby had found Rocky, who brought the curricle into the Park
in a clatter of hooves and jingling harnesses. Lord Latimer assured
Angelica he would find her mother's party and tell her her daughter was in
the care of Mr Asprey and his secretary and governess and would be
brought home later.

Ivor Asprey handed Angelica up into the curricle, her bonnet lost, her
hair dripping wet and tumbling to her waist. He passed his daughter into
her arms and she placed her on the seat between her father and herself.
Then he sprang into the driving seat and with Rocky up behind, drove back
to St James's Square at speed. He looked across at his daughter and Angelica, and the harsh anguish in his face softened to a smile. 'Miss Stafford and

Digby will follow on foot.' Angelica felt Elinor's small cold hand creep into hers.

Once they were in the house the true danger of the conflagration struck Angelica with force and she sat down on the hall chair, feeling the spirit drain from her. She was still wearing Lord Latimer's coat, her hair dripping on it and onto the marble floor. Mr Asprey called a maid and took his daughter upstairs to be dressed in warm dry clothes. He dispatched Goodall to the kitchens to mix up a paste of goose fat and honey ready for Miss Stafford to dress the burns.

As he descended the stairs, still wet and dishabille himself, he came to Angelica's side. 'Miss Leigh, you're soaked to the skin and cold. Until Miss Stafford returns and can lend you the necessary clothes, I can offer you one of my dressing gowns. It's essential you get out of these sodden clothes.' As he led her to the bedroom she had used when she was so mortally ill he smiled at her. 'You already know this house well. I'll bring through a gown for you.'

Within a minute he had returned with a purple brocade dressing gown. 'I've brought you my favourite as it's the warmest with its ermine trim.'

Despite feeling wan, Angelica could not supress a small giggle. Her eyes widened. 'Mr Asprey, I didn't know you for a dandy. This is very grand.'

'Put it on, Miss Leigh, and you will understand its charms. I'll go and change and will see you and Elinor in the library where there is a fire already burning.' Angelica slipped out of Lord Latimer's beautifully tailored coat and laid it reverently on the bed then peeled off her saturated gown and chemise and stays. She slipped into the dressing gown and was grateful for its warmth as she tied its voluminous folds tightly round her waist. She was taken aback at smelling the scent of Mr Asprey rising from the silk and hugged it close, breathing it in.

Angelica did her best to dry her hair with the towel by the dressing table but had no pins to secure it so left her damp curls falling down her back. Her shoes and stockings were also sodden so she padded barefoot down the stairs to the blessed warmth of the library. Here she settled herself into the corner of the sofa, tucking her feet under the purple silk folds of Ivor's gown.

The maid brought Elinor down, dressed in her nightdress with slippers and a woollen dressing gown. 'Oh, Miss Leigh! I'm so glad you're still here. But that's Papa's gown! It is very big on you.' She sat down carefully on the sofa beside her.

'Take care, Elinor, you don't want to bump your blisters. Miss Stafford will dress and bandage them then they'll feel better.'

'They aren't troubling me too much. Papa says being plunged into cold water was the best thing that could happen. Thank you, Miss Leigh.'

'We were just lucky that we had the Canal so close.' Angelica put her arm out and Elinor snuggled up against her on the sofa while they both watched the fire, feeling the warmth spread through their chilled bodies.

The door opened and Ivor Asprey walked in, completely transformed from the dishevelled figure who had brought them home. His clothes were once more immaculate, he had even tied a passable cravat. His dark hair was still damp and curling and his face had a softness about it as he stood and looked at his daughter, folded into Angelica's side. He was startled to see this beauty, like a golden-haired goddess, in his dressing gown and for a moment was overwhelmed by the incongruity of her luminous presence, here in his clothes, in his library.

'Oh, Papa. I'm so glad to be here with you and Miss Leigh. Can you sit next to me too?' His daughter shuffled closer to Angelica to make room and when he sat down slipped her other arm through his. 'Doesn't Miss Leigh look well in your gown?'

Ivor looked over his daughter's head and met Angelica's eyes, flickering green and gold in the firelight. 'She does indeed. But that garment could fit you both.' He smiled.

There was a knock at the door and Miss Stafford entered, her face concerned. 'Mr Digby and I returned as fast as we could. I'm pleased to see you, Miss Leigh, looking so well, and Elinor, thank goodness not badly burned. Come with me, missy, I want to dress those burns as soon as possible.' She put out her hand for her charge.

'Oh must I? I want to stay with Papa and Miss Leigh.'

'Elinor, it's very important you let Miss Stafford treat your legs. You don't want any scars, do you?' Her father had stood up and his voice was firm.

Elinor Asprey climbed off the sofa and in an impetuous moment kissed

Angelica on the cheek, then turned to embrace her father. 'Goodnight, dearest Elinor,' he said, holding her close.

'Goodnight. I'll see you in a few days for tea.' Angelica waved from the sofa.

As Miss Stafford left, she turned to say, 'Miss Leigh, after I've dealt with Elinor and put her to bed, I'll sort out some clothes of mine and leave them for you in your old bedroom.' She closed the door.

Unexpectedly alone, Ivor Asprey and Angelica looked at each other in the flickering firelight. 'I really ought to invite in a chaperone to protect your honour, Miss Leigh.' He leaned against the mantlepiece and smiled down at her.

'My honour and yours are rather compromised already, don't you think?'

'That may be so. And I dare think no one in my household will complain at the state of affairs. Are you happy for us to continue as we are?'

'I am.' Angelica was aware of every breath they took. 'Would you share the sofa with me, Mr Asprey?' she said, looking at him standing so imperiously at his fireside.

He hesitated for a moment and then sat down. She shifted her position to give him enough space and her small pale feet and ankles were suddenly exposed. Mr Asprey took them in his hands and she shivered. 'You're still cold, Miss Leigh?'

'Just a little, but I'm feeling much better now I have your dressing gown to warm me.'

'I don't think you should give it back; it looks too well on you.' His eyes were watching her with an expression that made her heart turn over. In a soft amused voice he said, 'I have missed you so since our last tetchy meeting. Do you think you can forgive a proud and arrogant man?'

'If he will forgive an insufferably interfering woman.' She laughed.

'Well, that interfering woman has possibly saved my beloved daughter's life, certainly saved her from further injury. I forgive all presumptuous meddling for that.'

His warm hands enveloped her feet but his thumb was slowly tracing a line up her instep and encircling her ankle. Angelica was exquisitely aware of the intimacy of this small movement and her skin tingled under his touch. She flexed her foot against his thigh and moved closer to him. 'Do you think you could put your arm around me to warm me up?'

He looked at her in the firelight, barely clothed, her hair quite undressed as if she had risen from bed, and love and desire crashed over him like a wave. He pulled her towards him and held her close, her head on his shoulder. 'What are we to do, Miss Leigh?' he asked. 'Could you bear to share your life with a politician who has a mission to improve the lot of others?'

'Could you bear to have people gossip about your liaison with a mere actress who prances on the stage for every man to gaze on?'

He pulled himself away so he could look her in the eye. 'It's not a *liaison* I had in mind, Miss Leigh. I want you for my wife.'

Angelica could not suppress a gasp as tears sprang to her eyes. For a minute or so she could not speak while he watched her with the most tender expression on his face. She hiccoughed and her words stuttered out, 'But I cannot bring any fortune or breeding to enrich your family name. I only have scandal and criminality to offer you.'

'But you bring your courage and intelligence, your great heart and beauty to enrich my *life*. That is more precious than anything.' His voice was thick with emotion.

With a cry, Angelica slipped her feet from his warm grasp and knelt on the sofa beside him, slipping her arms round his neck. She felt her breasts, pressed softly against his chest, and knew by his sharp intake of breath that he was aware too of their lack of constraint within the silk brocade of his dressing gown. The effect of her proximity on him excited her. Angelica watched his pupils dilate and his eyes grow almost black. His arm across her back held her closer as their lips met, gently then with increasing passion. She sank into the heady strength of him, sensitised to the fresh-air scent of his skin, the salty taste of him.

Angelica was the first to break away. 'No,' she whispered with a sob.

He extricated himself from her embrace with a sigh. 'Miss Leigh, if you continue like that I'll be obliged to reclaim my dressing gown and leave you undefended from my touch.'

She laughed, sitting back on her heels. 'You're right, Mr Asprey. I should go and dress and then Rocky can take me home.'

He pulled her to him again. 'Not just yet. I have something for you.' He removed the familial ring he wore on his little finger, an emerald carved with his family crest and the words TIBI SOLI, and slipped it onto her marriage finger. 'It says *to you alone* which is what I offer you. Everything I have is yours, myself, my heart, my soul. I hope, Miss Leigh' – he paused – 'Angelica, will you do me the honour of marrying me?'

The use of her name at last speared straight to her heart. Her breath came fast as she looked down at the ancient ring, glowing green and gold on her finger. *To you alone* expressed everything she felt about him, even when she feared they were but star-crossed lovers. She looked up, aware that he was still waiting for her answer. 'Ivor,' she said shyly. 'Ivor... Ivor... Ivor and Angelica.' She rolled their names round her tongue, smiling to herself. 'Yes, Ivor Asprey, I will be happy indeed to marry you.' With a shout of amused laughter, he pulled her into his arms and kissed her again and she abandoned herself to his embrace.

As she settled into the crook of his arm he said, 'Do you think, my beloved, my Mrs Asprey to be, that my interfering daughter could have had anything to do with this?'

Angelica sat up abruptly and looked at him, a question in her face. 'How could she? She could not have known about the tower bursting into flames.'

'No, not that. But she's been planning something with my mischievous nephew and insisted we all ended up in St James's Park to see the fireworks. And miraculously, it seemed, there you were with Charles and Miss Fitz-james and Dante Locke. Elinor's already giddy with success over Miss Stafford marrying my secretary. She considers it her doing, you know.'

'Oh, I know. She's got a lively romantic heart. And an over-developed sense of responsibility. Only she can secure the sun will rise and the world will turn; I wonder from whom she could have inherited that trait?' Angelica laughed, comfortable in his arms.

Ivor crushed her closer to his heart. 'Elinor's been agitating for me to marry you from the moment she first met you, you know,' he muttered against her hair.

'Well, I'm very taken with her and would consider it an honour to be as much a mother to her as she desires.'

He cupped her face in his hands. 'You really are the most beautiful woman I have ever seen,' he said, gazing deep into her eyes, which met his with matching emotion. He dropped his gaze as if unable to bear the intensity of the moment and began to trace with his lips her exposed breastbone from her shoulder to her clavicle. There he stopped with a deep sigh as Angelica held her breath, quivering with anticipation; he looked up, his eyes clouded with passion. 'I cannot vouch for my behaviour remaining honourable if I go any further.'

Angelica kissed his forehead. 'I really must get dressed and go home. I have rehearsals tomorrow. First night the day afterwards.' A thought struck her and she looked at him with a searching expression. 'You are happy for me to complete my contract for this play?'

'As long as you remain fully clothed for the duration. It was the sight of you barely dressed as Ophelia that inflamed my desire and stole my heart.' He sighed and looked away as if to dilute the intensity of his memory. 'From that moment I was lost, although I had no right to be. You were my nephew's love and I was there to admonish you. But from that first sight I was haunted by the vision of you, and could not admit it, even to myself.'

Angelica luxuriated in the delicious feeling of being desired, being loved by the only man she wanted to love and desire her. 'Despite our manager's best efforts, I remain costumed demurely throughout.'

'Well then, I can have no objections to Mrs Asprey being on the stage.' And they both laughed. At that moment the door creaked open and a small pale face appeared. Angelica hurriedly sat up and Ivor Asprey straightened his cravat and sprang to his feet. 'Elinor, are you all right?' He took a step towards her, his voice full of concern. The girl was a pathetic sight with her thin legs bandaged from knee to heel.

'Come and sit between us.' Angelica patted the sofa.

'I couldn't sleep,' she said in a wan voice.

'Are you in pain?' Her father sat beside her with an anxious frown on his brow.

'No, the bandages have helped. It's just when I close my eyes, I can still see the flames.' She turned her face to Angelica. 'Miss Leigh, I'm glad you're still here.'

Angelica shifted as if to get up. 'I have been meaning to go but it's just so warm and comforting by the fire.'

'And with Papa here, everything seems better.'

'Indeed it does.' Angelica smiled from daughter to father. The adults' eyes met, his with a question and she gave an almost imperceptible nod.

'Elinor, my darling girl, I have some news that I hope will make you happy, and perhaps help you sleep better too.' The girl sat up brightly, looking from Angelica's face to her father's. 'I am honoured that Miss Leigh has agreed to marry me.'

Her elfin face lit up with amazement and joy. 'Really? Oh Papa! Miss Leigh!' She put her arms around them both and held them close. 'I have so wanted Papa to be happy again, I so wanted you to be my new mama.'

'I know. Well, we're all very happy.' Angelica leant across and kissed her.

'We'll be a family again.' The girl clasped her hands together with an ecstatic expression. A sudden thought seemed to come to her. 'And Papa, will you hug and kiss Miss Leigh enough to give her a baby, so I can have a brother or sister?' she asked with a pleading look on her face.

Angelica suppressed a giggle, so taken aback was she by the question. Young girls were not meant to know anything about such things, let alone talk about them.

Her father leapt to his feet. 'Elinor! It's most improper to speak like this. What can you mean?' His voice was shocked, colour rising in his cheeks.

'Well, Miss Stafford has explained how baby sheep and goats are made and I thought it would be the same with people.'

'Damned advanced education!' he muttered under his breath.

Angelica leant across to take her hand. 'You are right, Elinor. Once we are married, your papa and I hope that we will have a baby to be a new brother or sister for you.'

'Will you promise?' she said, her face shining with excitement at the idea.

Ivor took his daughter's hand. 'I do promise. Now, my dearest, off to bed. You are the first to know our good news and have no excuse not to sleep well tonight.' He led her to the door and up the stairs to bed.

He returned to find Angelica ready to leave. He took her elbow to detain her. 'And you, most desirable, irresistible and wonderful of women, must go and get dressed in my governess's clothes and I'll take you home.' He paused. 'But first, I have something for you. It may not be your grandmother's necklace but I promise this is mine to give.' He slipped a scintillating river of stones from his pocket and Angelica gasped. 'May I place this round your neck?' He asked, his expression soft in the candlelight.

'Is this for me? It's too beautiful.' Her eyes filled with tears.

'I can't think of anyone more deserving to wear my most precious ancestral jewels. You are as nonpareil to me.'

Ivor Asprey stood behind Angelica, swept her hair off her neck and fixed the diamond necklace with its emerald clasp. 'Green for your eyes,' he murmured.

Her hands flew up to cradle the large oval stones against her throat. 'I feel like a queen. Thank you.'

He turned her round and folded her into his arms and then, to her surprise, slipped his hands inside the beautiful brocade dressing gown. Angelica felt his warm palms on her naked lower back, holding her body tightly to him; his firm touch on her skin made her tremble. With their faces close, she asked with a mischievous smile, 'So has my paladin of virtue turned very naughty indeed?'

'Well, if I have it's entirely the fault of a minxy actress who has bewitched me into loving her more than life itself.' He added, 'More than honour too.' Then he put his lips to her ear and whispered, 'If you don't go now, I'm afraid you'll find me hugging and kissing you so very much we may be presenting Elinor with her longed-for brother or sister rather sooner than expected!' They laughed as she broke free from his arms. She peeped out of the library and found the house silent.

He followed her. 'My servants are very discreet; they're all in their quarters. They've liked you since you first came to stay. Feel they had a part in saving your life, you know.' The candles in the candelabra were guttering low as Angelica ran up the stairs to her old room to dress. She paused on the landing and looked back at the man she loved, still standing there gazing up at her, his face softened in the candlelight, his eyes dark with desire.

A bubble of joy rose in her breast and with it a revelation about beauty itself. It had been her attendant throughout her life, awarding her great advantage but also unwelcome attention and fear. Now safe and loved, for the first time she realised her beauty was not just for others but for her; here could be found her own pleasure and power. In a moment of wild mischief she undid the tie on Mr Asprey's dressing gown and let it slip from her shoulders. Picking it up, she laughed as she tossed it down to him, his eyes still on her. She stood there in all her natural loveliness, free of artifice and any veil of propriety, the candlelight catching her breasts and gleaming off the curve of her hips. All she wore were the Asprey diamonds which glittered against her creamy skin.

'Oh, Angelica!' Ivor took a step forward as if to follow her up the stairs. Then he checked himself. She leant over the banister, her glorious hair falling like Rapunzel's, and reaching out her hand whispered, 'Marry me soon, Ivor. I don't want us to wait too long.' She turned and, in a flash of golden hair and white limbs, disappeared into the dim recesses of the house. This time he did not resist and bounded up the stairs, two at a time. Only the old owl in the tree outside Angelica's window heard her laughter stifled with a kiss.

ACKNOWLEDGEMENTS

Behind every writer is a team of professionals who bring a novel to the public but in front of every writer are their readers, who make it all possible. I have been amazed and touched by the thousands of wonderful readers of my books who have not only read but spent time to review, rate and comment. Thank you so very much, it means the world and encourages me as I beaver away at my solitary desk.

This is my third historical novel set in the Regency. *The Marriage Season,* was followed by *An Unsuitable Heiress,* and now I offer you my third, *A Scandalous Match* which I hope you'll enjoy as much, if not more.

I am so grateful to my publishers, Boldwood Books, for their continued enthusiasm and efficiency combined with a precious feeling of family. A brilliant young company on the move, they are led by inspirational CEO, Amanda Ridout. Particular thanks are due to my wonderful editor, Sarah Ritherdon, whose support is priceless and sensitivity to character and language makes her comments priceless. Nia Beynon and Claire Fenby and their inventive team are the wizards who work their magic in promotion, sales and digital marketing. The company is expanding so fast I can no longer mention everyone but every polished part of this Rolls-Royce machine works seamlessly.

I do want to make a special mention, however, of Candida Bradford's wonderful, insightful editorial input and the precise copy-editing eye of Rose Fox. I'm delighted to have the skills of Alice Moore for the jacket of this book. She added such distinction to *The Marriage Season* and *An Unsuitable Heiress* and I have heard nothing but praise from my readers. My heartfelt thanks to the whole Brilliant Boldwood team.

Behind all this creative activity is my agent, Jim Gill, and his assistant,

Amber Garvey, of United Agents. Jim is a passionate advocate of all his authors and their books, not least of me and mine, and it is a wonderful feeling to have him at my back.

Family and friends are both support and inspiration for a writer. Mine are essential and could not be more generous in every way. They all know who they are and how grateful I am to them for plot twists, equine information, medical know-how, literary sensibility. All have been subject to the phone call or zoom requesting help with some matter that demands their expertise. Thank you!

Love and thanks always to my husband, Nick, and my darling children, Ben and Lily, their partners Jess and Robin and wonderful grandchildren, who provide all the affection, literary advice, encouragement and humour any writing mother could ever expect. This support comes too from my beloved stepdaughter, Sophia, who together with her family brighten our lives.

Last, but never least, are the readers and book bloggers who have given me such support and feedback; reading, sharing, reviewing, I am so grateful for your time and generosity in contacting me and reviewing my books. Sharing the love in this way is one of the best everyday means of connecting with others. Thank you all.

ABOUT THE AUTHOR

Jane Dunn is an historian and biographer and the author of seven acclaimed biographies, including *Daphne du Maurier and her Sisters* and the Sunday Times and NYT bestseller, *Elizabeth & Mary: Cousins, Rivals, Queens.* She comes to Boldwood with her first fiction outing – a trilogy of novels set in the Regency period. She lives in Berkshire with her husband, the linguist Nicholas Ostler.

Sign up to Jane Dunn's mailing list for news, competitions and updates on future books.

Follow Jane on social media here:

ALSO BY JANE DUNN

The Marriage Season

An Unsuitable Heiress

A Scandalous Match

Letters from
the past

Discover page-turning
historical novels from
your favourite authors
and be transported
back in time

Join our book club
Facebook group

https://bit.ly/SixpenceGroup

Sign up to our
newsletter

https://bit.ly/LettersFrom
PastNews

Boldwood

Boldwood Books is an award-winning fiction publishing company seeking out the best stories from around the world.

Find out more at www.boldwoodbooks.com

Join our reader community for brilliant books, competitions and offers!

Follow us
@BoldwoodBooks
@TheBoldBookClub

Sign up to our weekly deals newsletter

https://bit.ly/BoldwoodBNewsletter